ACTS (
will inv
and int
It may make you. angry.

Its heroine is a woman so destructive of the men she loves, you may hate her. She is so lost, you may pity her, yet she is so passionate, you too may fall in love with her.

Its hero is a man so dogmatic, he may make you furious. He is so strong, he commands obedience, yet he is so warmly human, you too may fall in love with him.

But
ACTS OF LOVE
is compelling!

It has "raw power." This is "the way people *really* talk, argue, make up, lash out."

—*Kirkus Reviews*

It "demonstrates" Elia Kazan's "mastery of the novel." Each character "expands in all directions" and the "climactic act of love here is quite dramatic and unexpected."

—*Hartford Courant*

"The author's clear affection for the people he writes about makes the reader care."
—*New York Times Book Review*

And
ACTS OF LOVE

is "engrossing reading."—*Publishers Weekly*

is "vivid, passionate and immensely readable."
—*KFAC Radio*

Books by
Elia Kazan

Acts of Love
The Understudy
The Arrangement

Published by
WARNER BOOKS

Elia Kazan

ACTS OF LOVE

WARNER BOOKS

A Warner Communications Company

For my brothers,
AVRAAM, GEORGE *and* JOHN,
who will remember.

Acts of Love

one

IN August, on the Gulf coast of Florida, the heat doesn't ease when the sun goes down. It becomes more punishing; there is no shade. People go to bed with their windows closed.

Costa and Noola Avaliotis were asleep in their separate bedrooms when their son, Teddy, called from San Diego.

Costa, a restless sleeper, got to the kitchen, where the phone was, first. "What happened the other one?" he said after hearing why his son had called.

As he listened, he reached for a dish towel and mopped his forehead and neck.

"How I come there?" Costa asked. "Where I find that money?"

He listened again, glancing down the hall to where the lamp his wife had switched on threw a shaft of light under her bedroom door.

"Airplane, so forth, Teddy, that's a big bill. Where you get it?"

9

His son's response made him chuckle. "All right," he said, "that's your business. O.K., yes, I think it over."

By the time he dropped the phone in its cradle, he was completely awake. He walked down the hall past his wife's bedroom to the front door of their house, unbolted the Segal lock and swung the door open.

The impact of the heat was like walking into a wall.

Overhead the feather tips of the Australian pines didn't stir. If there'd been the least breeze, they would have caught it. Costa had planted these trees more than twenty years before, when he'd bought the place. Through their thinly covered limbs he could see the glint of the Gulf of Mexico on the other side of the shore road, he could hear its gentle tide lift the debris of shells, wash them again and drop them.

Now he heard his wife's slippers scuffing down the hall.

"What was the phone?" she asked.

"Teddy," Costa said.

"So? What's wrong?"

"Nothing. Go to bed. He wants to get married."

"Good."

"Not that one. A new one. This one, she's American. He wants me to come there look her over."

"Oh, Mother of God!"

"He's sending money."

"What happened to the other one?"

Costa shrugged.

"When you going?" she asked.

"I didn't make up my mind, going," Costa said.

"If Teddy is sending money," she said, "it must mean that—"

"Dzidzidzidzidzi," Costa said.

"I'll take care of the store, don't worry."

"Hear those? Summer bugs. Same ones at night in Kalymnos. *Dzidzikia*."

10

When Costa Avaliotis was a boy of ten his father had brought him to Florida from Kalymnos, an island in the Aegean Sea. Now, at sixty-two, he still spoke of Kalymnos as home.

"If he's sending money," Noola persisted, "he's made up his mind."

"He said it's all settled." Turning, he faced her. "Why don't you go to bed," he said.

"I imagine," Noola said, "he thinks he knows better than you what he wants."

"He pick out other one without showing her first. You see what happen?"

"Oh, Costa, he's a grown man now, twenty-three, what do you want? This time he's asking you to come look her over. Teddy's a good boy. Smart too."

"Smart in other things. Not this."

Costa turned his head away, dismissing her. He heard her slippers scuffing down the hall.

After a moment, he walked slowly through an opening in the hedge that flanked the entrance to their home, and passed over the burned-down grass to where a giant live oak stood. At the base of this ancient tree Costa had built a kind of day bed, and there he stretched out, looking up to the stars, which were sharp as diamonds. The limbs of the oak, round and heavy like the upper arms of well-fed matrons, were draped with Spanish moss.

Now he turned his head toward the house; Noola's bedroom light had gone out. Costa remembered he'd left the front door open and that field mice would accept the invitation to come in and scout for food. He raised himself up and, as if approaching an adversary, walked into the house, his knees stiff as those of a stalking dog.

A corner of the front room was graced with a soft light. On a high shelf were two wooden icons and, before them, twin oil lamps that burned day and night, their tiny red tongues fixed without a flicker. The holy figures were Saint Nicholas, who protects mariners if they are Greek and of the Orthodox faith, and Mary, holding the body of her crucified son. The paintings were dusky with age and from the smoke of the oil, but they glowed, the tiny lights reflecting off the blood of saintly robes and the gold of divinity around the attendant angels.

Beneath the icons stood the Avaliotis's large TV set. *Gunsmoke* was big that summer and *Kung Fu*. Idly Costa flicked the set on. Only the news, all from Washington. Costa switched the set off, passed by the saints, walking to the opposite corner of the room, where there were two photographs taken against the same landscape. The first was of his father, a captain, to judge from his hat and his posture, at the tiller of a sponge boat—the *Eleni*. By his side was his son, Costa himself, in his prime at twenty-four. A diving suit completely covered Costa's body except for his head. In the crook of his right arm, like a warrior of old, he held the helmet divers use. The mutual regard, the interdependence of father and son, was complete. Behind them, hung to dry, were long strings of sponge, a prize catch. Costa remembered the day.

Edge to edge with this picture was the same scene taken twenty-five years later. Old Captain Theo was gone and Costa stood at the tiller in his place. By his side was a boy of twelve, Teddy. Costa had his arm around the boy's shoulders but the story was different, the spirit changed. Two weeks after that photograph had been made, Costa sold the *Eleni*. The red tide left him no choice.

For some men it's an indignity to ask for help, even from the dead. Costa standing before these photographs looked more like a combatant than a suppliant. His toes were pointed straight ahead, like those of a boxer, his shoulders hunched, his head tensed. But the fact remained: he was searching into the face of his father. And what he remembered was what he himself had so often said: "My father always know what's right."

In a kind of reverie, he stood before these monuments from his past, waiting for a sign.

Costa was not a tall man, but his shoulders at the back were heavy, the muscles of his trade. Rounded now and softened, they'd retained some of their swagger. His buttocks came at precisely half his height, his body slimming there to half its width. Costa belted his trousers low.

At sixty-two he had a full stand of black hair. His mustache was that of the warrior of old, shading the heavy lips, then going past their corners to end in a swirl. His eyebrows, equally heavy, plunged to meet over his nose, locking the face into a single expression which was often a kind of warning that the man's patience was being tried, dangerously.

The eyes, which had looked out over the surface of the sea so many hours for so many long years, were black as black ink; not brown, that soft color. They, too, seemed to speak of suspicion or warn that a judgment was being reached which, if unfavorable, might release a great store of anger. Costa was not a friendly man. When he offered friendship, it was as an honor.

He could have been a brigand or a revolutionary, living the life of an exile high on a mountain. But what he'd been, in his prime, was one of a select company of sponge divers working out of the Anclote River. When the red tide killed the sponge, he'd turned storekeeper. His place, The 3 Bees ("Bait, Boats, Beer") was away from where the sponge fleet had harbored in the good times, on the other side of the river and west toward the edge of the Gulf.

Still, he had never lost the authority which sea captains develop: in his company you felt completely safe. He recognized only one force he couldn't deal with: the mysterious will of God.

"The only thing I ask that boy," he said to his wife the next morning, "he should marry one of us, a clean girl."

"Your eggs are getting cold," Noola said.

Even at breakfast, the kitchen smelled of olive oil and garlic.

Noola didn't eat any meal until her husband was finished. Perched on the edge of the other kitchen chair, a small Greek hen, she kept her eyes fixed on her husband to make sure he had what he wanted when he wanted it. She'd been brought up in a middle-class Greek ghetto in Astoria, Queens, a section of New York City, and this was the example her mother had set her.

"Good thing you're going," she said.

"I didn't make up my mind I'm going," Costa said, tapping his empty cup with a forefinger, an order. "Do me favor, don't try make up my mind."

"After all these years," Noola said. "Silly!" She scooted to the stove in her bedroom slippers, which she wore all day as well as at night.

"What is the problem over there, I'm wondering," Costa said. "All right, you're a young man, you need a woman. So you go, like we used to go, to Tampa, to Ybor City, you find a woman, you do your business, you come home. What's the problem?"

"If he's sending money," Noola said, "he must be in love."

"Love is in the movies."

"I'm still wondering what happened between them, the other one," Noola said as she filled his cup with coffee.

Teddy had sent them the rejected girl's photograph months before. It was on the sideboard next to the sugar jar. They both turned and looked at the girl, a Greek princess, hair to her waist. They hadn't met her, but Costa had instructed her long-distance on a few essentials. "Teddy quiet boy," he'd told her. "Likes home life, good cooking, so forth, so on. Can you hear me over there? Family life," he'd shouted. "You know what I mean. No nightclub business."

Costa couldn't remember what her response had been, but apparently his advice had not been effective. After a while Teddy was referring to her as "that Greek society bitch" and sometimes as "the pot roast."

"I know what happen," Costa said. "Too many parties! Daughters of Penelope, Philophtocos, Ahepa you, you heppa me, dancing American style, bingo, God knows what kind society business. One look I could have told him, 'Watch out!' Too bad. Her father, I understand, rich man."

"I suppose Teddy didn't really love her," Noola said.

"No, no, no," Costa said. "Many people marry without that. Like me with you. We didn't love each other when we marry. Remember?"

"Sure," Noola said, "we didn't love each other. Not like now."

"It happen slowly, proper way. You brought me son and I saw what you were, a fine woman, so I learn to love you."

"Well, anyway," Noola said, "I'm glad you're going."

"I tol' you don't make up my mind on that," Costa said. "What's the matter with you today?"

He got up and left the table.

"I only say something," Noola called after him, "because if he send money, it must mean he really—"

Down the hall, Costa had closed a door.

A few minutes later, when she was having her coffee, alone in the kitchen, she heard him call, "Noola, press my suit."

She found him in the bathroom, shaving.

"Since you worrying so much," he said, "I better go. Pack my bag. You got clean shirt?"

When Western Union called to inform Costa that the money had arrived, he was ready, dressed in his black mohair suit, a white shirt, starched at the collar and cuffs, and a maroon tie. He walked, carrying his bag and perspiring heavily, from their home in Mangrove Still, a scatter of stores and houses, to nearby Tarpon Springs, the center of the Greek community in Florida. There he cashed the money order.

He hadn't looked up the planes west, assumed one would be waiting for him when his bus got to Tampa airport. Costa believed in destiny. The plane was there as he'd expected and he wired his son to meet him.

He asked for an aisle seat, sat rigidly erect, head facing forward as if he were in charge of the plane's safe passage. When lunch was offered, he waved the distraction aside. Later the man at the window next to Costa engaged in a long debate with the man across the aisle as to whether or not the President should resign. They couldn't agree, disengaged. Costa had shown no interest. Out of curiosity his neighbor asked, "What do you think of all this, sir?"

"I got my own problems," Costa said.

Teddy Avaliotis was a petty officer third class at the Naval Training Center in San Diego. When he completed his training there, he had decided to stay on, accepting the duty of maintaining and operating the video gear used in the instruction of recruits. He was highly respected by command.

Teddy met his father at San Diego's mission-style airport, waiting for him at the gate, taking his bag and kissing him.

"Got your room all set, Pop," he said, "at the inn across the street from the base. O.K.?"

"Clean place?" Costa asked.

"Wait till you see. You'll like it."

16

Teddy noticed that his father had aged—or was it the long trip?

"You're looking great, Pop," he said. "Feel O.K.?"

"I hope so," Costa said.

"You'll meet her at dinner. There's a restaurant called the Fish Factory, which features abalone; she loves abalone. And you're going to love her." He threw his arm around his father's shoulders and squeezed him. "I can't wait to see the two of you together."

"I'm sure," Costa said. "But not tonight. No dinner, so forth, tonight."

"She's waiting to see you, Pop, so anxious and all."

"Tonight, you and me talk," Costa said. "Tomorrow, maybe."

"All right, Pop," Teddy said. "So she'll wait a little longer, right?"

It was a ten-minute drive to the base, along the edge of the peninsula. The water of the bay sparkled as though it were carbonated.

"See that big carrier out there, Pop? The *Coral Sea*. See it? San Diego is the most beautiful city in the country; everybody says so."

"Very nice, very nice," Costa said. "Where you get this car?"

"The Navy gave it to me. They give me everything." Teddy laughed. "How's Mom? Tell her I really appreciate those brownies and that halvah she sends me. What a woman! Where'd you find her?"

"She's good woman."

"I got a good one too. Wait till you meet her. I'm going to make a regular Greek out of her, Pop, you'll see."

"She listen to you, boy? Tell me that much. Because American girl sometime . . . This one listen what you say?"

"Like I was the law. Which I am to her. Look! That's the gate of the base. And there's your inn. Tomorrow I'll show you the works."

The corridors of the inn were scented with a heavy commercial perfume. "Smells like a Cuban whorehouse," Costa observed when Teddy showed him to his room; they opened all the windows. While his father was settling in, Teddy called his girl and told her that dinner was off. "Tomorrow," he said.

When she told him how disappointed she was, he explained that the old man was tired and would be in a more agreeable mood the next evening. "Like I told you," he said, "it's going to take a while."

"Meeting him?"

"Really getting together. He's very—you know—old-world. You won't believe they're still making that model."

"Well, I sure hope he likes me."

"If I like you, he'll like you. Don't worry. I spent my life studying the instruction manual that came with that old bastard. I can tell you what he's going to do before he knows it himself. Get a lot of sleep so you'll look real pretty tomorrow. He likes good-looking girls."

After Teddy and his father had taken dinner from the enlisted men's chow line, Costa announced, "We talk tomorrow. Now I'm going home, pray God I understand this situation. Then sleep. I need all my strength on this one."

Teddy saw him to his room, then called his girl again.

"Just checking up on you," he said, "make sure you're not out with some other guy." He laughed.

"Is something wrong?" she asked. "I've been worried."

"No, he's gone to bed. Jet lag. He's gotten older. Like now he's praying. Never used to, not that I knew about. All Greeks start as hellers, then as they get older they turn religious and pray their way through every goddamn crisis. Not that this is a crisis."

"He's got me jumpy, Teddy."

"Relax. If he comes on sorta gruff, remember you're

with me. I'm not going to let anything bad happen. Go on now—go to bed."

He kissed her good night over the phone, then went back to the base and sat in on a game of Dealer's Choice, walking away after an hour, apologizing, with ninety-one dollars.

In the morning, Teddy fired up his Ampex gear for a class and stood by during the instruction. Then he picked up his father and walked him around the base, showing him the installations. Neither brought up the subject that was on both their minds. They watched a class in marlin-spike seamanship. The old man said he wanted to inspect the tuna fleet—he'd seen it on TV—so they did. And came back to the base for a late lunch at La Cantina, service chow with Latino décor.

Teddy wasn't unaware that his father was proud of him; he played up to it. Every time they passed people Teddy knew, he'd speak to them in his command voice, then, after they'd passed, he'd continue with his father in properly deferential tones.

And why shouldn't Costa be proud of his son? Physically Teddy was perfect, combining in some inexplicable way his father's chunky power with his mother's delicacy. He didn't give the impression that he was tall, strong or muscular, although he was all three. Teddy kept himself in perfect shape with daily exercise. And he looked so damned good in his blues.

But his truest attraction was not his appearance, not his fine nose, his deep-set eyes, or the sweep of his forehead under the Mediterranean curls. It was the feeling he gave that he was capable of handling any situation. It's what had made him irresistible to any woman he'd chosen to court.

It was what Costa had, that same assurance. Teddy remembered an incident from his childhood. He'd gone

19

out in his father's boat and a sudden storm had kicked up a heavy sea. The Greek crew, not all of whom could swim, became uneasy. Costa had said, "Remember you're with me." Even the sea had calmed. Teddy was only ten but he'd never forgotten that day and Costa's words. "Remember you're with me."

"Tonight, Pop," he asked when they'd spent another hour watching drills, "can we . . . ?"

"Tonight, I buy you dinner."

"Then I better call her right away," Teddy said. "She's waiting for me to cut her orders for the day. She's a good girl, Pop."

"Tonight, just you and me, we have to talk."

"But, Pop, she's so anxious to meet you."

"The time will come for that," Costa said. "Last night, I pray God I understand this situation. Tonight I pray again. But first I want to talk to you. We didn't talk yet."

"All right," Teddy said. He pointed to a phone booth. "Excuse me."

She wasn't in. "She told me to tell you she'll be back in twenty minutes," her roommate told Teddy. Then added, "She seems a little upset."

"She's very upset," Teddy told his father. "She began to cry on the phone."

"Why, my boy—what's the trouble?"

"She doesn't understand why you don't want to meet her. 'Is something wrong?' she kept asking. It means so much to her, what you think."

"Well, then, what the hell, we take her out tonight."

"Let's give her a chance to calm down a little, then I'll call again. How about a cup of coffee?"

"No coffee. I buy you drink. Must be bar 'round somewhere."

"What do you mean, somewhere? This is today's Navy, Pop! We'll go to the Ship's Bell, right here on the base."

It was full of sailors getting an early start on their beer.

Their Commander-in-Chief had quit office that morning, but his men seemed unaffected, those who were discussing the event at all doing so without sense of loss, even frivolously.

"What this country needs is a Jewish king!" they heard as Teddy found a corner table.

"Now, Pop," Teddy said, after he'd ordered. "You want to talk, let's talk."

"Is she clean girl?" was the first question Costa asked.

"One look at her, you'll have your answer," Teddy said.

Costa felt better when Teddy told him she was a student nurse and her father a doctor. Thinking he might be on to something, Teddy boasted about his sweetheart's intelligence.

"Can she cook?" Costa asked.

"She's damn well going to learn," Teddy said. "I got her keeping a little notebook. Ethnic recipes. She cuts them out of magazines."

"I'm not old-fashion type Greek," Costa said. "If it was my father over here, you wouldn't bring up problem in first place. He say, right away, 'American girl for pleasure, Greek girl for family.' Your grandfather came to this country with no one. When he had money and a boat of his own, he knew it was time to find a wife."

"I know, Pop, I know."

"He went back to Kalymnos, pick out your grandmother. He believe in blood. Me too. But less. For your mother I only go to Astoria, Queens. That is why I pray God last night I understand your problem. Without prayer, my belief on that, I wouldn't come here. Easy to say no long-distance. But now when I say, Can she cook?, you have idea, I hope, that I am father you can talk to. Right?"

"I know all that, Pop. Look, maybe you better shave before we go get her."

"One more thing, Teddy, then we leave. Go 'head, get check."

"What's one more thing?"

"I want grandson my name. Is that possible?"

"Just tell me when you want him delivered," Teddy said.

"You're my only son. I don't forget that. Hope you same."

"How could I forget it, Pop, with you around? Now, is it O.K. if I call her and tell her we'll pick her up for dinner?"

"Why not?" Costa said. "Why you think I come here? I haven't much time. Your mother, poor thing, she's all alone back there in the store."

Teddy had to wait for his girl to come to the phone. On the wall next to the booth was an old-time poster of a lovely young woman. She was quoted: "Gee, I wish I were a man. I'd join the Navy."

"I got him in a great mood," Teddy told his girl. "You know he's a little nervous too. . . . About what? About meeting you. . . . Honest! Tell me what you're going to wear."

She gave him the possibilities.

"Wear your blue," he said, "with the long sleeves."

At sunset, they drove out to the suburban neighborhood where she lived in a big house with six other girls. The old-fashioned living room had almost no furniture. There were large bolsters and pillows all over the floor, and the girls and their boyfriends were sprawled on them.

Costa didn't like the look of the place or the company. Not one of the girls jumped to her feet to offer him a coffee or a glass of cold water. The hifi dropped another record down its spindle, as loud as the one before.

"Mostly nurses here," Teddy said.

Costa was still not impressed.

Then there she was, coming down the stairs, dressed in

blue and wearing her best turquoise earrings to match her eyes. Her hair, freshly washed, was unusually fine, and it was golden.

Score one for her. Costa trusted blue. It was the color of heaven, the color of Hellas, the color of feminine purity, the color baby boys wear.

She kissed Teddy, then, blushing, shook hands with Costa. Her hand was small-boned, fragile.

Score one against her: something about her figure disturbed Costa. Her legs were too thin all the way up. A proper Greek wife-candidate should be ample in the hips even before she was pregnant, but full-breasted—which this girl certainly was—only after.

Then Costa looked at her face. It reminded him of—he didn't know what: perhaps certain small sea creatures he'd seen, beings transparent and unshielded, whose way of life was to ride with the tide, whichever way it moved.

"Pop," Teddy said, "this is Kitten."

"Ethel," she said.

"She doesn't like her nickname." Teddy laughed. "She's only had it for—how many years? Ten?"

"I'm so glad to meet you," she said to the old man. "Finally."

She colored again, as if she'd been too forward or perhaps because Costa was studying her so gravely. In her embarrassment, she turned to Teddy, then back to his father.

"I also glad, miss," he said. "What I call you?"

"My name is Ethel. Ethel Laffey."

"Ethel then."

"I don't like Ethel either. It was my mother's idea. I never found out why."

"Well," Costa said, "which do you—?"

"Dislike least?" Teddy laughed.

"Kit, I guess," Ethel said. "That's what everyone calls me. Kit. Since high school. Or Ethel. I don't care," she

23

said, shaking her head and making little sounds of self-deprecation. "How silly," she said. "So silly! I mean, anything you call me is all right because I am so glad to meet you, Mr. Avaliotis."

Costa smiled at his son. "You teach her say my name very good!"

"She's been practicing," Teddy said.

"Do I say it O.K.?" Ethel asked. "Avaliotis?"

"Very O.K.," the old man rewarded her.

The music, flaring to a climax and making conversation impossible, gave Costa time to warn himself not to be diverted from the careful judgment he was there to make. He could see that Teddy was gone on the girl, but there were certain questions he had to ask and certain answers he had to hear.

He indicated the roaring hifi with a peremptory gesture, warning Ethel that if she didn't do something about it, he would.

Quickly she led the men to a corner as far from the hifi as the room allowed. There was an armchair for Costa. She and Teddy sat on the floor. Costa had his questions ready and wasn't going to waste any time.

"How you meet, Ethel, tell me that much," he asked with a smile to demonstrate his tolerance.

"We met at a dance." Ethel took Teddy's hand.

"What kind— Turn that damn music out!" Costa said.

Ethel jumped up and hurried to the other end of the room.

"Why she walk like that?" Costa whispered to his son.

"She walk like how?" Teddy asked.

"On toes and like this," Costa demonstrated, swaying his shoulders.

Teddy had never noticed Ethel's walk. "You like her, Dad?" he whispered.

Speaking to the girls around the hifi, standing erect and

quite still, she seemed to be swaying. The delicately turned feet and ankles, the long slim legs which came together and touched at the knees—a kiss before parting—seemed inadequate support for the torso of a mature, even voluptuous woman. Her head too, since her neck was long, seemed uncertainly balanced. Her whole person suggested a tulip yielding to a breeze.

"What kind color her hair?" the father was asking.

"Sometimes I think it's red," Teddy said. "Then, in another light, it's golden. I honestly don't know. It's pretty, though, isn't it?"

The music was brought to a compromise level and Ethel turned to her men. She was anxious and straining, but her eyes were steady, bits of soft blue velvet, a contrast to her hair and to the flame spots on her cheeks.

"What were you two saying about me?" she asked as she came back.

"He likes your hair," Teddy said.

"Very nice, very nice. Now tell me," Costa said, "what kind dance? Where you meet?"

"Oh!" Ethel offered her best kitten smile. "Where was it, Teddy?" she asked, sitting on the floor next to him and putting her hand in his again.

The veins in Ethel's hand showed like the tracery in a leaf.

"You know where, honey," Teddy answered. "At the enlisted men's hall, Pop, where we had dinner last night. Dime night—we met on dime night."

"Very nice," Costa said. He turned again to the girl on trial. "Why you don't stay with your parents?" he asked. "Where they live?"

Ethel didn't answer immediately. She'd begun to wonder what the old man was really trying to find out.

It was Teddy who said, "They live in Tucson, Arizona, Pop."

"Why she don't live in Arizona over there?" Costa

asked his son. "Beautiful. I saw magazine in airplane." He turned back to Ethel. "You fight with your father, mother, maybe?"

"Nothing like that," Ethel said. "I'm in training here to be a nurse."

"Your father, what he say?" Costa indicated his son.

"He hasn't met Teddy yet. He says it's up to me."

"He don't care who you—?"

"Of course he cares, Mr. Ava—" Ethel stumbled over the name, then righted herself: "Avaliotis."

"After all, Pop," Teddy said, "I'm marrying Ethel, not her old man."

"Everybody must know everybody first," Costa said to his son. "This is family business."

"That's why I've been so anxious to meet you," Ethel said.

"Family important to Greek people." Costa seemed to be scolding Teddy now. "Blood, you understand, boy? Keep family going. Clean blood, you understand?" He looked intently at the girl.

"Teddy and I want a family more than anything," she said.

Costa saw her eyes gleam and he believed her. He went on to the next consideration.

"You had sweetheart before? Other sweethearts?"

Ethel dropped her head as if she were suddenly exhausted. Then she looked up at Teddy and smiled a little.

"Tell him what you told me," Teddy said. "Don't be afraid."

"Yes, I did," she said, the effort visible. "I was sort of engaged before I met Teddy."

"What is that 'engaged sort of' business?" Costa asked.

"Well, I mean . . ." She turned to Teddy. "I don't know what to say."

"Tell him the truth," Teddy said.

Costa waited.

"Excuse me." Ethel got to her feet. "I have a little headache. Been so nervous all day about meeting you, Mr. Avaliotis. I'll run upstairs and get a couple of Bufferins."

After she'd disappeared up the stairs, Costa said, "She's nervous."

"Maybe you better knock it off, Pop," Teddy said. "Enough for now."

"O.K., boy," Costa said. "We go eat." He looked toward the other end of the room. "That damn music make anybody nervous."

Then Ethel was coming back and Teddy saw what his father meant: she tiptoed forward off her heels, the body's expression of her hope that she'd get by without being noticed.

"Feel better, Miss Ethel?" Costa asked.

"In a few minutes I will," she answered.

"Too many questions, I know. Come on, we go eat. I'm hungry."

"No; I want to answer what you asked." Ethel knelt on the floor in front of the old man and put her hands on his knees. Her face was that of a child making a difficult confession. "Since you asked," she said, "this other boy and me, we had almost decided to be engaged. In Tucson this was. Then I met Teddy. Fortunately."

"And that is all?" Costa asked.

"Yes. I mean . . . what are you asking, Mr. Avaliotis?"

"Almost engaged—what that mean?"

"Teddy was engaged himself before we met. You know that," Ethel said. "And from what he tells me, before that Teddy got around."

"He knows that, Kit," Teddy said.

"He's a man," Costa said to Ethel. "What you expect?"

"What I'm trying to say, I guess, is that neither of us is what you would call lily pure. That what you wanted to know?"

27

Costa dropped his eyes. They were all silent for a moment. Ethel sank back on her heels and looked at Teddy. He was watching his father digest the piece of information he'd dug up.

Then Costa spoke. "With man, you understand, it's different. He can't hold back. If he hold back, he get sick."

Ethel looked at Teddy, her face uncreased innocence. "I didn't know that," she said. "Is that true, Teddy? You get sick if—?"

"I just told you that, Miss Ethel," Costa said. "Yes!"

"Let's go to dinner," Teddy said.

But no one got up. There was a silence as each of the three tried to understand what had happened.

Costa broke the tension. "You know my boy's name?" he asked.

"You mean . . . Teddy?"

"His real name. Greek name?"

"Theophilactos."

"What it mean?"

"Guarding God. Isn't that what you said, Teddy?"

"Wrong! What kind protection God needs? *Following* God, it mean. This boy I brought up proper style; he always follow God's way—right, Teddy?"

"Not always, Pop," Teddy said.

"I don't want to hear about the other," Costa said.

They all smiled. Costa had thrown it out as a joke.

"Come on, we go eat." Costa stood up. "There's a place here, little birdie tell me, they have abalone fresh. I like abalone. How 'bout you, Miss Ethel?"

"I do. But honestly, I'm not feeling too well. I think I better just have a cup of broth and go to bed."

"No, no, no," Costa said. "No more questions, guarantee! Come on, young lady. I'm not so bad. Out of date, sure, sometime damn fool, but one thing sure—my family everything for me, you understand? I have one son, this boy here."

"That's enough, Pop." Teddy cut him off.

"And I want grandson on my name before I die."

"Pop, shut up for a while, will you?"

Suddenly Costa walloped Teddy across the back with his open hand, the bulk of his shoulders following the forearm with the power which comes from much experience.

Teddy, thrown off balance, took it with a smile. "Tough guy here," he said to Ethel.

Ethel wondered, was Costa mad at Teddy or at her?

By the time they got into Teddy's car, Costa had cooled. "Boy's right," he said as he showed her into the front seat and slid in beside her. "No more questions tonight. From now on, only good time tonight."

Before dinner Costa had a couple, and he had a double with the main course, and instead of lime pie he ordered brandy, which he compared unfavorably with Metaxa. But it kept the old man up and soon he began to boast.

"In those days," he told Ethel, who had been silent all through the meal, "it was Greeks against conks. Guess who won?"

"The Greeks, naturally," Teddy said to Ethel.

"Right," Costa said. "Whatsa matter, young lady? You say nothing."

"I'm fine," Ethel said.

"She's like that sometimes, Pop."

Costa took her cheek between the knuckles of his forefinger and second finger and shook it. "Damn pretty girl," he said, "especially after couple drinks."

Ethel pulled her cheek away.

"She has a headache, Pop," Teddy said.

"Never mind, never mind, it's nothing. What was I telling? Oh, the conks—crackers, maybe you call them. The people there, mostly in Key West, south Florida. They mad because we work their water, take out more sponge than them. They *vlax*. You know what *vlax* is, young lady?"

"How would she ever know that, Pop?"

"Country people. Stupid. Like donkey."

"Pop, the people at the next table are listening."

"O.K., I'm quiet," he whispered. "Well, one night in Port Everglade—Ethel, you hearing me O.K.?"

"Oh, yes."

"Teddy was baby boy this time, three year old. He never heard this story."

"I heard it ten times, Pop."

"So hear it ten more," Costa said. "And be quiet when your father talk. Also tell damn long-hair waiter bring one more lousy brandy over here."

Teddy looked for the waiter.

"We sitting—Ethel, listen!—in this conk bar. I always find bar my enemy where to drink. Their women too. I mean those cracker bitches my slaves. They wait for my boat to come, for me to—you know. Don't worry, Teddy, I don't say bad word. Teddy very good boy, miss. That's why I worry. Too nice sometime. People fool him. What you think?"

Ethel looked away. "Teddy, your father wants another brandy," she said.

Costa finished the one he had. "So listen," he said. "We were in this conk bar and I was singing—now I lost my voice—lotsa more too. You modern girl, nurse too, so I tell you those days I can cut my name in block of ice fifteen feet away with my water. Now like cow, excuse me, dear girl."

Ethel smiled. Then, as if she'd really just understood what Costa had said, she laughed for a long time in relief, like a child.

Encouraged, Costa burst into a Greek song.

"How you like that, Ethel?" he asked when it was over.

The middle-aged couple at the next table got up and left.

"Pop!" Teddy pointed.

"Not too hot, I see. Right, Ethel?"

"Well, I don't understand the words, so—"

"Roughly translated," Teddy said, "it goes: 'I'm a hell of a guy and my strength I will prove. I will have one more drink than I should. Never mind what my wife says.' "

"Better in Greek," Costa said.

"I've heard it sung better too," Teddy said.

"Don't be fresh front your father, boy," Costa said. He'd been brought his brandy now and he grabbed the waiter by the arm, holding him there. "Have one drink, young lady. Come on. I give permission."

"She has a headache, Pop."

"Let her talk, Teddy, for chrissake. All of sudden, she say nothing."

Ethel smiled faintly.

"When you have a headache, Pop, it hurts when you talk. Besides you're—"

"I talk enough for everybody, right?"

"Right. Let the waiter go, Pop. You're holding him."

"O.K., Mr. Waiter, go 'head." The waiter left. "Long hair, Ethel, see that? I don't like long-hair waiter; woman waiter too. No good. When they bend over, who knows what kind bugs, so forth, so on, fall on food. I like nigger waiter. Short hair, right? So. I been telling you. The conks, they burn our boats. That night, we go to the *limani*—beach in Greek, young lady—and we set fire to eight of theirs, pile one top the other. Then, quick, we put out to sea. There was big storm outside and those goddamn conks—" Costa couldn't continue for laughing. "Their boat no good, draw not even one foot water; they don't go down for sponge, you understand. Have long pole with hook on end. To go down, they don't have courage. They stay close to shore, we work outside, big seas, any weather. They can't follow us. Why I'm saying all this? You remember, Miss Ethel? Pretty girl? Eh? What's the difference? I remember that trip we had big catch sponge. When we get back to Tarpon Spring, three-day trip over there, people come down to docks, surprise how many sponge we take, like beads on every line we can tie on boat. And the smell! Sponge like you and me: when they die, they stink. My crew pound guts out of those sponge, boom, boom, boom, on deck. But not me. Number one diver, he bring sponge up, but cleaning, that's for crew. I get into my car—had fine car those days, Oldsmobile Eighty-eight. I go house my girl friend; Irish, but very nice. She waiting for me. 'How you know I come back?' I say. 'I smell you,' she say. 'No one stink up whole town like you, Avaliotis! Come on, take bath first.' "

"Then what did you do, Pop, you and your Irish girl friend?"

"Those things we don't talk front young lady. But I tell you this much, boy: when time come to marry, I went looking for proper-style Greek girl. I find your mother in Astoria section, New York City."

"But, Pop, you said all this happened with the Irish girl when I was three years old."

"Mistake," Costa said. And he was suddenly formidable. "When I marry your mother, boy, no more monkey business with other woman. Young lady, I been marry thirty years. In that time, I never touch other woman."

He was looking Ethel straight in the eye, as if challenging her.

"I believe you," she said. "Now may I ask you a question?"

"Anything you want, young lady."

"Wouldn't you be happier if Teddy married one of your own people?"

"You ask me that?"

"It's a natural question."

Ethel looked at Teddy. He took her hand.

"Yes," Costa said, "I be happier."

"Well, I wouldn't," Teddy said. "How do you like that, Pop?"

"I can't help it," Costa said. "She ask me question."

"Thanks for saying that," Ethel said to Costa. "I really do have a headache. I'd like to go home."

They let the old man off at the inn and he went up to his room and prayed. "I see she don't drink," he said to the One he hoped was listening. "Maybe because I'm watching, right? She's not clean girl, she told me that much. But to find American girl clean—will you let me live that long? What I see is this: Teddy love her. When she talk, which ain't much, he smile like crazy man. Meantime, I have idea she smarter than she look. But I don't understand young woman now. There is my problem. I don't have long time to live and Teddy twenty-three, so if I say no now, we should think over very careful, right?"

To clinch it, he prayed in Greek, in more formal phrases.

Then, having done what he could about the problem, he fell asleep.

two

THEY weren't speaking. Ethel's hand was on the door. Teddy swung to the curb in front of her house and jerked up the emergency brake as if he were trying to rip it out of the floor.

She opened the door.

"Wait a minute!" he said. "Tell me why you were looking at me like that."

He was talking to the back of her head.

"All night. Looking so disgusted at me."

Again she didn't answer.

From different parts of the house where she lived came sounds of music and sudden shrieks of laughter.

"You better say something now, and quick!"

"Why don't you do what he wants, marry one of your—"

"Why don't you go and fuck yourself! Close the door." He reached across and slammed it at her. "What's eating you now, for instance? Right now?"

"I never saw you," she said, "the way you were with him."

"What'd you want me to do when he hit me—punch him out?"

"You were pretending with him all night, and backing off, and when I needed help, you left me out there alone."

"He took to you, didn't he? I handled it the only way possible with him. You think he's easy? Try changing his mind sometime about something real heavy, like whether or not it's raining. If I hadn't thrown him a couple of curves this afternoon, you'd still be painting your nails up in your dinky room and wondering when he was going to break down and see you. I do what has to be done to get the result I want. What's wrong with that?"

She turned her head and appraised him as she might a stranger.

"Now what does that haughty fucking look mean?" he said. "I've been handling that man all my life, so don't give me lessons in the art. He's smooth as grass with you, sure. 'Miss Ethel!' 'Pretty girl!' All that shit. But cross him sometime, I dare you, then run for the emergency exit."

"Why don't you talk straight to him?"

"Because he's a rockhead. My mother does it the same way I do. We've both seen him charge off the edge of the cliff. Then there's something else, which you wouldn't understand because you were brought up rich. When I was in that junior college, he got it up, dimes and quarters, out of one lousy bait-and-beer place. And I'm going to pay him back in what he wants most—respect! That's why I paid his way out here. You think I need him to tell me what to do?"

She was still looking at him out of the coolest corner of her eye.

"What the hell do I have to do with you—prove myself all the time?" Teddy was fuming. "Is that the way it's going to be? Because you can shove that! Go on, get in your house. I don't want to bother with you anymore."

Turning the ignition key, he stepped on the accelerator. The motor roared. She ran.

The house she lived in was on the edge of a ridge and had been rather grand when it was built fifty years before. The twin towers, either end of the façade, had provided an impressive view of the harbor. Now they faced a row of condominiums built just off the side of the hill. That was the view Ethel had.

She occupied a small tower room with a girl whom she hardly ever saw. This young nurse, engaged to a lawyer, used the house only to wash her hair, change her clothes and receive her parents' mail. Most of the time Ethel had their room to herself, as she did that night.

She couldn't sleep.

The other bed was covered with the debris from her roommate's quick clothes change: discarded panty hose, several belts she'd tried on and decided not to wear, a mirror and several vials of eye shadow in slightly different colors, an eye liner with a broken point, a little plastic bottle of skin cleanser, a bag of cotton puffs to spread the liquid, two towels, one soiled with make-up, a hair dryer, the tube like a piece of white intestine, and the copy of *Photoplay* she'd read as her hair dried. All had been used in haste, left where they'd been dropped.

For some reason, the disorder, to which she was accustomed, depressed Ethel this night, perhaps because it suggested her roommate's eagerness to meet her lover.

From below, different music came from different rooms, a sound that further jangled Ethel's nerves.

She pushed her fingertips into her ears and got under the covers.

She still couldn't sleep.

Finally she called Teddy. "Hello," she said.

"I was just going to call you," Teddy said.

"I can't sleep when we're angry."

"Neither can I."

"I was thinking about what happened tonight."

"He was crude."

"I like him but he scares me."

"He had some nerve asking you those questions."

"He wanted to know if I was a virgin. It's a natural curiosity."

"Only for old-timers like him."

"No. A lot of people wonder about that but they don't ask. It still makes a difference to people. Doesn't it make you feel bad that I was with some others before you?"

"I don't think about it."

"Yes you do, Teddy."

"I used to."

"No, now. I think you feel bad about it now. I hate the idea of your having been with your little Greek pot roast. But the reason I called . . . I wanted you to know that I came back here and I couldn't sleep and I thought it over, you and me, and . . . what I wanted to tell you is that I love you a lot, right this minute."

"That's all I care about," Teddy said.

"I do. I love you. And you know what? My headache's gone."

"Now I can sleep."

"No, don't sleep. Because, Teddy, listen to me, Teddy. When we get married, I'm going to do everything you tell me to do. I'm going to obey you."

He laughed. "Obey! That I don't believe."

"I want you to beat me up if I don't obey you. That's

exactly how I feel, Teddy. You're so dumb. I'm trying to tell you that my headache's gone and I . . . Really, Teddy, you're so damn slow!"

"Oh. I'll be right over!"

A pot party had taken over the house, so Ethel waited for Teddy at the side of the road. She showed him where to drive; at the end of a dark street there was a beech tree whose branches hung down to a few feet off the ground. Another car was pulling out as they drove under.

Ethel had brought along a little pine pillow her mother had given her. They made love in the front seat, a trick the young can perform.

They were winging. Ethel forgot there was a world.

When they fell back to earth, they landed against each other, exhausted, happy and with nothing important to say.

Ethel spoke to herself, out loud. "We're going to make it work," she said with all the confidence in the impossible that follows lovemaking. "Teddy . . ."

"What?"

"I think he was nervous too."

"I told you; that's why he got drunk so quickly."

"Oh, the darling—he's a darling."

"He's scared your father and mother will find him too crude or too uneducated, what he calls a *vlax*. My old man is proud as anyone you'll ever meet, but he still thinks he smells of dying sponge, and do they ever stink!"

"I don't care what my father says, you know that."

"That's not the point. Costa Avaliotis cares."

"Maybe they'll like each other. Maybe."

She didn't see how they could. Her father, Dr. Ed Laffey, was a rigid professional, a surgeon. Her mother was an invalid for whom no cure seemed possible. Dr. Laffey ran his home like a sanitarium with a single patient.

"I have an idea," Ethel said. "Let's hop a plane tomorrow, all three of us, and fly to Tucson. Like your father said, everybody has to know everybody. We'll have the final score an hour after they meet."

"Then fuck 'em; we'll do what we want."

"Oh, Teddy," she said, wanting rapture again.

"But I do think he likes you. I want him to. I want him to be happy."

"I'll make him love me."

"That's the idea. Come on with him. Flatter him. Flirt with him. He's too old for pussy, but he sure can take a lot of kitten."

"I'll give him all he can take. And you too."

"Come here."

"Teddy, I love you so much."

"And shut up."

"Teddy, I didn't put it in, remember?"

When Ethel was happy, there wasn't anything else.

The rest of that night she dreamed about her lover. It was pretty childish, actually, and went like this: If she and Teddy could make it with his father watching—that was her fantasy—Costa would know how happy she made his son. Then Ethel saw it happening, exactly that, and Costa was being very serious about it, saying, "Proper way," or "Proper style," or something very heavy which made her laugh, and—

The phone woke her.

"He's agreed," a voice said.

"Who? What? Teddy? Is that you?"

"Who else you expecting?"

"I was asleep. Wait a minute."

She pulled the phone under the covers and, knees to chin, cuddled with it in the dark.

"Who agreed? He did? Good."

"On one condition: that you go first and he and I follow three days later."

"Oh, no."

"I told him, Hey, Pop, it's not going to take her three days to prepare her goddamn parents. 'You find out I'm right,' he says. He's got a hangover, by the way, which only makes him more stubborn."

Now she was awake. "I don't want to spend three days with my father," she said. "I don't want to spend three days in that house with my mother. I don't want to spend three days alone in Tucson."

"Well, you're going to have to."

"Why?"

"Because I say so. Now obey me and shut up. Because he wants it that way. 'Proper way,' he says. 'My father . . .' something or other. By the way, he does like you. 'High-class person,' he said. That's the way he talks, like you were running for mayor. 'Excellent person!' Ho-ho! Get up. There's a plane at eleven-twenty and I got your ticket."

"Will you drive me to the airport?"

"Got to stand by my Ampex."

"That damn Ampex. Let someone else do it."

"I don't want someone else to do it. Especially if I'm going to take three days off later. Now hurry up. Get dressed."

Before she got out of bed, she made him agree to drive her to the airport bus. Half an hour later he was under her tower, calling.

"Coming right down," she shouted through the window screen.

But she didn't come right down. Despite the fact that the old man stirred a quiver of fear in her every time he looked at her, which she said she liked and maybe did, Ethel was relieved not to have to see him that day. She gave in to a perverse notion. She decided to put on that one of her dresses which he would like least. The choice, after much deliberation, was a white dress of silk so light it floated when she turned. She augmented it with a yellow scarf which sparked her hair. The girls downstairs stopped her to say how intolerably sexy she looked.

"You're late again," Teddy said when she finally came out the door and ran down the walk to where he was parked. Then he noticed the dress. "You got a date in Tucson or something?" he said. "Some dude meeting your plane there?"

"Why do you say that?"

She got into the car and pulled her hem, gingerly, over her knees.

"Your dress!"

"What's the matter with it?"

"For a stranger, nothing. I can see your tits."

"I thought you liked them."

"What kind of an answer is that?"

"We're not going to see your old man, so what's—"

"My old man is standing in front of the inn this minute, waiting to say good-bye. You should have worn your little blue dress again."

"What would he have said about those little white drops you left on my little blue dress last night?"

Teddy had to laugh.

Costa's reaction to Ethel's dress was less tactful.

"What kind dress that, for God's sake. *À la Franka!*"

"Just a lightweight—it's almost a hundred degrees in Tucson. I called my father and he's looking forward so much to meeting you."

"I can see everything over there."

"Oh, the dress? This is the way girls dress now," Ethel said in her kitten voice.

"What kind girls?"

"Like the girls in the house where I live."

"Those girls getting married?"

"They hope to, most of them."

"Let them hope. Nothing doing over there, guarantee."

Then he spoke to his son vigorously in Greek.

To which Teddy replied, "We can't, Pop. We'll just make the bus as it is."

"I'm sorry," Ethel said as they turned onto the freeway. "If I'd known we were going to see him— What did he say to you in Greek?"

"He told me to take you home and change your dress."

"*You* take me home and *you* change my dress?"

"That's our boy! And if I didn't make a Greek-style woman out of you pretty damn quick, he'd do it himself."

"I don't want to go . . . I don't want to go . . . I don't want to leave you," she said again and again all the way into town.

"Three days," Teddy said.

"A lot can happen in three days. You can forget me in three days. What are you going to do? Tell me. Every day what?"

"My father. Every day. He'll talk, I'll listen."

They turned a corner and there was the bus station.

"I don't want to be alone ever again," she said. "I'm scared to leave you, Teddy." She leaned hard against him and whispered, "Teddy, really, why don't you take me all the way to the airport? We'll go back in the parking lot where we were that time—remember those broken-down school buses? Then I'll feel better."

"You said you don't like quick jobs."

"I like them better than nothing."

"What time is it?"

"Come on. Let's go. We can make it. Don't be so conscientious."

"Look, there's your bus loading." He pushed her gently off the steering wheel—he was so flattered—and turned the car to the curb. "Go ahead, baby, grab it. It's only going to be three days! And call me. Every day. I'll be waiting for your call."

Riding out to the airport in the bus, it occurred to her that these next three days during which she didn't want to be without Teddy were the last three days for a long time that she'd be without him.

She felt alone and unprotected. And in the kind of danger she had once enjoyed.

At Tucson she was the last off the plane, did not rush with the others to pick up her bag. She walked slowly into the unshielded sun, stood exposed to its weight. Having decided something, she went to the Avis stand and rented a car.

Ethel was not going home.

She drove slowly in the opposite direction, toward the mountains to the north. At the foot of the first hills, there was one long last street running off into the open desert. Where it ended, she stopped before a small white cabin. It looked deserted.

In the glove compartment of the rental she found a parking ticket which the previous user had not redeemed. On it she wrote: "Ernie, please meet me tonight at our Tex-Mex place. I need to talk to you." She signed it: "Kit."

She got out and walked toward the dingy frame building. There was an old Scout jeepster at the side of the house, but it looked out of service. The kitchen door was unlatched. When he was at work, Ernie left the door to his house open. And at all other times.

The outside of the place was shabby; much of the paint had been scoured off by wind-driven sand. But inside it was rather gay. The walls everywhere had been covered with clippings and photographs from newspapers and magazines, all with meanings special and private, pointed up by scribbles Ernie had added in the margins and corners. They ranged from the serious to the trivial, the trivial regarded seriously, the serious mocked. An obscene collage depicted Jackie Onassis on her knees servicing

General Charles de Gaulle, who was addressing his Army of Liberation in the distance. Ethel noted recent additions. One, on the refrigerator, read: "When the poor are born without assholes, shit will be worth money."

Ernie happened to be the son of a rich real estate operator and insurance tycoon.

The sink was loaded with unwashed pots and pans. The kitchen table had not been cleared of supper. Ethel noted that two people had eaten there the night before.

She found that the hot-water kettle on the stove was warm, and looking through the door to the other room—there was only one—she saw Ernie. He was asleep, naked, face and belly down, on his mattress on the floor exactly where she'd last seen him five months earlier.

Slipping out of her sandals, she tiptoed through the beer empties and let herself down on the edge of the mattress. There she was still.

She counted seven cats in the room—three additions since her time.

Ernie had the soft, rounded muscles of what he was not: a champion swimmer. He never exercised, but never gained weight. His skin was a golden brown, his hair even more fair, straw. The image of a modern Apollo, he was a young man so richly endowed by nature that he'd never been driven to prove himself.

Next to his head the sheet had been pulled back and she saw the place in the mattress ticking he'd set on fire months before, with an unattended cigarette. He hadn't even turned the mattress over.

An old alarm clock was busy: two fifty-two. Ernie, she recalled, had had a job, a sort of man-of-half-skills at the State Experimental Farm. But he often didn't bother to go in to work and the people there shrugged off his willfulness. Ernie worked when he needed money.

The area around the mattress was familiar to Ethel. The same books were there still, in piles, and everywhere magazines and newspapers. There was a new collection: small curious cacti in coffee cans and there were stones, cut open to reveal startling interior patterns.

"You're back." A murmur.

Ethel hadn't moved. Neither had Ernie.

"Yes."

"Bring the beer?"

"What?"

"You were going for a six-pack."

Ethel remembered. Five months ago she'd gone on a twenty-minute errand and hadn't returned.

Ernie turned over slowly and saw who it was.

"Oh, it's you. Kit!"

"I didn't bring any beer."

Ernie gave her a present, his gentle smile. He had what she remembered, a single dimple.

"You mad at me?" she asked.

"We do what we have to do, baby."

"You got my letter?"

"I got it, but I haven't read it all yet."

"In three months! It wasn't that long a letter, Ernie."

"I got the idea pretty quick. I didn't need a long letter."

"So you are mad at me?"

"What did you say you were going to do?"

"Get married."

"Oh, my God!"

"What's that mean?"

"Does he know what he's getting into?"

"That's not a nice thing to say, Ernie."

"Just a factual question. See if you can find me a cigarette somewhere, will you?"

Ethel got up and began to look around.

"I've told him everything," she said.

"If you did, you went too far. Look in my britches."

His pants were on the floor where he'd dropped them.

"Almost everything. Here. There's only one left."

45

"Now a match. When you go down to the store, bring me back a carton of Kools. Also beer, a six-pack, and maybe some Fritos. Also *Time* magazine and *Newsweek,* and if they have it, the new *Rolling Stone.*"

"What makes you think I'm going down to the store?"

"Everybody does, sooner or later."

She'd found a match and was lighting his cigarette.

"How come you're not at work?"

"I was reading this book last night, got real interested and wanted to finish it."

"I see you had a girl friend here."

"She fixed dinner. Then I told her to go."

"Same old Ernie. You want me to clean up for you?"

"If you want to. Don't do it for me. Let me look at you."

He did, through the smoke from the Kool, and smiled affectionately.

"You look O.K.," he said.

"I am."

"In fact, I'm glad to see you."

"I almost didn't come. I was afraid you'd be pissed at me."

"For what?"

"For disappearing that way. Are you?" Teddy, she thought, would have raised hell with her. "I wouldn't blame you, so tell me."

"We don't have to go through all that shit, do we?"

"I want to, Ernie; I want you to forgive me."

"I have. Besides, I expected it."

"Expected what?"

"That at the last minute you'd think better of the whole thing and pull out. I was kind of relieved. I'd thought of backing out myself."

"Really, Ernie? Or are you trying to make me feel better?"

"After you'd gone, I went to see that place you found. I

like it better here. It looks like hell, sure, but—well, think of the effort of moving all this art and wisdom I've put on the walls. It would be like moving the Sistine Chapel." He looked with satisfaction at the walls of his room. "I've got some beautiful new stuff. Take a walk around and— Are you crying? For chrissake, Kit, I'm not mad at you."

"I'm ashamed of myself," Ethel said, "disappearing that way, without a word."

"Ashamed! That's the most useless emotion there is. Shame and guilt—I don't know which is worse. See what it says there?" He pointed to a place on the wall. "Ingrid what's-her-name, the movie star, she said it. 'The secret of happiness is good health and a short memory.' Rip it off and take it with you. You did what you had to do. It wasn't a good idea anyway, our living together. If you paid the rent, which you'd certainly have to, it might make me feel obligated. I'd get to hate you. The strain of fidelity! And my cats! Here they're free. What would I have done there—clean up after them? No, we're better off here, the last house on a deserted street, the coyotes, the snakes and the owls feeding on the prairie dogs, the field mice and the quail, a perfect ecological balance— Kit, now cut it out, stop crying."

"I feel terrible, Ernie. But don't you see, we're too much alike. I wrote you all that."

"I honestly didn't finish your letter."

"You don't care about anything, baby."

Ernie sighed.

"What does that mean?"

"I can hear my father's voice," he said. "That's how he used to talk and that's why I left home."

"Well, it's true; nothing matters to you."

"That's right. But I'm glad for you. I really do like you." He caressed her face, softly, the way he used to. "That hasn't changed. You can rely on that."

She closed her eyes and was silent.

"I'm not sore at you," he said. "I'll always like you."

"Will you? Promise?"

"Yes. We'll always be friends. No matter what you do."

"Thank you," she said. "Really. Thank you."

Then, in relief, her eyes still closed, she lay down, put her arms around him, as if she were doing it in a dream, rested her head on his shoulder.

"I believe you now," she said. "That you're not mad at me. I feel better."

"So don't cry anymore."

"O.K."

Ernie did not move closer. They were quiet.

"I've really got somebody good now," she whispered.

"I'm glad for you."

"See, Ernie, I need someone to tell me how to be, what's right and what's wrong. He does that."

"So then good. Don't cry anymore."

"I'm crying now because I'm happy. Talking to you like this. I missed talking to you, Ernie. I kept worrying about you. Like whether you'd ever had this goddamn mattress fixed. Why don't you at least turn it over? Come on. Get up."

They turned the mattress over, putting it head to foot.

"Thanks," Ernie said. "It does look better. More work than I've done in a week." He stretched out again. "Come on now, tell me about him. What's his name?"

"Teddy. Cover yourself, will you?"

"Get in here with me and I'll cover us both," he said, throwing the sheet back and getting under it. "Come on, like we used to, just to talk."

She kept her panties on.

"Now tell me about Teddy."

She told him about Costa, his visit, Ernie listening intently and without interrupting, never challenging her interpretation of any event, never setting her straight on any judgment. Ernie knew how to listen. She told him how Costa had questioned her, how he changed when he was drunk, about the song he sang and how dangerous he looked when he got mad and how it had scared her. She told him how honest he was, that he'd admitted the truth when she asked if he wished Teddy would marry one of their own kind and how tight that family was, how close, she'd never known anything like that, her family was nothing. "And you . . . you know."

"I know," Ernie said. "Nothing. But look, you've been talking about the father. What's the son like? Teddy?"

"Oh, he's really fine. He always tells me everything. I always know what he's thinking. He bawls me out when he thinks I've done wrong. No one ever did that before —except my father. But I like it from Teddy because it means he cares what I do."

"And I don't?"

"Ernie, you never did. You never even got mad at me."

"You used to tell me you liked that."

"I did."

"I was your ideal, you used to say." Ernie laughed at the memory.

"You were. But it's all got to mean something, doesn't it, Ernie?"

"No."

"You see. We ride with the tide, wherever it takes us. But this damned old Greek, he's ferocious. Everything has to be a certain way for him. And I need that— Don't, Ernie."

Ernie, reaching down along her back to the nub of bone between her buttocks, had pulled her to him so that she lay close against him, her cunt pressed to his hipbone.

"I'm glad for you," he said. "You've finally found the right guy, I do believe."

"I know I have. Don't do that, Ernie."

"Lie still."

"O.K., but don't do that."

It felt good. Ernie was so perfectly relaxed, so passive! His indifference—oh, God! That still got her. It was really perfect lying there together that way, talking. Just as she remembered it, her face between his head and his shoulder. She noted again that despite the heat, over ninety, Ernie felt cool. On the hottest day, Ernie had a private breeze that played over his body. Teddy sweated when he was making love, especially before; she could always tell when he wanted to because he began to perspire. But Ernie was always so cool and easy.

"Don't, Ernie, please don't do that."

"I'm not." He put her hand on his penis. It was lax. "See? So go ahead, tell me about the son."

She moved her hand away.

Whispering because he was so near, she told him why she'd come back to Tucson. "He and Teddy are arriving day after tomorrow," she said. "The old man said I should come first and prepare my parents for their visit. Don't ask me what it all means—prepare my family, he said— or what I'm supposed to do. But what the old man orders, you obey."

"Why aren't you home now, doing whatever it is?"

"I had to see you. I've felt so ashamed, disappearing on you that way. You see, I don't understand how I am, Ernie. Like now, I still feel for you. My feelings don't lie down the way they're supposed to. But I know one thing—I really love Teddy. I really do."

She held him to her hard so he'd believe her.

"It's not just a crush, Ernie. I'm in love. Do you understand?"

"Yes. I do. Take these off."

"Ernie. No."

"Come on. I don't like it when I'm naked and you're not."

"I will not, Ernie. I'll dress and go home if you keep that up."

Ten minutes later, she pulled them off without being asked.

She took him in her mouth, pulling on him gently the way she used to, as he lay back with his arms folded behind his head.

He didn't get hard.

"You're mad at me, all right," she said, lifting her head off his prick, which was elongated but limp, then putting it back in her mouth.

There had always been that question, Ethel remembered, of whether or not she could rouse him. He was the only boy she'd ever known with whom she had to be the aggressor. She'd always had to go after Ernie, always hoping anxiously that, sooner or later, he would respond.

"You look well," he said, looking down at her.

She lifted her head. "Do I really?"

"Yes," he said.

She went back to it.

"So he must be good for you."

Ethel nodded.

Even when he finally did become aroused, Ernie didn't reverse positions. What he enjoyed most was to wait while whoever it was became engaged, then ardent, finally out of control. It pleasured him to hold back, to watch his partner come on, pressing, straining, waiting for him to be awakened, becoming anxious that he might not, wondering if something was wrong with what she was doing —then the thrill when he finally did move!

And now he did.

She reached down and put him in her body.

"I haven't anything in there, Ernie," she said.

"I won't come," he said.

"You been with a lot of girls, Ernie, since I left? There was somebody here last night, wasn't there?"

"Yes," he said, "there was."

"I don't care," she said.

She was crunched over him, her breasts pillowed on his chest. Frantically, she clung to him, doing all the work.

He still had his arms folded behind his head.

But now there was on his lips a soft-edged smile, the one she'd been waiting for, evidence that a mysterious feeling—not love, not passion, something closer to cruelty—had finally been awakened in him.

"I don't forgive you," he said. And at last he lowered his arms and put his hands on her working bottom.

This made her even more anxious and she held him harder, closing her eyes and pumping, working to make him come, as she was about to. For if he came in her body, that would really be forgiveness.

"Don't come in me," she gasped.

"I'll never forgive you," he said, "for what you did!"

Ethel was crying, but now it was with relief because as he said he'd never forgive her, she knew that he had.

"I know it," she said. "I know you'll never forgive me."

"You fucking little bitch," he said. "You fucking spoiled little rich bitch!"

"That's what I am," she said. "A spoiled! Fucking! Rich! Bitch!"

Suddenly, with all the force that had been slumbering inside his body, he became active and Ethel was screaming, "Oh, daddy! Oh, daddy, oh, daddy!"

When it was over, they rolled away from each other and the truth was in the space between them.

Happy and at ease, Ethel slept.

Clouds covered the sun. The room was dark.

Outside somewhere, a dog barked.

Time collapsed.

Ernie lay still, listening to the sounds of the going-home traffic on the thruway in the distance.

The largest of the cats stretched. It was his hunting time.

When a car drove up his road, Ernie did not move.

The car stopped outside his house. Ernie heard the car door open and close and footsteps come across the sand.

He didn't bother to stir.

A girl came into the house, the tomcat whisking by her feet and out the door. "Ernie," she said, coming to the bedroom door. "I'm back."

She saw there was someone with him. She stood in the doorway, a large brown paper bag in her arms. Then she turned, went back to the kitchen table. Out of the bag she took a six-pack of beer and a sack of Fritos, a carton of Kools, *Time, Newsweek, Rolling Stone* and the Arizona *Citizen*. She put them all on the table, picked up the barrette she'd forgotten the night before and left.

Then there was perfect silence except for a whistle of wind and a scurry of sand.

Ernie got up and went into the kitchen. Sitting on a chair he put his feet on the table, pulled back the foreskin of his penis and shook it a little, gently. Then he broke open a beer.

When the sun had set and the house was dark, when all creatures except the owls were still, Ethel woke.

"You want me to fix you something to eat?" she said.

"I'd like some ice cream but I have no money."

Ethel dressed and drove to the store. She brought back two quarts of coffee ice cream, the very best. They sat on the bed naked, ate the ice cream and talked.

She told him that with Teddy she felt her life, for the first time, had a purpose.

"I wish I'd found someone like that," he said, looking at her.

"Maybe you will," she said. "I hope so, Ernie."

They made love again.

Later she told him how Teddy did it, how he hurried, how anxious he became, how he perspired.

"You probably make him nervous," Ernie said, "like you might leave him any minute. Don't you do that?"

"No, no. I don't want to leave him. Ever!"

The tension between them altogether gone, strangers again, they made love for the last time, then fell asleep, their backs to each other.

When the first light came and she heard the birds, Ethel left his bed. Picking her way through the beer empties on the floor, dressed in an instant, she was about to make a successful getaway. She found her eyebrow pencil to scribble a farewell note on the side of a brown paper bag.

Then she changed her mind, tiptoed to where he slept.

"I'm going," she whispered.

"O.K.," he said.

"I won't be seeing you again," she said.

"O.K."

She waited, but he didn't say anything more; he was asleep.

She stepped into the suffocating desert morning.

There was a car between his and hers, an old Toyota pickup that hadn't been there the night before. In the front seat, looking at her with hate, was a girl, perhaps seventeen years old, with a thin face and the uneven skin of an adolescent. She didn't say anything until Ethel was climbing into her own car. "Leave him alone, lady," she said then. "Don't come back."

"Won't have to," Ethel said.

three

SHE didn't want to reach home before her father had left for the day, so she circled Tucson city, climbing above the smog line.

A hawk was looking for a meal in the flower garden around their swimming pool. She pulled her rental off the road, killed the motor and slumped down in her seat.

At exactly a quarter to eight, a maroon Mercedes rolled over the gravel drive and stopped inside the electric gate. Ethel saw her father's arm reach out of the driver's window and push the button on a metal stand which caused the gate to swing open. When the 280 SL had driven through, his arm reached out to press another button on the outside. As the gate clicked shut, the squat, powerful car turned in the direction away from where Ethel was hiding and plunged down the road.

To be safe, Ethel gave him ten minutes; Dr. Ed Laffey rarely forgot anything, but it had happened. He managed his home and his four hilltop acres meticulously. Each morning at breakfast he wrote the dinner menu, specifying what was to be taken from his walk-in freezer and large truck garden and what was to be purchased where. Quite as carefully, he oversaw the life in the stable which sheltered the riding horses, his single indulgence. This complex of instruction had to be passed on to his couple, Manuel and Carlita, and to his yard boy, Diego, before the doctor left for his day's work.

Satisfied that he wasn't coming back, Ethel drove through the gate, the barrier again making its double salaam, past the garage, where another Mercedes waited —this one white, a gift from her father on her twenty-first birthday.

She'd decided to slip in the back door unseen. Manuel would certainly be drudging in the stables, his first chore every morning. Inside the doorway she hesitated, heard from the laundry the rumble of their hotel-size washing machine. Each morning's load included everything washable that had been used the day before; no dirt was tolerated for longer than twenty-four hours.

It was one reason she'd taken up with Ernie.

Slipping through the pantry to avoid the kitchen, where she heard Carlita humming as she worked, moving on tiptoe with the speed of a fugitive, Ethel believed she had made a successful entry. But as she turned into the foyer and started up the darkly lit stairs, a two-story well with a tall window of colored glass, a quick look over her shoulder found her mother's face looking anxiously toward her from the living room below.

"Who is it?" Emma Laffey said, her voice trembling.

"It's me."

"Who?"

"Ethel."

"Oh! Kitten!" Relief gained from fear. "I'm so glad you're back."

Ethel went to where the woman was sunk in her

armchair, a loosely knit white throw over her knees, and did her duty, a quick kiss on the forehead. But the older woman seized the girl's hand and pressed it to her lips.

"Thank you," she said. "Oh, thank you."

"For what, Mom?"

"For coming back. It's not the same here without you, Kitten."

Ethel couldn't bear her mother's hysteria of gratitude. It was too painful. Mrs. Laffey didn't believe she deserved anything.

"You look tired, Sugar."

"I'm fine, Mom."

"You've missed your father. He just left. Sit down next to me and let me look at you."

Carlita came in with her mother's breakfast on a tray: Constant Comment tea, a piece of unbuttered toast, and at the side of the tray, slices of lime and a tiny Mexican silver receptacle containing a sugar substitute. No one was sure what ailed Mrs. Laffey, but all consultants agreed with her husband that her diet must be free of cholesterol and sugar. Dr. Laffey, convinced that sugar and cream were poisons, never used either.

"*Bienvenida,* Miss Ethel," Carlita said. "You just missed your father. Shall I call him and tell him you're back?"

"No."

"Oh, yes!" Emma Laffey said. "Do that, Carlita!"

"I'm awfully tired, Mom. I'll have a quick shower, take a short nap, then I'll call him myself."

"Of course. Don't call Dr. Laffey, Carlita. She must be exhausted. Long trips used to tire me so. She's come all the way from . . ."

She'd forgotten the name of the city.

"From San Diego, Mom. I'll see Father tonight and be down to see you as soon as I—"

57

"He may be late tonight. He operates almost every night now. He works much too hard."

"I know," Ethel said. She kissed her mother's forehead again. "I'll be down," she said, running up the stairs as if escaping a fire.

Closing the door to her room, she fell on the bed.

Teddy, she thought. Teddy is sanity.

She jumped to her feet, stripped off the dress that Teddy hadn't liked, and with a jerk and a pull, split it down the middle seam and let the pieces fall to the floor.

She douched. The last of Ernie.

Her shower was hot as she could take it. For ten minutes she stood under the heavy thrust of water, washing her tension away.

Eased finally, her body pink and soft, she wrapped a towel around her hair and walked into her bedroom. The sun had reached her windows and Ethel turned an armchair so that the amber flood filled it, then threw herself into the pool of light, spreading her legs and closing her eyes.

She was sore all over. She suspected she had marks on her body—it marked easily—but she wasn't ready to look at them now. She wanted to be still.

There was a discreet knock.

"Miss Kitten?" It was Manuel.

"What?"

"I have your mail."

"I don't want the goddamn mail, Manuel. Oh, wait a minute!"

She opened the door barely enough to look out, shielding her body behind it, so no extended conversation would be possible.

A compact little Chicano in his fifties, Manuel, with his wife, Carlita, had been "in the family" for as long as Ethel could remember. He was holding a pile of mail, deferentially. He was always deferential.

"It's so good to have you back, Miss Kitten," he said.

"I'm glad to see you too," Ethel lied.

"Congratulations. Dr. Laffey tells me you're thinking of getting married."

"I am getting married." She pulled back a little to remind the man she was unclothed. "Excuse me, Manuel."

Ethel had asked when she'd left for San Diego that her mail not be forwarded. It was quite a stack.

"And a telegram. It came last night. Dr. Laffey opened it, just in case. That's how we knew you were on your way. Your father thought you'd be here last night."

"Manuel, I'm right in the middle of my bath."

"Oh, sure, sure. You just missed your father," he continued, unabashed, "but Carlita called him and—"

"Why the hell did she do that?"

"Your mother told her to, I think."

"My mother told her not to, I think."

"Anyway, he said he'd cancel his operations tonight and be home in time for cocktails. 'Tell her not to go anywhere,' he said."

Ethel closed the door, saying, "I'm going to take a nap now."

She locked the door and flung the mail on the bed.

They'd be after her again in a minute, she'd bet on it. She pulled her dryer out of the closet, plugged it in and pulled the hood over her ears. Sitting on her bed with the throbbing helmet over her head, she picked up the telegram—it had to be from Teddy—held it to her breast and stared resentfully at the rest of the mail.

She was afraid to read Teddy's message. Suppose he'd tried to call her last night? She decided to save it till she got rid of the mess of letters.

They were mostly junk. An advertisement for a boutique's "End of the Line" sale had a covering letter: "Your daddy was in last week and selected some very pretty things. Did you like them? He said of course you

59

had a charge account here, you could have anything else in the place you wanted. He's really such a generous man and I must say extremely handsome."

So her father had a girl friend! Operating almost every night now, her mother had said; works much too hard.

There was an announcement from the hairdresser she'd always patronized informing her that he was moving his establishment to a new address, where, unfortunately, the rent would be higher, so his prices would have to go up. But for a few special people—she was one—the old rates would prevail. "So come by and see us!"

There was a large envelope from the Mercedes dealer. She'd had her car only five months but he was at her already with a brochure of their latest models, illustrated in dazzling color. "You'd look awful pretty in this one," the manager had written in a margin. "I'll bet you can tempt your father. And we'd be happy to help." No kidding!

Then there was an envelope with an Israeli postmark.

Aaron. After over a year of silence.

When she pulled out the letter, two snapshots came with it. One was of bathers in blue water, a swimming party of a dozen boys and girls in the sea. Aaron, who had been an Israeli transfer student at the University of Arizona's School of Mining when she was a sophomore in Fine Arts, had often told her how much he missed the salt sea. Now there he was, in the middle of a happy group, treading water. The swimmers, at a signal from the photographer, had raised their arms to wave them. They all looked delighted with the occasion and with each other's company except for the only one not looking at the camera—an intense young woman who was looking at Aaron. The other snapshot was of her alone.

"Dear Ethel," the letter read. "I'm getting married.

I want you to know. To Hannah, the girl in the picture."

Ethel looked at Hannah a long time. She had short-cropped black hair, combed straight back, eyes that came to a point, an olive complexion and a sharp-edged straight nose. Ethel hated her immediately.

She saw that Aaron had grown a mustache and looked older. But even his tiny image in the wide water gave off the warmth which had charmed everybody he met in Tucson and made every girl on campus want him. He'd awarded the prize—himself—to Ethel. It had made her proud.

Aaron had been the first boy who'd shown an interest in her other than putting his hand up her skirt. He'd been her first real friend, male or female. They'd taken week-long drives into the desert, sleeping out, wrapped in blankets, and he'd spoken to her about his country and its politics. "He talks to me," Ethel had remarked at the time, "as if I knew what he was talking about." She remembered a particular observation he'd made: "You Americans live on top of the desert and look at the sunset from your terraces as though it were a movie. We live in the desert because it's the last place left in the world for us. The earth is our mother; she protects us with her body."

He'd made Ethel sleep on the ground with him so she'd understand what he meant. In the morning he'd washed his hands in the sand as if it were water. The Arabs did this, he told her.

She became his disciple just as she'd been her father's kitten and was to be, for a time, Ernie's slavey. He pointed out to her that she'd been prepared for life only as a consumer, brought up with only one article of faith: that the refrigerator would always be full. But she'd never put anything in, he'd said; only taken out. Hers was the icebox generation, she the symbol of everything wrong with the United States and its ruling middle class, the reason it was doomed. "Your wealth has nothing to do with your goddamn know-how," he used to say. "It was all here. All you had to do was kill off the Indians."

"When I first met you," he'd say, "I thought, yes, she's O.K. Maybe. Then I saw what your father was doing to you. Why does he encourage her to spend like that? I asked myself. American Express, Master Card! Whenever she's bored, she goes shopping. Oh, Daddy, can I please have that? Sure, Kitten, what else you want? That! Take it! Then I understand something. That's what all American men do to their women, that's how they hold power over them. Make them altogether dependent. Reduce them to household pets. Kittens! Look what he's done to you! How would you get along if he stopped paying your bills and putting food in your mouth? Just once try earning your own living. I dare you. The first minute you're in trouble, you'll call, 'Daddy, Daddy, hurry!' and he'll come running with a nice fat check. But think of the price you pay for that check. Kitten! Do you have any idea what I'm talking about? Oh, forget it. What's the use?"

When his two-year exchange period was over and the time had come for him to return to Israel, he'd said she could come with him; he'd try to make a "real" person of her. They'd gone to the airline ticket office together and she'd purchased two one-way tickets to Tel Aviv with her American Express card. Ethel's plan was to vanish from her father's home, wire him from the airport, write him from Israel. Aaron told her not to worry: explanations were not important. Her father wouldn't understand anyway; her disappearance could mean only one thing to him: rejection of his whole way of life.

Ethel didn't know why she backed away at the last

minute. She simply didn't show up at the airport when she was supposed to.

She'd kept the ticket. She and Aaron had written each other passionate, desperate letters. "I think of you every day," she'd written, keeping him on her string. Had she lied when she'd promised that someday soon she'd vanish from where she was and turn up where he was? No, she'd meant it, as much as she'd ever meant anything. But the intervals between their letters became longer, and finally there was silence. The only news she had from Israel came from the tube.

"I waited for you many months," this, his final letter, concluded. "I kept thinking, tomorrow I'll hear. 'I'm coming,' she'll say, 'meet me,' give a date and the number of the flight. But I see you were playing with me. I'm not bitter about it now, but there were a few months when all I could think of was paying you back. One night when I was drunk I actually planned how I'd come to the States and I'd— Well, sooner or later, people get what they deserve."

Ethel put the letter away.

Of all the boys she'd brought home for her father to inspect, the only one Dr. Laffey had taken to, in the least, was Aaron. "He has a kind of authority, that little bastard," he'd said. "And some idea of what it's all about. Of course, he's a Jew—"

"So is Goldwater," Emma Laffey had chirped from her cave of oblivion.

"Half," Ed Laffey corrected. Then he'd laughed at himself.

The difficulty Ethel had with her father was that he was so often right, and that everyone else she'd ever cared for had some measure of scorn for her. Only Dr. Ed Laffey loved his daughter absolutely. Ethel needed that —half the time.

"I'm glad you're seeing that boy. Just be careful you don't go too far," he'd said about Aaron. "In your feelings, I mean. He's out of a totally different culture, one you'll never know anything about."

Exactly what Ethel had thought—half the time.

The same with other boys. "Perhaps I love you too much, Kitten," he'd said. "But I'm sure you'll do better than him. Give yourself a chance to look around."

After Aaron, Ethel continued as before. She would lie around with her classmates under the trees that lined the walks between the university buildings, listen to the gossip with what someone called a "bombed-out" smile, but when the campus carillon struck the hour and the kids moved inside for instruction, Ethel lingered, and when the class had assembled, she was not of its number. No one could have said when or how she'd disappeared. Or where to.

More often than not, it was to a movie. Marlon Brando was her hero that year; *The Godfather* had just come out. And during those first hours of the afternoon when the sun was a bully and people were either in air-conditioned offices or taking siestas in darkened bedrooms, she could be found, alone, in an enormous but nearly empty motion picture theater, the kind film exhibitors call "chair factories," sitting three or four rows from the screen, on the small of her back, her knees up on the chair in front of her. In this posture, she could see nothing except the image on the screen. Ethel saw *The Godfather* for what it was, a moral fable about a fine old Italian, bedeviled by ruthless enemies, a patriarch who loved his family so passionately that he sacrificed his life for them.

The scene she liked best was the wedding, where Brando dances with his daughter. She always stayed to see this over again. The old man was so graceful, so commanding, so protective. She wished she had a father who would dance that way at her wedding. When Brando died, she wept.

Ethel had other movie heroes: Clint Eastwood and Charles Bronson and Gary Cooper, mature men who spoke softly, bore hardship without complaint but, when the time came, struck back with all the violence they'd been storing in their souls. Ethel went to see their films for the same reason men go to fights: release.

In time Dr. Laffey got a note from the university authorities informing him that his daughter had not been attending classes. Then came a telephone call from Ethel's faculty adviser, warning him that it was unlikely his daughter would be promoted unless she embarked immediately on a program of intensive tutoring.

The tutor recommended was nearly forty, rubbery-plump, with a milky skin; he rarely saw the sun. He wore Indian jewelry and sandals and walked with a rolling gait. A missing tooth made his smile captivating. He'd lived all his adult life cradled in the university, an academic bum, making all he needed by tutoring the children of the rich at thirty dollars an hour. This allowed him four or five hours a day to work on the novel which was the purpose of his life.

Ethel was intrigued; she'd never known a writer, never seen anything like the piles of manuscript—versions, corrections and rewrites—all over the table, the window sills and the floor. She was also impressed by the scorn he showed for her.

"You talk as if you'd never read a book in your life," he said.

"I don't read books," she admitted. "Should I be embarrassed? Oh, my father belongs to some club and we get those books every month. I read the one about the seagull. About half of it."

"Then all you ever do is go to the movies and watch television," the tutor said. "You're a McLuhan baby."

"I don't watch television," she said. "The people on those programs are like the people around my family; they're not worth watching. But movies, they've got men. Like Gary Cooper. Did you see *High Noon?* I mean heroes. Marlon Brando! I've seen *The Godfather* seven times."

The tutor was a closet left-winger (what else in Arizona?) and tried to interest Ethel in social causes, the plight of the Chicano, the issue of peace, the nefarious activities of King Richard. Ethel's response was: "I don't understand politics. How can he shake hands with that Russian"—"Brezhnev," the tutor supplied—"and with that sweet old Chinaman"—"Mao," the tutor said—"and still bomb hell out of that country?"—"And seed their harbors with mines?"—"Aren't they Communists too?"

The tutor persisted. He was beginning to find her naïve candor engaging and her intelligence surprisingly quick in the narrow range of her true interests. But he did not succeed in stimulating Ethel's appetite for the studies she'd missed. "You could understand any of this stuff if you wanted to," he told her in a fit of impatience. "Your problem is you don't give a damn about anything."

"Why should I?" she said.

He found she had an exceptional memory, so he took to reading her the assigned books *(The Poems of William Wordsworth,* the Beards' *History of the American People)* out loud. He'd be tired in the afternoon, having spent much of the night and morning on his novel, so by the time she showed up at two, he'd be sleepy and assume his favorite position, stretched out on the floor. She joined him. That's how it started.

There she finally won his respect.

Dr. Laffey got a bill for these sessions too.

The tutor had a problem: episodes of impotence. Afterward, she noticed, he tended to be mean, mock her as stupid and ignorant, slash at her with his sharp tongue. But the next day, after he'd performed well, he was exceedingly friendly. There was a lesson there.

It was through him that she was introduced to certain drugs (including an aphrodisiac), but the discovery that he was dependent on an artificial stimulus alienated Ethel.

She'd met Ernie by this time and for a while she was seeing both men, the tutor in the early afternoon and Ernie when he got home from his job at the state farm. She'd leave her diaphragm in; "killing two birds with one stone," she called it.

There was no doubt which man she preferred; the moment to disappear arrived. The relationship with the tutor was easily dissolved: Ethel flunked all her exams. The university notified her father that they'd given up on his daughter, at least for that year. A note from the tutor, coming with his last bill, informed Dr. Laffey that the problem with his girl was not intelligence but desire.

Ethel joined the legion of dropouts.

Dr. Laffey despised Ernie openly. He was able to suffer the man's presence in his life only because he was confident that this relationship, like all the others, would not endure.

Late one night when Ethel had come back from an evening with Ernie depressed—"the curse" was overdue—he found her, teary and frantic, in the unlit kitchen.

"I had a hunch you were feeling sad," he said. Then he took her upstairs and tucked her into bed. He didn't ask what was wrong, which was a relief, and all she volunteered was, "Sometimes I feel so ashamed of him, Daddy."

"I'll have a suggestion for you in the morning," he said. Then he held her hand until she fell asleep.

The next day he gave her an airplane ticket to San

Diego saying, "Distance, you will find, has its uses." He explained that a former colleague was superintendent of a nursing school there and had given Dr. Laffey an assurance over the phone that he would make an opening for his daughter.

A month later, she'd written her father that she was in love with a boy at the Naval Training Center and this time it was for real. They planned to be married immediately, she said. "I'm very excited about my life and when you meet the reason, you'll see why. Anyone who doesn't like Teddy has something wrong with them."

Her hair dry, she took off the helmet, crawled under the covers and there, in the half light, she opened Teddy's telegram.

"Tried to call you but maybe this is better in print. You're a wonderful girl. You've been in our thoughts ever since you left. Arriving tomorrow afternoon, flight three-four-three. I love you but he loves you more. Teddy."

After a few minutes, she read the telegram again.

"Where will I tell him I was?" she asked herself. "He won't ask," she answered. "He won't even be suspicious. He's so damned good."

At her bedside was a princess phone. She dialed Teddy's number. She would tell him that she'd destroyed the dress he'd disapproved of and that she needed to hear his voice.

And find out if he suspected—

There was a knock, discreet and muffled. At the same time, Ethel heard, over the long-distance line, Teddy's phone ringing in San Diego.

"Miss Ethel!" It was Carlita, a whisper.

"What?" Ethel yelled. Then listened to the phone ringing far away. "Be quiet," she yelled.

Carlita whispered. "It's your mother. She wants to know what you'd like to have for lunch."

"I don't want any lunch. Now go away." Teddy's phone kept ringing, but no one picked up. "I'm trying to sleep."

Ethel knew that her short temper would be reported to her father.

Teddy wasn't there. He'd be somewhere, doing what he was supposed to be doing. She never doubted Teddy.

"All right, Miss Kitten," Carlita said in the insinuating tone of a child who means: I'll get even with you.

Ethel hung up the phone, pulled the covers over her face and got down into the belly of the bed. There, in the dark, she drew her knees up to her chest, put her hands, holding the telegram, between her thighs and settled to sleep.

The goddamn bed was hard, even in the middle, unyielding. Her father was convinced that a yielding bed was bad for the spine. The first thing she'd buy for her place with Teddy would be a very soft, very sinking bed.

Then she was asleep.

A knock woke her.

"Miss Kitten." Manuel now. "Your mother made me bring you some tea and a sandwich." It was a very cautious, very discreet whisper.

Ethel didn't reply.

"I'll just set it down outside the door," he said. Ethel heard the tray being put down. "Now be careful when you come out," Manuel finished, half whisper, half giggle.

It was four-thirty. She'd slept three hours.

The sun had passed over the armchair and was now on the wall opposite her bed.

That wall was covered with photographs of herself

69

from the days when she was seven and had only one goal in life—to grow up and marry her daddy. Since he liked to ride, she'd developed an equal passion for horses. Here, on display, was the record of that era of harmony: Ethel and her first pony, a gift from her father on her ninth birthday; Ethel and her daddy returning from a ride, the sun setting behind them; Ethel, now twelve, standing in the center of their corral, whip in hand, circling a colt at the end of a long line; Ethel with her favorite mare, one she'd seen through a difficult labor—she'd had to reach in and pull the filly's leg free.

To judge from her walls, Ethel's life had stopped at twelve. There were no photographs after that time. Abruptly, at thirteen, she'd stopped riding. At fourteen, she was fucking. At fifteen, she'd contemplated suicide, a children's game played by cutting one's wrists.

Ethel got up and put on a Chinese wrap of white silk. Who'd given her that garment? Was it that older man she'd met on a holiday in Mexico? No. Then who? It must have been that man. He'd taken her to the archaeological museum one summer's day. Had she gone to bed with him? She couldn't remember. She remembered he wore a diamond ring.

She began to take the photographs off the walls, yanking them down so the little hook nails flew. She wouldn't let Teddy see any of these; she'd give him an absolutely clean wall.

She tried to call him again. No one picked up.

She ought to dress and go downstairs. She felt pity for that abandoned woman below. Talk about disappearing! That's what Emma Laffey was doing—disappearing every day deeper into the shadow. Now she was waiting to be told about Teddy. Well, that's what Ethel was here for, to prepare Ed and Emma Laffey for Costa and Teddy Avaliotis.

She called another number that Teddy had given her,

a message center. There she left a message. "Urgent," she said.

How would she dress now? As Teddy's wife-to-be. Ethel, not Kitten.

On the racks of her walk-in closet were—she counted them—fifty-seven dresses. More than half were white: silk, cotton, nylon, Dacron, polyester; all lightweight, all "Kitten," "cuddly," cut and trimmed to attract attention and awaken desire.

Costa would bridle at all of them. Ethel was determined to please Costa even more than his son.

She wished she could talk to Teddy plainly, lay before him the complete history of her life—who, when, how often, why; the whole thing. But how could she tell him about last night, for instance, that it had all happened as a way of shutting down her past? She'd accomplished what she'd hoped to last night. Ernie was "dead" forever.

No, there would always be a part of her time she'd have to hide from Teddy.

What to wear?

She pulled the dresses off the racks, hangers and all, and threw them on the floor. None of them was appropriate now. Every one would betray her.

Look at these frilly blouses, gaily colored for the Arizona summer; tank tops and halters too, many in white, others in sky blue and yellow and orange, pastels, all calculated and chosen to show off boldly what she was now determined to conceal. How busy they were, how frantic for attention. "Look at me! Desire me! Come on! Come on!"

In long dustproof transparent bags were her white evening gowns, strapless or held up by a single thin ribbon which said, "All you have to do is slide me off the shoulder. It's so easy. Try it! See?"

Here, too, were little white jackets, one rabbit, the

other ermine, for contrasting dates: poor boy, rich boy. The rabbit had a faded flower pinned to it, a gardenia, the scent a memory. She remembered that night; she had not come home.

She would never wear any of these—dresses, blouses, tops, whatever—again. She flung them on the floor.

In the small triple-drawered bureau was her underwear: bikinis of the finest cotton, so trim, so light that their presence wouldn't show through the thinnest dress. "I'm not wearing anything underneath," they promised. "You don't believe me. Try and see!" There was a whole circus of what she'd once thought so "neat": panties with "Kitten" embroidered on them, others stamped in all sorts of places with slogans, song titles and promises, intimate advice and bold innuendo, the very stuff of intrigue and the delightful games of youth.

In the next compartment, bras, opening at the back or the front, some see-through, some deep-plunge, others of lace and mesh and fishnet, none padded. At fourteen, Ethel had already been ample. They were all single-clasped; no one had had to fumble long to open them. She threw them on the giveaway pile.

On a shelf were purses by the score, one for every occasion, one to go with every dress, matching colors. There was the one her father had accidentally opened, and found in it, along with her keys and a hanky, two Hershey bars and a condom. Ethel gathered all these bags in her arms and dumped them on the pile.

At the back of the nearly empty closet, on a top shelf, were boxes of souvenirs: love letters and report cards, programs and invitations, a confetti of little folded notes, those sneaked between school desks or snatched from boys passing in the halls, confirmation of dates, when and where. How much they'd all meant once!

There were a few newspaper clippings, one illustrated with the photographs of a horse: "The Surprise Winner."

And a close-up, herself on her mount: "The Little Champ." With them a couple of blue ribbons, lettered and trimmed in gilt, prizes she'd received at ten and eleven and twelve, soon after she'd started to jump. She'd become expert instantly, then quit cold. What had happened between her and her father? She didn't understand her life.

All these mementos, once so treasured, she dumped on the floor.

At the very back of the deep closet were two heavily loaded shelves, holding earlier treasures she'd saved. She began to pull boxes down, no longer pausing to look at their contents, flinging them on the floor, bottoms up, disgorging apparel she'd saved from her early teens, since forgotten. She kicked their contents onto the other discards, scooping up with her feet great piles of clothes, sending them flying in flutters, falling in tangles.

Out of one box dropped a little white skirt with a pert kick pleat. She carried it to the window and looked through it into the light. Not a trace of stain; the dry cleaner had done a good job.

She'd been unprepared that night long ago. The traveling amusement park had brilliantly illuminated a meadow at the edge of the city. She'd felt the flow begin as she was screaming with fear and delight on her favorite ride, Crack the Whip. When the little carriages were brought to a stop, Ethel backed off and sat on the first bench she found. She could feel the ooze between her legs. Sitting spread the satin. A quick look back—it was the size of a small tomato.

"I feel sort of sick," she'd said to the boy who was with her. "Could you get me a Coke or something?"

When he came back with the drink, she'd vanished.

She'd run the three miles home.

At school her pug-nosed escort spread the story of her behavior, the genesis of her reputation for disappearing on dates. This recollection, even now, raised a warm flush on Ethel's chest.

She remembered, on that night, saying, "God, why didn't you make me a boy?" A year later, when she got her diaphragm, she'd boasted to a girl friend, "Now I'm just like a boy!"

"Kitten! What in the world are you doing?"

Her father was standing in the doorway.

four

D R. Ed Laffey, a trim, compact man, was vain about his youthful appearance, and with reason. Proud of his belly, he'd tighten and loosen his belt, a kind of tic, check his weight every morning, his blood pressure once a week. They were what they should be.

"You're not giving all this treasure away, are you?" he said.

Did the pile of clothing amuse him?

Ethel waited anxiously for his further reaction.

But after a first faint smile, there was no hint of what he thought. His face, like the faces of most doctors, was a mask of composure.

Except when it came to his daughter. He cupped the back of her head in one hand and kissed her. "Whoever your new man is," he said, "he certainly agrees with you. You're looking particularly well." He examined her again, fondly again, then directed his attention to the giveaway pile, smiling over it as he might have at a children's game being played on the floor.

"I'm getting rid of all this," she said.

"I know the feeling. A new life begins."

Plucking up his well-creased trousers, he kneeled ranchhand-style, one buttock on one heel. "I've often wanted that, to get shucked of everything I own. Start over!" He flipped and stirred the clothing with long, strong fingers. "So many memories come back from all this, don't they, Kit? Was there ever such a time? Were we there? Oh me, oh my!"

Ethel didn't respond.

"What's he like?" Dr. Laffey got to his feet. "Your new man? I want to know all about him."

"Teddy. You're going to meet him, Daddy."

"And what are your plans? I need an avalanche of detail. Come riding with me the way we used to. We'll talk and watch the sun set. Then we'll dunk. I'll tell Manuel to make us margaritas and serve them poolside. In our own good time, we'll dress and have dinner by candlelight. Carlita will broil us a couple of New York cuts and I'll make my steak sauce. I have strawberries in the garden, imagine! What horse will you ride?"

"Daddy, I don't feel like riding. Or a dress-up dinner."

"Well, fine, wear anything you wish. We'll eat on the terrace off the dining room, listen to the coyotes and drink Mexican beer. I picked up some Dos Equis on the way home; it's being cooled this minute. Will you have dinner with me on my terrace tonight, Miss Ethel? I've missed you more than I can say."

"All right, Daddy."

"Good Lord, will you look at this!"

He stooped and came up with a little girl's nightgown of bleached-out cotton. He held it up, fingertips at the shoulders. Not quite transparent, it was modestly cut, the straps little white daisies all in a row.

"Remember when you were a little girl you used to come see me every morning, get in bed and talk, the nicest conversations I've ever had with anyone?"

"I remember."

"One morning you said, 'Daddy, is it true if you can kiss your elbow you'll turn into a boy? Because,' you said, 'I'd rather be a boy.' "

"How old was I?"

"I'd just given you that pony, Blazer, for your birthday, so you must have been—what? Eight? And I said, 'I doubt it, Kitten, but you can sure as hell try.' Thank the good Lord you got over that. You're a great success as a girl, Kit."

"You really think so?"

"Look at you! My God!" He was running the soft fabric of the gown gently through his cupped palms.

"You didn't tell the end of the story," she said.

"Because the end is a little sad—like all endings. Overnight you metamorphosed; suddenly you were a young lady and—"

"It wasn't overnight. It was suddenly one morning, years later. I remember that morning. I pressed up against you because I guess I knew it was coming to an end, all that, and you held me hard because you knew it too. And then—" She paused.

"Yes?"

"You pushed me off, saying—remember what you said?"

"So many years ago, how could I?"

He'd spread the gown over the bed and was smoothing it with the palm of his hand.

"Don't do that!" Ethel said, a distinct harshness in her voice.

"Why?"

"That's what you said that morning, and how you said it. When I pressed against you and you pulled away, you said it in the voice you use when you give orders to the yard boy. 'Don't do that!' "

"Kitten! Have you been holding that against me all these years?" He laughed.

"I'm not that silly," she said. "But I can still hear how you said it."

"My dear, don't insist on a more graphic explanation; it would embarrass me." He was still laughing. "It might even embarrass you. Let's ever so gently draw the curtain, as we must from time to time over so many things, and move on."

"Then the next day you were reminding me, ever so gently, that I was an adopted child, a fact you'd hardly ever mentioned before."

"What was there to say about it beyond the fact? I told you that when you were maybe five or four. I remember the day. I said to you, 'Mummy and I wanted a child, so we looked and we looked and we found—who do you think?' And you said, 'A kitten?' " He laughed. "You were so cute. Remember?"

"I was right. A house pet. Why didn't you adopt a kitten instead?"

"Oh, come on. Actually, the fact that you were adopted was never important to me."

"It turned out to be important to me. The reason I'm bringing all this up now is so you won't worry about me. I'm all right. Since meeting Teddy, I've gotten over a lot of things. All I have to say to you, as I mosey over the horizon into the sunset, is: 'Thanks for loaning me your name. Here! I'm returning it!' "

"You're not going to get away from me that easily. Or that quickly."

"I'm getting married as soon as I possibly can."

"Well, I'm certainly dying to hear all about him." He looked at his wrist watch. "Sunset in twenty-five minutes."

Once again he looked at the pile on the floor. "You

won't mind, I'm sure," he said, "if I ask Manuel to pack all this in dustproof cartons. We'll store them in the attic and—"

"Daddy, I don't want to see this stuff again."

"You won't have to. Not until that day, years and years from now, when I'm foolish and feeble and in desperate need of warm memories. Then we'll open everything in the company of my grandchildren. It'll be such fun. I'll tell Manuel what to do. . . . Now, sure you won't come with me? They've extended the trail to the top of the second ridge. It's wild and it's beautiful and there isn't an anthropoid in sight. Come on. Please." She shook her head. He still urged her. "For old times' sake. For my old sake! *Vamanos, chiquita!*"

"Daddy, I haven't been on a horse for five years. I hate the animals and—please don't crowd me."

So he didn't. He left, all smiles, his confidence undiminished.

Standing still in the middle of the space where the light was fading, she heard the echoes of his energy below: a door slamming, his voice summoning Manuel, then, a little later, shouting at Diego, the yard boy. Now she waited, still without moving, till she heard his horse's hoofs on the cattle guard, clopping through the break in the fence where his property bordered the ridge trail.

Only when she was certain that he'd be well out in the desert did she call Manuel and Carlita to her room and tell them to burn the papers and the photographs.

"The frames too, Miss Kitten?" Manuel wanted to know.

"Everything. Quickly! The dresses and all, they're yours. Do what you want with them."

"Did you ask your father?" Manuel said.

"No, goddamn it; I didn't ask my father."

"Because he said—"

"I don't care what he said."

79

"He said he was going to tell me what to do—"

"Now I'm telling you what to do. Are you going to do it?"

The couple looked at each other.

"I don't think she has to ask," Carlita whispered, her eyes on the clothing.

Suddenly Ethel was being showered with thanks. "Enough clothes for a village," Carlita said, scooping up great armfuls and rushing out of the room. "Come, Manuel, come!"

When they'd taken everything and the floor was as bare as the walls, Ethel fell on the bed. She was trembling.

Her princess phone, that little pink bitch, so cozy in her cradle, was amused at Ethel's upset. She had the temerity to offer advice and, doing so, revealed an unexpectedly coarse character.

"Tell me, cunt, why you're getting so hot and bothered? Let them fuss and say unforgiveable things. You stay cool. Give them that upside-down smile. See mine. See how it goes? No matter who yells at me, did you ever see my expression change? All you have to live through is two more days. Then you'll be out of here. For the rest of your life. Why holler and hassle? Two days! Try to do something right for a change. Like tonight, have dinner with your daddy and be sweet, be feminine, be cunt-wise. Kiss him two for one, tell him how handsome he is and that you adore his steak sauce, even tell him you're sorry you burned the fucking photographs without getting his permission. What's the diff? They're gone, aren't they? Then tell him you want his advice about men, other men. That always gets them. And when he gives it, nod and smile and say, 'Oh!' like that. 'Oh!' and 'Oh, yes!' and 'Oh, I see!' and 'Oh, of course!' and 'Oh, why didn't I think of that myself?' and even go so far as to say, 'Oh, Daddy, Daddy-oh, what will I ever do without you?' He'll eat it up. He still has a hard on for you. You can still make that man do anything you want. It's a cunt's life, baby. Instead of fighting, we smile, pretend to give in, then go our own way. Or make believe we're awful dumb and give them lots and lots of hero worship. Some girls get along and that's all they know how to do. That's why nature makes us short: so we can look up at the dopes. And why she made men naïve: so they'd never suspect that after they take us home, we have a late date. But you got to keep that cool pink front up at all times. You got to make them wonder, those dumb studs, what the hell you're really thinking. Ah, that's the mystery of life, ah, that they write songs about! Are you listening? Don't fall asleep on me now. Just get through this one evening. Then, before you know it, Teddy will be here and that crazy old Greek with him. That will be the main event. Costa Avaliotis versus Dr. Edward Laffey. Sit back and watch the show, kid; you got the best seat. You're the door prize, baby. All you have to do is stay cool and look pretty. And when you feel yourself going over the brink into girlish hysterics again, remember how I sit here, playing pink poker, and say to yourself: A couple of days in the life of a cunt, that's all it is."

The Laffey home, from the public road, appeared to be nothing more than a wall of some concrete-based material, the color livened with a tint of ocher. This wall was fenestrated by a row of small casement windows, a story's height off the ground, but no front door was visible. The drive could be seen, leading around the side of the house and disappearing to the rear.

There was the entrance and there a deep U, a place of shelter and family leisure, its inspiration, of course, the inside court of the landed Mexican's hacienda. Symmetrically flanking the imposing entrance door were two ceiling-to-floor windows, actually double doors opening onto twin terraces, banked with flowers. One terrace led off the dining room, the other off the parlor, which was rarely used by anyone except Emma Laffey, who sat there before a large TV set every night of her life.

On the other side of the driveway, behind a hedge of tropical shrubs, a thick but well-ordered growth of blooms surrounded the swimming pool. Behind and a little below this area was another garden, Emma Laffey's particular devotion, a cultivation of desert flowers and cacti with their prickly fruit.

At the end of the day, this was the quiet place. Four great saguaros stood guard at the corners. Where lines between them might intersect was a rattan sunshade, suspended over a floor raised a few inches off the hot sand. Here Ethel sat in the light the sun had left behind, waiting for her father to come out.

She could see her mother, alone on the terrace off the parlor, eating her supper from a tray. Emma put down her knife and fork as if they were too heavy to handle, sighed, then saw her daughter looking at her and quickly brightened. The two women waved to each other across the space, then Mrs. Laffey looked at her wrist watch and what she saw there caused her to make a series of gestures and signs in Ethel's direction. Ethel decoded the message: In a few minutes there would be a darling show on TV and Ethel was to come, please, please, and watch it with her.

Ethel called, "I'm waiting to have supper with Daddy," accompanying this information with signs and gestures which said the same thing.

Emma nodded, understood why she had to be alone again, and looked as pleased about it as anybody possibly could.

Then he was there, striding out onto the other terrace,

the one off the dining room, dressed in a navy blazer of coarse Irish linen fitted with gold buttons and, under it, a shirt open halfway down his chest. He waved gaily to his wife on the terrace opposite, threw her a kiss, then gestured impatiently for Ethel.

She was already rushing to him. In his arms she said, "I forgot to tell you, Daddy, that you really look wonderful."

Pleased, "Better, I'm sure, because you've come home," he said.

"And that I'm awfully happy to be having dinner with you."

Manuel was lighting two hurricane lamps, one a rich burgundy, the other the heavy green of holly leaves.

They had margaritas. There was guacamole. They smiled at each other. There was no need to talk. In that silence, everything was perfect.

Then in the distance they heard the first coyotes.

"Diego told me one of them got the poodle," Ethel said.

"More likely a bobcat. They have a taste for dog meat. By the way, what's that car in the driveway?"

"I rented it at the airport."

"Your own car is in the garage." He waited for an explanation. Ethel didn't offer one.

Manuel came out with two more brimming margaritas, the golden liquid lapping at the crusty salt edging.

"Ah, thank you, Manuel," Dr. Laffey said. Then, "Manuel, there is a peculiar acrid scent in the air, like shellac burning. What is that?"

"It's my photographs," Ethel said. "I asked Manuel to burn them."

"Oh," Dr. Laffey said, "I see." He looked at Manuel. "The wind is coming toward us, what wind there is, and it just hangs here, the smoke."

"Yes, sir," Manuel said. "I'm sorry." And he left.

Ethel reminded herself what she'd come there to do. She remembered Costa's instructions.

"I didn't mean to hassle you before," she said. "I mean, I did and I'm sorry."

"About what?" her father asked.

"My being adopted. I'm sure you did me a favor."

Carlita came out with the salads. "Your father made the dressing, Miss Kitten," she said as she put the wooden Oaxaca bowls on the table at the side of each place mat. Then she hesitated.

"Yes, Carlita, what is it?" the doctor said.

"I just wanted to ask Miss Ethel, are you sure you want to give me all those clothes? They will make many people wonderful happy, of course, but . . . Dr. Laffey, what do you say?"

"Why, Carlita, they're Kitten's clothes; she can do anything she wants with them."

"Thank you, sir, thank you both."

Relieved, she rushed off.

"I love your salad dressing, Daddy," Ethel said, "and the steak sauce. How did you learn all that?"

"Had to. Your mother, it turned out, was not very good in a kitchen."

"You must give me both recipes. I've started a little notebook."

Manuel came out with the steaks on a large wooden plank. Around the edges were baked tomatoes and piles of tiny onions sautéed in butter.

Dr. Laffey put on the half glasses which hung from a silver chain around his neck, and carefully ran a sharp knife's edge through one of the sirloins.

"As I thought," he said to Manuel, "they're too well done. Put another pair on the flame."

"I'm sorry, sir, but it will take time, you know; they're frozen."

"I took four steaks out of the freezer. Just in case.

You'll find another pair in the refrigerator, waiting. You can't expect us to eat these, can you? Now hurry. And, Manuel . . . Never, never again destroy anything that is my property without my permission. Is that understood?"

"Yes, sir."

"And, Manuel, after you've put the new ones on the fire, bring us another round of margaritas. Doesn't Manuel make perfect margaritas, Kit?"

"Yes, he does."

"Thank you, thank you." Manuel rushed off.

"I made them do it," Ethel said. "I'm sorry. I know I should have asked permission. But the pictures were mine, so—"

"Well, it's of no consequence, but they were taken with my camera, which exposed my negatives, and I had them developed, printed, cropped and framed. It's not a point I care to argue, but by any definition of property that I know of—"

"But they're of me. I am the subject. I didn't ask you to take them or to frame them or put them up on my wall. I know you did it out of affection, but I don't want any old pictures of me around."

"It doesn't matter, it doesn't matter. It's done and you're happy. Well, now, you can't avoid it anymore: Tell me what he's like."

"He's very old-fashioned, the father. I'm supposed to be preparing you for his arrival."

"Is he that formidable?"

"He is incredible." She remembered Costa and laughed. "Literally so."

"But you are marrying the son, not the father, aren't you?"

They laughed together.

"More like marrying them both. I'm being taken into a family. The old man is the last of a breed. And he cares about his offspring, he really cares."

"And I don't?"

"Why, Daddy! I didn't mean that!" She leaned over and kissed him.

"I was joking. Now! About your new young man?"

"Teddy is—I really believe it—a saint."

"I suspect saints, I enjoy bastards. Is he very good-looking?"

"Very. But you have to look twice. He's second-sight handsome. But all that never really mattered to me, believe it or not. Teddy is just what I need."

"What is it now that you need so badly?"

"So badly that I have to get married?"

"I didn't say that."

"Order."

"What was that again?"

"Order."

"A new taste you've developed?"

"At last."

"Is that good in a lover?"

"Daddy, I've been talking about a husband."

"Still . . . ?" He took her hand and kissed it.

"Yes, Teddy does have another side. Real Navy. When I first met him, he was servicing hundreds of girls, it seemed, and doing it so you'd never know. Always very correct. Even about that. But I finally figured out that that big blue stance of his was a technique, the one he used to make girls unclench their knees. Oh, the uses of command! The bastard!"

"But now? He's true to you?"

"I absolutely believe so."

"He'd better be."

"He's like no one I've ever known, Daddy. In some fundamental way, he's decent. And I love him."

Manuel's arrival with two fresh margaritas gave her a chance to turn her head away. She was on the edge of tears.

Together they broke the salt crust around the rims of their glasses and sipped the sweet golden liquor.

"I miss him, Daddy," she said, "even after a day and a half."

"What are those marks on your neck?" her father said.

"I visited Ernie last night."

"Oh, for chrissake! Well, in the name of God!"

"Now may I ask you a favor," she said. "You see, whatever I hope for from life now, I hope for from Teddy. Please, when he gets here, no matter what you think, be nice to him."

"I'm disturbed that you feel it necessary to ask that."

"I just thought I'd say it."

Manuel rushed out with the steaks.

"I think these are perfect," he said. "I mean, I hope."

Dr. Laffey put on his half glasses, took the sharp knife and sliced through a quadrant of the steak, inspected the cut, then looked up at Manuel and nodded, dismissing him.

The meat was good and they were silent.

"What are you thinking?" he asked.

"That we both like our meat the same way."

"You're like me another way. You double think. What else were you thinking at the same time you were thinking about the steaks?"

"I was wondering," she said, "when you said that about Ernie just now, you said, 'Oh, for chrissake!' And, 'Oh, in the name of God!' Remember you said that?"

"Yes?"

"Were you really upset or just pretending?"

"Do you mind if I don't answer that question? It's insulting."

"Well, I did wonder about it. Sorry."

"Apology accepted. By the way, you didn't tell me how you like nursing."

"Daddy, I know too much about your profession to like being a nurse."

"So it was just a whim?"

"No. It came at a time when I needed it. Thank you very much for that."

"Kit, give it a chance; don't jump to—"

"Daddy, nursing is not for me!"

"Well, then, what are you going to make of yourself, now that you've reached your maturity?"

"Nothing. Be a wife. Which is not nothing. Have children. Help Teddy be all he can be. That's my main hope—that I will be good for him."

"Well, you certainly are a changed girl. What's brought all this about? Your new man?"

"By the way, his name is Teddy. I'm going to do everything I can for *Teddy*. Including giving children to *Teddy*. *Teddy*'s father made me promise that, a sacred oath. And I did."

"That's wonderful. But—forgive me for bringing it up —the first thing you do when you come back here is go see that—"

"I had to do that. I finished Ernie last night. You were right what you once said, that I was more like Ernie than I knew. A drifter, you said. And there was a reason for that. But as of last night, the drift is over."

"Good. You are different, Kit. Tougher. You used to be so sweet. But now—well, you're an adult, I guess."

"It's because of Teddy. Do you know, Daddy, that I never really had a friend? The boys were always after you know what and the girls resented me because the boys were after mine, not theirs. But Teddy is a friend. Aside from everything else, he likes me enough to fight with me and not walk away."

"That quick little Jew, he fought with you."

"I just got a letter from him, by the way."

"From Israel, I hope."

"Yes. He was very insulting, but when I thought over what he said, I decided he was right."

"What did he say?"

"That you spoiled me rotten. That I'm nothing more than a household pet."

"Son of a bitch!"

"I think he's right. The only thing you ever taught me, Daddy, was to sit straight on a horse and grip with my knees. But all that's going to be changed. That's why I asked you to make Teddy feel you like him whether you do or not."

"If you mean behave cordially, I always have, always do. But if you mean set aside my critical faculties—"

"You know what I mean. I don't want him to feel resented."

"I've never not—"

She rushed on. "Another thing. The old man talks about bloodlines as if he were breeding a mare. It will sound primitive to you, I know. Because it did to me. But it's serious with them, their pride in the family, and—"

"Are you going to tell him that you're adopted?"

"I don't dare tell the father. But if I could get it out to Teddy, along with a few other items, I'd feel better. I don't want secrets under a cover that might blow off later. Especially since we're going to make a kid as soon as we can."

"I wouldn't tell about it. Not the way they sound."

"I'm going to. And since we're talking, I wish you'd take that goddamn photographic album, the pictorial history of my life, off the coffee table before the Avaliotis family comes."

"Oh, now really! That album means a lot to me!"

"Just do it, Daddy; just do it because I'm asking you to

do it. Because if you don't, I sure as hell will. And I'll burn it myself this time."

She got up, cautioning herself too late not to quarrel with the man, to just get through these two days, stay cool. But it was too late. She'd blown it and she was about to blow it again.

"Excuse me," she said. "I'll be all right in a minute."

She walked off the terrace, across the driveway, into the flower garden, around the edge of the pool and down into the garden of cacti, where she sat under the sun shelter, her back to the house.

Which is where her father found her when he brought her white mint in a snifter.

He leaned over and kissed her, then sipped the brandy he held.

"The coyotes," she said. "They're closer now."

"As it gets darker."

"It's a wonder, with the thruways and all, that they're still here."

"They'll survive man," he said, "which is more than man will do."

"I'm awfully sorry," she said, "the way I was at dinner."

"I understand. It's a nervous time."

"I guess it is and I didn't know it."

Then she said it, very quietly.

"Why have you never really spoken to me about the adoption?"

"I asked your mother to tell you everything we knew about it."

"She can tell you everything and tell you nothing, your wife. Who were my parents? Who is my real father?"

"The service people were particularly strict about not telling us that."

"Did you ever ask?"

"Yes, I did. They said your father in biology was some kind of artist, talented and—since you want to know—a bit wayward. But they wouldn't tell me his name. Or where he lives."

"If you'd cared enough, you could have found out."

"Let's say I preferred not to know."

"But I want to know. I want to meet them. I want them to be at my wedding."

She could see how much he resented the idea.

But she went on. "Tell me, did you have to pay for me?"

"What they call a service fee, that's all."

"How much?"

"What's the difference?"

"What did I cost?"

"Twenty-five hundred dollars, I believe it was."

"So you did buy me."

"It was more like a—"

"A rental?"

"Why are you being so mean to me?"

"Because I haven't seen you in a long time."

"Is that a reason?"

"I want to know who I am and you won't help me find out."

"But why, all of a sudden, this anxiety about it?"

"I'm marrying a man and I'd like to be able to tell him who I am. Not Laffey. That's a name I borrowed from you, which I am now returning to you. Many thanks. But who the hell am I?"

"Do you really expect me to institute a search?"

"Don't you owe me that?"

"Wouldn't you rather have it to hold against me?"

Again she had to choke down anger and turn away.

"I'll tell you why you're so mean to me," he said. "Because you can get away with it. You're safe insulting me because you know I'm not going to hit you back."

He was going to say more, but Manuel came to where they were, bringing a tray with two bottles, one of the white mint, the other of brandy. Setting the tray down on the low table between the contestants, he asked permission to go to bed.

"I'm sorry, sir," he said. "About what happened today."

"We'll have the strawberries for breakfast," the doctor answered. "Refrigerate them."

Manuel left.

When all was quiet again, he spoke to her. Quietly.

"About what you did with Ernie, I hope what you said is true, that it's over. You've always had a self-destructive streak. Perhaps you can control it now— Don't look at me that way! I am not the cause of everything unfortunate that ever happened to you. On the contrary, I've given you everything good you've ever had!"

He filled his glass with the brandy. When she reached out her glass, he said, "I think you've had enough."

She filled her own.

"I want to ask you a favor, Daddy, just a plain old favor."

"Anything I can do, I will. As always."

"It's not going to be easy for you."

"Allow me to judge that."

"With Teddy, for the first time, I believe I have a chance. Don't try to break us up."

"What did you say?"

"I said don't try to break it up like you have all the others."

"All what others? When have I ever—"

"I'll tell you when. Quote: 'I think he's a weakling.' Quote: 'Remember he's Jewish!' Quote: 'See how clumsy he is on the tennis court. Ha-ha!' 'He's a mama's boy. Ha-ha!' 'He's a faggot. Ha-ha!' 'I think he loves his car more than he does you.' 'I'm sure you can do better than that, Kitten, much better!' Now you've started on Teddy.

'I suspect saints,' you said, 'I enjoy bastards.' You haven't yet said his name. 'Your new man!' It's Teddy. Teddy. Teddy! You can't help it, I know. That's why I said it was going to be hard for you. But I won't let you louse me up this time. I'm asking you please to control yourself. I'm also warning you that I'm on to you. No side-swiping, no undercutting, no subtle slurs. I'm alert, I'm on guard!"

"Go to bed," he said, getting to his feet. "You've had far too much to drink. Sleep may clear your head."

"It's clear now."

"No comment. I told an old friend who's giving a party that I might drop in after dinner."

"I don't believe that. But it doesn't matter. Good night. This is not the way I wanted our last conversation to go. I guess it's my fault that it did. Sorry."

When he bent over to kiss her, she moved her face away, then turned and looked at him.

"Teddy is a fine man," she said.

"I'm glad. That's what we all need." Then he touched the place in her neck where the marks of her encounter with Ernie showed. "The danger, my dear," he said, "is not from anything I might or could or even should do. The danger you fear is from yourself."

He went into the house, controlling an unsteadiness. In a few minutes, she heard his car, the gate open, the gate close. He was gone.

The coyotes seemed to be closer and there were owls in the hollow below the cactus garden, the coyotes complaining, the owls seductive, talons ready.

When the desert began to cool, she went into the house.

She heard music, thirties jazz, feet shuffling on a wooden stage, little cries of "Hey! Hey!" As she progressed, the front of the TV came into view and Ethel saw the image of a middle-aged man who looked far too distinguished for the work he was doing, teaching a line of girls in rehearsal clothes a dance step.

Seated in a heavy plush armchair and leaning forward, Mrs. Laffey gave the impression that she was anxious not to miss a word or a move. But as Ethel came closer, she saw that Emma was asleep. There was a stupefied expression on her face and her mouth was open.

Ethel leaned over and kissed the top of her head.

"Good night, Mom," she whispered.

Startled, Emma looked up. "Kitten! Oh, Kitten darling," she said.

"Are you all right, Mom?" Ethel asked.

"Wonderful. Is there anything more tiresome than self-pity? Here"—she moved over—"sit next to me. You look tired, dear. Rest."

She opened her arms. When Ethel did not respond, she reached out, and taking hold of Ethel's elbow, gently pulled the girl to her.

"I miss you so much," she said. "Come sit and talk with me."

"Tomorrow, Mom," Ethel said, wriggling her arm free.

Emma reached for the girl again and pulled her with a strength that was frantic.

"Don't do that!" Ethel said. Her voice—impatient, ugly—surprised her.

Emma's hand flew off and remained in the air, trembling.

Then she began to sob, and as Ethel's rage with her father had been the accumulation of years, so were Emma's tears. Her heart cracked and she had no pride.

Fumbling, she reached for her cane, pulled herself up, leaning over the arm of the chair, then walked toward the hall and the stairs, sobbing bitterly.

Ethel didn't move, didn't watch her go. When she heard

the bedroom door close upstairs, she sat and put her face in her hands.

She'd said the same words to her "mother" that her "father" had said to her years before, and in the same heartless voice.

Jumping to her feet, she ran up the stairs. But there was no light in Emma's bedroom that she could see under the door. She tried the handle. The room was locked. She called through. There was no answer.

Well, what the hell could she do or say to help that woman? It was too late. The truth was that no one in that house could help anyone else there. Or should.

In her own bedroom, Ethel went to the phone. Teddy still wasn't in. She wished she could distrust Teddy a little; it would relieve the guilt she felt. But she knew where he'd be—at a movie with his father.

"They told me someone had called from Tucson, a girl," Teddy said when he woke her in the middle of the night. "I figured it might be you."

"Might be me! How many girls do you know in Tucson?"

"The entire high school graduating class of girls."

He didn't sound angry; Ethel was relieved.

"Oh, Teddy, darling," she said, "will you, for chrissake, come take me away from here?"

"We're coming. The day after tomorrow."

"I want you now."

"What happened? Somebody hurt your feelings?"

"No. Everybody's been very patient. It's me. I go bananas here. It all comes back; the way it was when I was a girl and— Sorry; it's nothing for you to worry about. How was the movie?"

"How did you know we went to a movie?"

"I know everything you do, so be careful."

"No kidding, how'd you know?"

"I have second sight because I love you. Move your

flight up! I don't know what the hell I'm going to do here tomorrow."

The next day, Ethel slept till two in the afternoon, or pretended to, Emma made her monthly trip to town to visit her personal doctor—a professional her husband had selected for her—and Dr. Laffey didn't come home for supper. It was his evening for bridge; he was a player of tournament rank.

five

THE following day, in honor of the occasion, Dr. Laffey canceled his appointments, including one orthopedic operation that would have brought him a very substantial fee, and drove with Ethel to the airport.

She wore a high-buttoned sky-blue shirt; there were still red scuffs at the side of her neck.

The encounter was undramatic. Costa sat in the back of the car with his son. Dr. Laffey drove, Ethel beside him. To make conversation, the doctor described certain landmarks. He went out of his way to take them by the new civic center.

"Plenty money over here," Costa observed.

He was even more impressed with some of the homes they passed on the way to the Laffey hilltop.

"I always tell my son," he observed, "just as easy marry rich girl as poor girl."

"There speaks a Greek," Teddy said.

When they got to the Laffey place, there was a problem.

"What is this?" Costa said.

"Where we live," Dr. Laffey answered. "Is that what you're asking?"

"Very nice, very nice, but . . ." Costa was balking at something. He started back toward the car.

"Your rooms are ready for you," Dr. Laffey said. "Aren't they, Ethel?"

"Come on, Mr. Avaliotis," Ethel said.

Costa stood his ground. Apparently what was troubling him could only be discussed between fathers, so he approached Dr. Laffey, indicating with a sweeping gesture that they should step to one side.

The children waited.

The consultation they could not hear was a short one. They saw Dr. Laffey nod, heard him say, "Of course, if you'd prefer that."

The man returned. Costa seemed untroubled, but Dr. Laffey clearly had had a first discomforting glimpse of what was ahead.

"Mr. Alavotis has told me—"

"Avaliotis," Costa said, "Ah-vah-lee-oh-tis. Very easy."

Dr. Laffey spoke to Teddy. "Your father prefers that you stay at a motel," he said.

"Proper way," Costa said. "Till we settle, you understand," Costa said. He turned to Ethel. "You understand, young lady? Your father and you will have many things to discuss. Teddy and I, same problem."

"I won't be able to find you a place and take you there myself," Dr. Laffey said.

"I'll find them a place," Ethel said.

"Unfortunately, I have an office to take care of and hospital rounds to make. I operate tomorrow and—"

"No necessary explain, Dr. Laffey—correct, Laffey?"

"Yes. I'll run along now. Ethel has her car and she—"

"Don't worry, don't worry," Costa said.

"But tonight," Dr. Laffey said, "I insist that we all have dinner here. Will that be all right?"

"Proper way," Costa said.

"Fine. So I'll run along—"

"Before you go, I want meet your wife. Could we trouble you introduction?"

"Ethel will—"

"It take one minute." Costa seemed anxious that it be Dr. Laffey who introduced him to Mrs. Laffey.

Which he did. And left.

Costa sat with Mrs. Laffey, complimented her on her beautiful home and on how well her daughter had been raised.

"Truth is," Emma Laffey said, "I had very little to do with either."

"Dear lady, I cannot believe that."

"I think they want to be alone," Ethel said, pulling Teddy out the garden door. "Come, I want to show you our flower borders."

As they left, they heard Emma telling Costa about her "weakness." It was the first time in years anyone had been ready to listen to her.

Something was troubling Ethel. The morning paper had a piece about the increasing number of VD cases in the community. There was a tiny sore spot inside her. Ernie never locked his door.

She'd considered telling Teddy the truth, decided against it.

"I have to admire your father," she said, "the way he wants to do things. By his tradition, you know? So I thought maybe we shouldn't . . ."

"Shouldn't what?"

"Make love again until—"

"Are you kidding? Until when?"

"We're married. Or, at least, everything's settled."

"Keep me off, let's see you." He began to laugh.

"What's so funny?"

"What do they do with horses? You told me once."

"Oh, Teddy, be serious."

"What do they do? Tie a—"

"A stiff brush on the underside of the stallion's belly so when he—" She was laughing too. "It's known as the stallion shield. You'd look so cute in one."

"I'd do a lot for my old man, but you just found the limit."

"Teddy, I'm sort of serious. So when we marry, it'll mean more."

He pulled her to him and began to kiss her.

"Women control these things," he said. "Go ahead, control me."

"Teddy! Look out. Your father's coming."

Mrs. Laffey and Costa had walked out of the house. He was supporting her at the elbow and she was looking up into his eyes.

"I think my old lady is flipping for your old man," Ethel said.

"I'm as happy as most people," Emma was saying. "I love my garden and . . . my room and . . . my daughter." She hesitated and smiled bravely, as her tradition demanded. "And I hope I'm not too much of a burden to him, to Dr. Laffey."

"I'm sure, nothing."

"We've had wonderful times. Dr. Laffey used to take me to Europe every other year. But lately he's been much too busy."

"Important man, what can you do?"

"You know what I miss most in the world? An old-fashioned shopping spree, the kind I used to go on. Oh, the shopping I've done!" She began to speak very rapidly and with unusual animation. "The French have very soft leather goods. In Scotland it's woolens. If you see something you like in a shop, buy it. It might not be there when you get back. Remember, there's a season to these things. About bargaining. In England there's no point in it. But east of Paris, offer half and stick to it. Dr. Laffey used to admire my skill at bargaining"—she laughed like a girl—"but that's all there was to it: offer half and hold on. Remember that."

"In my family, my wife buy everything," Costa said.

"How nice! I do look forward to meeting her. I have some beautiful clothes upstairs I'll show her. Many I've never worn. Probably never will. Though I haven't changed size."

"Mom," Ethel said, "he's not interested in your size."

"Zooo-hut! Ethel!" Costa said. "Let woman talk, God's sake. Please, Mrs. Laffey, again, your size?"

"Oh, it doesn't matter. I'm still a six. A junior, not a miss. Ethel, here, is a miss. See how much bigger she is?"

"Mom! We'd better get you a place to stay, Mr. Avaliotis," Ethel said. "Before tourists grab all the space."

"Don't worry, Ethel, they always have room for me. Wherever I go, dear Mrs. Laffey, people look out for me. But it's not them, it's God. He look out for me. I will bring you His blessing. I will ask Him to give you your strength back, you will see how quick."

He raised up on his toes and filled his chest with air. "Well, why we waiting here, boy?" he said to Teddy.

"Waiting for you," Teddy said, "who else?"

Costa laughed. "He get fresh with his father sometime, he answer back. But that is your country, Mrs. Laffey. Thank God your daughter understand respect, right, Ethel?"

"Sometimes," Ethel said. "Come on or we really will need God's help."

She drove them to several motels which Costa didn't like. "Where is river, some water, something?" he asked.

"Pop, for chrissake, this is desert. The water here is a thousand feet underground."

"There is a motel out in Palm Canyon," Ethel said. "That's quite a ways out, though. There's sort of a stream there."

"Sort of, again!" Costa said. And when he saw it, he said, "You call this river?"

"In the spring it's full," Ethel said.

There was a frame-built motel. Costa made a face.

"We really better take a room here, Mr. Avaliotis," Ethel said, "if there is one."

They registered, then Ethel excused herself so the two men could shave and clean up.

"I have problem," Costa said to her. "No car."

"I will call for you at six and bring you out again after dinner," she said.

"No, now. Few minutes. I must find store."

"I have shaving stuff, Pop. What do you need?"

"I want to buy dear mother something," he said to Ethel.

"It's really not necessary, Mr. Avaliotis——"

"I cannot come to dinner without present for your mother."

At a drugstore the old man bought a two-pound Sampler box of Whitman's chocolates. "No more problems," he said.

The dinner that night went very well, every detail, from Costa giving Mrs. Laffey her present, to the cocktails, the compliments about the house and grounds—everything until Costa told Dr. Laffey what he expected.

"We are Catholics," Dr. Laffey said, his lips drawn tight. "Ethel is going to be married in our church."

"That is not possible," Costa said.

"Anything is possible, Mr. Avaliotis." Dr. Laffey had been put through a practice session on the name by Ethel.

"Maybe for you. Everything is not possible for me. We

have family and that is our way. We don't change when we come to this country. Our boys marry Greek girls and our Greek young ladies marry Greek boys. I am not old-fashioned type man. I understand the world is changing. But on this one thing we don't change."

"Neither do we," Dr. Laffey said, more succinct, quite as definite.

"So . . ." Costa let it fall, with a turn-out gesture of his palms. "You have your right, I have my right. We see what happen."

There was the kind of silence a hostess dreads.

"We have beautiful flowers in the desert," Mrs. Laffey said. "Desert flowers."

"He knows that, Emma," Dr. Laffey said.

No one spoke.

"When suddenly everybody quiet in conversation, like now," Costa said, "people in old country say, 'A girl is born!'"

No one got the point.

Costa turned to Mrs. Laffey. "Very nice dinner, Mrs. Laffey," he said. "How you get fish like that here, so fresh?"

"I had nothing to do with this dinner, unfortunately," Mrs. Laffey said. Then she looked at the doctor.

"The mountain trout," he said to Teddy, particularly to Teddy, "are flown in from Denver."

"Did you hear that, Pop?" Teddy said. "The trout are flown in from Denver."

"Very nice, very nice," Costa said.

"Now why don't you two gentlemen," Teddy said, "start getting along?"

"All K. with me," Costa said.

But Dr. Laffey didn't talk to Costa anymore that night except as part of the group. At about nine forty-five, he looked at his watch and stood up. "You will have to forgive me," he said. "I am operating in the morning."

Ethel did not forgive him for that, any more than she had for a hundred other things.

"Of course," Costa said. "We don't want to be problem here. Operation very important. Call taxi, boy."

"I'll drive you home," Ethel said.

"Too much trouble. Also I think proper thing, you and your father maybe discuss situation—"

"There is nothing to discuss," Dr. Laffey said. "Good night." He did not shake hands with Costa, but smiled at him with the grim admiration one reserves for worthy antagonists.

The Avaliotis men took a cab home.

By the time they'd gone, the light was out in Dr. Laffey's bedroom. Ethel had to wait till morning.

She got up early, waited at the breakfast table for him.

"I want to tell you," she said, "I am going to marry Ted Avaliotis and I don't care where the ceremony is performed."

"I'm aware of that, Ethel," the doctor said. He always ate a whole pink grapefruit in the morning, opening it like an orange and eating it in sections. "But I am not going to be bluffed. You don't know Greeks the way I do. They are a nation of traders. The first position a Greek takes is never his last. Thank you, Manuel."

Dr. Laffey's breakfast was a small steak cut very thin. His diet was protein, carefully regulated. He took three tablespoons of granular lecithin every day.

Ethel had three cups of black coffee.

"That coffee will make you very jumpy," Dr. Laffey said. "You certainly don't need additional stimulation, my dear."

"You know what's making me nervous," she said. "I want to settle this."

"Go ahead. Run off, leave your usual note, disappear, don't come back, get married, do anything you want. But whatever you think of your father, you must know by

104

now that I am not a fool. You are not here because you want my permission. You're here because that old man wants my permission; that is also part of his code. Am I right?"

"So?"

"I will not allow myself to be bullied."

"He's not trying to bully you."

"You are. And I will not have it."

"Please, just this once—please!"

"Now that tone I prefer. Can we talk sensibly? Remember, always, that I know a lot more about you than Mr. Whatever-the-hell-his-name-is. For instance, right now I know you're not in a position to bully me either. So quiet down and let's talk sense."

"Go ahead."

"I have made many trips to the Orient and I have never been in a shop there—Greek, Egyptian, Turkish, Armenian, Syrian, Lebanese or plain old woggy-wog—where the owner did not expect me to bargain. The owner, in this case, gave me an idea of what he wanted. He will not get it; not from me. I also have an idea of what he'll settle for and in time I will offer him that."

"What is that? More coffee, Manuel."

"I suggest"—Dr. Laffey had finished his steak and his decaffeinated coffee and was wiping his lips—"I urge you, in fact, for your own happiness, to find five minutes today when you can be alone with the young man—whom I like, by the way; he seems adaptable—and urge him to speak earnestly to his father and tell him that two people can play at being adamant. Tell him that he's got to learn to bend a bit, because if he doesn't, he'll break. Let's bend together, shall we?"

"Dad, you're really so full of shit!" she said.

Dr. Laffey left the room.

Ethel stopped him as he was backing his car out of the garage. She did it by standing in the car's path.

"Well, what is it?" she said at the driver's window. "Your proposal."

"To have two ceremonies: one in his church, one in ours. It is intolerable for him to believe he can dictate to me. What the hell is he, anyway? He has no education, not one bit of humor, he smells of sweat, yet he's all pomposity. And arrogance. I won't stand for it. Now tell Teddy to take it or leave it. It's a perfectly acceptable compromise, one that can do what all good compromise solutions do: leave everyone as happy as they can be under the circumstances, which is—you will find out— all you can expect of this life. Teddy, to judge by his ever agreeable expression, already knows that. Good-bye."

He pulled away, very fast. Stopped abruptly, backed up to his daughter again.

"Do you agree or not?" he asked. "May I have something on the record?"

"I think you're very clever," she said.

"Years of experience," he said. "By the way, tonight, do we have to again?"

"Oh, Dad, cut it out, Dad!"

"I'm sorry, I really am. You just got my goat before. I'm at his disposal tonight. What is he going to do with me?"

"Take us to dinner."

"May I humbly request that it be to a restaurant where I can eat the food?"

"I don't know how he's fixed financially—"

"I'm sure Teddy saves."

"If I know anything about him, the old man won't take money from his son, not for an occasion like this."

Costa took them to Dr. Laffey's favorite restaurant; he'd asked Ethel to suggest it. She had hinted that it was expensive, but the old man waved his finger violently across his pursed lips and she got the message.

Costa escorted the two women into the place and Dr. Laffey had the instant he wanted alone with Teddy.

"What I don't quite understand," he said to the young man, "is what you see in Ethel. She can be quite difficult, you know, perplexing and unpredictable. Are you prepared for that?"

"Dr. Laffey," Teddy said, "the truth, I'm afraid, is that I'm a dull man. I certainly wouldn't want to marry someone like myself."

Inside, they found Costa, as was proper, sitting at the head of the table.

He spoke of the sponge. What it was, how it lived, what it ate, how it reproduced. He talked about the red tide that had come in and, for ten years, killed the whole industry. He talked about the advantages of the natural sponge over the synthetic. He made Mrs. Laffey another present, a box carefully wrapped and tied in fine blue paper, and told her what it was, placing it carefully at her feet: "Two perfect sponge for your bath," he said. "I look over thousan' piece."

Then he spoke of his father and of his father's grave in the yard where the old Greek Orthodox church had once stood—it had burned down, arson suspected, but all the Greeks in Tarpon Springs still considered the ground hallowed. On his father's stone marker was an oval-framed photograph, not as he'd been when he died, but the way he'd looked in his prime, the very strongest photograph of the man they had, so he'd be remembered as he'd been before age reduced him and death cut him down. Then he told them something that even Teddy didn't know, that every other Sunday he took potted flowers, blue nasturtiums or white lilies, to the grave site, left them there, on top of the mound which covered his father's body, and then, after a fortnight, took the old flowers home, dug a hold for the bulbs, filled it with

107

dehydrated cow manure mixed with loam and bark mulch —Costa went into every particular—transplanting the flowers to his own yard to keep his father's memory alive.

"That is why I cannot agree anything except my father's way, these two children be marry in church his religion. Anything else, he will not forgive me. Eh, boy?" he asked Teddy. "Isn't that the reason, boy?"

No one else had said a word for over half an hour.

Now Teddy spoke. "That's the reason, Pop."

Mrs. Laffey was sniffling. She was in love with the old Greek. "Can I say something, dear?" she asked her husband.

"Of course," he said, "but may I ask a question first?" He turned to Teddy. "Did Ethel tell you my suggestion?"

"Yes, sir, she did."

"It seemed very fair to her," Dr. Laffey continued, "as it does to me." He touched Teddy's arm. "Look at me, please, young man, and tell me, truly, what did you think? The truth."

"I try to speak only the truth, Dr. Laffey. Why do you think I would dissemble?"

"I don't know why. It doesn't matter why. What do you think?"

"It's up to my father," Teddy said.

Dr. Laffey turned to Costa Avaliotis. "Isn't their happiness the only important thing here?" he asked with the greatest show of certitude he could muster.

"No," Costa said. "Something more important. At their time in life, twenty-one, twenty-three, these children know nothing. That is value old age. Otherwise what use we live long time and be put in position respect? You American people have other ideas. With you most important thing is happiness, success and happiness, good food, happiness, automobile, so on, always happiness. But your children they leave home quick. Usually for—excuse me, nothing personal—usually good reason. Our children stay close. So you can see, what we have more important. Over many thousan' year, it prove itself."

"What is it you're talking about, may I ask?" Dr. Laffey was becoming quite impatient.

"What our fathers think, what they did, what grandfathers think, what they did. What you call that?"

"Tradition," Dr. Laffey provided. "But traditions do not remain like the mountains, never changing."

"Ours don't change," Costa said.

Dr. Laffey turned to Teddy for help.

"He speaks for me," Teddy said.

"Don't you have a mind of your own, young man?" Dr. Laffey said.

"I just spoke it," Teddy said.

"Do you every think for yourself?"

"I am now. It's going to be his way."

"Or not at all?" Dr. Laffey looked at his son-in-law-to-be scornfully.

"I didn't say that; you did. But I'll tell you. Yes!"

"I blame you for this," Dr. Laffey said to his daughter.

"She had nothing to do with it, sir," Teddy said. "She argued very well and very hard. I told her the same thing I've told you. I'll only marry with my father's permission. And he won't give his permission unless Ethel has your permission."

"Emma, why don't we go home."

Mrs. Laffey began to gather her wrap. She remembered there was something she'd meant to say in praise of the Avaliotis family, but it was too late now.

"Oh, no, no," Costa said. "Delicious dinner, now cognac, brandy, something. Maybe they have Greek brandy, very strong, for men, something sweet for ladies. Call waiter here, Teddy."

"I have to operate tomorrow."

"Never mind, never mind, how often your daughter marry? Once in lifetime, I hope, Greek style!"

Teddy got the waiter and they ordered drinks. The issue was not brought up again.

When the bill was presented, the old man reached into a shoe he'd taken off and produced some money. Ethel also noticed that he didn't blink at the size of the bill, and while he didn't have much money left when he got through, he tipped with a flourish.

Dr. Laffey dropped them off at their motel and said good-bye with practiced politeness. He didn't mention what was on everyone's mind.

Neither did Costa. Ethel had the feeling Costa wasn't even thinking about it anymore. He'd had his say, was sure of his position. It was not up to him now; it was up to the others. He would sleep perfectly that night. She would not.

The next morning, Costa made a dramatic announcement and created a crisis.

"Tonight finish!" he said. "Such matters don't need more than three days decide. I hear him, he hear me. So? Now we go to what is next, good or bad, move forward in the life, pain can be endured, other connections made, right?"

"Not in this matter," Teddy said.

But Costa didn't hear. "Also tonight I make dinner. Bring Ethel with car. I make my salad tonight, we see what kind markets they have here."

Ethel drove over as quickly as she could; Teddy had told her today was going to be it, one way or the other.

"All right use your mother kitchen?" Costa asked her.

"Of course," Ethel said. "Just tell Manuel and Carlita what you want and they'll be glad to—"

"Want only one thing, they get out. After, they wash dishes. O.K.?"

The gathering of materials for the great Greek salad was a ritual. A day-long pressure was created by Costa's insistence that each of the ingredients be the best available. He was disappointed in Tucson, Arizona; its supermarkets came in for serious criticism. "What kind people we have here?" he demanded. "Barbarians!"

The feta cheese, perhaps the one exceptional ingredient, was finally found in a specialty store, in the richest section of the city. It was packed, dry, in a tin—"canned goods"—not in brine in a barrel. Costa took time out to explain to the owner of the store, a plump middle-aged woman in a paisley skirt, what the loss is when a food of delicate flavor is packed in a can.

There were tomatoes and cucumbers in this store, but Costa didn't like their looks. He did find, on a neglected shelf, a bottle of first-quality olive oil, imported from Greece, not Italy. On the bottom of the bottle's straw cradle was a stamp which read "Itea." Itea, Costa informed them all, is the port of Delphus, that one-time navel of the world. This, he affirmed to Ethel, was a good augury.

In the Mexican barrio he bought some gentle green peppers and two sweet Spanish onions. He didn't like the tomatoes here either, but at least, he observed, they were not four identical unripened fruit, in a cellophane-faced carton. He carefully selected six for purchase, kept shaking his head as he did. It was evident that he was seriously dissatisfied, even discouraged.

In desperation, he entered the largest supermarket in the city. To his surprise he happened on a little gourmet corner, where he found the kind of wine vinegar he wanted and, to his great relief, some tins of bitter anchovies. In standing wire baskets was a variety of breads, not wrapped in plastic. After a great deal of pinching, Costa bought a dozen crisp-crusted, soft-hearted clover rolls.

Here he also discovered—"Oppa!"—some wrinkled black olives.

In the vegetable department he came on something labeled "burpless cucumber," bought it distrustfully, suspecting that when you take the burp out of a cucumber a lot more goes with it. "This not cucumber," he was to say later. "We have here squash."

Finally Costa concerned himself with that delicate matter, Mrs. Laffey's palate. He insisted that Ethel drive him to the best butcher in the city. "Maybe Greek salad, garlic, anchovies, so forth, too strong for dear mother," he said. "I find something in case." In the butcher shop he quickly made friends with the owner, explained that he wanted three tender chops of baby lamb. Rejecting what the butcher first showed him, he accepted an invitation to enter the walk-in freezer closet and himself select the niblets he preferred. He carefully supervised these as they were trimmed of fat and wrapped in brown waxed paper, then shook the butcher's hand.

On the way home they stopped at a liquor store, where he found neither Mavrodaphne nor Hymettus, the wines he wanted, but the Italian Soave Bolla, which he purchased with a generous show of tolerance.

At the Laffey's home, since there was at least an hour and a half before it was proper to start making the salad, Costa escorted Mrs. Laffey to the twin white wicker chairs at the side of the swimming pool, where they could watch their children bathe.

"Leg too skinny," Costa said to himself as he measured Ethel in her bikini. He could not understand his son's passion for this young woman. But he'd prayed God for patience and understanding and it had been granted him. He was doing everything correctly, giving the Laffeys, particularly the head of the house, every chance. Perfectly at ease, he fell asleep with the sun on his face.

He snored. Mrs. Laffey smiled and stole away to her air-conditioned bedroom.

The arrival of the doctor woke Costa. The surgeon strode onto his terrace carrying a double vodka martini, straight up, sat down next to the Greek and began to boast in well-modulated tones. He showed Costa, using the old man's heavy hand for a model, the operation he'd performed that afternoon. An affluent client had lost his thumb in a home shop accident. Dr. Laffey had, successfully, taken the first finger and moved it so it could serve as a thumb.

When he'd finished with the description of his knife and needle work, he let drop that for this one job—three and a half hours it had taken—he would be paid a fee of four thousand five hundred dollars. "I am the only man," he said, "between Los Angeles and St. Louis who successfully performs this operation."

"Very nice! Very nice!" Costa said.

Dr. Laffey that afternoon was full of confidence and energy. He'd made the same resolve Costa had: Today was going to be it. Vodka fortified this decision. He offered to provide Costa with equal strength from the same source. But Costa told him he didn't want to drink until their difference had been settled. "When I drink," he said, "I get soft heart."

It was time for Costa to go to work. He went into the kitchen and asked Manuel and Carlita to leave. Carlita pleaded to be allowed to watch, but Costa said, "Too many people in kitchen no good." He did want Ethel's help. "You will learn exactly, this," he said. "Teddy likes very much."

Any fine chef does only the planning and measuring, the combining and flavoring. The routine work—slicing, peeling, washing—is done by pantry help. Ethel worked under Costa's instruction, slicing the burpless cucumber, dividing the tomatoes in eight, unfolding the lettuce leaves, washing each one separately to make sure there were no brown spots. Costa allowed her to make notations of each ingredient, how much to use and what to watch for when buying it. He had no secrets from Ethel.

It was to the kitchen that Dr. Laffey brought Father Corrigan when he arrived. Costa's hands were greased with the oil of Itea, so he could not shake. As Costa washed, Father Corrigan and Dr. Laffey discussed golf, to which they were both devoted. Then Dr. Laffey turned to his daughter.

"Ethel, I wonder if you and I might have a chat before dinner," he said to her. She was about to object, but a look from Costa, whom she'd begun to obey without question, sent her off.

The priest and the Greek were alone.

Costa gave him a few olives and a bit of cheese to settle his nerves. Then he told him the story of his life.

"For first ten years," Costa revealed, "I no see my father. We wait in Kalymnos, small island over there, for him to bring us to Florida, my mother, my brother, my sister, me. One day he don't send message, he come his self. With money in pocket. 'Pack up,' he say to my mother. 'We go.' Sudden, like that." He snapped his fingers. "We sell house—for nothing; drachma buy nothing—pack grandfather picture, holy icon, virgin, Saint Nicholas, so forth, so on, and we come to Florida.

"I young boy this time. But my brother strong, he learn sponge quick. After, he teach me. Then terrible thing happen. My brother die. No propeller guard those day, prop cut his air line. My brother on bottom with lead weight on feet. Finish. So my father say, Come on, take his place. I begin go down. Ten fathoms. More. Soon I bringing up plenty, one day two hundred seventy-four pieces."

"That's a lot," Father Corrigan said, "isn't it?"

"You damn right, a lot. You bring up two hundred piece someday, see how you feel after. I lean forward 'gainst tide, big tide below, you understand, I show you, look, like this, see, like this, I never stop, pick 'em up, pick 'em up, pick 'em up."

"Must be hard work," the priest said.

"That's what I'm telling you. But O.K. America I understand right away. Work hard here, you make good living. Go 'head, work hard in Greece, you die all same poor. I own my house here, take plenty time, find nice wife, Greek girl, Astoria section, Queens. She bring me one son. Then finish. Who knows why? Ask God. You see my boy?"

"A fine lad!"

"You damn right! My father raise me certain way, I raise this boy same. Teddy. Real name Theophilactos, means 'Follows God,' you understand?"

"He looks like a God-fearing—"

"He don't fear nobody. Officer, U.S. Navy! Third class!"

"You go to the Greek Orthodox church, Dr. Laffey tells me; he says you are very devoted."

"I am religious man, don't go to church. We have new priest now, he's like woman! They have womans on committee too! Also bingo over there! Bingo, for chrissake! I say to this priest, next Sunday take money from church, go dog track, gamble, same thing! Many priest, you understand, racketeer. Too rich, too fat, forgive me, nothing personal, I see you eat plenty."

Father Corrigan put down the cheese. "I want to tell you about the Laffeys," he said.

"I talk with them three days now," Costa said. "Smart man, plenty money, very fine wife, too bad sick, daughter love my son, I see that, so far everything O.K."

"I want to talk to you about their faith," the priest said.

"Why not? But before you must understand certain things my faith. O.K.?"

"Of course."

"First thing! The seed is carried by father, am I right on that?"

"What? Oh. Yes. Yes."

"Yes. Also father put seed inside woman body over there, right?" Costa illustrated with a gesture. "There it finds home and grows nine months, you know that much?"

"Well, actually, that is not the present scientific—"

"Problem with your religion, dear sir, priest don't marry. Our priest marry, so forth, so on, have children, they know they carry seed, they see many times."

"I'm talking about science."

"I don't need science this subject. You must take word people who have experience from life, right?"

"It's common knowledge; every TV station has had scientific programs—"

"Who put seed in Mary's body over there?"

"Mary who? Over where?"

"What's matter with you, what kind priest? Mary, mother God, who put seed over there, her body?"

"Why, God, of course."

"Correct for change! God."

"But—"

"No but business. Jesus son of God. Not son Mary. God's son, no half-half sort-of business. We are created God's image, me, my son! God's image! You should read Bible, my friend—"

"I know my Bible very well—"

"You come here convince me something, right?"

"Just this: Don't you think you should have some consideration for Dr. Laffey's family and their—"

"I don't see any family here. We do them favor bring

their daughter in our family. We don't need them, they need us!"

"I don't think one side needs the other."

"Then why they ask me here? I come from Florida, plenty Greek girl for my boy over there. But he want this one. O.K. I come here protect my family. That's my business. Your mind your business, Father, better way. With me you waste breath!"

Father Corrigan had come to the same conclusion. He sighed deeply. He doubted he had the strength to continue this absurd debate. But he made one last try.

"I did hope to have just a few minutes of your listening—"

"Why not? Only we must talk truth, right?"

"That's what I propose to do. We are living, you do realize, in a democracy, which means we live in a condition of equality, everyone has his or her rights. So what we are proposing is that there be two wedding ceremonies, one in your—"

"My dear friend, tell me truth. Miss Ethel, she go your church?"

"She went to catechism school."

"I talk now. She go now?"

"I don't really know."

"You know. She tol' me. Nothing! She tol' me she marry my son if her father say O.K., also if her father say no O.K. What kind belief is that? She lucky my son wants her. She believe in nothing. She don't listen to her father. Why? I can smell what goes on over here. I know what she is. She is not clean girl. Am I right?"

"Oh, now, come—"

"You listen one time her confession, so forth. Tell me truth."

"Oh, come, come; we can't reveal—"

"I don't need your opinion on that. I have plenty

experience, know many women, many time. Cracker girls, so forth, so on. *Gameso.*" A gesture. "You know what I mean?" Another gesture. "But this girl, when my son marry, I will help her, I will teach her proper way. That's my gift to her."

At this the priest lost control. "You are, Mr. Avaliotis, the most bigoted, the most arrogant and without a doubt the most narrow-minded man I have ever met."

"O.K., from priests I take insult. But God knows my heart is good. He listen when I pray—"

"I am going to recommend to Dr. Laffey that if he can possibly influence Ethel not to go ahead with this—"

"Have some more cheese."

"No, thank you," Father Corrigan said, and left the kitchen.

In the pool garden, Ethel was slipping a small rose into the buttonhole of her father's lapel.

"I called my gynecologist today," she said. "His line had been taken out of service."

"He made so much money," Ed Laffey said, "he couldn't afford to work anymore."

"Can you recommend another man?"

"There's my old bridge partner Julian Moseley; he's been here to the house."

"When you speak to him, tell him I'd prefer if he'd keep my visit confidential."

"I don't have to ask that. All doctors—"

"I've heard some of your conversations, Dad."

Father Corrigan appeared on the other side of the limpid blue water. As he approached, he threw his hands into the air, a gesture of frustration.

"Would it embarrass you," Ethel said, dropping her voice and speaking more quickly, "to use your friendship to get me a quick appointment? Tomorrow morning, please, right after their plane leaves?"

Father Corrigan was laughing as he came up.

"Is anything wrong?" Ed Laffey asked Ethel quickly.

"Very pretty," Father Corrigan said. "Father, daughter and a red, red rose."

"I'll call him for you," Ed Laffey said to Ethel, "but in return I'd like your help. I haven't been able to make a dent in Mr.—I'm still not entirely comfortable with that name!"

"No deals, Dad. Just do what I said." Ethel turned to go.

"I have never met anyone like that man," Father Corrigan said. "He has his own theocracy, his own biology, his own medical science. Ethel, are you sure you know what you're getting into?"

She looked at the priest a moment without answering. Then she said, "Why do you pretend to care whom I marry or where?" and walked into the house.

Father Corrigan, laughing and gibing, told Dr. Laffey about the conversation.

"I felt I was taking part in one of those corny TV daytime dramas. I've seen this same scene a dozen times— the bigoted, but somehow lovable father from the old world who cannot be moved. I was trying to remember during our conversation how those TV struggles are resolved. I thought I had it. I told him it was the democratic way that both sides be given equal respect. That works on TV. But not with this man. I'm afraid I've let you down. I'll take another crack at it tomorrow, if you like, invite him to the parish house and have a go at him over a heavy lunch."

"Ethel tells me he's going east in the morning."

"I'm afraid if it's to be settled tonight, you have to do it. I wouldn't budge. Absolutely not. By the way, I thought the man was rather insulting about Ethel. I didn't care for what he said about her, not one bit. But I can

119

tell from one look at the boy that he loves your daughter very much and that's he a reasonable lad. After all, he's an officer in the United States Navy."

"What did the old bastard say?"

"It may even be the occasion for a display of anger; you certainly have every justification."

"What did he say about Ethel?"

The priest told him and drove away.

Ethel and Teddy set the table under the meticulous direction of Costa. He wore an apron now and carried a cotton kitchen towel. He'd found an old Bavarian cow bell that hadn't been sounded for years; he used it to announce dinner.

Costa wanted Teddy at the head of the table, Ethel at the opposite end, facing him, Dr. and Mrs. Laffey side by side opposite the kitchen door and his own chair close to that door since he would be serving. He dismissed every offer of help. "All you do, what I bring, you eat," he said.

He poured the Soave Bolla and raised a toast to Mrs. Laffey, wishing her what he knew she didn't have, health and happiness. The woman laughed in a treble, then, blushing like an adolescent, turned to her husband to see what he thought of all this gallantry.

Meantime, Costa had disappeared. But now more familiar than anyone there with the resources of the pantry, he came back with five of the Laffey's wedding present dish set that he'd discovered at the back of a top shelf, ornate pieces, their scalloped edges in gold.

"Oh, Edward, remember?" Mrs. Laffey twittered.

"I remember," Dr. Laffey responded. He leaned over and kissed his wife on the forehead, a sentimental gesture performed without sentiment.

Then came the eruption.

"I wish," Costa said as he cleared the heart of the

table for his great Greek salad, "I only wish golfer-priest was here. Now I remember many things to say to him."

"He's a very fine man," Dr. Laffey said. "I was hoping he'd convince you—"

"He convince me nothing," Costa said. "Maybe I convince him something."

"What, for instance?" Dr. Laffey said. He knew the moment for head-to-head confrontation had come.

The area in the center of the table was cleared.

"Greek ideas don't change," Costa said.

"Then why do we continue to meet?" Dr. Laffey grabbed the bull's horns.

"We are waiting you see proper way," Costa said.

"That's pretty damned arrogant of you," Dr. Laffey said. He knew the time to slash. "Don't you think so, Teddy? Don't you, Ethel, really?"

"I don't," Ethel said.

"I know what you think," Dr. Laffey said scornfully. "I haven't expected anything loyal from you in years—"

"Don't say that," Emma Laffey cried, with surprising force. Then, in a whisper, which she leaned forward to deliver properly: "Edward, please don't. Say. Anything like that!"

"Be quiet, Emmie," Dr. Laffey said. "There is no use putting this off. I wish you would recognize that you are no help whatsoever, and leave this to me."

Mrs. Laffey tipped her head on its side and looked up at the ceiling. One eyelid began to quiver.

"Dr. Laffey," Costa said, "not polite talk your wife that style in front strangers! She is fine woman, very sensitive—"

"Kindly do not intrude yourself into this area of my family life too," Dr. Laffey answered. "I won't tolerate it."

Then he turned sharply in his chair, giving the side of his body to Costa, and addressed Teddy.

"May I speak to you and only to you for a moment. First let me say that I respect your uniform. I assume you are what you appear to be—Navy, a petty officer third class, in good standing—and that you respect the creeds of this society as you must those of the woman you've chosen to be the mother of your children."

"Daddy, what crap!" Ethel said.

"Please shut up," Dr. Laffey said. "Just shut up, all of you. Let me talk without interruption to the boy who is asking to be my son-in-law. May I do that? Just for once?"

"Who's stopping you?" Costa asked.

"You are. You terrify your son. He's afraid to have an opinion of his own. I cannot see, unless he liberates himself from your domination, how he can be an effective naval officer."

"Very high respect, don't worry, effective too!"

"Dad, please, I want to hear what Dr. Laffey has to say, please."

"You heard, we all heard."

"I want to hear him now and I want to answer him now."

"O.K., O.K., yes, what, Doctor, what? Talk!"

"First of all, sit down, please, sit in your chair."

Costa looked quickly back toward the kitchen door, where his salad was losing its crispness in its bath of olive oil, lemon juice and vinegar.

"Never mind the goddamn salad, Dad—" Teddy said.

"Don't talk that way to me, boy, Teddy. Don't forget who you are and who I am!"

"I want to forget it. I respect your wishes, but you are not the problem now. Dr. Laffey is. So please shut up and sit down."

Costa was impressed by his son. He sat in his place.

"Dr. Laffey, you were saying something about my uniform." Teddy smiled at the doctor and waited.

"I want you to know," Dr. Laffey began, "that I was Navy too, in the last war, a lieutenant commanding three medical corpsmen who landed on Tarawa with the first wave. The dead were slung like cordwood over the beach of that island we've all forgotten. We operated by the light of four flashlights in a small Jap pillbox one hour after the marines had cleared it. We treated more than a hundred men during those first thirty-six hours. Only four died. So I don't ask for your respect, I command it."

"I'm giving it to you," Teddy said.

"Me too," Costa said, "but for God's sake, say something."

"What we fought for then and what your uniform symbolizes still is democracy. Equality. How can you on the one hand say that you love my daughter, then ignore her wishes, scorn everything she believes in? That is not democracy. Your father is a relic of a dead past, he is antediluvian; but you, what about you?"

"In this matter, I intend to satisfy my father."

"But what he respects is bigotry! How can an officer in the United States Navy take him seriously?"

"I take him seriously," Ethel said.

Everybody knew that was it.

"I'd rather do something illogical, even downright crazy, for him than something sensible for you. Where do you get off making fun of his tradition? It's better than yours and it's better than mine."

Dr. Laffey stared at his daughter.

"And how can you expect me to go for all that shit about our religion? We religious? You! The man who just killed his wife with a few well-chosen words. Look at her, sitting beside you. Dead by your hand. Look at her. I dare you. Forgive me, Mother, but—"

"No, you're right, you're right." Mrs. Laffey burst into tears."

"I'm sorry I said that," Ethel said.

"You're not sorry," Dr. Laffey said. "Don't pretend that!"

Mrs. Laffey got up awkwardly and slowly, took her cane and, refusing all offers of help, left the table.

There was silence.

Costa remembered the salad, but he didn't do anything about it.

"There's a greal deal I could say to you and about you," Dr. Laffey said to his daughter. "But I choose not to."

"Say anything you want!" Ethel challenged him.

Dr. Laffey smiled at her, then left the room.

Teddy went to his father and kissed him.

"It's all yours, Kitten," they heard the doctor say from the parlor. "Do whatever—"

He stopped. He'd heard Ethel sobbing.

She made a dash, not for Teddy but for his father. Just as instinctively, Costa pulled her onto his lap, her face against his thick, muscular neck.

Costa kissed her cheek, he kissed her moist eyes.

Teddy stood over the girl and stroked her hair.

"Fine girl," Costa said.

"When she cries," Teddy said, "she looks ten years old."

Slowly Ethel began to ease, gasping at intervals until she was quiet. But she didn't lift her head, didn't open her eyes.

"Boy!" Costa whispered. "Pay 'tention here. Tell me this much—we can have wedding proper way, in Florida?"

"Pop, I can't break off my duty on the base."

Costa nodded, then looked at Ethel. For the first time he understood his son's feeling for the girl.

"We'll have to do it in San Diego," Teddy was saying.

"Then there is problem," Costa said.

Her body's perfume was reaching him. Her buttocks,

plumped out under her weight, felt heavy between his legs. And warm.

"I have to bring Avaliotis family there," Costa said. "My sister, her family, my dead brother wife, so forth, few dear friends. . . ."

Her breasts were pressed against his chest, her abdomen, twisted outward at the waist, fitted his hand. There was a roll of flesh, the one Greek men like, just below the belt of her dress.

"They saw you baptize," he said to his son. "Now they must see you marry."

"I understand," Teddy said. "Sure, Pop, sure."

"Cost lotsa money," he said, not looking at his son.

"I'll help out," Teddy said.

"No, no, not possible," Costa said.

She was awakening the life in him.

He shifted her weight so it was on his knees.

"Tell me, Theophilactos," he said, "we have Greek church San Diego?"

"A fine one. Saint Spiridon. They brought the marble all the way from Mount Something near Athens. The Greek community in San Diego is rich and highly respected."

"Naturally. O.K. So I change my plan, go back with you and Ethel San Diego. I look over this church, talk to priest, so forth. Hope no goddamn bingo priest over there. Then I go home."

He looked at his son.

"Going get up now," he said.

Teddy nodded. "But you like her, Dad, don't you?" he said.

"Fine girl," Costa said.

He got to his feet, Ethel in his arms, and moved toward the parlor. She didn't turn her face to see where he was carrying her.

Dr. Laffey was reading *Time*.

"Put down magazine, damn fool," Costa said.

Dr. Laffey turned a page.

Costa put the man's daughter on his lap and left her there. They were two oddly fitted pieces of crockery, brittle, unyielding.

Costa went back to the dining room and poured himself a glass of cold wine.

six

E D Laffey was rarely depressed and never so in public. Behavior that might evoke the pity of others was abhorrent to him. That evening he retired to his bedroom quickly, leaving Ethel and her men to celebrate their victory. When he heard them leave the house in her car, heard the sounds of their laughter and the gate doing its double duty, he entered Ethel's room. The walls were pockmarked with holes in the bare plaster, like the marks shrapnel leave. He sat on her bed and wondered how it had happened so quickly. On a table was her suitcase, only partially unpacked. Suddenly it was over, their life together, and behind him were the opportunities he'd let slip. There was nothing to do but go to bed.

He'd often boasted to his friends of his ability to fall asleep anywhere within minutes. At an age when most of his friends woke two or three times a night to confront insoluble problems or to urinate, Dr. Laffey slept right through, got out of bed each morning perfectly refreshed.

But not on this night. For one thing, there was a peculiar odor in the air, faint but penetrating, the smell an animal's body produces as it begins to disintegrate. It occurred to him that it might be his imagination. But that unique sweetness was familiar to him; it reminded him of the smell that had saturated the Pacific island for weeks after the invasion, that cloying evidence that bodies were decomposing, invisible under the debris of palms or at the bottom of foxholes half filled by the rain or flung grotesquely about the rubble of pillboxes destroyed by the guns of the fleet. There had been nothing to do about it then but wait for time to pass, and there was nothing to do about this disaster except to endure it.

Ed Laffey had taken seriously the job of raising his child, particularly so because she was adopted. It was he who'd chosen a girl rather than a boy, it was he who'd read books on child rearing and, early on, taken over the child's stewardship from his wife. One book had been especially reassuring. A parent, its author stated, always has another chance. But now Ethel was a woman and the speed of her development frightened him. If he'd once had that "other chance," he had it no longer. All that was left was to lie there, alone in his bed, and try to figure out what he'd done wrong. She was going and he was about to be left behind in a house with an invalid wife. The story was over.

He assumed Ethel had driven the men to their motel, but an hour had passed, then most of another. It could not have taken her that long. Finally he heard her car drive up. Quickly he moved to the door of his bedroom, opened it about a foot, then hurried back into bed, turned on his reading lamp and picked up a magazine. He wanted her to poke her head in—without being asked—and wish him a good night.

But she didn't and he had to shame himself calling after her. She turned back. Her face was pink. Exhilaration! The doctor saw it all: The old man had retired, leaving the young people alone in the car, and they . . . and so forth. Now he didn't know what to say. He couldn't say, "Please talk to me," and he couldn't say the truth: "I'm damned jealous of you and those Greeks!"

What he said was: "You smell something strange in the air tonight?"

"Just the desert air," she said, giving him the smile of one in possession of a secret. She still didn't throw the little footbridge he needed across the chasm which had opened between them.

"I made you a doctor's appointment for tomorrow," he said.

"Thanks," she answered, "I'm staying another day," and was off to bed.

He couldn't sleep.

"Well, goddamn it, there certainly is a bad smell in the air," he said to the space she'd occupied. "Whether you smell it or not, I'm going to find out what it is." He jumped out of bed and pulled on his terry-cloth robe. Leaving his door open and the hall lights blazing, he ran down the stairs, pushed open the door to the terrace off the dining room, slammed it closed, clumped down the steps to the patio. The smell was still there. He turned off the Italian fountain and looked over his shoulder. The windows of her room were dark. She must have jumped into bed immediately. The weariness that follows victory? Or love-making?

In the stable he went straight to Maria's stall. His new mare was O.K. Diego called her The Bitch and the doctor had picked up the name, a tribute to her temperament. He fondled her soft nose. She swerved her head and bit at him. He cuffed her but it was affectionate play. No one else rode The Bitch.

Back of the barn, the smell was heavy. There was no light: the waning moon had risen but it was behind the second ridge and produced no more than a glow silhouetting the edge of the hill. He gave up the search.

At the pool, he took off his robe and, naked, holding his testicles, jumped on the diving board, seeing how high he could leap in the air, then came down as hard as he could, pounding the thick strip of laminated wood, making it creak and complain. In time past he'd called Ethel out to go swimming at night this way. He threw himself into the water—not a dive, but a great noisy splash—and swam from one end to the other, again and again, blowing out water each time he lifted his mouth. He did eighteen laps. The light in her room did not go on.

He was ridiculous. Once when he was a kid of seventeen, in love and losing out, he'd ripped open the back of his hand with a wood screw to show and shame a faithless girl. It had gained him nothing. The memory embarrassed him; it also made him laugh.

In the den, he poured himself half a tumbler of whiskey and drank it down. It was the knockout he needed.

He woke later than his usual time, showered, dressed for the office and ran down the stairs.

He poked his head out onto the terrace. The smell was gone, the air clean. It had been his imagination.

"Good morning, Carlita," he said, opening his grapefruit. "Where's Miss Ethel?"

"She had two cups of coffee and left twenty minutes ago. She said she was going to have her breakfast with Mr.—excuse me, I can't say it—then drive them to the airport. But what a handsome young man! Congratulations, sir."

Manuel had his car ready, the motor running.

"Dr. Laffey," he said, "did you smell something last night?"

130

"I thought I did."

"It's the dog pack," Manuel said. "They got a deer a few days ago. We found what was left of it in the gully below the cactus garden, a fawn. Diego buried it this morning. That dog pack! I'd like to pack eight hardnose shells into the M-1 you gave me and pour them into that lead Doberman till he was hamburger."

This conversation heartened the doctor, he didn't know why. He decided to drive to the airport instead of to his office. He would not surrender the field in a sulk.

They were at the gate and the flight had been called.

Teddy saw him first. "It's nice of you to come see us off, sir," he said extending his hand, Navy to Navy.

Costa didn't turn; he was occupied with Ethel. Ed slapped him across the back. "I'm not through with you yet," he said. That got a smile out of the Greek. But nothing more. He led Ethel away to one side, seemed to be giving her last-minute advice.

"Better get him on board," Ed said to Teddy. "Mr. Avaliotis!" he called.

Ethel wouldn't hurry. "Hold that plane, Daddy," she cried. Then she was telling Costa how grateful she was. "I'll do anything to make you happy," he heard her say. The generous victor answered, "Now you fix up everything good with your father proper way." When they kissed, Ed noted how she held his head, her fingers sliding through the hair at the base of the old man's neck. Then they were gone.

Standing behind Ethel, he watched the heavy jet lift off. It might fall. It didn't. When Ethel went on looking after it, he said, "Don't you have a doctor's appointment?"

"Oh, God," she said. "When did you make it for?"

"Nine o'clock."

"It's nine now."

"Run! I'll call and tell him you're on your way."

131

He got to his office late, took a quick look at his mail, called in his secretary and instructed her to cancel the two operations on his schedule for that day.

"What reason will I give?" she asked.

"That if I were to operate today, my knife would slip. Now call the tennis club; I want to speak to the pro."

That was his day in the office. He went home, changed into his shorts and sneakers, looked for Ethel in her room, then around the rest of the house and the grounds. Finally he called Manuel.

"Diego says she went riding," Manuel reported. "She took The Bitch. The mare you ride, sir. Diego is plenty mad, I can tell you."

"Tell him to stop whatever he's doing and come up here. I'll be back in ten minutes."

He jumped into his Mercedes. He always carried field glasses and a pistol in his glove compartment. When he arrived at the overlook off the second ridge, he climbed on top of the car and swept the area with the glasses. There was no sight of her.

When he got back, Diego was waiting.

"I told you no one was ever to get on that animal except me, Diego!"

"You ever try to stop that girl?"

Diego was a short, thin man who looked like a former jockey and may have been; no one knew anything about his past. At fifty-six, his face had baked-in creases.

"Where is she now?"

"Out on that trail somewhere. Wearing an old pair my pants, for chrissake, she's wearing my goddamn dirty pants. I told her, 'Your daddy give me hell if you take that horse.' I don't want to tell you what she said to me. It means like mind your business. Including you, sir."

"Did the mare behave?"

"I told her, 'She don't like nobody on her, that Bitch, except your daddy.' I told her, 'Don't use spurs.' But she found an old pair of her boots in the stables, spurs too. I said, 'Don't touch her side with those. And be light on her mouth.' First thing she gets on and jerks the mare's head around and that goddamn Bitch, she feels Miss Kitten's legs not tight like yours, and I holler, 'Don't lay those spurs into her side.' Well, I don't have to tell you what happen. That mare, in a minute she throws her. What does the girl do? She sits right back on and they ride away. What the hell could I do with that?"

"Stop her. Same as you'd do if she were your daughter."

"You mean beat hell out of her?"

Dr. Laffey considered riding out to find Ethel; she might need his help. But he also knew that in her present state his act would be interpreted as interference, not concern, and would make her resent him even more.

At the club, he asked the pro to take him to the end court. He smashed lobs for half an hour and felt better.

She was still out when he got home.

He called his friend the gynecologist.

"I took a smear, Edward. Absolutely negative."

"She must have been relieved."

"I couldn't tell. I may have trespassed on your jurisdiction, Edward. I said to her, 'The real punishment for infidelity is what you've been going through, that anxiety. Now tell me truthfully, was it worth it?' "

"And?"

"Quote: 'It sure as hell was!' "

"Oh, Julian, she was spiting you. She's getting married. Did she tell you? To someone else."

"She told me. Edward, I've known that girl since she was a child playing on the floor. I remember how she used to sit in your lap and how she'd look at you. God and his angel. And how she looked at everyone else, as if they might steal you away from her. What happened to all that? What happened to her? Is she the same person? Sit that girl down, Edward, before it's too late, and have one hell of a heart-to-heart talk with her. There still are standards of behavior, aren't there? Goddamn it."

He was the one who hung up.

Ed admired Ethel for not playing humble.

When she came back from her ride, he was in the pool, and to his delight, she joined him.

"Teddy was very impressed that you came to the airport," she said. "It was damned generous of you, he said, and I don't appreciate you, he said. He bawled hell out of me."

"Well, that's a side of him that I didn't appreciate."

"I thought we might have one last evening together. I'd like to get gently drunk. I mean, intelligently and gracefully drunk, in a companionable way. Would you like that?"

"I owe this kind offer to Teddy?"

"It was his idea and now it's mine. I don't automatically do everything he says, you know. Will you drink with me tonight, Daddy, on the old home ground? Our farewell party?"

That evening, after her mother had turned off the TV and, whispering apologies, had left to go to bed, Ethel and her father killed a quart. They talked like two friends who needed nothing of each other, approval or affection, so felt completely and surprisingly friendly.

"Don't you really have to like him?" Ethel was talking about Costa. "Sort of?"

"What am I supposed to like about him?" Ed said.

"His smell, for instance. It's seductive, vaguely foreign, very romantic."

"I smell sweat."

"Yeah, a little. But also—what? Cinnamon? Cloves? Teddy tells me old-time Greeks sometimes put whole cloves in their mouths."

"Sweat," Ed said.

"True, it's all pleasantly soured in perspiration."

"You're getting drunk."

"Not the way I want to be. Let's keep going."

"I'm going to get a refill. Want me to do yours?"

"Yes. Let's break down a wall or two tonight, Dad. It may be our last chance."

"Well, I'll tell you the truth. He's stupid. I don't like stupid people. How about 'naïve'? That's a kinder word. Will you go for 'naïve'? He's so confident of all that nonsense he spouts."

"He's the only man I've ever met who believes in anything."

"But what nonsense," he said, walking her drink to her.

"Well, here's to your— What do you still hope for, Dad?"

"As you said, nothing. About that old man, what I see is stupidity and energy. I find that combination particularly hard to take. And that bastard is a bully. He'll be asking you to give up what you most don't want to give up."

"Like?"

"Your independence."

"Which one are you talking about?"

"They're one and the same. A family like that is a dreadful thing. You'll find yourself in a prison with no windows."

"Is that what you predict?"

He drank his fresh one, one swallow.

"By the way," he said, "that's a bad horse you were on this afternoon."

"We got to like each other. She's like I feel."

"Now do you want to know what I predict?"

"Yes."

"I need another drink to enter the prophetic condition."

"My tongue is getting thick."

135

"There's an old Greek proverb, or should be: 'A thick tongue tells the truth.' "

They drank, sizing each other up. Old lovers, new antagonists.

"Predict me," she said. "And I'll predict you."

"I start?"

"Go ahead."

"You, my darling daughter, will be divorced within a year."

"Wrong."

"You don't like Teddy as well as you did a week ago. Tell the truth."

"Wrong again. What makes you say that?"

"Is he always so correct? So dutiful?"

"Depends whom he's with. Teddy is adaptable. He's a good Greek son to his father, he's Navy all-American with you, he's one plenty tough noncom on the base, and he's bossy as a bastard with me."

"But I saw your face last night. You lost some respect for him last night. I saw it."

"Not one bit."

"Oh, yes. And you'll lose the rest within a year. I've watched you. You've spent your life so far looking for someone who's got the answers. Your boy Teddy does not."

"The answers to what?"

"You tell me. First I was it. God. Very uncomfortable position, I assure you. Then you drop me. Because of three words, according to you. Am I supposed to believe that? Now comes the Jewish hour. Others in between, I can't be bothered to keep track of them all. Your Aaron had something. A little something. But suddenly you're trailing him as if he's the original grasshopper-eating prophet, ready to follow him to his homeland, live in one of those horrible Jewish communes, kiss the mezuzah, learn the language. Anything!"

"How did you know that?"

"Guessed it. Guessed right, it seems. Now comes Ernie. Anybody else could smell the rot there. But for you, for a time, he's the back of the book, where the answers are. What this time? Dirty dishes in the sink, work when you feel like it, Bohemia too late. O.K., that didn't last. You give him one more night, what men call a mercy fuck, and come away with black-and-blue marks on your neck, which you have to hide from your current Jehovah. Teddy with the sunburst behind him. Order. Control. Command. Well, let me tell you, if he's ever going to be in any kind of command position—even with you—the first one he's got to learn to command is his father. Were you trying to tell me that you actually like the way he buckles in to that old fool on absolutely everything?"

"He's kind to his father, Dad, that's kindness, Dad; it's so long since you've seen it that you don't recognize it, Dad."

"All right, all right—"

"And I like him physically."

"What I don't see is why he likes you."

"Why shouldn't he?"

"He must sense that you'll kill him. Within a year. You're already looking around."

"I am not."

"What about the old man? Whatsisname? He knows the secret now, it seems."

"Come on, you're kidding."

"Oh, you won't go to bed with him. It's always idealism first with you. But you were giving him that old starry-eyed look at the airport. What you haven't learned yet, baby, is that no one knows the secret. We all live in the dark. Did you ever think of that?"

Ethel didn't answer.

"Your turn," her father said.

She sipped her Scotch, looked at the man who'd raised her, tried to see him clearly and plainly. She wanted to tell him the truth finally and finally didn't fear the consequences: his pain or his rage. Maybe, she thought, that's all an inspired state is: the removal of the censor from the top of the throat.

"You, my darling father, will be remarried in a year," she said.

"You mean you think . . ."

"Don't you?"

"She may hang on for ten years."

"Not the way you're going."

"What do you mean by that?"

"She's already crucified; you want her dead. Mummy has always been a most obliging person and she will soon oblige you. I can't think of a single reason for her to want to continue living, can you?"

"I resent that."

"What's so bad about what I said? Most married couples wish each other dead."

"What I resent is your accusation that I am killing her."

"You'll admit you killed her a little last night."

"All I said was that she'd do better to leave—"

"Quote: 'I wish you'd recognize that you are no help whatsoever.' You left her no reason to live, Daddy."

Dr. Laffey turned away from his daughter and slowly finished his drink.

Ethel saw his hand tremble. The naked man was boiling up.

"Come on," she said, "say what you think now. The truth. I dare you."

"To you? No, thanks. But do tell me one thing: why you feel so much pity for your mother and not a breath of sympathy for me. Have you ever looked at my side of it? Do you think, for example, that this, the way I'm living, is a normal way for a man to spend his best years?

Your mother no longer has an appetite for life. I have. I'm only fifty-four. That seem old to you? It's not. Not in my case."

"I didn't say you were old, Daddy."

"I can read your face, Kitten. You know what I want most in the world, the single simple thing? Start laughing. I'd like to fall in love again. Why do you smile that crooked way?"

"Because I happen to know that you have a mistress for whom you buy pretty trifles at the Saint Tropez, that boutique."

"Those weren't for her. They were for her daughter. And she's no longer my mistress. O.K.? You want to know one reason I was so impatient yesterday? You did think I was extra mean yesterday, didn't you, Kit? Even for me?"

"I did, yes."

"She came to see me that afternoon, my mistress, while you were finding your Greek islanders their motel, came to my office, where she has not been since we took up with each other. She said I had to get a divorce, promise her that, or we'd come to *der Tag*. She said she didn't propose to sneak in and out of motels anymore."

"Who is she?"

"The wife of a close friend. Well, what's the difference? You know them. He's our representative up at the legislature in Phoenix. Millard Hoag. His wife is Martha Hoag. You remember Martha. She and Emma were friends years ago."

"I remember. Oh, my! If there was one couple among all your drunken friends who I thought would make it, it was those two . . . hand-holders. She's a nice woman."

He laughed. "The tone of surprise in your voice is not flattering," he said. "Doesn't matter. When he was up in Phoenix tending to our legislative business, she and I would spend evenings at this motel on the edge of town.

But—and here is what became the problem—he used to call her at eleven from Phoenix; it was their good-night ritual. So at ten thirty-five she'd leave me to go home for his call and there I'd be, alone with Johnny Carson. You see we couldn't even leave together, couldn't be seen in each other's company, even for an instant. She got sick of it—and I can't blame her. Can you?"

"No, I can't."

"She said she was too old, too nice and too rich for that kind of thing. And that it had been going on too long—four years! So she delivered her ultimatum. She was ready to get a divorce. Was I? What do you hope I said?"

"I hope you said you'd get a divorce right away."

"That's my darling daughter!"

"So what did you say?"

"I said good-bye. Can you see me, as big a bastard as I am, telling your mother, your crucified woman, that I was leaving her? Now? I'd do better to slit her throat. She'd die; not in a year, which is your timing, but in a week. I'd be the murderer, in everybody's eyes. Including yours."

"Not mine."

"You said it two minutes ago."

"What I'm sorry about it that you didn't make the break long ago, when she might have—" Ethel stopped.

"Might have what? Answer! You can't. There was no such time. And don't feel sorry for me. Because, since we're telling the truth tonight, I'm not. Sorry. I've been with Martha Hoag four years and—we are telling the truth, aren't we?—I'd like, believe it or not, a younger woman."

"Martha is younger than—"

"Only six years. Also, in many ways, a great deal older. She's settling everywhere. I, on the other hand, am not an old man. I'm talking scientifically, charts and

140

records. Blood pressure one fifteen over seventy, all internal organs perfect, the skin of a boy. Have you any idea, my smug daughter, how much unused energy your old man has? I'm the best tennis player over thirty at the club. I can't beat the kids, but all the others. . . ? I play three sets of singles and don't puff. What I'd like now is a girl, not a dowager; someone your age, Kit, not a woman at menopause. Forgive me, Martha dear. All right, laugh. I dare you."

"I'm not laughing."

He was at the bar, pouring himself another drink.

"I know what you're thinking," he said, his back turned. "But you're wrong. You young people are so patronizing, so mechanical. I could do it every night if I had the right girl wanting me. That is all it would take, someone I wanted wanting me."

"Daddy, I hope you find her."

"And believe me, if I can't find the real thing, I'll engage someone to simulate it. I'll pay her on a sliding scale: the better her performance, the more I'll pay her. After all, that technique, convincing someone you see every day that he is just as desirable as he was at the beginning, is what marriage is all about, isn't it? For a woman? Martha has been playing that role with Millard ever since—at least all during our four years. Every time he came home from Phoenix, she had to pull her act together. 'How did you do last night?' I used to ask her. 'Quite convincing, I believe,' she'd say. Then she'd explain to me, because I was curious, her ways of reassuring her husband that she was still ardent and he still desirable. But an odd thing happened. These same techniques, the tricks of the marriage trade, began to pop up in our intercourse. I was ready for them; in fact, I'd been expecting them. So when she came in that afternoon with her ultimatum, I couldn't help thinking: Martha, my darling, you should have spoken this piece three years ago, when it was still for real. I'd have rushed to a divorce lawyer then. And let whatever might happen to your mother happen. But to go from one enacted ritual to another, no! I'll tell you, if I find someone who reawakens me, I'll devote my life to her. I'll give up my profession, lock up my office, tear down my sign, take my name out of the phone book. I have annuities, tax-free bonds; I'm not swine rich but I have all the money I'll ever need. I will never work another day in my life. I'll travel and read, go back to school, explore the regions of the earth and the races of man, go to Africa and China, take piano lessons and look at myself with wonder again—but here I am, the victim of a bully."

"Mother?"

"A bully! Threatens me every day."

"With what?"

"Suicide! She sends Manuel out for sleeping pills. By the gross. Fortunately, I've kept a tight hold on Manuel, so he tells me immediately. I provide him with placebos, in all colors, and he brings them to her. The night before you came back, she took forty of them, emptied the bottle. When I came home, I found her in her bath, her skin white and puffed. She'd been there, in a foot of water, for hours, waiting for my placebos to take effect. What she said was that she didn't have the strength to get out of the tub. Did you ever try to lift a will-less woman, and a very slippery one, out of a bathtub of lukewarm water?"

"How long had she been there?"

"No way of knowing. Her skin was loose. I see that shocks you. I'm glad. The worst part of it, for me, is that I am trapped psychologically. Tell me why I should spend my life in a quicksand of guilt, living with a person whose every attitude and inflection and glance accuses me. I don't know why I tell you all this; you don't give a damn."

"Daddy, I do."

"I don't believe you. If you did, you would have noticed some of what I'm telling you years ago. Her cruelest weapon is her goodness and her patience. No matter how late I come home at night, she's sitting waiting for me. Or she's fast asleep —fully dressed, mind you—on the sofa downstairs. With the trace of a saintly smile still on her face. So I'll know both that I'm very late and that she's forgiven me. So then I have to waken the martyr, who's a bully, get her upstairs and put her to bed. There, for an instant, she brightens, says something like, 'What kind of a day did you have, Sugar?' You know, normal husband-wife talk, which, of course, I can't answer. I can't tell her that I was with Martha, can I? Well, that's over. But what can I say? I used to try to answer, tell her about some operation and so on. But she'd fall asleep, smiling that all-forgiving smile, in the middle of my second sentence. So I finally get her undressed and into bed and she says, 'Tuck me in, Sugar.' She calls me Sugar, just like she did when we were newlyweds. 'Tuck me in, Sugar!' I know I sound cruel to you, but I don't care anymore."

"I'm sorry for her and I'm sorry for you."

"Which is about as patronizing as you can get. Bless you for that! But maybe you can see that she is punishing me when she plays the martyr? When she acts the victim who is so patient, so generous, so gallant, enduring the incredible villainy of a man who—what? What?"

He was at the bar.

"I didn't say anything," Ethel said.

"Well, say something, for chrissake!" he yelled. "Answer my question. Do you see that?"

"Yes, I do."

"I doubt it. I really doubt it."

He poured himself a double.

"I keep remembering my father," he said. "Toward the end of his life, his blood stopped circulating. First his feet got cold, then numb, then green. The doctors cut off one leg to save his life—so they said. Then it began to affect his brain, which wasn't being provided its oxygen. I remember him, sitting on the sofa, staring across the room, saying, 'Here comes Shep, driving in the cattle!' He'd point as if he was looking through a picture window onto open range. Shep was the collie on his father's ranch. I used to think, looking at him dying: Here's this man, trapped in a totally unreal universe. But mine, here, is just as unreal. And with the added horror that I am healthy, horny and very curious. I'm just as trapped as he was. Period. Your mother is my jailer. She's in the right and I am in the wrong, and this is my punishment. I can't ever again have the normal pleasures, not as long as she lives. I'm not talking about adventures, just the ordinary pleasures of life."

He finished his drink, then turned and pointed into the distance. "Here comes Shep," he said, "driving in the cattle." Then he burst out laughing, saw something on her face, stopped abruptly.

"What?" Ethel said.

"You're smiling that way again."

"Not that way again."

"Sure I wish her dead sometimes. Can you blame me? Sure I'm on edge and unfair, even unprofessional. A couple of days ago, I almost let my knife slip during an operation, the one on that bastard's hand. By that one slip, the smallest part of a millimeter, I could have ended my career and all the pretense that I have nerves of steel and a hand that is always perfectly steady. That slip would have freed me. I wouldn't have had to do what I'm finally going to do—explode through the top of my head. Just that tiny slip! Can you understand that?"

"Yes, Daddy."

"Yes, Daddy! I don't believe you. The only way you can see it, my darling daughter, is that I am the villain and she is the saint."

"I don't think that."

"So go to bed. Go gently out of my sight."

Ethel didn't move.

"What I don't understand about you," he said, and now she could hear the pain in his voice, "is why you hate me."

"I don't, Daddy, I really, really don't."

"Oh, dear, you do. You were once the only thing in this world that I cared about, and suddenly— What did I do to you? It can't be that one unguarded phrase, three words, spoken so long ago. Or even the way I said them: *Don't do that!* You expect me to believe that you still hold that against me? It has to be more. But what? What did I do for you except break my neck trying to help you, trying to solve the riddle of why you were suddenly fucking every pimplehead in the sophomore class of Northside High."

"Oh, Daddy, there weren't that many."

"Which I still don't understand," he went on, as if she hadn't interrupted, "except that in some involuted way, you're convinced it was my fault."

"How can I blame you for that, Daddy?"

"We're telling the truth tonight?"

"You were a good parent."

"Thank you. I'm glad to hear you say that, even though I don't believe you mean it. You're pretending, but doing it rather well."

"Stop that shit, Daddy. Even when I was sore as hell at you, I loved you. And now I'm free of you and I love you still."

He didn't speak for a moment. She had no mask on now and at last he dropped his.

"Say it again Ethel," he said, not looking at her, barely getting out the words. "Say what you said again."

She threw her arms around him and kissed him.

He held her in silence, hiding his face in her shoulder.

"You're just disappointed, Daddy," she said.

145

"In you? Never."

"In yourself. Or in Teddy. Who he is. I don't know. Come on, we're telling the truth."

"Well, a father, you know, he's an insane man. The way I see it, you could have been the wife of the President of the United States and done him honor. What do you expect of me? Fairness? Sure I'm disappointed. I'm also crazy."

"I understand."

"May I say one thing, please? Before it's too late?"

"You better."

"Think hard! I may just be right about your Greeks. The father I'm sure about. But after all, you're not marrying him. But the boy? Can he stand up to you? You're —however it happened—a strong woman. Is he your equal? Is he—what's the word? I can only think of a very snobbish one. Is he elite enough for you? It's so important. Not the marriage part of it. Simply whom you spend your days with. Is that very nice, very decent boy man enough for you?"

"I'll say he is! You don't know him."

"As I see it, you've got it all, now that your years of adolescent nonsense are coming to an end: brains, taste —no, not that, not yet that, but looks, energy, curiosity, courage, everything. It's hard for me to see what his attraction is. He's steady. Reliable. I suppose those are virtues I don't sufficiently appreciate. I see him as a rather overcorrect petty officer, third class, without the itch to be anything more. I like strivers. Disrupters! He's too damned agreeable. He even likes me. That's not natural. He should have an uncontrollable antagonism toward me. As I have toward him."

He hesitated a moment, then walked to her and stood, looking down at the ground.

"Don't pay me any mind," he said. "I'm drunk."

It appeared he was going to kiss her. But perhaps he

wasn't sure she'd respond, because he turned away and walked to the dark well through which the stairs rose.

Halfway up, he stopped, smiled at her and said, "Here comes Shep, driving in the cattle."

Then he was gone.

seven

TEDDY and Costa met Ethel at the San Diego airport. She was dressed like a teen, knee socks under a baby-blue skirt. When she saw them, she raised her arms high. Each hand held the string of a balloon.

"I'm taking off," she said. "Hold me. Hold me!"

They did. She kissed them both, released the balloons.

"I've got a surprise for you," she whispered in Teddy's ear.

Costa was flying east in an hour, so they found a dark corner of the airport bar to celebrate one another.

"You don't look pregnant," Teddy whispered, as he put her in a chair.

"I'm not," she said. "And that would be a surprise!"

Costa had not been impressed by the Greek church in San Diego. "They lock door over there," he objected.

"Pop!" Teddy said. "San Diego is not Tarpon Springs. It's a modern city."

"Too damn modrun," Costa said. "Church door must stay open day and night. Church is God's heart."

After another drink, he added, "Also that priest over there, my opinion, Jewish."

Teddy had to laugh. "Pop," he said, "you're an anti-Semite."

"What kind compliment is that?" Costa said.

"You don't like the new priest in Tarpon either."

"Has no whiskers."

"What's whiskers got to do with it?"

"You ever see picture God? Plenty whiskers over there."

"This man will grow them. Give him time."

"Never. He try, he try, everybody sitting there, waiting, every Sunday. Nothing come out. So one by one, they leave, the old timers. Therefore this problem: Only old men give money to church."

"What about the women, Pop?" Teddy said. "They still go?"

"Women have no money. You ever see woman with money? They get from us. And young men? Nothing. Selfish. Meantime leak in roof, electric bill go up, bad situation. So then they all waiting old man Xenakis, when he's going to die. Very rich man, Ethel, Simeon Xenakis. This priest goes sit by his bed every day, says prayers, eats Mrs. Xenakis's *goorabyeh*, hard like rock. Old Xenakis, by this time, he don't hear, he don't see, but he's not a donkey. 'Why you don't grow beard?' he say to priest. 'I'm trying.' liar priest say. Xenakis put hand on priest face here"—Costa ran his fingers lightly along Ethel's chin—"and he made a sound, 'Tst, tst, tst!' Day after he die, they read will, he leave church zero. So what damn fool priest do?"

"Bingo!" Ethel shouted. "But he had to do something, Dad, didn't he?"

"Dad?" Costa said. "You call me Dad?"

"O.K.?" Ethel said. "May I?"

Costa shrugged. "Why not?" he said. "So now, where's my kiss?"

She kissed him, then begged him to stay another day, promising to prepare her southwest specialty, tamale pie. "I'm sure you'll like it," she pleaded. "You better. It's the only dish I can make."

"Do me favor, first learn Greek cooking," was Costa's reply.

"I'll buy every Greek cookbook ever written!"

"No books! I put Noola teach you everything, don't worry on that."

She kissed him four times when he left, couldn't stop covering him with affection. His arms were heavy, his shoulders thick through, she loved his neck, how strong and straight it was. When he stood to go, she adored his short muscular legs. Oh, the storms survived at sea!

As for Teddy, it was one of the happiest hours of his life. He had successfully brought them together. The classic matchmaker, at once relieved and delighted, he watched them gabbing and jousting, flirting and fondling. He laughed till he cried.

"What the hell you laughing, damn fool?" Costa said.

"I don't know, I don't know," Teddy said. Then he'd be off again.

When Costa's plane disappeared into the purple clouds to the east, Teddy and Ethel were left with each other. They didn't want to go to a movie; they were too perfectly, too tenderly drunk.

He drove her out to the Naval Training Center, she ducking out of sight as they passed through the gate. This installation, flung over a breezy waterside plain, always seems too big for what's happening on it. Teddy walked his girl to the foot of the bridge leading to Camp Nimitz, the island where the "hamburgers," the raw recruits, receive their first instruction. They stood at the rail and he kissed her, more in gratitude than in passion.

She pressed hard against him.

"What are you doing?" he said.

"I love your father so much, I want you," she said, laughing.

"Weren't you the one," he teased, "who said we weren't going to till—?"

"I changed my fucking mind, Teddy. O.K., Teddy?"

"That your surprise?"

"No," she called as she ran to the car and jumped in the driver's side.

The breeze had quickened, coming off the harbor to cool the air.

"Let's go to Mexico!" she said. "What do you say?"

"When?"

"Now. Quick! Tonight. Let's have our honeymoon before we get married."

"How about there's a place right here, quick, by the estuary under the flight approach lights? No one goes there."

Where he showed her, she stopped the car, turned off the lights.

Her quick fingers found him.

A great plane lumbered overhead. Then it was quiet and they could hear the new breeze kicking up ruffles in the water.

He lay back, head on the back of the seat, eyes closed.

Would it ever be that good again?

The car windows fogged with the heat.

"I wish we had somewhere to go," he whispered.

She was too busy to answer.

"Wait!" He was getting near.

She raised up slowly, smiled down at him, the conqueror measuring her treasure. Then she turned in place, put her head under the steering wheel and toward the front of the seat. He lifted, freeing the arm she needed to wriggle out of her panties. She left them hanging from one ankle.

He rocked her till she and he were both exhausted. Her feet in their teen hose pushed frantically against the window glass.

It was the first time she was done before he was.

For an instant too short to measure, they slept.

Then woke together.

"What happened to you tonight?" She whispered her admiration.

He laughed, proud of his power.

"Let's go somewhere," she said.

Every floor of Ethel's house was jammed with girls. She suggested Teddy sneak her into his barracks.

"I got a roomie too. Remember Big Jack Block?"

"He'll be asleep."

"He sleeps light."

"Let's go to a motel."

"Twenty bucks."

"You're a cheap son of a bitch."

"Besides, I like it here in the car; more and more I like it."

She turned in the seat, pulled up her baby-blue skirt and offered two perfect pink buns. In the dark, they glowed like night flowers.

She clung to the wheel. He clung to her.

Finally they cooled, content to lie against each other and talk.

"I have a wedding present to tell you," she said. "I was going to wait but—are you ready?"

"This it? The surprise?"

"I enlisted."

She waited.

"In the Navy," she added.

He still didn't get it.

"Teddy," she said, "I enlisted in your Navy."

"When?"

"Last week. The day after your father arrived. That made me sure."

"You're kidding."

She laughed nervously. "I'm not," she said, "kidding."

"What the hell did you do that for?" he said. She saw him straining to control himself. "You crazy or something? Why'd you do a damn thing like that?"

"Because I don't want to let you out of my sight," she said. "Because where you are, I'm going to be."

When she tried to touch him, he pulled away.

"You're really crazy," he said. "For what fucking reason?"

"Because I like the clothes in the Navy; for that fucking reason."

"Ethel, come on," he said. "What's the real reason?"

It was their first serious contest.

"It's like an instinct," she said.

"What is that, an instinct?"

"I'm scared."

"Of what?"

"Of myself. Of the way I've been. The Navy's maybe what I need—"

"Did you really do it, Ethel?" he interrupted her.

"Yes," she said, "and I don't know the reason. Like that better?"

"I'm trying to get with you, Ethel. Talk straight to me."

"So when you go to sea," she said, "you'll know where I am and what I'm doing. Don't you want to always know where I am and what I'm doing?"

"Sure," he said. "In my house, looking after my son— that's where and what."

She touched the middle of his forehead. "You frown all the time," she said, "you'll get a crease there, Teddy."

"Did you hear what I said?"

"Yes. And I'll be where you said. I'm going to work right into the eighth month. A lot of girls here do that. He'll be born in the Navy, your son. They promised me I'd be stationed wherever you are or in your home port. Maybe I'll specialize in cryptography. We can send each other secret messages, ship to shore. We'll put our salaries together, we'll have our own home. And that's where he'll be. Teddy?" she waited.

His head was down; he was swallowing his anger.

"If you wanted that other kind of wife, Teddy," she said, "you should have married your Greek virgin."

She moved closer, cradled his upper arm between her breasts.

"You saw my mother and father, how they are," she said. "He leaves before she's down in the morning. She eats her dinner on a tray before he comes home at night. Once a week she tries to kill herself. I'm not getting married to be that way. I'm going to be with you, night and day. That's the point of the thing, isn't it?"

She leaned forward and kissed the middle of his forehead. "You're frowning again, sweetheart. I'll kiss it away. It's so sweet. You do it when you're fucking too. Don't be worried. I'll make you happy, Teddy. I'll do more than that. I'll make you proud of me."

"I'm proud of you now, for chrissake."

"I mean really proud. I've been a useless person all my life. I never had a profession, Teddy. I mean a real profession. Not like nursing. I want to be capable at something. I got good marks at school. Even in math. I got B's. In math! So you see, we'll be working together in the day, and at night, every night, we'll be—like we are tonight. See how good it will be? There's only this that's bad: I've got to go to boot camp for nine weeks. And that's in Orlando, for female recruits. In Florida."

"Holy shit!"

"Only for nine weeks. First I thought we'd get married before, but your father said he needed time, two months minimum, he said, to get things together. That's why I didn't object. Don't worry. Even the sidewalks there are segregated by sexes. I'll write you every day, and when I get back we'll be married and never again be apart."

He still looked downcast and even resentful. But she didn't allow him to sulk, clinging to him and kissing him again and again. There was a wild light in her eyes, as if she were watching a conflagration.

"Well, that was some surprise!" he said.

"That wasn't it," she said. "I've got another. I'm going to tell you the real, real reason."

"Which is? What? Ethel? Come on, what?"

"I'm scared," she said. "Well, here goes. I want you to be an officer. I mean a commissioned officer. At least. No, listen, please. When I walk around this base and see the jerks everybody salutes! You're better than any of them! So I found out what it takes to get there. Just work. No one ever worked harder than you. You must have thought of this yourself, one time or another. It's the natural next step."

"But I don't want to be a rate-grabber, Ethel; I'm happy where I am. And I sure as hell don't want you pushing me like those officers' wives I see."

"That's the kind of wife you got yourself, Teddy. When our kid grows up, I want to hear him say that his father is an officer. Doesn't that sound better than petty officer? Third class?"

"You been talking to Dr. Ed Laffey. Haven't you?"

"What makes you say that?"

"Because every time he said 'petty officer,' he said 'third class,' quick. I didn't like the way he said it or the expression on his face when he did."

"This has nothing to do with him. I want it for you. And for Costa. Wait till I tell him——"

"Don't you do that!"

"I mean when."

"Not when. If. Then I'll tell him. Don't manage me, Kitten."

"Hell be so proud of you."

"I'm not living for him, no matter what you think."

"You're mad at me, aren't you?"

"I sure as hell am."

"Well, since you're mad at me, I might as well tell it all, Captain Theodore Avaliotis."

"What?"

"That's right, Theodore. A wife's supposed to tell the truth, isn't she? You ought to change your first name. Theophilactos, that's a paralyzer for these Navy people. I can't even say it right myself."

"Are you nuts? After all my father told you?"

"Teddy, I'm saying all this because I'm a believer and what I believe in now is you. Teddy? Teddy . . . ?"

He didn't answer. He was frowning again.

"Well," she said, "that was the surprise. I'm relieved I got it out and over with."

"O.K., you got it out. Now forget it."

She seemed totally deflated, then suddenly began to laugh.

"What the hell is so funny?"

"I'm wondering what he'll say, your old man, when he hears about me, a sailor. A girl sailor!"

"Give him a grandson," Teddy said. "That's all he cares about."

Costa had taken a bus from Tampa to Tarpon Springs, then walked the distance home, not to The 3 Bees, deciding that Noola should remain behind the counter—they'd need every dollar—while he made family plans.

The first question was: how much money would he

need? Whom would he ask to make the trip, and if they couldn't pay their transportation, should he? And what else would he have to pay for?

For the next few days, Costa did little except sit at home, glower, mumble and curse, scribble names and sums on the backs of brown grocery bags.

"Are you sick?" Noola finally asked him.

"I don't get sick," he said. "Go on, go to the store, don't bother me."

"You suddenly got very funny," she said as she left.

Noola didn't mean "funny," but she was right. Something strange was happening to Costa, something unprecedented. He'd begun to dream about Ethel. It was fortunate that he and Noola had decided years ago to sleep in separate rooms. Twice during the first week he was back, he had to get up in the middle of the night to remove from his sheets the evidence of his "sinful" feelings.

By day, over the phone, he lined up the pilgrims for the hegira west: his dead brother's wife and family, his sister and her family, his two oldest and best friends and their wives. They all acknowledged him as head of the clan, were ready to make the trip, but as Costa had anticipated, made it clear, with appropriate apologies, that he would have to get up every cent for every expense, including new dresses for the "girls."

"Don't worry," Costa pronounced on this historic occasion. "I pay everything!"

When he'd done the addition, Costa applied to the bank for a loan. It was denied. In a grand stroke, he mortgaged The 3 Bees, doing it over Noola's hysterical objections. "You're throwing our money away," she said. "What's the matter—this thing got you crazy? Just you and I go. Enough! We'll tell everybody all about it when we get back."

"How many sons you give me?" he replied.

A few days later, he was able to grumble that she and his fat sister-in-law were pretty damn quick to buy fancy new dresses. Talk about wasting money!

"You want me to look good, don't you?" Noola said.

"Wear that black dress, you look good enough!"

Noola didn't take this remark as a compliment.

Sitting on a bench in the public square, the sun in his face, his cronies around him, Costa said, "Cost me fortune, maybe more, but what they bring out will be continuation my name. What is more important over there, tell me that much?"

Nobody could.

Nine weeks of time can be any length.

It wasn't long in this case because everyone was intensely occupied.

Ethel, a "female recruit" in boot camp on one side of the continent, had never worked so hard physically in her life. She was too continuously tired to make the trip she wanted, south to Mangrove Street to meet her future mother-in-law. So they exchanged tiny notes on Hallmark notepaper, anticipated love.

But Ethel was never too tired at night to write her fiancé, and at length. She told him everything. At the same time, there was nothing to tell. Ethel lived alone, in mind and in body, and, by God, for the first time in her life, liked it.

When she came back west, she would be, she told him, a seaman apprentice. "Wait till you see me in my blues," she wrote.

Teddy, his confidence puffed up by Ethel's adoring letters, went in to see the education services officer on the base and informed him that he was no longer satisfied to be a petty officer, third class, and wanted to go for a commission.

The man whose help he was asking sat squarely at his desk propped up on both arms as if he were on a ship riding a heavy sea. Known as "Coach" to his "shipmates," he was an old-time line officer, put out to pasture. He always wore his combat stripes. At the moment he was working on a crossword puzzle.

"I want your help, sir," Teddy said.

"What's your background?" The ed officer finished writing in a word.

"Junior college. One year. I dropped out."

"Why?"

"Couldn't afford it. And to tell you the truth, I didn't give a damn."

"What's different now?"

"I'm getting married."

"When?"

"In seven weeks."

The ed officer sighed. He was looking at the puzzle.

"What's the matter, sir?"

"You think a honeymoon is a good time to study?"

"I don't need a honeymoon, sir."

The ed officer smiled and began to write in a word.

"Don't you believe me?" Teddy said.

"Why should I believe you? Who's your wife? To be?"

"She's at Orlando. A female recruit. This was her idea. She's all for it."

The ed officer looked up. "You mean," he said, "that we're not going to let our split-tail shipmates get in the way of work?"

"What I mean, sir, is I'm not. If you'll help me, I'll study till my eyes fall out. Just tell me what to learn and where to get the books."

"It's my experience"—the ed officer returned his eyes to the puzzle—"that dropouts drop out."

"Not me!" Teddy had raised his voice. "You want me

to help you with that puzzle, sir, so we can talk for a minute? I need your help."

The ed officer smiled at Teddy's anger. "I'll tell you the truth." He leaned back from his desk. "I don't like the young men coming into the service now. They've never been required to see anything through, so they don't know how and never will."

"You're talking to me now, sir."

The ed officer nodded, unconvinced but in some way impressed. He told Teddy that the first obstacle was to pass the college board exams. That done, he could apply to enter any one of a score of universities which offered naval reserve officers training.

"I'll be able to tell very quickly how serious you are," he said.

"Just watch me work."

"Not by that. By your wife, when I meet her."

Ethel had even affected her father. Dr. Laffey had found a new mistress, this one in her mid thirties. "She's made me feel like a buck in the spring," he told his daughter over the phone.

When the day came, Costa arrived for the ceremony (the same black mohair suit) shepherding what Dr. Laffey later described as a delegation to a greasy spoon convention. Ethel found herself being kissed by people she'd met only three minutes before, all of whom had the same peculiar but not unpleasant smell that Costa had.

Teddy had arranged to put them all up at a "housekeeping" motel near Saint Spiridon, convincing the manager that it was quite the custom for five Greek men to sleep in one room, five women in the other. These connecting chambers, full of food packages and baggage, suggested a refugee camp after a disaster.

The night before the wedding the Greeks threw a party. The five women did their duty in the kitchenettes. They went to work at dawn and by seven there was a four-course feast ready to serve on paper plates of a creatures-of-the-sea design.

Ethel found herself the vortex of a whirlwind of affection. The Greek women used any excuse to touch her. When she sat, they would sit next to her, offering bits of food to tide her over till mealtime. They stroked her hair in admiration—"Look, like gold!"—arranged her dress and skirt, tidied her lap of crumbs. Then, taking her hands, they examined her fingers and palms, turning to one another to compare impressions, nodding, smiling, agreeing that she was O.K., the one they'd hoped for, a good choice for Teddy.

Ethel got the idea. Their future was in her hands.

For the first time in her life she had what she'd wanted: a family which revolved around her. She liked being the center of all their hopes.

Finally she understood something else: they were treating her as if she were already pregnant. That's why they kept telling her to sit down, to rest, to allow herself to be coddled. And fed.

The only guest from Ethel's side was her father. Mrs. Laffey had remained at their hotel room, sent greetings by her husband, which Dr. Laffey forgot to deliver.

"Where's your wife?" Costa asked. "She's like a mouse, where she hiding, so quiet?"

"Back at the hotel. She's indisposed."

"Thank God she's not sick, right?"

The journey from Tucson had taxed Mrs. Laffey's strength, but that wasn't the reason why, soon after she and her husband had checked into the Sheraton Half-Moon Inn, she'd told him she had to have bed rest. There was another, secret cause.

It was the first time in years that Emma and Ed Laffey had occupied the same bedroom. The instant the bellboy closed the door, the doctor disrobed to shower and clean up. Seeing him naked was a shock to Emma. His abundant vigor, his evident sexuality, depressed and frightened her. She knew that what she'd suspected for a long time had to be true. Dr. Laffey had another, a mistress. It was this recognition that collapsed her. Dear Mr. Avaliotis, she thought, would never do anything so disloyal to his wife!

Dinner in the motel was a tumultuous affair. Everything that happened, Ethel soon saw, was directed at her. The tribe of Greeks, all originally from the Dodecanese island of Kalymnos, told the young woman who was entering their world the legends of their place. The topography was described, the rocky hills, the olive groves, the harbors, the beaches. The history of the Dodecanese was detailed, all important dates. The villainies of the Turks were recounted graphically; those of the Italians, humorously. One of the men who'd fought against the Italians in '42 told affectionate stories about their cowardice, how those rascals ran toward their Greek opponents at top speed, couldn't wait to surrender.

Inspired by drink and by looking into the bride's loving eyes, they began to sing, first the songs of Kalymnos, their home island, then those of Simi and Halki, their Aegean neighbors. Expanding their circle of memory, as they ran out of material, they recalled the songs of Samos, then of Mytilene, so moving into the Cyclades and finally to the Peloponnesus itself. That night all of Greece was celebrated in a San Diego motel.

Finally Costa sang. "Happy are the eyes of the groom/ That selected this beautiful bride." Then he toasted Dr. Laffey. "May you live long enough to pay for this wedding."

Dancing followed. Ethel was initiated by Costa. She felt his heavy arm around her, pressing her delicately framed rib cage against his barrel chest. She looked into his eyes, the lights of a fulfilled man.

It was their hour. They were the family, he the upholder of the tradition, she the womb of the future.

At the end of one dance, as Teddy laughed, Costa held Ethel captive, breathless. Dr. Laffey excused himself and left for home. Ethel understood perfectly that her father's sudden departure transferred her to this new family more finally than any ceremony would.

She wanted to spend the night in the motel with Teddy, whispered this to him. But Teddy thought better; Costa would know and wouldn't like it. The last thing Ethel wanted was to chance upsetting this old man; his approval was now her central concern.

The ceremony the next day seemed a pale continuation of the party—except for its climax, the event which Costa was later to call the happiest moment of his life.

He'd been disappointed in the way the marriage ritual had been chanted. The young priest, born in the U.S. and beardless, trained at a seminary erected by funds donated by guilty Greek millionaires, spoke the old language with a callow American accent. The traditional vows, while correct in the letter, were delivered without their traditional fervor. An old-time priest would have fulfilled God's purpose, intimidating everyone, particularly the young couple, filling them forever with the fear of wrongdoing.

But obviously that kind of catharsis was not happening. Costa kept looking around dolefully, making baboon faces, growling in Noola's ear, then yapping out loud until his wife told him to shut up, he was spoiling the service.

What more than made up for everything wrong inside the church was the ritual performed outside.

During that part of the *gamos* when the priest holds twin crowns of orange blossoms (bound with a white ribbon: Union) over the heads of the bride and groom, ten of Teddy's friends sneaked out of their pews. At the end of the ceremony, as everyone was gathered around the priest to kiss his hand (for Costa, a bitter taste; where was the heavy tallow-feel proper to a priest's hand?), the young men had lined up either side of the exit walk. As the newlyweds appeared at the door of the church, these gallants in blue raised swords and crossed points, creating an arch of honor.

Costa had once seen this in a film—was it *The Long Gray Line?* Was Tyrone Power its star? Was Mr. Power, over there, Greek? Proferis into Power? Costa had once expressed to his son a wish that they could have this particular piece of pageantry at his wedding and Teddy had answered that it was impossible. The base commander, however, granted permission, a contribution to the Navy's new effort to make its service more attractive to career designates. Teddy's friends had borrowed Japanese trophies from officers, redeemed other swords from a downtown hock shop, borrowed the rest from a local dramatic company.

As soon as Ethel and Teddy had passed through the arch, she turned to watch Costa following and saw his moist eyes gleam. She ran and embraced him with all her might. He did what she'd been waiting for, kissed her on the mouth.

How thin and tight my lips are, she thought, how heavy and enveloping his!

The signal that the post-wedding party was over came from Costa. No one saw him get to his bed. Everyone heard him snoring.

Noola hustled the company into the other room.

When Ethel kissed Costa good night, he smiled but didn't open his eyes. He knew who it was.

eight

THE new couple spent the night at the Breakwater Inn, a motel. Neon signs pulsed across the front and the sides. *"The Place to Stay, The Place to Play"* was proclaimed in green calligraphy. And below, in more modest characters, "Waterbeds Available on Request."

The relief of orgasm put them to sleep immediately. At the first light, Ethel slid down under the covers and roused her husband. Afterwards they slept again.

By the time they got to where the party had been, it was two o'clock and Costa's people had disappeared, beating the check-out time by taking an early plane. The manager of the motel complained bitterly about the noise the night before and the mess left behind. It took a twenty to stop his mouth.

Back at their room, sitting on the ever-yielding waterbed, they opened presents. The afternoon sun caught Ethel's wedding dress where she'd flung it over a chair the night before. Some of the guests had pinned five- and ten-dollar bills to the skirt; they fluttered in the fresh breeze off the bay.

Ethel found a tea-for-two set imported from Jamaica, a large wicker tray of candied fruit, two monster Rock Island sponges, a jumbo box of pralines the size of dinner plates, and—

"Just what we need!" she said as she pulled the wrapping from around a table lamp made all of shells.

"Hey, Kit, look at this," Teddy said. "From your old man."

He read the note. " 'Dear Children. The enclosed is to help launch you on your merry course. Come visit us soon. We love you.' "

Teddy handed her the check. It was for two thousand dollars.

Ethel looked at it as if it were a curio. Then she tore it up.

"What are you doing! Kit! What the hell are you doing?"

"I'm not going to take money from him anymore."

"Well, it was for me too. 'Dear Children,' it said."

She nodded but didn't answer. She was opening a box which contained a tablecloth-and-napkin set, embroidered by hand.

"Will you look at this needlework," she said. "Oh, that poor girl's eyes! Isn't there anything from your father?"

"He gave me his when I said good-bye. Not a present; advice."

"Which was?"

" 'Make Greek wife out of this woman, quick, my boy, take my advice.' "

"So go ahead, I'm ready; make a Greek wife out of me."

"O.K. Why the hell did you tear up that check?"

She thought a minute, then she said, "I had a friend once, Aaron, a Jewish kid who—"

166

"Will you relax all that about your old boyfriends, Kit? Didn't you ever have any girl friends?"

"No, actually. Never. Aaron used to repeat an old saying his father liked: 'If you take with one hand, sooner or later you're going to have to give with the other.' I'm never going to take one cent from anybody again. Not even from you. When you take money, it gives the giver power over you."

"It's all right if I take from you, isn't it?"

"Oh, yes, I want power over you."

She pounced on him, knocking him back on the bed, which wallowed around them in heavy waves. Straddling his body, she held him captive.

"I'm going to give you your thousand dollars' worth right now," she said.

"We just did it, for chrissake!"

"That was this morning. I want it again! Oh, God, you're so scary! Come on, Teddy, make me a Greek wife with your big fat Greek tool."

"You're going to have to wait, little girl, because it ain't big and it ain't fat; it's resting."

"Then I'll wash my hair."

"You washed it yesterday."

"It's got your stuff all through it from this morning."

She rolled off the bed, onto the floor, crawled on all fours to a corner of the room where her belongings, everything she had left to wear since that big giveaway day, were in an old-fashioned leather suitcase, a hand-down from her mother. Close by were two satchels, holdalls. She opened the one she wanted and as he watched, scrambled through its contents. There was a clinking of glass and a stir of plastic. When she didn't find what she was looking for, she turned the bag upside down on the bed and emptied out her collection of aids for the feminine toilet.

"Jesus, look at all that shit!" Teddy said.

"You never saw this before, did you? You thought I was just a natural beauty with a complexion that needs no help. Like one of those Ivory soap models on TV or—"

He interrupted her. "I've got to talk to you about something."

"You know there's stuff here I forgot I had! What?"

"A budget. That stuff must have cost a fortune!"

"I suppose it did."

"Well, in the Navy, you—that is, we—can't afford this kind of splurge anymore."

"Teddy, we just got married. Can't we go a few days without a budget?"

"O.K. Next week." He picked up a bottle. "Is this what you're looking for? Earth Born pH Balance Natural Shampoo? Strawberry flavor?"

"No. But it will do."

"Here's Raspberry too, if you prefer raspberries. Do you wash your hair with this stuff or drink it?"

She took the small bottle, held it between her teeth as she unbuttoned her blouse.

"What's this? Soap for the feet? You need special soap for your feet? And milk bath! What are you, some kind of secret Roman?"

Stepping out of her skirt, she was naked.

"Where's your bikini?"

"Girls aren't supposed to wear pants on a honeymoon. Hasn't anybody ever told you that, Greek?"

She disappeared into the bathroom.

She liked the water very hot. Soon Teddy saw wisps of steam floating out from under the door.

He stretched out on the bed and thought about his happiness. He'd married a live one: no bra, no pants, always ready, full of sass and struggle—some kind of wife! He didn't mind that she'd torn up the check, he told himself. He didn't really want Dr. Laffey to have a two-thousand-dollar edge over him.

It occurred to him to surprise her in the shower and let her know how happy she'd made him.

Soaking wet, exhausted again, as happy as they'd ever be, they lay on the waterbed and made it roll like the sea.

"I wish," Ethel said, "you'd learn to like it on a bed. I mean an ordinary, comfortable bed. Any weird place, there's no way to stop you. In a shower? Wham! Bang! In a car with my head squeezed under the steering wheel, upstairs at a party, preferably in the nursery with a sleeping kid in the crib, in the cloakroom of a crowded restaurant during a thunderstorm, in a classroom ten minutes before they all come in, on the floor of the aisle of an abandoned school bus, in the john of a Boeing 707 flying over Albuquerque—oh, no, that was another guy. Sorry."

He turned and topped her, his hands around her throat.

"Leggo!" she cried. "You're strangling me prematurely. Wait till I do something bad."

"Bitch!"

"I can't help it. You're so tough! I can't help teasing you. And you're so childish!"

"Well, which am I?"

"Both. That's why I love you. I do love you. I never, ever, loved anyone else. I never will."

"Tell me more and I may let you go."

"You are the one, the one big one, you!"

"Go on."

"The funny part is that I mean it. Only I still don't understand how come in an ordinary, sensible bed—"

"This is not an ordinary, sensible bed. This is a foul old bladder that's given support to one thousand whores of the port."

"But it's fun." She pulled loose and turned over. "Why can't you—?"

"I can't get a good hold on you. I've got to chase you all over the bounding main."

"That's what I want. Chase me. Chase me!"

"And when I catch you, there's no bar at the bottom to push against."

"When you've got something to push against, you come too quick!"

He reached for her again, but she slipped away and he was in the belly of a wave, rolling from side to side, overdoing it, laughing.

"I hate this old belly bag," he said. "When we leave here, I'm going to stick my stainless steel Swiss knife into its flabby side and let it leak to death. Oh, God, oh, God!"

"What's the matter, baby?"

"I'm so sleepy."

"Come here. Let your mummy hold you."

He moved up close against her. She took his thigh between her legs and rested his head in the soft place between her neck and shoulder.

"Teddy, couldn't we stay here?" she said. "Instead of a honeymoon, which I really don't want. Teddy, couldn't we?"

"It's forty dollars a day here," he said, "which times thirty days comes to more than we both earn a month in today's Navy. Look, you got a week before your classes start. Find us a place, will you, twelve dollars a day maximum. That'll leave us money to eat on after we've paid the rent. Now you got time to look for an apartment. Because once your studies start, you won't have. O.K.?"

"I'm your obedient Greek wife."

When he came home late the next afternoon—the honeymoon of a day and a half was over; he'd gone back to his Ampex and his studies—Teddy found Ethel parked in her car, waiting for him.

"We've moved," she called out through the window opening of her car when he pulled up parallel.

"Where to?"

"Follow me."

"What does it cost?" was the first question he asked about their new quarters.

He was at the window, one floor above the ground, looking across at an identical honeycomb of bedrooms facing the one they were in. Below him was the community's pool, servicing, at that moment, what seemed to be the entire population of the twin motels.

"Eighteen-sixty a day," she said. "How's that?"

"Better," he said.

"Now look."

He turned and saw at her feet, throat wide open, the bag which had been full of bottles and jars and tubes the previous afternoon. She turned it upside down. There was nothing to fall out.

"And I closed down my charge account at the drugstore. O.K.?"

"You didn't have to do that," he said. "For chrissake, I was just kidding. I'm sorry."

But he kissed her in thanks.

And they were happy.

The fact that she hated the place meant nothing to her.

The first day in the life of a newlywed couple that comes to an end without the performance of an act of love is a shock, a cause for wonder and private speculation on both sides.

Two weeks and five days had gone by. They both enjoyed that sense of safety which comes from being locked inside a routine. Relieved of the burden of choice, they informed themselves each morning, by a quick look at a mimeo sheet, where they were supposed to go, first, second and third; what they were supposed to do when they got there, and in Ethel's case, what lessons she was expected to have learned.

On the Saturday that brought the third week of her training to a close, Ethel decided to cook. The kitchen alcove, two burners and a corner sink, was a one-person accommodation. It was an acrobatic trick to prepare a steak dinner there. They'd been eating mostly in the motel coffee shop below—plus a couple of junk-food bed picnics. She knew that Teddy thought it an expensive way to go. He'd said nothing about it because, like her, he was too happy to chance disturbing their private order.

Ethel had had only one class that morning. Then a long formation drill, marching up and down and across the sunny plazas of the base in her "blues," with pauses for instruction, correction and, occasionally, reprimand, delivered with appropriate scorn by a huge drillmaster. To avoid his critical attention, Ethel had managed to bury herself in the middle of the mass of girls. As soon as the marching was over, she'd rushed home, douched, showered, reordered the place, then gone shopping. By phone.

As soon as Teddy got home, Ethel rushed him a cold glass of beer, offered with a kiss, and the information that they were going to eat in. "Steak," she said. "Stay out of the kitchen."

She had frozen spinach, too, and frozen French-fried onions. She'd read the directions carefully, just as she had the directions in her brand-new *Joy of Cooking* on how to prepare a steak for the fire.

Teddy was mumbling something from the other room. "I ran across one of your instructors. He tells me you're doing great."

"It's just memorizing," she called back. "Lists. I've always had a quick memory."

"Understanding and appreciation of the fundamental workings of democracy, right? Navy systems and traditions, right? It'll get tougher. Wait."

"I know."

He came into the kitchen behind her.

"What about your physical fitness marks?"

"He said I was top-heavy. His idea of a joke."

Teddy lifted her skirt, cupped the bottom of her belly and pulled her to him.

"Teddy, I'm cooking."

"So am I. Let the steak wait. Don't put it on."

"I just now put yours in. You want it well done, don't you?"

"Take it out. Put it back after."

"Teddy, I've got a good dinner; I worked all afternoon getting it ready. Let go. We haven't eaten in for a week and you squawked about that the other day. Now come on, we're going to have one beautiful meal. I got wine too."

"What'll I do with this?" He pushed it at her.

"Take a shower."

"I don't need a shower." He walked away. "I saw you walking around the base today," he said, "through the education officer's window."

"My drillmaster, he's a maniac. He marched us up and back for almost two hours, going nowhere. I'm turning your steak over."

"Burn it a little first. I meant walking by yourself. Every time I've seen you, you've been by yourself. Haven't you made any friends yet?"

"You're my friend."

He'd seen her marching too, striding as if with great effort, overcoming her unsteadiness, head and neck tensed, like a schoolgirl going somewhere to be scolded.

"I've never made any friends," she said from the kitchen.

Only lovers, he thought.

Outside, around the pool, it was Saturday night, cook-out time. Families were spread on blankets around braziers and little Japanese hibachis. The pool was jam-packed with bodies and the smell of chlorine on the wind reached one flight up. There was a continuing chorus of shouts and squeals, the laughing frolic of kids mixing with the commands and protests of their parents. Over all, rock music and the ball game on a score of portables.

She came in with French bread wrapped in foil, out and back with chili sauce and butter, then the salads in wooden bowls.

"I didn't put the dressing on the salad yet. I learned that from your father."

"That goddamn pool out there, it's a madhouse."

"I don't hear it anymore."

"I remember your father's pool, how quiet and clean it was."

"I remember it too. I'd rather be here. With you. Sit down. Pour the wine."

There was the sound of cars crashing just as Teddy sat. He rushed to the bathroom window, which was over a parking lot. A man had backed his car into another. There was yelling, a duet. Both men were drunk.

"What happened?" she called out from the kitchen alcove.

"It's Saturday night."

"I want to ask you something," she said as she put the meat on the table.

"Which is mine?"

"The black one. Teddy, why can't you study here?"

"I got used to studying in my old room."

"I thought they put a new roommate in with Block."

"He's mostly there at night."

"But you mostly go there at night."

174

"Hey, Kit, you're not going to tell me where I can study now, are you?"

"Of course not."

"Because I know where I can study and where I can't."

"Sure. Don't get mad. But, Teddy—"

"That's my business. See?"

"You're mad."

"No. If I was mad you'd really know it."

"I only wanted to say this is your home. Why can't you study here after dinner while I clean up? I'll read in bed and wait for you."

"I tried that. I keep thinking: She's waiting for me to come to bed. And you're over there looking at me that way. So then I do. And there goes the evening. I'm too sleepy afterward to ready anything."

"So I won't look at you. I'll turn my back."

"You know you started all this, about me being an officer."

"I know. And I thought we might work together on—"

"No, thanks. Really. That's not the way I am. But thanks."

"O.K. Anyway, I said it. How's the wine?"

"Good. What did it cost?"

"Don't ask. I paid for it out of my savings."

"I don't want you to do that anymore. We're just fooling ourselves when you do that."

"I wanted you to have wine with your steak. 'Proper way,' you know?"

He was critical of the melon. "You buy this over the phone?" he asked.

She admitted she had.

"You can't buy melons over the phone. A melon you have to hold in your hand, put it to your nose and press it where it's supposed to be soft, the navel. Even then, you're guessing. But one thing sure, they'll send you one like this one if you order by phone. My old man would call this a squash."

"But that's a full-time job, shopping for melons. I'm all day over there, telling them back the lists I've memorized the night before, that I'm going to forget right after I've said them. Then they got me drilling up and down, up and down, and by the time I get here—"

"I'll buy the melon next time, on my way home. What did this one cost?"

"I don't know."

"What do you mean?"

"It was a charge."

"Didn't you ask? What did the steak cost—do you know that?"

"That was a charge too."

"Jesus!"

She drank her wine in two gulps.

"I think maybe tonight," he said, "we ought to have a talk about our finances. I don't want you paying for things out of your savings. I don't know how much money you got, but I don't want us living on it."

"Why don't you take your shower while I clean up?"

"How much money do you have—do you mind my asking?"

"Right now? A few hundred dollars. My father used to give me a hundred a week allowance."

"But your clothes and all that stuff from the drug-store?"

"Charge accounts. He gave me charge accounts."

"Isn't your mother rich?"

"Her family owns mines south of here. When she dies I'd be sort of rich if I'd take her money—which I won't."

"So we'll just have to learn to be careful, right?"

"Right."

"That's what I want to talk to you about."

176

As she was scrubbing the oven pan with Brillo pads—steak grease, she made a mental note, cooks into metal—Teddy came to the kitchen with Ernie's letter in his hand.

"Did you mean me to read this?"

"No. But sure, you can read it."

"It was open and over on my side of the bureau, out of the envelope, so I thought . . . Who's Ernie?"

"Fellow I used to know."

Ernie had run into Carlita on the street, charmed the news of the wedding out of her—and Ethel's address.

Teddy was rereading the letter.

"I told him about you," Ethel said.

"When?"

"That time."

"When you went home to get your parents ready for my old man?"

"I think so. Yes."

"You saw your old boyfriend then?"

"We used to talk a lot and I wanted him to know that I'd found the one I wanted."

"What's he mean here: 'I know there's plenty he can learn from you'?"

"In general. About living. I guess."

"I think he meant something else."

"Oh, no. Ernie's not a sly man, he's not a tease."

"Did you fuck him?"

"Of course not. What do you think I am?"

"But you did tell him all about us?"

"Anything wrong with that?"

"I don't like you talking to other men about us, especially your old loves."

"Look, Teddy. I don't want to hide anything from you ever and I don't need you to hide anything from me. Ever. Let's not have any dark figures in our life that might come to light some sorry day. What do you say tonight, instead of talking about the budget and all that boring shit, why don't I tell you everyone I've ever been with and you tell—"

"I don't want to hear about them," Teddy said.

"I want you to trust me and if you knew exactly what—"

"I don't want to hear all that!"

"Well," she said, "if that's the way you want to go."

"I do."

"But it isn't 'all that.' Really it isn't, the way you said it: 'all that.' "

"We're happy now. Let's leave it alone."

"O.K."

"And don't get any more letters, and if you do, don't leave them out for me to read."

"I didn't leave it out for you to read."

"Sure you did. You like to tease me that way. It's one of your goddamn tricks. Just don't do it anymore. I don't like it; it's not cute and it's not funny and I don't want it. O.K.?"

"O.K."

"If you put aluminum foil under the steak you won't have to do all that elbow work."

"O.K. Now I want to ask you something."

"What?"

"I don't want you to call me 'Kitten' anymore. Or 'Kit' either."

"Do I?"

"Most of the time. Let's drop it, O.K.?"

"O.K., we're starting clean."

When she got through with the dishes, he was in bed backed by all the pillows, a mimeo book on his lap— he was using the back of the curriculum pages—and a Razor Point pen in his hand.

"You want coffee?" she asked.

"It keeps me awake. Let's get some Sanka."

"It's expensive," she said.

"Less than coffee. Come on, get in here with me."

She sat on the side of the bed with her clothes on.

"I've been meaning to do this for a while," he said.

"I know."

"It's not boring shit, like you said, and it's not an attack on you. Will you get into bed?"

"I don't take it that way, like an attack. I want to meet our money problems as much as you do."

She went into the bathroom and undressed—except for her panties. It turned him on to take them off. She left the bathroom light on and the door open an inch or two—a compromise she'd worked out between his preference for making love in the dark and her pleasure at watching his face when he came.

She got in alongside him and watched him work at his figures.

Then some sounds from overhead distracted her.

"Listen to them up there!" she said. "He's at that thing again."

"Which one is he, anyway? You know?"

"I read his name on the list next to the bell buttons downstairs. Jack something."

"Probably Rabbit. Have you seen him?"

"I think so. He's that skinny little guy, bald as a cue ball. Not more than five foot six."

"I've seen him. Yeah, that must be him."

"Did you notice his hands? He's got enormous hands."

"That's a superstition about hands."

"Not hands, thumbs. And nose. The nose, if it's big—"

"I got a big nose and I got small hands, so what does that make me?"

"Sometimes it's big, sometimes it's small."

"Come on, look at these numbers, will you?"

They covered a page.

"Can't we do this in the morning?" she said.

"We said that last week, then we started playing around—"

"Let's do that again."

"And it was practically morning by the time we fell asleep. Then it was Sunday afternoon and—"

"There was the football game, two of them—"

"So we didn't do much figuring or looking for an apartment either. You know we've just got to find an apartment— Don't do that."

"I'll just hold it."

"That's the way it starts. Don't. Let's do this tonight, then it will be over. We've got to, I'm worried."

"And you're mad. What are you married about—I mean"—she laughed—"I meant to say, what are you mad about? Ernie's letter?"

"No. Pay attention. No, I'm not. I want you to pay attention. Here. Look at this page."

"Listen to them up there."

Through the ceiling came sounds of scrambling and teasing, whispers and laughter.

"You've got to admit," she said, "that's a pretty cute little guy, even if he's bald and wears glasses. I wonder who's he got up there now?"

There was an edge of admiration to her voice, Teddy thought, even envy.

"Seems like it's always a different one," Teddy said. "Some squeal, some grunt, some shriek."

"And some go 'gobbledee, gobbledee, gobbledee,'" she said. "That little bastard!"

"Now come on," he said, "pay attention. On this sheet, here—Look! No, that's the wrong one. Here. My base pay is four hundred and fifty dollars and sixty cents. Your base pay is four hundred and seventeen dollars and thirty cents."

"I wish I could watch them," she said. "Don't you?"

"No. This figure is our basic allowance for quarters, ninety-nine-thirty apiece, which comes, for both of us, to one hundred and ninety-eight sixty. Got it? So far?"

"That's pretty good money."

"Christ!"

"What?"

"I mean it's not. You have no idea what our living expenses are."

"So tell me."

"I'm coming to that. I wish that guy would shoot his load and get it over with."

"He starts right up again, like he did the other night, half an hour later."

"Well, that would give us half an hour," Teddy said. "Come on."

"Why don't we wait till he's done and then—"

"He must be some sort of sex freak. Maybe he's twins. Maybe there's two of them up there. Here, will you look!"

"What's this? What is 'COMRATS'? An animal?"

"It stands for, I don't know why, subsistence allowance. We each get two dollars and sixty-five cents a day, which for a thirty-day month comes to seventy-nine-fifty times two."

"Why times two?"

"Because there's two of us. There's you and there's me. That adds up to two. You're not paying attention."

"Teddy, do we sound like that?"

"I hope not. Sounds like he's hurting her."

"I don't think he's hurting her."

Lying on their backs, side by side, they were both looking up at the ceiling. Now he lifted his paper again.

"Now I'm adding." He pointed. "It comes, as you see, to one thousand two hundred and twenty-five dollars and fifty cents."

"A month? That's a lot of money."

"Money, baby, is a subject you know very little about."

"I've spent money all my life, so I must know something about it."

"Exactly! How to spend it. Now you're going to have to save it, which is different. This sheet, now, is our expenses. Our rent in this paper-wall, paper-ceiling box is eighteen dollars and sixty cents times thirty, which comes to, with tax and extras of all kinds, including this fucking no-go TV set where it's always snowing, to almost six hundred dollars a month. There goes half of our twelve hundred and twenty-five dollars, right there."

There began a rhythmic pounding, culminating in cries like those of extreme pain or of exultation, it was difficult to say.

"I tell you, he's hurting her," Teddy said.

"That's him making that sound," Ethel said.

"It's her."

"It's him. That's the way some men sound when they come."

She knew immediately that she'd said the wrong thing. She didn't have to look at Teddy's face to know that.

"It's over," Teddy said. "You think maybe we can go on with this now?"

"Sure!"

"So our rent accounts for at least half of what we get from the generous U.S. Navy. Now here's another page, on which I've put down—"

"Teddy."

"What?"

"You better get your mathematics done before that little son of a bitch starts up again."

"I said don't do that!"

"I didn't know I was doing it."

"Here. Look here! This is for transportation. See? We're going to have to figure a way to use just one car."

"Why? And whose?"

"Why is obvious. Whose? Whosever."

"We can't do that."

"We're going to have to."

"Now I wish I'd kept that check. I'm kidding. Oh, is that why you're mad at me? That I tore up——"

"I'm not mad at you. Here. Look. This item is the money we're going to need if we take the trip to Florida later on. This is for the bill from the supermarket. I wish you'd cancel that charge account too."

"O.K. So that's why you're mad at me."

"I told you I'm not——"

"You've been p.o'd at me all night."

"But if you want to know what I thought of you tearing up your old man's check, I'll tell you. I notice that only the very rich and the very poor have these pure ideas about money. Beggars and billionaires. My old man and you. But for me there's no psychology mixed up with money. It's just money. Like what I win at the poker game. That has no face. And it's better to have it than not. What would it have hurt you to take that check? Why would it bother you? You don't have to feed it, it doesn't make dirty-dirty, so you don't have to take it for a walk three times a day. It just sits there and waits for the day when you need it. You. Not me. For that day when I really get mad at you."

"What the hell are they doing up there now?" she said.

The sounds were of laughter and of quick intimate talk. Then more laughter.

"Congratulating each other, no doubt," Teddy said sourly. "O.K. You didn't hear what I said. O.K. Now look, there's a whole list of stuff and when you add them all together, which I have here, then subtract the sum from the sum of what's left after I have subtracted the rent from what the Navy gives us and then divide that remaining figure by thirty——"

"Thirty?"

"There are thirty days in a month and sometimes thirty-one, which leaves us about fourteen dollars a day, as I make it out, to eat on. Food. Do you understand that much?"

"I got dizzy in the middle somewhere."

"The only point is that we have to get an apartment. We have to stop paying half our income to live in a dump with a filthy community pool and a greasy-smoke barbecue on one side, a twenty-four-hour parking lot on the other and a jackrabbit at work every half hour overhead. Goddamn it, Ethel, I want some help from you on this; I want you to help me hold the line."

It wasn't that they were mad at each other. Neither could have said what made it impossible for them to love each other that night. But for the first time, they lay side by side between cool sheets, said good night, and fell asleep.

Next morning, she made the coffee while he put on his robe and went down for the papers. He read the ball scores while she made pancakes. They were good and when she saw he was satisfied and pleased, she knelt at the side of his chair and said something that made him feel even better.

"Why don't you run our finances?" she said. "Give me each day whatever the number is. Tell me that's what I have to spend that day and not another cent. I'll hold the line if you tell me what it is. There won't be any more steak because you won't have given me money enough for steak, and I'll go to the store and look for bargains and I'll forget all about wine. O.K. It's all in your hands now."

"You sure that'll be all right with you?"

"It's what I always wanted—to be told what and how and when and how much. So you tell me."

He still hesitated. He thought it a loss of face for her. "You really want that?" he asked.

"It's what I want," she said. "That way you will be

happy, which is all I want in the world. For you to be happy."

Now she was his baby bride again and he liked her again. She was pleased that he wanted her in the middle of the day. He even turned off the Rams game for her.

They didn't get out of bed till three-thirty in the afternoon. Then it was pretty late to go looking for an apartment.

On the front page of the *Hoist*, the naval training center's weekly paper, the headline read: SEAMAN ETHEL AVALIOTIS PICKED BY SEABEES AS QUEEN TO REIGN OVER GALA EVENTS NEXT MONTH. Under it, at the side of two fetching photographs, there was this: "The twenty-one-year-old Centerite has been named 1975 Seabee Queen for the San Diego area. She will begin her reign at two gala events next month, the Amphibious CPO club announced today.

"This your wife, Avaliotis?" the education services officer asked. They were meeting in his office.

"Yes, sir," Teddy said.

"She's a looker," said the education officer.

"Yes, sir," Teddy said.

The lieutenant from public relations, who'd asked for the meeting, said, "Look at those pictures, Coach."

"I am."

One was of Ethel eight feet off the ground in a boatswain's chair—the cameraman below, shooting up. The other, from close up, effectively silhouetted her figure.

"What's the problem?" The education officer put down the paper.

"She said it was O.K., that she'd do it, sir," Teddy said. "Then when she saw those pictures, she changed her mind."

"I even reasoned with her, Coach," the lieutenant from public relations said. "I gave her Admiral Zumwalt's line, how we must bring our service into the mainstream of American life and so on. I snowed her good. But honest. She just shook her head, which I don't mind telling you, Avaliotis, is a very pretty head. I hope you appreciate what you got there, kid."

"I appreciate," Teddy said.

"I still don't understand what the problem is," Coach said.

"Well, here, sir." The lieutenant from PR picked up the *Hoist* and read: " 'She will reign over the San Diego Sea-bee ball two weeks from tomorrow and then, three weeks later, over the Navy Civil Engineer Ball.' These fellows have already committed themselves, publicity-wise, Coach. We'd have a hell of a time backing out of this one."

"Nobody's going to back out of nothing," Coach said. "Isn't this still the Navy? You say you reasoned with her? Christ! Reasoned!" Coach's face went red, a biological display which informed all who could see that the man's short fuse was about to burn out. "Why do we, all of a sudden, have to reason with somebody in the Navy? Tell her it's an order and that's that, boy!" He looked at his wrist watch.

"I don't think that will work, Coach," the lieutenant from PR said. "I think what we have here is a home-job." He turned to Teddy. "This one's up to you to do something about, Avaliotis."

Teddy nodded, then looked at his education services officer anxiously.

"Coach," the PR lieutenant said, "I want you to understand why I'm so hot and bothered that I brought you into this. We will get more ink in the press with Avaliotis, female, than with any other E-One I've seen aboard this base this year. I mean, they will publish these pictures"—he slapped his copy of the *Hoist*—

"anywhere! This goddamn girl is beautiful!" He hit the pictures again. "I mean beautiful!"

"Leave it to my boy here," Coach said. He smiled at Teddy affectionately. "Because this boy here is a Greek boy and they're maybe the last to hold out against the female wave which is about to swamp us all." He stood up; the meeting was over.

"She can swamp me anytime," the lieutenant said to Teddy as they went out the door.

On his way home, Teddy tried to figure out how to approach Ethel. It was not going to be easy. This was the second time she'd had her picture in the *Hoist*. She hadn't liked it the first time. Neither had he.

Two issues earlier, before all this Queen of the Ball fuss, the *Hoist* had featured their picture together on its front page. Teddy was standing by his Ampex, Ethel at his side, looking up at him admiringly. Teddy, hand on a "pod," looked like the best the Navy had to offer, Ethel like what she was called, a Kiwi, meaning "sexy kid." All that was all right.

It was the print that infuriated Teddy.

The headline read: THEY PROBABLY DON'T STUDY TWENTY-FOUR HOURS A DAY. The lead paragraph continued the thought. "But at least the opportunity is wide open to them. They are Teddy and Ethel Avaliotis. He's heading for NROTC. She's in radarman 'B' school and making excellent progress in her studies."

Then Ethel was quoted. "I think it brings us closer together that we are both here. If I wasn't in the Navy too, I wouldn't have any idea why he comes home so distressed sometimes and I wouldn't be able to help him."

"When the hell did I ever come home distressed?" Teddy had demanded.

"I didn't say distressed," Ethel had said. "That's their word, distressed; they made that up."

"No way they could make that up," Teddy said. "Me, distressed! Christ, everybody on the base reads this paper."

He'd gone on, storming about it, saying there was not to ever be any more goddamn his-hers bullshit publicity, not ever again.

Which was going to make it difficult, now, for him to reverse himself and talk her into what he'd promised his education services officer he'd talk her into.

They were eating supper in the motel's coffee shop.

Some Greek male instinct told Teddy that his tactic should be to make Ethel feel guilty about something, then come at her from the side.

"How's the Swiss steak?" he asked.

"Not bad," she said. "How's your cheeseburger?"

"Awful. Precooked. Soggy." He pushed away the half he'd not eaten. "I'm ready for some home cooking."

"As soon as we get a place—"

"I'm beginning to believe you like this goddamn motel."

"I don't."

"I saw one of those little bastards from the other building pissing in the pool this morning."

"Well, we don't go in the pool. About the home cooking, I'd like to. But they run me all day on the base. I don't know where I'd find time to move us if we did find a place we liked. By the way, I did what you said: I cut off our charge account at the supermarket."

" 'Bout time. Let's really look this weekend—will you do that for me? By the way, I don't think that apartment we saw last Sunday was so bad."

"No?"

"You seemed to like it too. At first. You stood at the window and looked out; you stood there a long time."

"No swimming pool under that window, which was a relief."

"Then it seemed like you changed your mind. You know you're not going to find a place you like as much as what you're used to, you know that?"

"You're telling me again I've been spoiled? All my life everybody's told me that. I'm beginning to believe it. . . ." She sighed. "God, I'd like to hear some music tonight. Let's go upstairs and see if we can find some old funky music on the radio, something from way back under."

"What about what I was asking?"

"I haven't got any fight in me tonight, Teddy. You find a place, tell me you really like it, and we'll move in. I'll go anywhere you want me to go—is that all right?"

"I wasn't scolding you, Kit."

"Ethel. You sound like you think it's my fault we're still here. Maybe it is."

"By the way, they were on me about you changing your mind on that queen deal."

"Teddy, please. I don't want to hear about that tonight."

"Did you read the article in the *Hoist* or just look at the pictures?"

"I read the article. As much as I could take. Why do they shovel the same bullshit at you in the Navy as they do outside?"

"Because it's the 'new Navy—part of the mainstream of American life.'"

"That PR man went on and on about that. I couldn't tell if he was serious."

"They're trying to make the service attractive to a lot more people, with the draft gone and all. Which is good, you got to agree. So maybe you should think again about—"

"I thought you didn't want me to do that stuff."

"Well, I don't generally, but—"

"But this time they've been talking to you."

"Yeah. So, what the hell, maybe you should think about it again."

Ethel got up and walked out of the coffee shop.

Teddy ate his strawberry shortcake. Then he ate Ethel's.

"She's not coming back?" the waitress asked.

"She got mad at me," Teddy said. "Now I'm mad at her. How'd you stay married all these years, Ginny?"

"He's Portuguese. He'll break my bones if I fool around. That's all that holds any marriage together. Terror."

Upstairs, he saw her, clenched like a fist, on her side of the bed, her back turned to the side he slept on.

He decided the waitress had a point. Terror, the quiet kind. He opened the bottom drawer of the bureau, pulled out the extra blanket, went into the living room, closing the door after him, and stretched out on the sofa.

He slept in the raw and the green nylon blanket was scratchy. But Teddy had a gift; nothing kept him awake.

Ethel, crouching at the side of the sofa an hour later, had trouble waking him. "Teddy, don't be mad at me, Teddy," she whispered. "I can't sleep when you're mad at me. Come back to bed now, please, Teddy."

"Don't you ever do that again to me," he said when he'd picked up on what was happening. "Don't you ever walk out on me again! In a restaurant full of people! So everybody in the joint, even the goddamn waitress, laughs at me! You made an asshole of me down there, Kit."

"I'm sorry. I'm on edge tonight. Maybe I'm getting my thing. No. I don't know what's got me this way. Come on back to bed, Teddy. Please come on back."

"You go back. I'm going to sleep here."

She lifted the green cover and stretched out next to him. She pulled up the gown she'd put on and pushed one thigh between his.

He could feel her yearning.

"You're the only reason I'm here, Teddy," she said. "You're why I live."

She was kissing him, her lips soft and yielding.

"Stop it," he said. "I don't want that now."

"Yes you do. You always want me. That's the only thing in life I'm sure about. But I want to tell you, I didn't pose for those pictures. That cameraman, he just seemed to be monkeying around and I had my coat off and he snapped at me from here and from there, walking around like he had no idea what he was doing till he had the sun behind me and that's how he got me sticking out front that way."

Gently she pulled him to her again.

He still held back.

" 'Lift your hand,' he said. 'Stretch your neck up.' And like a big dope, I did what he said. You saw the result."

"You look like some little tramp, not my wife. And that other picture—you can see clear up your dress."

"I know. I'm sorry. Let's not talk about it anymore. Let's find some music—"

"But those pictures—that's what goes on today, you know that! That's the way the world is now."

"What really got me was the article. 'With Avaliotis, you always know who's coming on board before you have the verification of her face.' "

"I know. But you've been around; why does that bother you? That much? The Navy's no different from anywhere else."

"I thought it would be."

"What is wrong with what you did is that you agreed

first, then after they got everything organized around you—I mean, why the hell did you agree in the first place?"

"Those Seabee fellows cornered me, nice plain guys, sort of rough and all, and one of them had a cute smile and he put it to me and then, all of a sudden, I was saying, 'Sure, swell, be glad to, that'll be cool,' and all that girly-girl rap which I hate worse than anything when I hear it from someone else. I guess it's just a habit, me being so agreeable, saying yes when I should say no and seeming to be so easy to get when you know I'm not. Then, when I saw the pictures, I realized I was doing something again because somebody else wanted me to, not because I wanted to."

"But, Ethel, now look—"

"And I remembered how angry you got the time before when they played us up that way in the paper and you said you didn't want us in that kind of shit ever again and I thought you were right. Don't you still feel that way?"

"Yeah. But this time, just this time, since you said you would—"

"Because if you really feel that way, let's stick to it because the way you think is right. That is what I would respect."

"Yeah, but I don't think you should go back on your word."

"Well, then—if you want me to. Do you? Really? O.K. If you do. Then I'll do it. Maybe that is the easiest thing. Do it and forget it. Get it over with. Is that what you mean? Take it as a lesson?"

"Yeah. Come, let's go to bed. Get up."

"O.K. If that's what you think, what you really think."

"Come on, honey, get up."

"All right. Let's see if there's any decent music on the radio. I looked before and there was nothing. But it's

192

later now and all the freaks are listening; that's what I like, the goddamn subculture. I miss my hifi more than anything, Teddy. Wait a minute—let me get some music on first."

But he pulled her into bed.

A couple of minutes later, he said, "Go put it in."

"I don't have to anymore," she said. "I started on the pill. So I'll be ready anytime you want me. I know you don't like to wait. See. Like everything else, I did that for you. Anytime you want me."

The odd thing was that Ethel rather welcomed the *Hoist* incident. It broke up what was becoming routine. She wanted Teddy at many different times, but it was turning out that he wanted her always at the same time, which was a couple of hours after supper, after his period of reading and study. This regularity had begun to disturb her. Before they were married, she had some say in when, and where, and even how. Now he named the game, only he, and it was always at the same time and in the same way. In fact, it had become part of his professional routine, its purpose to relax him into a restorative sleep.

So she thought.

The one time she'd complained about it, his answer had been: "Sex, sex, sex. Don't you ever think of anything else?"

Teddy couldn't have articulated it, but what he really expected of Ethel was that she should leap to her feet when he entered the room, approach him with an attitude of unmistakable worship, and offer him the kiss of familial veneration. In the morning before he went out, she should inspect him carefully to make sure he showed every evidence of perfect health, check his clothing to see if all his buttons were firmly attached, his shoulders to make sure they were brushed clean, even his shoes, so he would appear to the rest of the world to be what he was to her: perfect in every respect. At breakfast his coffee should be waiting when he occupied his place at the head of the table, the milk added in the proportion he favored. While he ate his breakfast—or any other meal —she should watch, preferably on her feet, to make sure he found what she'd set before him acceptable, guard vigilantly that his plate was refilled as necessary and if, in the end, the food had pleased him and he chose to reward her with even the most offhand commendation, she should be extravagantly—and visibly—grateful for his praise.

In other words, Teddy was his father's son, and his model for a wife was his mother, Noola.

The next morning, Teddy went into the education services office and told his mentor how he'd handled the situation, every detail.

Coach laughed. "You got to rough 'em up once in a while," he said. "Otherwise they forget who's boss."

The following Sunday, he took Ethel back to the apartment he'd found which she hadn't responded to. This time, perhaps because he'd been very loving the night before, she said she liked it. At any rate, she agreed that they should sign a lease immediately.

Teddy remembered, later, how happy she seemed about it all.

"Now we can really ease up on the budget," he said. "Let's for instance go out tonight. Let's go to a restaurant where they have your abalone, the Fish Factory. How about that, the place we took Pop to the first night you met—how about that, Kit?"

"Ethel," she said.

The rental agent insisted they deposit the last two

months' rent when they signed the lease. The Navy, he said, had a way of shipping out without warning.

"How long's the lease for?" Ethel asked.

"A year," the agent said. "That O.K.?"

Teddy said sure it was, and that they'd come back with the money at the end of the next day, which was a Monday, and sign up.

The next morning was the morning Ethel disappeared.

nine

WHEN Teddy got home at the end of the afternoon, their place was silent, the stove cold. He didn't worry at first, figured she'd gone downtown to a movie. But then he went across the hall, out on the fire escape balcony, and there was her car, with the windows raised, in its slot below.

There was nothing to do except go to bed and study. She was probably mad at him for some silly woman's reason and staying with a girl friend. But she didn't have one. Well, he'd worry about it in the morning.

He woke at a quarter to six without the aid of an alarm, made his breakfast and left the empty motel room to attend to that morning's electronics instruction. He still wasn't worried; what he was feeling was more like embarrassment. Suppose someone asked him where she was?

Soon someone did. "Her mother's seriously ill," Teddy

told Ethel's instructor in naval history. "She suddenly got worse." He let the man guess cancer.

He drove home shortly before noon; the place was deadly quiet. Perhaps something bad had happened. He bought a newspaper. There'd been a kidnapping and the usual traffic deaths. Nothing about Ethel. He decided to go to the police, asking their discretion. He wanted to keep the matter in the family, he told them. They didn't know where to start looking. He had no suggestions.

He had lunch at La Cantina on the base. People were already asking him how Ethel's mother was.

When he got home, there was a telegram. It was not from Tucson but from Tarpon Springs. "Don't worry. I'm fine. Letter in the mail. Always, Ethel."

He could have called her in Florida, but didn't.

Teddy needed someone to tell him what he should be feeling. He went to see the education officer.

"She seemed so happy yesterday morning," he told him.

"That's what I mean," the ed officer said, "about women in the service. They're unstable."

"What the hell am I supposed to do now, Coach?"

"Did she give you any warning she might pull something like this?"

"I remember one conversation. 'Is this the way it's supposed to be?' she asked me. It was at breakfast, she was pouring my coffee, I was studying. Calculus. I didn't look up. 'What are you talking about?' I said. 'Married life,' she said. 'Is this it?' 'Guess so,' I said. 'I was never married before.'"

"That all?"

"I didn't think anything of it at the time."

"Well, if it's any comfort, may I inform you that this is not a first. Unauthorized Absence—the Navy has a name for it. You see, the services are tough going for our split-tail shipmates. They want equality, but then they don't. Chew them out like a man gets chewed out and they can't take it. Mother Navy's not the glamour queen they expected her to be."

"Coach, should I go to Florida and talk to her?"

"Worst thing you could do. Don't chase her; she'll come to heel. May I give you some psychological advice?"

"Wish you would."

"Get mad. Kick ass. You'll feel better. I need a drink. How about you?"

In the ed officer's quarters they hoisted a few, then the old seafarer took off his shirt and showed Teddy his tattoos.

The next morning there was a letter.

DEAREST:

I'm sorry I've caused you worry. Please don't be upset. I came here to talk to your father. I trust him more than anyone I know. I'm calmer now because I'm near him. I've even begun to figure out a thing or two.

The Navy didn't turn out to be what I hoped. What I was doing, mostly, was memorizing lists of names and figures and learning to read dials. It didn't have a lot to do with the sea. Like that landlocked destroyer on the base.

But it suits you fine. So I had to ask myself, "Wouldn't he be better off living in the barracks, back where he was before I messed up his life?"

You study better without me near you. I've been in your way. You don't say so because you're a saint.

When will I be back? I don't know. Tell them that the Queen will not attend the ball.

I love you and always will.

ETHEL

The ed officer had prepared Teddy for such a letter, prepared him to feel angry, and that anger was a comfort. He was sleeping very well when the phone woke him at two-thirty the next morning.

It was Noola. Collect. "What happened?" she asked in a whisper.

"Don't worry about me, Mom," Teddy told her. "I'm fine."

"But what happened? She's here but she says nothing. Why did she leave all of a sudden?"

"She says she's working something out."

"What does that mean?"

"In her mind, Mom—working something out in her mind. Don't ask me what. But I'm all right, so don't worry."

In Florida, it was five-thirty. Noola had left her bed early that hot morning so her call to Teddy would be private.

Noola's first duty every day was to make a fresh supply of yogurt. She boiled the milk now, remembering how Ethel had burst in on them, night before last. Costa had been sympathetic. "Women should stay inside the family," he'd said. As she poured the hot milk into the jelly tumblers, Noola thought of how she'd been polite despite what she'd felt. Then she stirred in spoonfuls of the yogurt remaining from the day before and recalled the frantic look on the girl's face as she got out of the taxi that had brought her all the way from Tampa airport. How much did a taxi from there to Mangrove Still cost? Noola wondered. She covered the full tumblers with old soft dishcloths. She hadn't liked what Ethel had done and, no matter what Teddy said, she still didn't.

Costa had announced he was going to show Ethel the town that morning and his instruction to Noola had been: "My black suit, get ready!" It was much too hot for that suit, but Noola had long since given up trying to talk

Costa out of anything. Since Ethel had arrived, his temper had been even shorter.

When she heard her husband groaning and sighing in his room—the first sound Costa made each morning was a complaint to Fate—she hurried to put the coffee on. Costa required that it be ready when he walked into the kitchen.

Yes, Ethel's presence there was a puzzle; her son had explained nothing. But Noola knew his voice when he was hurt.

"Coffee," Costa said, entering the room. She scuffed to the stove in her slippers, picking up a coffee cup on the way.

"I will show her Tarpon today," he said.

"What's there to see?" Noola said. "The street along the dock, a few old stores, that park full of loafers!"

"I will describe, when we walk along the dock, what used to be. I will paint the picture so she sees it like it was in the good days. You press my suit?"

"Costa," she said in spite of herself, "black suit in this heat?"

"Who's going to wear it, you or me?"

She set up the ironing board.

"You have clean shirt for me?"

"In your bureau drawer."

A moment later, he came out with the shirt and showed her, as if she'd snipped it off on purpose, the place where a button was missing. His gesture, as he pointed to the empty spot, made a reprimand unnecessary. "I will eat couple eggs today—two, not one," he said.

She put the eggs to boil. Then bit off a piece of white thread, put the end in her mouth and pulled it sharp enough to pass through a needle's eye. She needed glasses for this; her eyes had been giving her trouble.

"The mortgage money is due today," she said.

"So give it to them."

"I don't have it."

"How much they asking?"

"Same as every month. Sixty-two dollars."

A grand gesture of his hand stirred the air. "What's sixty-two dollars?"

"It's what the bank is waiting to receive from us this morning."

"How much you have?"

"I need thirty-two dollars to make it."

"Tell them next month sure. Speak to Mr. Mavromatis, president over there; he's old friend from my young days."

"You speak to him; he's your old friend, from your young days."

"I'm busy today. I have to show Ethel our life here."

"Mr. Mavromatis will say speak to Mr. Cotter and Mr. Cotter—"

"Oh, Cotter! Don't worry! He's crackerboy, sure, but fine man. Explain everything."

"What's there to explain? We haven't got the payment, that's all there is to it. How much money you got?"

"I have enough, maybe, to show this girl good time today. She's our daughter, Noola, right? First time here, right? Make hot water ready: suppose she want bath!"

"She took a bath last night. Why don't you give me the thirty dollars, Costa?"

"Noola, there are more important things my life than bank. Thousan' time I tell you. We have five years to pay goddamn mortgage. Explain that to son of a bitch, Mavromatis, may the Devil fuck his mother! Tell him not to bother me anymore. I have other problems. He's old friend, you understand. He admire me very much."

The button reattached, she bit off the end of the thread.

"I hope he behaves like your old friend today," she said.

"I hear her. Quick! She's getting up."

"Quick what?"

"Put coffee."

"It's ready. You've been drinking it."

"Please, Noola, no fighting now. Keep everything nice in front Ethel, do me favor. Oh, my eggs! I will not eat them hard!"

As Noola was serving him his eggs, which happened to be just right, Ethel came in and kissed them both.

"We make big tour today," Costa said, "so eat plenty —eggs, dear girl, all you want, toast, coffee, piece cheese, honey, gives strength."

"Sometime today," Ethel said, "I want to wash a few things."

"Give to Noola," Costa said. "She wash 'em."

"Costa, Noola has enough to do without washing my underwear."

"Come on, have your breakfast, hurry up before it gets too hot. I will show you Tarpon Springs today. You want bath?"

"I didn't put the hot water on," Noola said. "I told you."

A look from Costa to remind her not to quarrel with him in front of Ethel.

"I had a bath last night," Ethel said. "I'm fine."

"So come on, giddyap horsey, we go, dear girl."

It took Ethel a while to dress, but not half as long as it took Costa to shave, apply polish to his black shoes, put on his shirt, tie his tie and don his black suit.

They left as a couple, Ethel's arm hooked around Costa's elbow, walked from Mangrove Still ("Old-time cracker make liquor here," Costa explained) to Tarpon Springs ("One time bay here full tarpon fish laying eggs. Now all gone").

As soon as they were out of the house, Noola made the three beds, tidied the rooms, washed the breakfast dishes. Neither Costa nor Ethel had put their eggs dishes to soak in cold water—Costa from arrogance; Ethel, Noola guessed, because she was used to servants. Noola had to scrape the plates with a knife.

In Ethel's room she found the underthings Ethel wanted washed. Noola looked at them. How light they were! And transparent. No cover at all. How did they hold together? Or hold anything up, those two net slings?

There were no servants here; let the girl do her own. She went into her own room.

Noola opened the bureau drawer where she kept her stockings. In the back she found the rolled-up grays inside which she hid the money she saved for the mortgage payments. These were also the stockings she wore each month for her visit to the bank.

Three tens, tightly folded. Her father had always had money to avoid embarrassments like this. To be fair, Costa had had money when she'd married him; it wasn't his fault the red tide had come. That was God's work in league with the Devil.

She'd better go. Despite what she'd told Costa about the heat, she decided on her black dress. It was more dignified. Taking off her robe, she dropped the dress over her shoulders, pulled it around and zipped up the side. She examined the gray stockings for runs, then crossing an ankle over a knee, she ran her hand gently up and over the enlarged vein at the back of her calf. Her mother had had varicose veins, worn surgical stockings and complained everlastingly about the pain. Noola expected nothing better.

Suddenly she stood and it happened. The doctor had told her it was nothing to worry about. When she'd been sitting awhile, he told her, if she got up suddenly she might have a short dizzy episode. She remembered "episode," and "You're not a kid anymore, Mrs. Avaliotis."

She sat back on the mattress, dropped her head, waited for it to pass.

She didn't want to go to that bank, she didn't want to beg those two men—neither Costa's old friend Mavromatis, nor that good old crackerboy Cotter. That's what it amounted to, begging them for pity. She didn't even want to go downtown. She didn't feel like cooking a big dinner: "Make something special," Costa had commanded.

Not for a girl who'd left her son without an explanation.

Noola was breathing hard again, but because she was angry, not because she was dizzy.

She was in a trap and there was no way out of this one, the trap called wifehood and motherhood, the trap called kindness to all, understanding always, patience without end. She didn't feel loving or kind, understanding or patient. Not one damned bit.

It was a quarter to eleven and she was already tired.

She rose slowly, holding on to the bed as she went to the closet, bent over, half kneeling to pick up her shoes. She had difficulty pulling them on, had to twist, wrench and squeeze because they were too tight. Noola hadn't been out of her slippers for almost a week, not since Sunday, when, without Costa, she'd attended mass at Saint Nicholas. Her walking shoes felt tight once they were on, which was probably the reason her ankles were swollen.

She'd better go and stop feeling sorry for herself. She used the mirror to put on her little purple hat with its flourish of feathers up front. They looked as if they'd had a fright which had brought them up on their quills. She winked at herself and began to hum a march. Back in high school, Noola had been in the chorus of *Babes in Toyland* and one of their numbers, "March of the Toys," had been a strut. Now she did it in place, watching herself in the mirror. She was so ridiculous. "Stop being a baby, for chrissake," she said out loud. "Cry baby!"

On the way down the hall, she passed the open door to

Ethel's bedroom. There were the pastel flimsies, waiting to be washed. "Oh, what the hell, just this once!"

Standing before a sink full of suds, the sleeves of her most dignified dress rolled up, the purple hat with its startled feathers pushed back off her forehead, Noola washed her guest's underclothes.

Who wouldn't forgive her for pulling hard on the elastic band around the waist of the panties? No waist should be that small, no abdomen that tight! Who would blame her for feeling a small secret satisfaction when the stitches holding the elastic gave, first a little, then so that a length of it came loose from the rim of the garment?

Noola was human.

A neighbor saw her walking along the highway—there was no sidewalk—picked her up and dropped her at the *kentron*, the park of dusty shrubs and benches at the center of the town.

Walking the short distance from there to the bank, she passed a large grocery that featured imported specialties, goods in cans and in barrels, packed in oil and in brine, most of them from the mother country. The store was filled with a crowd, in the middle of which she could see, as the people surrounding them shuffled, the two heads— her husband's coarse black, her daughter-in-law's fine red-gold. She could judge what was happening from the sounds, could imagine the scene: the owner of the place asking Ethel to sample the variety of his olives or the feta cheese he'd forked out of a wooden keg, dripped of its brine, sliced and offered on a piece of wax paper. Or was it a can of *yalanji dolma,* stuffed grape leaves imported from Greece, that had been opened and offered to the visitor? The owner, it seemed, wanted the honor of making small packages of Ethel's favorites if she'd promise to do him the honor of accepting these poor gifts.

"You must take them," Noola heard her husband shout.

"Otherwise he get insulted, right, Manoli? Manoli, give her, never mind what she say, she's too polite over there, American style. Give her!"

Noola hurried on. As she went down the street, she heard the cascade of flattery, then Ethel's "oh"'s and "ah"'s, the bursts of laughter and the cries of astonishment, homage to Ethel.

Were they sincere? Was Ethel really that pleased? Her daughter-in-law, it seemed, was expert at receiving gifts in a way that made the donor happy.

Noola decided to do her shopping in another part of town.

The breeze kicked sparks off the water and the sun was warm. A triumphal procession was entering the dockside street along the Anclote River. People came to their windows to watch it pass, merchants stepped out of their places of business, cardplayers, holding their hands against their chests, came to the doors of coffeehouses, sailors raised themselves out of the holds of their fishing boats. Even the tourists, who understood nothing, stopped and studied.

Costa, carrying the shopping bag he'd been given to hold their acquisitions, walked slowly and gravely at Ethel's side, not a step ahead as he did with Noola. He hovered over the girl, protecting her, as he pointed out landmarks and made introductions. Around and behind them were the curious and the idle—kids too young to work, old-timers too old, as well as those others who had work to do but didn't feel pressed to attend to it that day. An old black man who spoke perfect Greek had attached himself to them and carried the bulkier gifts. Dogs protected the flanks.

Anyone who didn't get to meet Ethel that day was marked as a second-class citizen. "My son, the officer, his wife," Costa would say. Then all would listen to everything Ethel uttered, with the kind of attention no one deserves, laugh more than was called for, comment often and in two languages on the girl's grace and wit, on her insight. How sweet she is, they gurgled, how modest, how correct! She could have been a Greek girl, to judge by her manners. They paid her this final compliment.

It was evident that there was one person Costa especially wanted to show Ethel off to. He was standing in front of his tourist shop, a man taller than Costa and, even at this distance, more monumental. Here was the glamour figure of the community.

"Ethel," Costa said, "meet Johnny Gonatos. Johnny, my daughter over here."

"Daughter-in-law," Ethel said. "Awful glad to meet you, Mr.—"

"Gonatos, Johnny Gonatos. Hello, young lady. So you're the one everybody's talking about. No wonder. Beautiful girl, Costa."

"My son, Teddy, he can pick 'em! Ethel, you talking now to real number one old-time diver, Tarpon. Not me. This man, here, Johnny Gonatos! Famous man. He was in Hollywood picture over there, everybody know him, coast to coast."

"You were pretty good on the bottom yourself," Johnny said.

"How's Virginia, Johnny boy?" Costa said. Then to Ethel, "His wife, fine woman."

"She was just here," Johnny said. "Now she's home fixing dinner. How's Noola?" He turned to Ethel. "Fine woman," he said.

"She certainly is," Ethel said.

"Home fixing dinner," Costa said.

"And how's Teddy doing in San Diego?"

"Fine! Wonderful!" Costa turned to Ethel. "Johnny's son went to the same place."

"That's how Teddy got the idea," Johnny said.

"Oh, he had idea by himself, all right," Costa said.

"He used to hero-worship my son, Michael," Johnny went on. "Everything Michael would do, Teddy would do. If Michael wore a certain sweater, wait a week and you'll see Teddy wearing the same sweater—"

"For chrissake, Johnny, Teddy could pick his own goddamn sweater!"

"He used to follow my boy around like a dog."

"Hey, Johnny, hey, Johnny, watch yourself!"

A wave of tourists went by, Midwesterners, the men loaded down with cameras, the women fresh out from under dryers.

"Tourist!" Costa said with a sour sound. "Like flies over here. Kansas City, Kansas City Madzouri! Johnny, how man like you can live here, whole town gone to hell, tourist, tourist, tourist?"

"They're my living," Johnny said. He turned to Ethel. "But you should have seen this place in the old days, young lady. Two hundred sponge boats docked along that river. And the men." His fist made a gesture to Costa, back to himself, then hit Costa a hell of a shot. "Like us! Not like these—"

"*Skoopeethi,*" Ethel said. "Means 'garbage.'"

"Right, young lady. Hey, Costa, smart girl. I like her."

"Why don't you move where I am?" Costa said. "Beautiful there, you don't hear a sound."

"Because when I don't hear a sound, I don't have bread on the table. I have heavy responsibilities, Costa. Not like you. I got three children. You got one. Five grandchildren. You have nothing. No offense meant, excuse me, young lady, I'm talking about so far!"

"Don't worry on that," Costa said. "Right, Ethel, pretty soon, right?"

"I'm not worrying about this girl here," Johnny said. "I wish I was a young man again, this girl here!"

"I sometimes have same thought over there," Costa said.

"Then you should have seen them," Ethel said. "Noola, they were laughing and punching each other, these two old goats. I thought any minute they'd jump on me."

Ethel was unwrapping a rather large present, a cut-out figure of Christ, whose eyes followed sinners from side to side.

"Oh, look! I didn't know they gave me this. Noola, look!"

"That's to remind you He's watching you every minute, so watch your step," Costa said. "Noola, let's eat, for God's sake."

Noola was at the stove, ladling the dinner, tender young okra stewed with lamb and tomatoes, into a serving dish.

"So sit down," Noola said.

"And we got—look, Noola—three kinds of oranges, that woman at the citrus ranch—"

"Grace," Noola said, "that big horse. His one-time girl friend."

"Zoooo-hut! Noola, we don't talk these things at the table."

"And grapefruit too," Ethel said. "I shouldn't have taken them all."

"You were doing her a favor," Costa said. "She will boast on this someday. Where's yogurt, Noola? Ethel, sit down here. I don't eat unless you sit down first."

Ethel sat but didn't eat. She was looking through the contents of an old shoe box. "Go ahead," she said, "don't wait for me. Noola, please, sit."

Noola didn't. She'd filled Ethel's plate with okra and lamb. "You want yogurt on top or on the side?" she asked.

"Look at these!" Ethel said. "Everybody was giving me photographs of Teddy when he was a boy. What did you say? You people put yogurt on everything!"

"Gives strength," Costa said.

"Noola, here's one of you—you look so young. Here, look!"

"Later. Go on, eat your dinner."

"Oh, this is wonderful, just wonderful. Noola, please sit down."

"I'm getting the rice."

"But when do you eat?"

"When we get through," Costa said.

"Does Teddy expect me to do that too?" Ethel asked, as a joke.

"I hope so," Noola said.

"Too hot this damn black suit, Noola, for God's sake, sweating like pig yesterday. Give me something light today. Noola!"

So began the second day of the honeymoon. "Costa, listen while she's still asleep, let's go down to the water and clean the boats. They're filthy. The people that rented them yesterday, you should have seen them, gorillas."

"You want me stink from fish all day, is that your idea?"

Costa hadn't gone near The 3 Bees the day before.

"All right, I'll do it myself," Noola said. "You didn't ask me what your boyhood pals at the bank had to say."

"What's difference. What?"

"No. They said no."

"That man, Mavromatis, he's not a sincere banker. U.S. Government should send him back to Kalymnos. He gives me lousy five thousand dollars, now he's getting eight back and insulting my wife same time."

When Ethel came in, she kissed Costa, who'd offered his cheek.

Noola noticed Ethel kept touching her husband.

As soon as she'd sent the pair off, Noola went down to the water's edge with a pail, an old broom and a stiff hand brush. The boats were badly fouled with the remains of bait, the debris of lunches, beer cans and cigar butts and, in the *Boston Whaler,* vomit.

Noola hitched up her dress and scrubbed the boats clean.

Meantime, Ethel was being taken for a ride on the river. She was shown where the diving boats used to tie up, fifty, sixty in a row. Their names were a collage: the *Eleni,* the *Andromache,* the *Poseidon,* the *Venizelos,* the *Eleftheria,* the *Nereus* and *Symi,* the *General Van Fleet,* all recalled with a kind of reverence, like memories of beautiful and well-disciplined girls.

During the "big" war, a boat had been named the *Joseph Stalin,* but in time this had been corrected.

A group lunch followed. Over the fried pompano, one Aleko Iliadis, a quirky-faced man in his fifties who did nothing one day he had not done the day before, including going to the track every afternoon, offered them his car and his services as chauffeur. He'd take her to the track, he told Ethel, and, en route, regale her with the glorious history of the Greek in Tarpon Springs.

"She must win every race," Costa warned the man.

Ethel hunch-bet eight races, won two, lost none—that she heard about.

On the road back, they were boxed in a traffic jam and Aleko took the opportunity to boast to his captives about the achievements of those pioneers who first set foot on the floor of the Gulf of Mexico, then went on, despite hostility and hardship, to make their fortunes.

"How about you?" Ethel asked.

"I wasted my life," he said, "happily. That was my talent."

He asked her in a whisper if she'd honor his girl friend with a visit. "She stays in Clearwater," he said. "We go right by."

Costa was not happy with the idea but finally condescended. "Married man," he muttered in Ethel's ear. "Damn fool. That's why they call him the Levendis. Aleko the Levendis. Means lives only for pleasure. Son of a bitch!"

They stopped before a house in a neighborhood of identical houses. The "girl friend" proved to be a gracious woman in her fifties. She had grown children from an early marriage to an opera singer, a basso who'd left her to work an unplowed field, a soubrette of eighteen.

That had been forgiven. What made the lady's mouth turn down was that her pleasure-lover had not divorced his wife to marry her. She was beginning to believe he never would.

After spoonfuls of cherry preserves washed down with tumblers of water, Aleko the Levendis pulled his girl friend to the piano, where she displayed a lovely voice, thin but true, a voice for the month of May. Her lover led her through "Dalla Sua Pace." As she paid her tribute to Mozart, Aleko looked up at her from over the keyboard and there was evidence of genuine sentiment in his eyes, even a kind of adoration. Clearly he loved the woman—at least when she sang.

Ethel began to cry uncontrollably, reaching out and taking Costa's hand. They held hands through "La Paloma" too.

"She's thinking of her husband in California," Costa said.

"I haven't even got a reason to cry," the soprano said.

"Why don't you two marry?" Ethel pleaded. "I want you to marry."

"Come on, Costa, we go," Aleko said, looking at his watch.

"You come in, you make your cross, now you want to leave," the woman complained.

The Levendis had Costa out the door.

"He's ruined my life," the fifty-year-old girl friend told Ethel as they parted. "Tell him to marry me. Maybe he'll listen to you."

Ethel hugged her, said she'd do all she could.

"How could I have ruined her life?" Aleko asked as they turned onto the Tarpon road. "It was ruined so many times before we met."

"But you made her hope," Costa said.

"True, I did her that disservice."

"You lied to her, damn fool."

"But the truth is what she said: Her life is ruined, my life is ruined; tell me whose life is not?"

"My son," Costa said. "His life is not."

When they got home, Noola had dinner ready.

Aleko kissed Ethel's hand as they parted.

"Never mind that stuff," Noola said. "Go home, Levendis. Your wife is waiting."

Teddy called that night.

There was nothing dramatic about their conversation. "Your mother is going to teach me how to cook," Ethel said.

"When are you coming back?" Teddy asked.

"I'll let you know," Ethel answered. "I love it here. It's so peaceful and I love your parents. Thank you for your parents."

"Do you love me?" Teddy asked.

"Oh, yes, yes," Ethel said. "Believe me. Wait; your father wants to talk to you."

"Hello, Teddy boy," Costa said. Then he listened, smiling and nodding to Ethel. "Don't worry, don't worry down there," Costa said. "We take good care of her, here's your mother."

Noola spoke Greek in a whisper. "Your son sounds worried," she said to Costa when she hung up. She didn't look at Ethel.

Ethel offered, as she had the night before, to help with the dishes. This time, when Noola refused, it seemed like a rebuff. Noola avoided her eyes.

There were two heavily upholstered chairs in front of the TV. The one Costa dropped her into was broken down in the springs, so the heavily cushioned sides seemed very high. Costa's was just as deep but he filled it.

The shooting—there was a western on television—didn't keep Costa awake. Ethel knew his evening pattern now: three beers around a heavy meal, the first hour of sleep inside his chair.

When she saw that he was asleep, Ethel went to the kitchen; she'd noticed the hostility in Noola's manner and wanted to mend it. Leaning against the side of the door frame, watching Noola scrub the pots, she tried to make conversation.

"I think I met everybody here today," she said. "It was like walking with a god! He owns the earth here, your husband."

"He can give that impression."

"What's his secret? He never doubts himself."

"He leaves that to us."

"Are you mad at him tonight?"

"Oh, no, no."

"I know he says silly things sometimes, but . . . I'd really like to find out his secret. How come he's so sure that he's right? About everything? My father is a brilliant man and behaves as if he's absolutely sure of everything, but when you really know him, he's not. He made fun of Costa at first, but in the end—"

"Finish here," Noola said. She turned off one light, put her hand on the other switch and waited for Ethel to leave the kitchen.

Ethel went back to the chair Costa had given her. Noola went to the table between the two armchairs, reached down to its low shelf and lifted out a sewing basket.

"I'm in your chair, I guess," Ethel said.

"Stay there." Noola went to the sofa, sitting under the official photograph of her son's graduation. She put a wooden egg inside the coarse-thread white stocking she was going to darn. She didn't speak.

Ethel had time to examine the room. At each end of the sofa where Noola sat were two carnival kewpie dolls. On the wall behind the sleeping Costa was a large color-tinted photograph of Teddy on his graduation day, with his parents standing proudly at either side. On the table between the sleeping father and herself, there were two large photograph albums: Teddy's athletic career in high school. Behind them was a Bible squeezed between the tusks of rampant iron elephants.

The windows were closed; the shades, Ethel had noticed, stayed down day and night.

Again she tried to stir up some talk.

"I'm dead tired," she said.

"You walked a lot today. And yesterday."

"It wasn't the walking."

"No? What then?"

"All that flattery, it was a strain. I'm not as sweet as those people think I am."

"Nobody is."

"I was pretending. All day."

"Why do you do it?"

"I was brought up that way. By my mother. That's another reason I admire Costa so much. He's always himself."

"Next time be yourself."

"Then they won't like me."

"Probably not."

Ethel waited, but Noola left it at that.

So, sure, Ethel thought, she's mad at me.

Along with everything else, Ethel noticed how stale the air was. No wonder! Not a window open. She wanted to go out. The day was not over. Was it? Now? At nine? But where would she go? And how would she explain the impulse to this woman, sitting so clenched and silent?

And why the hell did she feel apologetic about it?

"I so much wanted you to like me, Noola," she said.

"It doesn't happen quick with me," Noola said. And nothing more.

Ethel felt trapped between the heavily bolstered sides of that overstuffed chair, transfixed by the images shot from the TV screen. How to escape? Forget it.

Well, goddamn it, say something, Ethel thought. This is some character, she thought. When she gets mad, she hides it.

"Well, Teddy, what did Teddy say?" Ethel cranked up once again.

"He's all right." Noola looked at her sleeping husband.

"Is he worried?" Ethel persisted.

"Well, that would be natural, wouldn't it?" Noola said. "He says you left without telling him. Why?"

Christ, I can't explain this to her, Ethel thought.

Costa was snoring lightly. Ethel turned and looked at the bulk of the sleeping man, watched his chest rise and fall.

"Why aren't you with him; why are you here?" Noola said.

She hadn't lifted her eyes from the wooden egg over which she was darning her husband's heavy white sock.

"To know you better," Ethel said.

Then Noola did look at the girl and she said, "My men, they're children, they know nothing. But I went to school in Astoria, Queens, and I know that no woman leaves a man—even for a day—without a better reason than that."

Tough talk, Ethel thought. O.K.

"I don't want to be in the Navy," she said.

"What do you want?"

"I want to be like you."

Noola laughed.

"Don't you believe me?"

"I'll believe you when I believe you."

"What does that mean?"

"You're a different piece of cloth from me. I don't know how or why, but I know you're different. I don't understand you."

"I never had a family. I want to live in a family."

"Have children. Make your own family."

"In the Navy now you can do that. But is it the right thing? When I have children I don't want to work."

"I don't care," Noola said, "if you're in the Navy or not. But if you do anything to hurt my son, I'll not forgive you."

"I'm trying to be—" She stopped.

"What? That's what I don't understand. Tell me the truth."

"What he really wants."

"I hope so. He's a good boy and doesn't deserve to be hurt."

"Who's hurting him?" Ethel burst out. Then she made herself speak quietly. "He's so good he doesn't ask me to be what he really wants—someone like you."

"You think you can be that for him—what he wants?"

"The truth?"

"If you know it and if you can speak it."

"I don't know. I get awfully discouraged some days and want to smash everything. You ever feel that way?"

"No."

Costa got up without warning and went off to bed. Noola followed. Ethel had been surprised to find that Mr. and Mrs. Avaliotis, like her own parents, slept in separate rooms.

The next day, Noola took time off from the shop and introduced Ethel to the Greek kitchen. She taught her how to make her own yogurt, how to stuff young zucchini with lamb (never beef!), how to make rice so it was dry, each kernel separate, how to make egg-lemon soup and Turkish coffee.

217

Ethel wrote everything down in a little book and at first Noola seemed encouraging. But that didn't last. She's just doing her duty, Ethel thought, and it's a hell of an effort.

Noola made Ethel uncomfortable.

Ethel made Noola uncomfortable.

She'd become fascinated with her mother-in-law's plump belly. She imagined it unclothed. Did Noola wear some kind of corset or girdle? The bundle of fat and flesh seemed so well-packed, so evenly and symmetrically shaped. Like the ballet dancer's heavy calves, the tennis pro's overmuscled forearm, the cowboy's pigeon-toed walk, the dowager's hump, this abdominal exaggeration marked something: the surrendered housewife.

Is that what they all wanted *her* to be?

Is that what *she* wanted to be?

The next morning Ethel announced she was going to cook dinner that night.

She insisted on doing everything alone: the marketing, on foot, preparing and spicing the meat stuffing for the young zucchini, stewing the lamb bits in olive oil, onions and tomatoes before adding the string beans.

The rice she left for last.

Exhausted and satisfied—but not ready to repeat the experience the next day—she asked Noola to keep an eye on her rice, forced the windows in her bedroom open and stretched out.

The smell of burning food woke her.

In the kitchen her fear was justified. The rice!

On the porch she went after Noola.

"But didn't you smell it?"

"No. What happened?"

"The rice burned. It's all stuck to the bottom of the pot."

"Maybe you didn't put enough butter."

"I put in what you told me. I thought you were going to watch it for me."

"A cook, Ethel, should never leave what she's put on the fire in anyone else's care."

"You wanted it to burn, didn't you?"

Noola got up. "Don't worry," she said. "I'll make some more rice."

"You wanted that too."

Noola went into the house.

Costa was not impressed by the meal. "Teach her more," he instructed his wife.

"Try again tomorrow," he told Ethel.

Ethel didn't think much of the meal either.

"Noola, coffee," Costa said.

"I'll make it," Ethel said. But Noola was gone.

"Let her do it," Costa said. "Try again tomorrow," he repeated.

A command or a suggestion? Ethel wondered.

"Tomorrow I'm going to Tampa," she said.

She hadn't known it till she'd said it.

"What for?" Costa wanted to know.

"To find a beautiful dress to go back in."

"Whatsa matter that dress?"

"I want to look wonderful."

"Whatsa difference how you look? He be glad to see you."

"You think so?"

"Sure. What's the matter with you?"

She was doubting everything now. She knew what was coming: one of her bad days; she'd been there before. Trouble.

"Go to Clearwater," Costa commanded. "Tampa bad city. Plenty nice store, Clearwater. That's where she bought dress for your wedding. You don't like that dress? Hah? Clearwater!"

"O.K.," Ethel said.

I'll go any damn place I want, she said to herself.

The next morning Costa hurried off to The 3 Bees, muttering something about the live bait having to be replenished. "Noola don't understand that there," he'd said in a gruff voice.

The honeymoon was over. Noola must have informed Costa that Ethel had left their son without explanation or apology.

Unexpectedly Aleko the Levendis appeared. "Costa wants me to carry you to the Clearwater bus," he said.

Escort or guard? Ethel wondered.

ten

THE bus was full. She found a seat by the last window. A young man, reading a book, was on the aisle.

Ethel felt relief at being alone, being loose, being by herself; she felt released from confinement.

The movement of the bus woke her body. She opened her window to the breeze and laid her head back on the top of the seat. She uncrossed and relaxed her legs. She let the bus seat cradle her.

She became aware that the boy next to her was "accidentally" pushing his knee against hers. She didn't move away. Pretending to look at the road on the other side, she examined her neighbor out of the corner of her eye.

He had a long nose and his eyes were close together. The ends of his upper front teeth showed under his lip. He was trying to raise a mustache. She waited for him to look at her.

He didn't. He preferred to be guilty.

Ethel knew why she pressed her knee back against his. Her perversity was on her. She wanted to see how far he would go. The boy was pathetic, begging for crumbs that way! What woman would respond to that?

Now his knee was trembling!

If that boy had so little confidence in himself, what she was doing would destroy what he had. She'd better stop it now.

She stood up. The bus had arrived at a crossing where the road to Tampa leaves the road to Clearwater.

She had meant, until that instant, to go to Clearwater.

"Excuse me," she said.

"Sure," the young man said. He cleared the frog in his throat, said "Sure" again, smiled without looking at her.

Ethel walked across the road to where the traffic was moving toward Tampa. She thought of the boy in the bus with compassion. How lonely he must feel now. She wondered if he'd had an erection. She knew the movement of a bus could do that to a young man.

It had affected her.

The day was hot, getting hotter.

She decided to hitchhike to Tampa.

Why did she feel this way? That boy was so unattractive, it couldn't be him. The thing that had happened was entirely within her own body.

"God." She breathed deep. "Oh, God!"

What did she need? What was she looking for? Something she didn't understand.

She knew if Noola could see her now with her thumb out, asking anybody and everybody to pick her up, she'd have no pity. The plain fact was that Noola didn't like her and Costa did. Well, men had always liked her better than women did. All Noola could think of was Teddy boy. A sure way to ruin a son.

Well, she'd be the same way herself, if she ever had a son.

Noola had asked her what Costa had not dared—or didn't know how to: did she use a contraceptive?

"I'm on the pill," she answered.

Noola had nodded.

"I don't want a baby in the Navy," she'd explained for the third time. Why couldn't Noola understand that?

"When then?" she'd answered.

"When I'm out."

"That will be a long time."

"We discussed it," Ethel had said. "Teddy agrees."

"Teddy agrees but Costa is getting impatient."

That broke them up, both laughing.

Later Noola had walked her to her bedroom door and there had clinched it. "Maybe it would be better if you were out of the Navy, like you say. But now he is there. You should be in the same place. Married people living apart, it's very dangerous."

Well, what the hell could she have answered to that except what she had, "Good night," then let Noola close the door after her.

A car stopped for her. It was a pickup truck. That should be safe, she thought.

The driver was a man of about thirty, a Latino of some kind, not like the Mexicans she'd seen around Tucson, but Puerto Rican, maybe Cuban, something.

It seemed he'd picked her up to scold her.

"What the hell you doing, picking up rides like this? Don't you know you get in trouble like this, picking up rides? What's the matter with you?"

"Oh!"

"Oh, what? What does that mean, 'Oh'?"

"What I mean is you don't look like that kind of person."

223

"How do you know? I'm not, but how the hell you know?"

"By looking at you. I can tell."

"You trying to tell me that when you saw me driving down the road before with the sun on my windshield you could tell what kind of person I was? What you think, I'm an idiot?"

"I certainly don't think that."

"What are you anyway—some kind of tramp?"

"Let me out here, please."

"I can't stop here. I'll let you out at the next light; there's a bus stop. You going to Tampa?"

"I guess so."

"You guess so! Jesus Christ! What you going to Tampa for? That's a very bad city."

"Shopping."

"For what?"

"A new dress. My, you're nosy."

"Well, you take a bus, hear!"

"You know, not everybody you pick up is a tramp."

"I got my own ideas."

"Well, they're wrong. I'm a married woman."

"Who isn't? What's that got to do with it?"

"A lot."

"Spending your husband's money, huh?"

"It's my own money. I earned it."

"Yeah? How? O.K., O.K. You earned it, never mind how. What's your husband think of you doing this? What he say about it?"

"I don't know."

"Does he know you do this?"

"I just happened to do it today. He trusts me."

"It isn't a matter of trusting you. It's me, the guy who picks you up. What about that? You trust me?"

"Now I do."

"Well, this time you're right, but—"

"People don't generally bother you unless you lead them on."

"What's the matter with you—don't you read the papers?"

"I'm not interested in politics."

"Who's talking politics? Don't you read what's happening? Everybody's going crazy this country. Here, look!"

He handed her the newspaper he was sitting on. She took it but didn't look at it.

"May I ask where you're from?"

"Santurce."

"San . . . ?"

"You so dumb you don't know where Santurce's at?"

"I'm pretty dumb about geography, yes."

"What are you?"

"A nurse."

"A nurse! My God! See what I mean, what's going on? A nurse! A pickup. Jesus!"

"So I haven't had a chance to travel much."

"You heard of Puerto Rico?"

"Of course I heard of Puerto Rico. I'm not that dumb."

"Anybody, I mean a lone girl, who stands out on a corner . . . ! If I was your husband, you know what I'd do with you?"

"Well, let's not go into that."

"I'd take you home right now and beat hell out of you."

"Are you married?"

"Sure I'm married. But my wife, she went crazy too. Everybody's gone crazy. Especially the women. You bitches!"

"Don't talk to me that way; you have no right to."

"Anybody who picks up rides on the open highway, I got a right."

"What happened to your wife?"

"I don't want to talk about her. She went home. She loves her popi more than she loves me."

"Well, it's nice to love your parents, but not more than your husband."

"Right, for a change."

"Is that really why she left you?"

"Well, what else you think?"

"I don't know. I was asking you."

"She don't like it here. She never made any friends, she says, nobody to talk to, she says. I told her, but I can't make a living in Santurce. Here maybe I can save a dollar."

"You seem to be . . . this is a nice pickup truck."

"I do pretty good, don't worry. Except today. Today's a shutout. Goose eggs. Zero!"

"I'm sorry."

"I want to kill everybody today."

"Is that why you've been so mean to me?"

"I'm only trying to make you understand how dangerous what you're doing is. For your own good."

"Oh, yeah; well, thanks."

"You just got me on a bad day."

"I can see that. What happened?"

"None of your business. Look in back."

Ethel turned in her seat and looked through the cab window. Then she turned and looked at him. She looked at his hands on the wheel. They were very strong and very heavy. Like Costa's hands.

"O.K."

"O.K. what?"

"I looked back."

"You seen those window bars?"

"Is that what they were?"

"You are stupid. Even for a girl. What do they look like to you?"

"Window bars, right?"

"Right. That's my trade. Here."

He reached up to where there was a hook over the windshield, ripped off a bill and handed it to her.

She read it out loud.

" 'Julio Ramirez—' "

"Say it 'Who-lee-oh,' for chrissake; say it right."

" 'Julio Ramirez. Ironwork. Made to your specifications.' "

"Go ahead. Read the rest."

" 'Screen porches, window bars, barbecue grills, custom-made, balcony railings, staircases—' "

"That's my specialty."

"Ninety-nine dollars! Is that for . . . ?"

"That sound like a lot to you?"

"I don't know."

"The way you said it, I thought maybe . . ."

"No, no."

"That is very cheap for the work I do. Look at those things."

"I can see there's a lot of work there."

"I get plenty orders, that's the proof. I got work for six months ahead. I'm making a beautiful staircase now, curved, like you could climb to heaven that way. But mostly window bars. See, this country now, she's full of criminals. Just like Puerto Rico. People are catching on what they have to do—bar everything on the ground floor."

"I see what you mean."

"What do I mean? You don't know what I mean."

"Well, maybe not exactly."

"Then what do you say it for?"

"I meant about the world being full of unhappy people. I see what you mean about that."

"Not only unhappy. Liars, thieves, terrible people. Criminals. Like this man"—he indicated his cargo in the back—"he had his house broken into four times. He

227

goes fishing, he comes home, the TV's gone; he goes to the track with his wife, her hair dryer's gone. So he comes to my shop. I show him what I been doing for this other fellow and he said O.K., me too, go ahead. So today I go there to put up these bars and he says, 'Take 'em out of here! You're making my house look like a jail,' he says."

"Oh, I see."

"You see nothing. So I said to him, 'You ordered them, here they are.' So he says, 'I don't want to live in a jail. I'd rather be robbed every day.'"

"I see."

"What? What you see?"

"About living in a jail."

"For chrissake, he ordered them! I showed him what they'd be!"

"I see what you mean."

"You see shit, excuse me. But *nada! Niente!* Nothing! You're so stupid. 'You live in a jungle,' I told this man, 'what do you want? You can't sleep, you look terrible, you got black circles under your eyes. When I put these bars in your windows, you and your wife sleep good for change, it's worth ninety—'"

"I know. Sleep is everything."

"You're so dumb. You American girls are so dumb."

"Puerto Rican girls are smarter?"

"No, they're worse. They love their popis more than their husbands."

"So why pick on me?"

"But at least with them, we keep them in line. You don't see any island girls picking up rides! Do you?"

"You didn't keep your wife in line, it looks like, excuse me."

"Don't play games with me, young lady, don't make fun of me!"

"I'm not making fun—"

"I ought to take you home and beat hell out of you so you don't go around getting picked up. I don't want you to do that again, ever again."

Ethel looked back through the cab window.

"You do nice work," she said.

"How can you tell? What the hell you know about nice work?"

"I just look at them and they're nice."

"You should see my staircase I'm making. Then you be right. This is nothing, this in the back. Heavy! Clumsy! What the hell can you do artistic with window bars? The man was right not to want them in front of his windows. I made them too heavy."

"That's nice."

"What's nice?"

"That you admit that, that you turn around."

"I don't turn around. They're good enough for him. He's built like a pig, you should see, a big heavy man; those bars perfect for him."

Ethel burst out laughing. This freak delighted her. He freed her of worries.

"What you laughing at?" he demanded.

"The way you talk. You're an artist, all right."

"What do you know?"

"Can I watch you work?"

"What?"

"I'd like to—"

"No."

"Just for a little while."

"What've you got in mind?"

"Nothing. I think that stuff is beautiful, the way those bars are turned."

"I thought maybe you had something else in mind."

"What else? Oh, that? No, I don't do that."

"Because I don't have time for that stuff."

"I know."

"And I don't like—" He stopped.

"What? What don't you like?"

"Fresh girls. You know, smart?"

"I'm not a fresh girl."

"All the girls around here, they come inside my shop, hang around, hang around. 'What the hell you want!' I yell. 'Nothing,' they say. 'Nothing. Just looking, O.K.?' They just looking shit, man."

Then he noticed she was crying.

"Now whatsa matter with you?" he demanded.

"You have no right to be mean to me. Why do you talk to me that way? I haven't done you any harm. How can you be so rude to me?"

"I'm sorry," he said, "but you know what I mean?"

"No, I don't know what you mean. I don't like that, when people are rude to me. I don't know why people can't be decent to each other. It's tough enough living anyway, without all that rudeness all the time."

"You can say that again, kid."

"So just be nice to me, will you?"

"O.K., come watch me."

"No, forget it."

"I like you to come watch me, please O.K.?"

"Only if you really—"

"I really want you to, O.K.?"

She didn't say anything, looked out the side window.

"You married, or something?"

"I told you."

"I mean the truth."

"I really am."

"You love your husband?"

"Very, very much."

"I hope so."

"He's a wonderful man, my husband."

"Then what the hell he lets you run around getting into trouble?"

"I'm not getting into any trouble."

"Because you're lucky, because it's me, because I know what's right. But suppose it had been someone else? Bang!"

"If it was somebody else, I wouldn't be going to his house—I mean, where you work."

He didn't say anything for a while, then: "You better get off here. Bus stop. O.K.?"

Ethel didn't answer. She laid her head back on the top of the soft warm seat, closed her eyes and let the jogging of the truck take her over.

He didn't stop.

His place was an abandoned horse barn that had been turned into a garage, then given up because it was made of wood and didn't have metal fittings or the concrete base necessary for the heavy machinery used in a modern garage. But the place was perfect for Julio.

He was pounding a four-by-four iron bar into flat pieces, which he cut and fitted to the sides of his curved staircase, working at an open coke fire, with tongs and an anvil, a hammer like a metal fist and a great container of water. Always a confident man when he worked, he was now showing off a little for Ethel.

"I can get along without her, all right, my wife. But my kid, I miss hell out of my kid, all the time, goddamn her—my wife, I mean."

He pounded the piece, flatter and flatter, then held it up, then put it down and pounded it again.

"What's her name?" Ethel shouted.

"My daughter? Ciela."

"That is beautiful. See-el-ah!"

"Right. You got any kids?"

Pound, pound!

"We just got married."

He threw his hammer down, inspected the piece of flatware and approved of it.

"Ciela! You know what that means?"

"Tell me."

"See that?" He held it up for her to see. It was red hot. "See that curve? Perfect. Even, man! Smooth!"

"It's beautiful."

"Ciela! Heaven. Like you say heavenly, right?"

"That's beautiful, Ciela."

"I'll show you her picture later."

"You look hot," she said. "Can I get you a drink of water?"

"Yeah. Upstairs. I live upstairs. Go ahead up. Nobody there."

While he was working another strip, she tiptoed around his living quarters. There was a little kitchen where he ate and a bedroom. The bed was unmade. She made it.

As she did she remembered that the panties she'd put on that morning were old and frayed and the waistband had come loose.

On the bureau was a picture of a young woman, also Puerto Rican, she thought, holding an infant child. Ciela.

"That's a pretty kid you got there," she said to Julio as she gave him his drink.

"Yeah, a good kid. She's four years old by now."

"Your wife has a nice face?" Ethel said, asking a question.

"I used to think so. But she go home to the island. She says, 'When you save enough dollar come get me; I'll be there.' Meantime, I hear she's already with someone else. Women got to have somebody. That's how they are. The truth is she likes her parents better than me. So all right, stay with them, do what you want, be happy, like you said, tough all over. Right? Look out!"

He plunged the turned piece of strip metal into the water. It sizzled, then hissed, then it was still.

"Right," Ethel said.

"Where's your husband?"

"He's in the Navy."

"You like him?"

"I told you. I love him. What do you think?"

"I think what I still think. When you have to go?"

"What time is it?"

"One. I stop for lunch now."

"I have to go."

"Just when I'm stopping? Wait till after lunch. O.K.?"

"O.K."

"I wash my hands."

He pounced on the stairs; they shook as he mounted them.

Ethel knew it was now or never.

"Come up here," he called.

Ethel didn't answer.

"Come on. Come on. I haven't got all day. . . ."

Costa was speaking to her. "So what you do all day?" he said. The dinner was stewed lamb, covered with greens, the inevitable rice, and yogurt.

"I took in a movie."

"Foolishness." Costa chewed. "Waste of money."

"What'd you see?" Noola asked.

"Frank Sinatra and Cary Grant pulling a cannon all over the place. Spain, I think it was supposed to be."

Ethel couldn't tell if Noola believed her. The woman wore a veil in front of her husband.

Costa ate without speaking. Ethel noticed his hands again. They were big and heavy and strong like Julio's.

Why should Noola believe her? She'd seen the film in San Diego months before and noticed it was advertised in yesterday's paper.

Or was it in Sunday's paper?

"What's the matter, Ethel? What you dreaming?" Noola was judging her openly now.

"Why?"

"The way you looking, at nothing? What you thinking?"

Ethel hoped the film was still playing. Did Noola know enough about movies to know whether or not . . .

"I was thinking how nice you two are," she said.

"Compliments aren't necessary in a family," Noola said. "Besides, we're not all that nice. Nobody is."

Ethel reached across and gently ran her palm over Costa's hand.

"I love your hands," she said. "They make me feel safe."

Costa shrugged, picked up a chop bone, gnawed on it.

She had to get rid of that Sunday newspaper. She knew where it was, the amusement section—on the TV, folded to the page where the week's programs were listed.

"When you going tomorrow?" Noola asked.

"My plane is at five. Costa, maybe you could drive me."

"Costa doesn't drive. Didn't you notice?"

"I find that damn Levendis," Costa said without interrupting his ingestion of food.

Had Noola noticed her new dress? Ethel wondered. She'd found one very close in cut and color to the one Julio had ruined. Noola's eyes hadn't lingered on it. She probably hadn't noticed.

"What you thinking now? Dreaming again?" Noola was smiling—was it affectionately?

Ethel hadn't realized how long they'd gone without talking.

"There are terrible people in that city," Ethel said.

"Clearwater is a very nice city," Noola said.

"Plenty Greeks over there." Costa kept on eating.

"I'm talking about Tampa."

"I tol' you don't go Tampa." Costa stopped chewing and looked at her sternly. "Didn't I tell you that?"

"Well, I went. But when I saw the people in that city, my God! You're right."

"Sure I'm right."

"Where'd you buy the new dress?" Noola asked.

"I forgot the name of the store. Right in the middle of the city. There's a label in the back, if you really want to know."

"You didn't bring the other dress back, the one you were wearing."

"I threw it away. I was sick and tired of it. Who's Saint Jude, by the way?"

Costa broke off a heavy crust of bread and began to wipe up the gravy on his plate. "Who knows?" he said. "Some kind Roman saint."

"Oh, Saint Jude!" Julio had said. "Oh, God! Mother of God!"

"Who's Saint Jude?" she'd asked him. "I know who the other two are."

He was lying on his back, she up on an elbow, looking at him. She knew there was something mocking about her expression, because what she was thinking was: How did I ever come to take up with this man?

"Saint Jude is the saint of the impossible. That's you —impossible!"

Ethel, at the dinner table, smiled. She remembered she'd been pleased.

"I thought a girl like you, she was impossible for me to get," Julio had said.

"I think he's the saint of lost causes," Noola said.

"My beautiful new girl." Julio smiled at her. He was already possessive, Ethel noticed.

"Why do you ask that?" Noola said.

"That what?"

235

"Why are you asking about Saint Jude all of a sudden?"

"I saw a lot of him in Tampa, in the windows there—pictures and little statues and tall colored glasses of wax, like candles. A light for Saint Jude. We all need him."

"O.K., finish!" Costa announced, and pushed his plate away.

"You finished?" Noola asked Ethel.

Ethel handed over her plate.

"You didn't eat much," Noola said. She was about to scrape what Ethel had left onto her own plate so she could stack them. "You sure you had enough, Ethel?"

"Yes," Ethel said. "I'm finished."

"I'm not finished," Julio had said. "Don't get up."

"What time is it?"

"What's the difference? You know something? Your cunt, it's orange. I seen a lot but I never seen that before—inside, I mean. And you have so little hair there, like a baby girl, like my Ciela, almost. And inside it's orange too. Our women are so heavy there, the hair, so dark and thick."

Noola got up from the table, carrying the dishes into the kitchen.

Ethel remembered it was then she had got up to go.

"Don't go," Julio had said. This time it was more like an order.

"I've got to."

"You don't got to do nothing."

He'd tried to pull her down onto the bed again.

"Don't. Please. That hurt."

He'd let her go and was quite apologetic; he hadn't turned mean yet.

"Stay awhile," he'd said. "I won't work anymore today. I won't ever work again if you stay with me. How about that?"

She was looking for her bra in the rumpled bed.

"I really have to go. Excuse me."

"When you coming back?"

"I'm not."

"Yes you are. You have to."

"I don't have to do anything."

"What's the matter—you don't like me?"

"I like you all right."

"You better."

"You know the thing I like best about you?"

"What thing?"

"Your hands."

"What's the matter with the rest of . . . you know?"

"Nothing. I just like your hands. Here it is. Excuse me."

He moved so she could pull her bra from under the pillow. She noticed when she'd said that about preferring his hands, his cock had suddenly grown smaller. What a strange little device a penis is, she thought. So easily upset. Now she remembered she'd laughed when she'd noticed it shrinking as if it were beating a retreat.

"What are you laughing at?" He covered himself there with a sheet.

"Oh, my own crazy head."

"You ever been fucked before like me? Tell me the truth? I'll bet you never was, huh? What you say?"

She bent over and dropped her breasts into the cups of her bra, then straightened up and reached behind for the clip.

"You looking for compliments?" she said.

"Sure. Why not? The truth."

"Well, which? The truth? My experience is that most men do it just about the same way, a little frantic, as if they don't really like it or aren't sure it will stay up. So they pitch as fast as they can; we catch if we can."

"So that's the way God made us."

"Blame it on God."

"Nature."

"And nature." She was looking for her panties.

"Well, kid, leave us face it, you got nothing to fuck with."

"I could say something, but I won't."

"What the hell are you—one of those women wishes she was a man?"

"Probably." She'd found her shoes.

"That's what I think—you're one of those."

"I'm really not one of those anything."

Oh, forget the panties, she'd thought. They're shot anyway. She picked her dress off the floor and turned it around in her hands.

"I know what you are—you're one of those women who needs a different guy every night to turn her on. Maybe that's it, huh?"

"I told you I'm not one of those anything. Don't! Don't ever do that!"

Up out of bed, he'd tried to grab her.

She'd pulled her hand out of his grip.

"I knew what you were the minute you climbed into my cab."

"Well, you were wrong."

She was putting on her dress, buttoning it quickly.

"All you cracker bitches are the same. I knew what you had in mind from the first minute."

"I really didn't, you know. I didn't have the least idea—"

"I feel sorry for your husband," he said, pulling on his trousers.

"Good-bye."

"You better fix your hair, because now you look like what you are."

She went to the mirror quickly.

He'd gone to the open sink in the corner. Standing on

tiptoe, he had his cock out through his fly and was soaping it.

"Yeah, I pity your husband," he said. "If you really got one."

"I really have one and he doesn't need your pity."

"He must be some kind of faggot!"

She picked a bottle up off the floor and flung it at him.

"Don't you dare say that! He's worth twenty of you, any day, any day. There isn't a mean bone in his body!"

That's when he'd come after her again, and she didn't want to remember that.

Noola came back from the kitchen to gather up the rest of the dishes.

"Most people are mean," Ethel said to her, "but you know, there isn't a mean bone in Teddy's body."

"So then why did you come here?"

"I told you: I just wanted to know you two a little better. But I'm going back tomorrow." She'd had her fill of Noola's prying.

"Get to know Teddy better first," Noola said.

"Noola! Stop it!" Costa intervened. "Go fix coffee!"

The table was clear and Noola left the room.

"She love her son," Costa apologized. "She's a good woman." He looked at his watch. "Nine o'clock. Wrestling," he said, and left the room.

"What happened to you today, Ethel?" Noola was back, folding the tablecloth. "Something happen to you today?"

"Just what I told you," Ethel said. "I don't know what you mean."

"I don't know what I mean," Noola said, "but you know. You look so pale. Eh? What happened? Nothing? O.K., then nothing."

She put the tablecloth in the heavy oak cabinet and went into the kitchen.

Ethel was alone again and her breath was coming faster. She looked at the framed photograph of Teddy on the wall.

"Maybe your husband don't need my pity," Julio had said. "Maybe he needs yours—what you say to that?"

"Nothing."

She'd done the best she could with her hair, but it was still a mess. She'd stop and buy a hairbrush and go into the ladies' room of the bus station.

"Good-bye," she said on her way to the door.

"You forgot your pants."

"Where are they, you know?"

"Maybe you don't need them, huh?"

He'd washed off his cock and was drying it in a towel.

"Look in the bed," he said.

Ethel pulled the sheet off.

"Hey, what the hell—don't throw that sheet on the floor. I got to sleep on that damn sheet!"

"Sorry."

"There they are, on the other side, on the floor."

He was looking his cock over before putting it away.

Ethel turned her panties right side front and began to put them on.

"What you so high-class about? Turning your back, for chrissake. I seen your front; it's orange. Why all the manners suddenly?"

"Next time," she said, "wash before you make love to a lady, not after."

"I don't notice no lady around here, just a bitch dog in heat; maybe you mean her?"

"What does that make you?"

"Never mind about me. I know what I am. Shit, like you."

"Speak for yourself."

Picking up her purse—she'd almost forgotten that too —she was ready to go.

"You're just like my wife, look like one of those baby angels over the altar in the church. Can't wait to get home to mummy and popi. 'I'm waiting for you,' she writes me. Then I get the news. She waited, all right; two weeks she waited."

"Maybe part of that was your fault. Ever think of that?"

"She goes for the whole thing—mass every Sunday, communion, confession, catechism school, every night pray before she get into bed. You think she pray before she give it to this fellow?"

"So we're all phonies, but you men, you—"

"Yeah, I seen them all, but no one as big a phony as you, baby. You really stink!"

She turned and hit him across the face with her purse.

"Good shot!" he said, smiling. "Yeah, you're the champ! 'I like to watch people work,' for chrissake. How many times you said that before, lady?"

"Good-bye."

"You like to watch me work again? Hah?"

"I know how you work."

"But if you hit me, that mean you want to watch me work some more—what you say to that? Hey, I'm talking to you."

He took her by the arm, pulled her around, looked at her, nodding his head in recognition.

"I think I treated you too good before. Now I'll show you what you really are."

"Don't do that."

"Because in your heart you're a pig, see? 'I like to see how people work,' for chrissake! O.K., you asked for it."

"Stop it, stop it! I don't want you anymore."

"Yeah, you're just like my wife—turn me on, turn me off, like a faucet. Now! Not now! Come on! Stop it! Shit, lady!"

"You're ripping my dress."

"Fuck your dress."

He pulled at her and she kneed him in the groin.

"Stop it, goddamn you," she said. "What do you think I am?"

"I know what you are. Good, hit me. Go on. Hit me again!"

"Don't! I won't be able to go out on the street—"

"I'm ruining your dress? So take it off."

He let her go for an instant. She dashed for the door. He caught her and flung her on the bed.

"O.K., then don't take it off. Leave it on. I don't take off my pants either. See, here, here, see it? Now come on."

He stood her on the back of her neck as he pulled off her panties. Her legs flailed in the air.

She lay back, covered her eyes with her forearm. What difference did it make now? If she fought anymore, she'd have marks on her face and body she wouldn't be able to explain. The other would wash away.

Eyes closed, silent, she waited for it to be over. . . .

Eyes closed, silent, she could hear the wrestling matches from the other room.

"I made for you too," Noola said as she passed from the kitchen to the front room, carrying coffee to her husband.

"Thank you," Ethel said, following to where Noola had set down the small gilt-rimmed cup full of the sweet thick coffee.

"I'll help you with the dishes," she said to Noola.

"Not necessary. They're almost done," Noola said as she left the room.

Ethel reminded herself to be sure to take the amusement section of the Sunday paper when she went to bed.

The coffee was too hot to drink. Costa blew across the mouth of his cup to cool it, then sipped noisily. He was fascinated by the gross jolly giants slamming each other to the mat and clubbing each other with fist and elbow. Ethel knew it was a fake, but the contestants performed cleverly, struggled convincingly.

She'd struggled when he'd turned her over and pushed her, face down, on the bed. "You're an animal," he'd said. "This is how they do it to animals." He'd clubbed her across the shoulders with his fist to make her hold still.

"That hurts! Don't do that. I hate that!"

"Now you won't forget me, bitch!"

"That hurts!"

"Remember next time wash before you fuck a man, not after."

Ethel put her hand in her mouth and bit down on it.

"Now where's your popi, bitch? Come on, let me hear you holler. Popi! Popi! Help! Help!" Then he was screaming his rage in Spanish and Ethel didn't know what he was saying.

Below, someone was knocking at the door.

"Ramirez! Hey, you crazy Ramirez, you gone crazy again? You all right up there, Ramirez?"

"Get the fuck away from my door. Sure I'm all right. Get away!"

Ethel's face was buried in the sheet. She didn't move.

Suddenly Julio got off her, sitting up and examining his cock.

"Goddamn it! Look what you did!"

He went to the open sink, let his trousers down over his buttocks, spreading his legs to hold them up. He soaped again, rinsing himself, then examined a small cut, frowning and cursing.

She was going over her dress. It was badly mauled and she'd not worn a slip.

"Goddamn you," he said. "You cut me."

"How'm I going to get out of here?" Ethel said, speaking to herself. "Look at this dress!"

"Bitch! You bitch!" Holding his wet and bleeding cock, he walked to the industrial medicine cabinet on the wall near the open toilet bowl, found a roll of inch-and-a-half gauze, began to wrap it around his penis.

She needed to use a washcloth. Turning to the open sink, she saw what Julio was doing.

"What happened?"

"I'm cut. The zipper."

"I suppose that was my fault."

He put his cock, now a roll of bandage, back in his pants and zipped up. "Come on, get out of here," he said. "I got work to do."

"Could I use the sink for a minute?"

"No."

"Look at this dress. Have you got a pin or something? How'm I going to get out of here?"

"The same way you came in. Come on, get out before I kill you."

Outside, the sun was a bully.

Walking in small steps down the street, she could feel his stuff running out of her. Her whole crotch felt sticky.

At the bus stop she adjusted her dress again, getting a new hold to keep it together.

She took the first bus that came by. It took her to the heart of St. Petersburg, deserted at this time of day, a square without shadows, surrounded by a department store, an office tower and a great newspaper building, all of a light color. They flung the sun's heat at whoever was exposed in the middle space.

The new dress she bought was the nearest thing she could find to the one she had to throw away.

When Costa was asleep in his chair, Noola, who'd been darning his heavy white socks, got up and turned off the wrestling matches. The only sound in the house came from the hot-water heater in the kitchen.

The quiet disturbed Costa. He rose to his feet and, like a child going off to bed already asleep, he left the room.

Noola began to pick up the coffee cups.

"When I was a girl in Astoria," she said, "there was a terrible accident in our neighborhood. I was in the house and I heard the crash from the other side of Ditmars Boulevard and I ran out and down the block. It was a Greek boy, who went to the same school I did. He'd driven his uncle's car into the telegraph pole in front of old Saint Demitrios, our church where it was those days by the Pennsylvania Railroad tracks. The *despoti* pronounced it a miracle from our saint because the boy walked out without a scratch even though the car was a complete wreck. I remember how he was, the boy, standing on the sidewalk, his face white as a sheet of paper, as pale as you are now, that's what reminded me. You didn't drink you coffee."

"That's all right, take it. Was he drunk, the boy, because sometimes when they're drunk . . . ?"

"No, he was just accident prone, they call it, because about a year later, he had another accident, only this time it wasn't in front of old Saint Demitrios church and there was no miracle. They had to take the boy out of that car piece by piece."

She took the cups to the kitchen, came back, picked the weekend amusement section off the top of the TV cabinet, said, "There's plenty of hot water, why don't you take a bath?" and followed her husband into the back of the house.

While the tub filled, Ethel went over her body, looking for giveaways. She didn't fine any, only some reddish spots which she knew from experience would be gone in the morning.

She washed her hair in the sink, using Johnson's baby shampoo, after which she lay in the tub, her fine hair floating on the steaming water. She eased the soreness by pressing a hot washcloth against the place.

Then she turned over, face submerged, and stayed that way as long as she could hold her breath. She felt the way she felt all the worst times of her life when she didn't know for weeks at a time why she did what she did.

eleven

THE next morning, Costa found a way to prolong her visit.

He arranged to take Ethel to the Tampa airport by boat. "Not exactly there," he told her, "but from where I put you down, you will take taxi easy."

"Won't Noola be angry?"

"How can she be angry? Noola!"

"You've hardly been to the store since I got here."

"For thirty years who brought the bread? And the meat and the oil? She know those things, she say nothing."

They went down the Anclote River at half throttle. Their crew was Aleko the Levendis and an old sponger captain with one eye. The surface of the water was smooth as a piece of taut gray cloth.

"Hot day coming," the one-eyed man, at the tiller, said.

They made the turn south and followed the coastline

about half a mile offshore. Ahead, on their left, was Dunedin beach.

"I used to own most of that beach, damn fool," Aleko the Levendis muttered. "Thirty years ago, I sold her for nothing. Oh, the mistakes I made are many and when I remember them they bring me sorrow."

Ethel walked up front, where she'd be alone.

There were fishermen in small skiffs and a couple in an ordinary rowboat. Occasionally she saw them bring up fish.

Her body still felt sore. She wished she had another day before she had to report home.

Ethel had had experience before with the self-destruct button in her psyche. Now she was feeling the morning-after panic.

Noola hadn't kissed her when she left. That was the tradition, the double kiss; it was routine. But Noola hadn't offered.

And the big man sitting on the stern rail watching her, calm as the belly of water they were on. He was on her side now, but if he should ever turn against her!

When they talked, Ethel wondered, what did Noola say about her?

After all, Noola had been brought up in Astoria, Queens, had gone to a New York public school, had heard the talk in the girls' toilet. Some of her classmates must have been kids like Ethel.

Costa moved closer, sat on the cabin top.

"I wish you'd brought me up," she said to him.

"So now I bring you up," he said.

"I will do anything you want," she said. "Only tell me what you want."

"You know what I want!"

"As soon as I'm out of the Navy! But I'm talking about every day. That is what I need from Teddy, that he tells me every day how he wants me to be. Like the double line in the middle of the highway on a curve that says don't cross over—"

She stopped; she was getting close to a total confession and Costa wouldn't . . . couldn't . . .

"He will tell you."

"He doesn't."

"Not in words. What you expect? I don't tell Noola in words. But she knows. So you must know what Teddy want. You're a woman, you can tell. You sleep with him, you eat with him, you know when he's happy, now you know his father, you know how boy was when he was young, what I taught him—"

"Yes, yes, I see, but— Yes."

She turned her head and looked over the heavy still water and the birds working it. Tucson, of course, didn't have this variety, so she didn't know their names. Except for the pelicans. They looked so awkward, so ill-put-together in the air. But the instant they made that half turn and tipped over to plunge, great beak first, into the sea and out of sight, they were the perfect fishing machine.

There were others, gallant little birds, flying patterns as erratic as those bats fly at night, and nipping at the surface. Like tiny broken kites they were; she felt close to them.

"What are those little ones?"

"Terns."

"And what are they after?"

"Big fish chase bait fish to surface. Birds wait."

Completely at ease now, she stretched out on the deck. Overhead, the gulls kept a course.

"The gulls fly straight," she said, "as if they're going somewhere. How do they know where to go?"

"God teach 'em," Costa said.

She turned over and lay on her belly, hung her head over the side and watched the furrow of water being turned up.

How safe she felt with Costa. There wasn't anything in the world she wanted at this instant except to stay on that boat.

She was about to say, "I don't want to go back," but she didn't. He would take it as what it was, a slur on his son.

"The men in the little boat, they're getting some fish," she said. Costa was smoking the cigar she'd brought him from Tampa.

"Soon, nothing," he said, pointing.

Some large fish were breaking water, not so many as a school, a family.

"What are they?"

"Porpoise. They clean out the fish, leave nothing. Vacuum cleaner. See?"

Several of the fishermen had sighted the porpoise. They were starting their outboards and leaving the vicinity.

The porpoise were all around the boat now. Ethel pulled herself forward on her belly to the very prow of the boat. She hung her head over the rail and there was one of the mammals swimming in perfect formation with their boat. And now another at its side. She could hear them breathing. How effortlessly they moved. She thought they were making some kind of reach for companionship, the way they stayed alongside, rolling from side to side to catch her eye.

"They're looking up at me," she said. "I mean, they're looking right at me."

There were sounds of a squabble from the men in the back.

"What are they fighting about back there?"

"Foolishness. Woman been dead twenty year."

Again the lead porpoise looked up and directly into her eye.

"Oh, they're trying to make friends!" she said.

"When we came to this country," Costa said, "they

were our first friend. Everybody else 'gainst us. When we were on the bottom and we see porpoise in the water, we know, right away, no shark come near."

Then she said it. "I don't want to go back."

He didn't say what she feared he might. He didn't say anything.

"I never had a real family before," she said.

"You make your own family now," he said. "This is your chance."

This is your chance? Of course. Noola had spoken to him.

She decided not to push the subject.

The porpoise had vanished.

Costa got up and walked to the stern of the boat. She heard him talking to the others in Greek.

The motor stopped. Costa came forward and threw the anchor over the bow. "There's reef here," he said. "We catch lunch."

The first few they used for chum and strip bait. Then they began to fuss around the reef, Costa looking through a glass-bottom barrel, till they found a good spot. In ten minutes they had thirty fish, most of them, Costa said, baby grouper.

A big black pot was steaming over a brazier of charcoal; she could smell the bubbling olive oil. The one-eyed tillerman threw a couple of handfuls of flour into a bowl. The fish were powdered, then dropped into the hot savory oil. The men ate the fish, head and all. The head of the fish, Costa explained, is good for the human brain.

Wine they all drank out of the same bottle.

After lunch, Ethel fell asleep on the foredeck. When she woke they were passing under a great bridge, arched high enough to permit oceangoers to pass through.

She turned her head and there was Costa, smiling at her. But his eyes were stern.

"Where are we?" she asked.

"Tampa Bay," he said. Then he said what he'd been thinking. "Most things we have to do in life, we don't want to do."

She looked around. They were getting close. To something.

"I've got to talk to you," she said. "You can help me."

He nodded, waited.

"Let's pretend we have an accident," she said, trying to sweep him along with something like gaiety. "We'll spend the evening together, go to that Spanish restaurant, the one in Ybor City with the beautiful light fixtures where you used to go for girls when you were young—"

"Who told you that?"

"Ted."

"How he know what I do before he was born?"

"What about what I said?"

"Teddy waiting for you."

Still she could see he liked the idea.

"I'll call him," she pressed. "He's home studying every night. You'll talk to him, he'll know it's legitimate. We don't have to explain everything, do we?"

"Your husband, you have to explain everything."

She got herself together and made a fresh start.

"I don't want to go back," she said. "I want to stay here with you."

"You have to be where your husband is, what are you talking?"

She'd overstepped, but she didn't care.

"I'm afraid something bad is going to happen."

"Trust Teddy, tell him, you can always trust Teddy."

She could see that the old man was bewildered and puzzled; he was out of his depth. "Go back," he said. "Find out what he wants. Do it."

She was on the verge of telling him everything.

"I'm not strong, you know, I'm not a strong girl."

"You be all K. when you have children."

"You really believe that?"

"When you have children, it's simple, the life."

"I came into the world without a book of instructions," she said. "I keep thinking there is something I should be doing that I'm not."

"No one knows what they supposed to do. But for a woman, more easy. She's suppose continue the family. Make new ones better than the old ones, little smarter, little stronger. When you done that, you die happy."

"You think I can teach children how they're supposed to be when I don't know myself?"

She could see that for the first time he was frightened.

"Tell me," she said. "Tell me the truth."

"When you look into child face, you will know what you must tell him. Everything will be clear then because your purpose in life will be clear. That is what you've been put on earth for."

"Just that?"

"Just that. Whatsa matter your father—he teach you nothing?"

"You teach me. I don't believe him. I believe you."

"Otherwise you go each day like the weather—here, there, every day different. You believe one simple thing, the rest easy. You are here to continue my family. In the church, you said O.K., I take that job. That is very important for me. I know my family, who it was, the names, the places, the houses, the work they do, for hundreds of years. When you marry in my family, that is what I expect from you. That! Nothing else! Don't play games with that! Don't fool around! Or, believe me, I—I don't want to be mad at you."

She looked at the heavy gray water.

"You understand what I say to you?"

"Yes."

"You believe?"

"I do."

"Give me your word you believe, and because you believe that's what you will do."

"I will do my best."

"Never mind your best! Not good enough so far. You have to grow, be bigger, stronger, in my family, bigger, stronger."

"I'm afraid all the time. Why am I afraid? Of what?"

"Of yourself."

"That's right."

"And because you are alone. You marry in church, O.K., but in your heart, not yet. You must go back and marry in your heart. Don't need damn fool priest for that. Now I want your word."

"What word?"

"That you will do that."

"I will try."

"Never mind those American words: 'I will try!' 'sort of'—that's monkey business over there. Let's hear: I will do it. I promise, I will do it."

"O.K."

"No. 'O.K.' monkey business. I want the words, the same words I say."

They were inside the bay now. A little wind had come up and the water was lively without being rough.

"I will do it," she said.

She kissed him. That settled it.

As they moved in to dock, she went close to him and said, "I love you."

"I don't want you love me," he answered. "I want you obey my son."

twelve

S HE saw Teddy was thinner. As he drove, street lights passed in strobe slow motion across his face and there were hollows under his eyes.

As she churned on, she considered his hands on the wheel. They were not Costa's, they were Noola's; not a sailor's, an officer's. She ran her hand over his as she talked on about her cooking lessons and Costa's reaction to the one meal she'd prepared.

At their intersection, Teddy turned the car away from their old place.

"Where we going?" she asked.

"Home."

"Where's home?"

"You'll see."

Content to leave it at that, she told him about each Greek dish she'd made, each kitchen technique she'd learned.

As she went on, she imagined his hands on her, hers

on him. This fantasy took place in a soft, dark place where lights were deflected and sounds muffled.

"Everything your mother taught me, I wrote down. I'll show you my notebook."

She'd make him know she loved him. Did she? She could. They still had a chance.

"It all starts with olive oil," she said. "Every dish!"

She'd run her hands slowly over his chest and along where the ribs showed. She'd pass down his slightly raised belly, back up, then down into the pubic hair which sprouted out of the pale olive skin. She'd be gentle with his cock, fondle it lightly. She'd run her fingers under his bag, scramble his stones gently.

Was he smiling? Had he guessed what she was thinking?"

"And if it isn't onions, it's garlic. I love garlic now."

And when it came up, his cock, she'd let it go down again. She'd teach him not to rush. A girl in Tucson had told her it was like training a dog to wait for its food. You had to train your husband not to gobble. Call it tease, call it technique; she'd tease him, she'd change his technique.

"Yogurt! I can make our own now," she heard herself saying. "It's better than the stuff that girls eats on the tube. You'll see."

They'd couple, not fuck. She'd make him different from all the others she'd known. She'd make him into the lover she needed.

"I learned to make the plain kind. No flavor is the flavor I like best."

Not like Ernie, not like Aaron, not like Julio—oh, God, no! Teddy wouldn't—well, he never had, he never took her that way. What a word: "Took"! All those male fantasies. Bang her! Ram it in! Split her with your tool. Fuck her to death! No; they'd couple, they'd join in love.

"I'll make some tomorrow," she said. "You'll see what I mean."

She'd start anew and he'd start anew. She saw the tableau of their joined equal bodies.

"And I think I finally learned the trick of rice."

Not an animal pitching as hard and as fast as he could, she catching what she could. She'd make everything right. This was their big chance, maybe their last chance.

They were winding through green now. He hadn't reacted to anything she'd said—not that reactions were called for. He looked determined and she had no idea about what.

Now she recognized the surroundings. They were climbing into the Mission Hill district, an area of old houses and new condominiums.

Still filling the void, she told him about Aleko and his mistress.

The condominium they were approaching was the one she'd been supposed to sign for the day she'd disappeared.

"He'll never marry her," Teddy said. "Greeks don't divorce. Did she sing for you?"

"Oh, yes! It killed me, the way they were together!"

He banged on the brakes. They were in a slip marked by two heavy yellow lines on the ground. He got out of the car, pulled out her bag and slammed the door. He seemed wrought up, ready for a fight.

She knew where she was now. The elevator whistled as it mounted; she remembered that and how the corridor was lit by units in the baseboard so people passing by seemed to float.

He opened the door and, as he pulled out his key, stepped aside, an officer at a ceremony, opening a passage for an honored guest.

She passed through and found a lamp.

"Can I put this on?"

"Sure."

He'd furnished the place entirely with unpainted furniture.

She crossed to where he waited, at attention, and put up her lips.

He kissed her quickly, then turned on the overhead light.

"Want to see the rest of the place?" he said.

"In a minute."

She sat on the sofa, indicated the place at her side by laying her palm on it, and waited for him to come to her.

He sat on the armchair opposite, the light from the one-hundred-fifty watt bulb beating down on his head. She saw he was still getting up steam for something.

Then he went out of the room and when he came back he was holding a large Manila envelope. Pulling out a typed form, he laid it on the coffee table in front of her.

"It's for a year," he said. "I signed it."

"Well, then, fine," she said.

He slid the form back into the Manila envelope and again sat in the armchair opposite her.

"How do I look?" he asked.

"Thinner. Beautiful."

"Beautiful, for chrissake."

"You're becoming an officer."

"Not yet. But I'm studying. Hard. The ed officer has really taken an interest in me."

He did look different: crisper, tauter, better put together, very determined, an elite person. All of which made her want him with his clothes off as quickly as possible. They had to break down the fences between them.

"We're going to talk first," he said.

It was an order.

"O.K.," she said. "Can I turn off this bright light?"

"I'll do it."

She watched him move through the unpainted furniture, arranged at right angles, the area in the middle bound by heavy wooden arms and straight, square-cut legs.

"What did my father say?" he asked as he sat again.

"What about?"

"You wrote me you went there to talk to him."

"Oh, yes, sure."

"Is that really why you left here?"

She saw he was struggling with an unreleased question.

"Did you . . . ?" he said.

"Did I what?"

"See Ernie?"

"Ernie!"

"I'm trying to find out why you suddenly ran out on me the way you did; I mean, the real reason."

"Baby, Ernie lives in Arizona. I went to Florida."

"You said you did it to find out what you wanted— something like that. Did you? Find out?"

"Teddy, give me time. Don't crowd me, Teddy."

"O.K."

"Want some coffee?"

"Why not?"

She put the kitchen light on. When she'd first seen the breakfast alcove, she remembered, she'd liked it; it had a wide window to the east. Now it looked crowded, with an unpainted table and four straight-back chairs.

"Where's the measuring spoon?" she called out.

"I've been guessing," he answered from the other room.

"Turn on some music, why don't you?"

She heard him get up and move.

"How do you like the place? You didn't say."

"I like it."

"But you didn't say that."

"Before I left, I said it."

"But then you disappeared. How do you like the way I got it fixed up?"

"All this furniture—you bought it?"

"There was a sale." He came to the kitchen doorway. "I got it cheap. I thought maybe painting it all white . . . You don't like it?" He laughed. "It's like a hospital, huh?"

"Can I push it around a little?"

"Do whatever you want. It's your place."

"Same stuff in the bedroom?"

"Yeah. I put a sheet of plywood under one half of the bed. I know you like yours soft."

"Let's take a look. Come on."

"I have something to say to you first."

The coffeepot was on and the heat under it. She turned to where he was standing in the doorway and leaned against him, putting her knee between his, and kissed him. His lips didn't give.

"Can't we talk after?" she said. "It's always nice when we talk in bed. I missed you, Teddy; I've thought about you a lot."

"I want to talk now. Right now."

She sat in the armchair he'd occupied. He sat in the middle of the sofa, on its edge, and leaned over, elbows on knees, head down.

"O.K.," she said. "Go ahead."

"A lot happened to me while you were gone."

"What's her name?"

"Not that. But something like."

"Like what?"

"One night I was sitting in the Ship's Bell, at that table in the back where we used to sit—remember?"

"I remember."

"I guess I was looking kinda sad, because she came over, this girl, sat next to me and put her lips against my cheek and kissed me, and God, I thought, God, there was so much sympathy in that kiss, it was so tender, like you might kiss a sleeping infant."

"Then you went home with her?"

"I didn't need to. That was all I needed."

"What was all you needed?"

"The touch of another human. Do you understand that at all?"

"Baby, that is all I ever wanted from you."

"You stopped being that way . . . right after we got married."

"So did you."

They sat in silence.

"Was she as pretty as me?"

"No. But all that doesn't matter. She was simply telling me she knew I needed a human touch, the way you— Stop dancing around, Ethel."

"I'm sitting here."

"Your eyes—they keep dancing. What the hell are you thinking?"

"The coffee. It's perking. It must be by now."

She got up. Then she stopped. She was very angry and very tired of it all. It wasn't going to be anything like she'd hoped.

"Take me back if you're going to," she said, "and if you're not—don't!"

He didn't answer.

"Tell me what you want; you never tell me what you want. I'm not a mind reader. How am I supposed to know what you feel? Sometimes I wish . . ."

"What? I'd like to know. What?"

"I wish you'd yell at me. I wish you'd beat me. Slam me around, if you're mad."

"What good would that do?"

"You know what I worry? That you won't say anything and you won't say anything, then one day, years from now, when I'm asleep, you'll chop me up in little bits—"

"What are you talking about?"

"I'm trying to tell you I don't know what's in your head. You can't be all that controlled all the time! Come on. Take a chance. Tell me what you want of me before it's too late. Or if you don't want anything, tell me that! Say something, please, Teddy, now, Teddy, please."

It was an effort. "I like this place," he said.

"And?"

"I'm going to stay here."

"And?"

"In the Navy."

"I know that."

"In what we started together. Remember how you talked?"

"So what do you want of me?"

"I want you to make up your mind. I can't live in your kind of uncertainty. It upsets me. I can't work. I don't want to live with someone who—"

"You want me to stay here or don't you? Tell me!"

"I'm trying to be fair to you," he said. "Maybe I'm not what you want."

"Fuck what I want. I want what you want."

"But you don't. You just showed me that."

"The coffee's done."

She ran into the kitchen, turned off the coffee, then came running back into the living room and was on the sofa with him and kissing him with all her need to wake him to her feeling.

"I love you," she said. "I really do love you."

"Don't, goddamn it, Ethel, don't. Because you had no business walking out on me that way. That was a terrible thing to do, humiliating me in front of everybody, leaving me to cover up after you with lie after lie after lie."

"Why didn't you tell them the truth—that I'm a no-good bitch?"

"Don't do that, that kissing. That doesn't answer a goddamn thing."

"When she did it, it answered plenty."

She kissed him again and again, not to trick him or seduce him, but because he looked so earnest and so pure; she was kissing a bewildered child.

"I've got to get this settled," he said, "so I'll know it's not going to blow up in my face again."

"It's settled."

"Not for me. I'm going to take a walk. And you think about it. If you want to go, go now. Not six months from now, not when I don't expect it, not when it's going to hurt me. I can take it now. You don't have to do anything for my sake, or because you feel sorry for me. I can get along without you, I found that out, maybe better—much better as far as my studying goes."

He got up and stood there, rather formally.

Ethel was crying.

"Stop it," Teddy said. "Stop it! Please." Then he said, "When I come back, if you're gone, I won't be mad at you, I'll admire your honesty. I will understand why you've gone."

"You're so good, Teddy."

"I'm not! What good means to you is weak! I found that out. So, tonight, it's going to be settled one way or another. Tonight! I'll go out and—"

"You don't have to go out."

"I want to."

"I'll be here when you come back, so why make the trip?"

At the door, he stopped.

"Do you know," she said, "this is the first time since we've been married that you've ever truly told me how you felt?"

"I guess so."

He didn't go out.

"You had to hurt like hell to do it. But it's the first time you've broken your silence and it's the first time I've felt close to you. Can't you see, baby, how it was for me?"

She got up and walked very slowly to where he was. She stood in front of him without touching him.

She spoke the next words as if they were a message of love. "Living with someone and you haven't the least idea of how he feels about anything. When he keeps up this iron front."

"I'm sorry."

"Hard-working! Industrious! Studious! Dutiful!"

"I'm sorry."

"Disciplined! Always correct! Never speaking his mind! How am I supposed to know what to do? That's why I say, Take charge of me."

"I'll try."

"Be like your father! Boss me! I want it!"

There was an extra room, a bedroom or a nursery-to-be, unfurnished. It was dark in there and the last tenants had left a carpet on the floor. Ethel got him in there and undressed.

When they were through, Teddy left the room.

She followed him. He was in the bathroom, standing on tiptoe, washing his cock at the sink as he always did. When he began to towel it, she went to the bedroom. He'd made the bed barracks style. She got between the cool, smooth sheets.

She could hear him brushing his teeth, then there was a silence; he was using the floss. Teddy did what the base dentist told him to do.

"I couldn't work right the last few days," he said as he climbed into bed. "I was thinking about you coming back."

She got up against him, put her leg over his.

"Thanks," he said, "for understanding."

"What?"

"Me. I had to get things settled, you know."

"Hm-hm."

He smiled and kissed her.

"I'm trying to get ready for my college boards," he said. "They're tough. I imagine you've fallen behind."

"Behind where?"

"In your work."

"I imagine I have," she said. "Far behind."

"I'm glad you're back," he said.

"So am I," she said.

She thought he'd fallen asleep, but he said, "You know what I kept wondering while you were away? Why the hell you ever joined up here."

"So we could be together."

"We could have been together without that."

"And because in the Navy they tell you exactly what to do and I thought I wanted that. But it turned out I didn't. I didn't want to do anything the Navy told me. I wanted to do what you told me. And your father. I want to be part of your family. But mostly of you, baby, altogether of you, in every way, of you and no one else and nothing else. That's why now I want out of the Navy, because I want to be with you altogether and in every . . ."

He was asleep; she heard his breathing. He didn't snore like his father did. The sound he made was that of an infant, the same soft, regular in and out.

She was awake a long time, listening to the sound his body made. And she remembered Julio, standing on tiptoe before his sink, soaping himself.

Why did these very different men perform the same after-fucking rituals in exactly the same way? Why were they in such a hurry to be "clean"?

Well, she'd heard girls talk about "cleaning themselves out after," too.

265

Now Ethel's effort went into being a wife. She decided to go to work on that unpainted furniture. When Teddy came home from work, she determined he'd come into an atmosphere as different as it could be from that at the Naval Training Center.

She bought the homemaker magazines: *Woman's Day, Ladies' Home Journal, Good Housekeeping,* even *House and Garden.* In one of them, she found a sketch of an inexpensively furnished living room where everything was low, the chairs little more than backrests and one whole side filled with a low divan, a mattress covered with an Oriental throw. To create a mood there were Indian blankets on the wall (she'd substitute the batik prints she'd seen in the window of a local hippie store), and the lamps hung from the ceiling to within two feet of the floor. What light was admitted from outside filtered through reed screens.

In one of Ethel's favorite TV movies, *Morocco,* with Marlene Dietrich and Gary Cooper, all window openings were covered with strip screens and all light on all faces was patterned in stripes. *Morocco* became her inspiration.

Dinner was to be served on a table no more than a foot off the ground; the head of the house could stretch out between courses like an Oriental king.

It was a big gamble to take—Teddy might hate the whole thing—but she decided to take it. She planned a bombshell.

Piece by piece, she accumulated the materials she needed in the condominium's basement storage room. She bought a small crosscut saw to reduce the legs of the tables and chairs, and some little rubber feet to shoe the stumps. And finally a pack of colored bulbs; no white light was to be tolerated.

The day came. She said she felt sick, couldn't go to class.

When Teddy came home that afternoon, he entered a — "A seraglio, for chrissake," he said, laughing nervously.

He told her he liked it and that the dinner, curry of lobster tail, was great and it was nice to lie on the floor, head on a pillow between courses, even between swallows. They could both lie on the same side of the table and the dinner could be interrupted for personal games.

The Soave Bolla made everything go down easily, as well as reminding Teddy of what she'd wanted him to remember, their wedding.

But in a few days, Ethel noticed that Teddy again was studying in his former roommate's quarters on the base. And when she asked him how come, his reply was: "Isn't this place more for screwing?"

"I study O.K. here."

"Well, good."

"I'm glad you like the place for something."

"It's great at night," he said.

Teddy couldn't reasonably object to it, because Ethel, who studied there (he didn't know when, couldn't understand how), was doing well in her studies. What he'd slaved over for days, she mastered in hours and later repeated back to her instructor. At first the man thought she couldn't actually know what she was saying, her tone was that "feminine." But when he asked her to explain the assignments, she did, perfectly.

Easter time was a vacation for them both. They flew to Florida.

"You won't believe this, Dad," Teddy said to Costa, "but her marks are better than mine used to be."

"You're right," Costa said. "I don't believe."

They were eating dinner. Ethel, Teddy could see, was familiar with their kitchen and its rituals. She helped Noola serve the food, particularly kept Costa's plate provided. Teddy was happy to see how easy his wife was with his father.

"Feel any magic?" he asked when they were in bed. "Because a couple of days before we got home, my father consulted that old priest he favors down in Tampa and this sainted geezer came up here with a young boy and, while the priest said the appropriate prayers, the kid rolled back and forth over our mattress, the one we're on. Feel any magic?"

"Doesn't Costa know I'm on the pill?"

"They didn't have the pill on the island of Kalymnos."

The next day was Sunday, the day Costa visited the grave of his father. He announced to Teddy that he was going to take Ethel along, part of her indoctrination into the family.

They walked the distance to Tarpon Springs. For Easter the fences in the Greek community were freshly painted white. Crossing a superhighway, they went around and behind a liquor store, found an old road down an incline through live oaks where the Spanish moss hung like tattered shrouds. Past the trees, Ethel saw a small pond and, above it, a graveyard. Some of the graves had lamps on poles, "eternal lights," fed by propane gas. No one was there.

Costa went straight to his goal. On the stone marker, behind a glass shield, was a photograph of Costa's father and beneath the likeness there were offerings: a flowerpot holding narcissus and a smaller one with African violets.

Costa sat at the foot of the marker, indicated a place next to him for his daughter-in-law. Then he turned to his father's face.

Ethel studied the image. It was even more fierce, more obdurate, than she'd expected, the eyes permanently narrowed from looking at the hard, bright sea.

"Tough guy," Costa said.

"He looks like you, Dad," Ethel said.

"Better man than me. Sometime I have trouble making my mind. Him? Never. He know everything. What he need to know, I'm talking. He don't read books, so forth, didn't bother with all that there."

"He died here?"

"He died in the bed where you sleeping now. When he die I gave the room Teddy boy. That was my father's name, too, but no Teddy business over there! Theophilactos! Captain Theo on the boat."

"He looks very old-world," Ethel said. "You know what I mean?"

"No."

"Like you sit at the table: 'Noola, the soup! Noola, the meat! Noola, my coffee!' She is there to serve you."

"My father worse. When you sit table with him, no one else talk. Look at him!"

Instead Ethel looked at Costa. Impulsively she hugged him.

"Why you do that?" he asked.

"Because I love you, Dad, and I want you to know that I'll do anything to make you happy."

"One way."

"I know."

"I speaking for this man too." He indicated the photograph and the stone.

"I know."

"Noola tells me you put something over there," he said.

"I take the pill."

"Pill?"

"That's right. But the day I'm out of the Navy, I'll stop," she said.

"Promise?"

"I can't wait. I told Teddy—"

269

"Now I tell you secret. Noola mad at you. She think you hurt boy. You know how she is. Noola is lion, you see that."

"I wish she liked me."

"Don't wait for that from mothers. Greek womans even less! Now, listen me."

"I'm listening."

"Navy for woman? I can tell you, no good! I want you quit tomorrow. Because then I know I have grandson."

"What you want I want."

"Quit. I tell Theophilactos, explain him everything very good, don't worry."

"The problem isn't Teddy, it's the Navy. Once you enlist, you can't just walk away."

"This is too important for that. Tell them I said—"

"It's not that easy."

"Then I tell them. I come over there, fix up everything."

She laughed. "You think you can do anything, Dad, don't you?"

"Only what's right," he said.

She went into her purse and pulled out a little blue plastic container. "I promise you," she said, "the day I quit, I'll—"

Embarrassed, he'd turned his face away. "O.K., O.K.," he said.

"The day I quit, I'll throw this away."

"If they make trouble, leave. Come here. Where the hell they find you here? Tell me that much."

"That's just what I was thinking," she said.

"So, finished?" he said.

"O.K., Dad."

And as far as he was concerned, that was it. He produced a little whisk broom from his back pocket and swept the gray stone marker.

"Go bring water," he ordered, pointing to the pond. "Be careful snakes."

An old coffee can was held by a nail to a tree. She didn't see any snakes, but there were fish, quite large fish, breaking the surface of the water.

"Mullet," he told her when she returned. "I don't eat those fish. For nigger."

He took a handkerchief out of his back pocket, soaked it in the water and carefully washed the glass cover of the photograph. As he did this, he told her about the line she was to continue.

"Greek people in what they call Greece over there, they all mixed up, who knows what, Albanians, Rumanians, Bulgarians, Egyptians, even Turks. God knows what kind barbarians! Serbs too, Syrians, Yugoslavians, Italians, all kind garbage, right? But in Kalymnos, island where I born, she lay right next to Turkey and no matter who come there, soldier, sailor, merchant, we mix with nobody. Now you!"

He stopped work and looked at her, measuring her. She could feel the chill.

"You. First time new blood. I watch you careful, you remember, before I say O.K. My father, I guarantee you this much, he don't give permission. He say *no*. Right away. One look. No! Look at him."

Ethel looked at the photograph and she knew Costa was telling the truth. It was beyond imagining that old Theophilactos would have accepted her.

"You see what you are," Costa said.

"Yes. I see."

"The first from outside."

"I see. Yes."

She sat there, head bowed and silent, while he washed the stone. She had a family now, one that had survived wars and invasions, conquest and slavery, famines and

271

plagues. It would survive her if she failed. But she would not fail. By that grave's side, she accepted the role she'd been selected to play.

They told Teddy at supper.

He was furious.

"You cannot do that," he said.

"Why, dear?" Ethel said.

"Because you made a contract, you gave the Navy your word. It's not something you can walk out on this way. Besides, they'll come after you."

"How will they know where I am?"

"They'll ask me."

Then Costa spoke. "Don't tell them," he said.

Teddy turned on his father. "I knew this was your idea," he said.

Costa repeated, "Tell them you know nothing."

"I can't do that."

"O.K., then."

"O.K., what?"

"Let them come after her."

"Yeah, I knew this was you, Pop. From the first time you saw her, you made my life impossible. How could I play up to her the way you did, take her around town, everyone kissing her ass—"

Suddenly, Noola broke in. "He's right, Costa. You spoiled her. Everybody giving her presents, like it was an honor to know her, and that old fool Aleko Iliadis, her private chauffeur with his broken-down Chevy, and telling me to wash her underwear."

"How could I expect her to come back to the base, where life is disciplined and honest?" Teddy said. "Well, I don't anymore. But I'm telling you, when the Navy comes hunting her, which it sure as hell will"—Teddy turned to Ethel—"I am not going to lie and lie and lie for you, not again. You're doing something wrong and it's against my wish and I won't be part of it."

They ate in silence. Every so often, Teddy looked from Ethel to his father, and they could see how angry he was and how bitter, and that it was permanent.

When Noola got up to clear the table, she kissed her son.

Costa had nothing to say. As usual, he sat before the TV set and watched a western. He had what he wanted and he didn't doubt it was right.

Later, when they were alone in their bedroom, Ethel tried to make it up to her husband. But he wouldn't have her.

They lay in the dark, side by side, not speaking.

"I don't want you to do this," he said, finally. "What you're doing."

She didn't answer.

"Are you asleep?"

"No," she said. "I heard you."

That was all she said.

A little later she heard him laugh, a kind of snort-laugh, and she asked, "What's so funny?"

"Something you said a long time ago."

"Which was what?"

" 'I want to obey you.' Remember you said that? 'I wish you'd beat hell out of me,' you said, 'slam me around when I don't do what you say.' Remember?"

"Well, here's your chance," she said. "Go ahead."

He didn't move.

"Too late now," he said. "Maybe yesterday, but after—"

"Maybe you don't really care that much," she said.

"That could be it."

"Teddy," she said, turning to him, "what I'm doing—it's for you."

273

"For me!"

"For your family. So I don't think you should be mad at me."

But he was. Through the last four days of his stay in Florida, he didn't make love to her.

At the end of the week, he went back to San Diego alone.

The day after he left, his wife gave her little blue case to his father.

Costa kept it for a day examining it secretly. The next morning he passed a rubbish fire behind the row of stores along the Tarpon Springs waterfront and threw the case into the flames.

thirteen

ETHEL settled into Costa's house, slept in old Theophilactos's bed, behaved like a woman expecting. Waking late and alone—husband and wife having departed, she for work, he to meet his friends over coffee —Ethel enjoyed a slow breakfast, washed everybody's dishes, made her bed. Then, still in the spell of self-pleasure, prematurely pregnant, she cleaned the house, leaving it as neat as a magazine illustration.

Never before had she been able to tolerate being alone. Now every silent moment was a treasure. Her only problem was how to get together with her husband to produce the child for which they were all waiting. And this problem she was happy to postpone. If only she could impregnate herself!

She bought a secondhand car, explored the west coast of Florida. On wheels, she was even more alone than sitting at home; no one could approach her. Within a week, she'd fallen into a routine of solitude. Packing a lunch—a single sandwich and a handful of small, chewy olives—she'd fill a Thermos with a day's supply of herb tea sweetened with honey, and drive to the first beach south of Tarpon Springs. There, at Dunedin, she'd find the smoothest piece of sand, spread an old pink sheet Noola had given her and set up her green umbrella.

Curled in this tinted circle of shade, she spent the heat of each day reading about the lives of women. She went from Anne Lindbergh and Eleanor Roosevelt to the girls in Iceberg Slim's stable of prostitutes. She was particularly interested in the responses of these women to bad fortune and what made the ones who succeeded succeed.

Alone in the heat, she'd read till she got drowsy, slowly eat her lunch, sip her sweet tea, watch the heavy sea roll and the birds skim over it, sleep, wake refreshed and at ease. Then she did what the pregnant wife of a soldier on overseas duty might do: wrote a long, chatty letter to her husband, a catalogue of trivia, comings and goings, doings and thoughts, detailed by the hour and put down so carefully that Teddy could not possibly complain: She doesn't say what she did between four and five on Thursday, what was she doing then? Every hour was accounted for—not because he'd asked for it, but because it was what she wanted to do.

Having covered her entire day, she sealed the envelope with her tongue, then with a kiss-cross, and stopped at the post office to send it off to California. This duty done, she reconnoitered the perimeter of Tarpon Springs's *kentron,* the park of dusty green shrubs backing a circle of benches, to see if the old man was still sitting with his cronies—Costa ended his day as he began it—and if he was there waiting for her, as he usually was, she'd drive him home.

These were her habits. Slowly she was making it up

to Teddy; she was even winning over Noola a little; and with Costa, what was there to win? He'd been hers from the beginning.

For a month she never missed dinner at home. She even offered to help out during the day at The 3 Bees. But tourist time was waning; they were disappearing, those birds of season. Noola thanked her but declared that Ethel's help was not needed, not now, thanks again.

Several times in the middle of the night, Noola thought she heard sobbing through the walls. But she wasn't sure. Each morning Ethel looked more radiant, so Noola said nothing to her husband.

Gingerly Ethel tried to communicate some of this to Teddy, but she tore up the letter. She couldn't explain why she felt that the quiet, passive life she was leading was bringing her into peril.

But she did know that this new kind of danger attracted her. Danger always had.

She only hoped that Teddy believed one thing—that she had not now, as she might have not long ago, turned to another man.

"I am true," she signed her daily letters.

But she had a secret life, which wasn't true. Why this, for instance: Despite the terrible things he'd done to her, she thought back on Julio with some respect. She had no idea why she respected him and she didn't like herself for it. But there it was. She even felt oddly close to the man. Oh, she certainly wouldn't want to see him again, not ever; he was too dangerous, too sick. But how could she not respect a man carrying that much pain? As for what he did about it—to her surprise, Ethel defended him to herself. What should the man do with his pain? Mask it? Keep silent like Teddy? Pretend he was agreeable? Pass as happy? Be civilized? The simple fact was that his guts were unprotected.

She often felt closer to him than she did to her husband.

This, of course, she did not try to explain to Teddy.

He was answering her letters briefly, didn't have the time she had, or the ear for what she was saying. His exams had been tough, he said; he hoped he'd done O.K. His future ("theirs" is what he wrote), whether or not he'd get to go to the university at Jacksonville and become an officer, depended on how he'd done.

In one letter he told her rather formally that he'd been questioned about her and where she was. "I told them the truth," he said, as if that made it O.K. He didn't tell her what they, the authorities, were going to do about her desertion. "You've been away more than thirty days now," he wrote, "and that's what it is now, desertion—a serious matter, I might as well tell you."

She didn't give a damn what they did. She didn't tell Teddy that.

They grew apart. With each daily letter.

But the time was coming, she knew, when they'd have to face each other and try to make a new start. She didn't rush him and he hadn't pressed her. She suspected strongly that Teddy liked being alone as much as she did. He'd hinted that. She knew he believed he did better in his studies when she was nowhere near. She'd witnessed this. But now she also knew it because of how she herself felt when she woke in the morning, alone in the old house and with a whole precious day of unbroken silence ahead of her. She realized how much of a person's vital force a permanent relationship siphons off.

This was the fact: They were able to stay together now only because they were not together in body. This pleasant indifference, this friendly but total separation, might have become their permanent relationship, except for pressure from Costa.

One day he demanded to know when she and Teddy

would start meeting their family responsibility. She side-slipped him, said she'd write Teddy and see what he suggested.

Teddy answered that since there was no vacation ahead on his calendar, it was up to her; she'd have to visit him. He didn't press her.

This being a family matter, Ethel discussed it with Costa. His judgment was: "Never mind what he say, I want you go there now! I'm getting old waiting down there."

As head of the tribe, he spoke law. Ethel had to agree. But clinging to the solitary life she'd found, she avoided setting a departure date, said she wasn't quite ready to go.

"Why not?" Costa broke in.

"For one thing, I have to find a new dress."

Costa ordered Noola to go with her immediately, this time to Clearwater, not Tampa, and buy the damn dress.

Up and down the shopping street they scouted the racks for two hours. The dress they bought was a shade of delicately powdered rose.

"You look so pretty in that dress," Noola said, "I'm proud you're my daughter."

Ethel blushed. It was the first nice thing Noola had ever said to her.

"Look who's blushing. Like a little girl!"

"I know," Ethel said. "I still do that. It's so embarrassing."

"It means something good," Noola said. "Your heart must be clean, what do you think?"

On the way back to Tarpon Springs, Ethel revealed to Noola that she was calendar-calculating. When they came to a red light, she took a tiny calendar out of her purse and pointed to the dates she'd circled, her fertile time.

"See? There's no hurry," she said. "These three or four days only."

Then Ethel asked Noola what she'd always wondered. "What did you use?"

"Nothing," Noola said.

"Ever?"

"Never."

Ethel could see how hard it was for Noola to say even those two words, so she didn't press. But Noola, on her own, added, "After the one—a boy, thanks to God —I dried up. Costa wanted more, he kept pushing me and pushing me. But that was all God would give me."

"Still, you're happy," Ethel said. "Teddy is a fine man."

They'd come to another stop light.

"I'm happy enough," Noola said. "Why should I be happier? Is a woman ever really happy? I have Costa. He's the story of my life."

Ethel hugged her before the light changed.

One noon, at the time of the heaviest heat, Ethel saw two men walking aimlessly along the beach at Mangrove Still, skipping flat pebbles over the sheet of gray water. Ethel knew the uniforms. Shore patrol.

She was lying on her belly with her bikini bra off. Deliberately she didn't replace it, did stand the book up so it partly covered her face, and pretended to be sleeping. The pair passed at twenty feet, and being properly mothered young men, they didn't stare at the topless young woman. At a decent distance, though, they sat and appeared to be killing time. She could feel their attention, though it lecherous, not official. After twenty minutes of pretending they weren't looking at her, they brushed the sand off their blues, adjusted their arm bands so the initials "SP" would show, and strolled off.

Stopping at the first phone booth she could find,

Ethel called The 3 Bees. "Yes," Costa said, "two men from Navy, they come by, give me question. Very fine boys, I'm sure. I tell them you out of town. Where? they ask me. Tucson, Arizona, try over there, I say. Maybe she gone see her family."

They claimed to have positive information, Costa told her, that she was living with her in-laws. Could they drop by his home that evening? Not that they doubted his word, but they'd have to report they'd been there. "Why not?" Costa said. "I give you coffee. Noola! Fix some coffee here! Look gentlemen, beautiful shells!"

They had bought two sponges as well as the shells.

"I guess my time's come," Ethel said. "Tell Noola if she'll look in the back of my closet, she'll find my suitcase all packed and ready to go. I'll leave my car at Koundoros's garage. Maybe you can talk Aleko into picking me up there and taking me to the Tampa airport."

Ethel hated to leave. By a series of accidents she'd found the life she thought perfect; she resented this meaningless intrusion of uniformed authority.

By the time Aleko drove up in his Chevy, she was in a quiet rage.

Costa was in the back seat. He reached out to help her in. "Down, down, get down," he said, making a big drama out of the thing.

She did what he ordered, but with bad grace.

"What's the matter, you don't feel good today?" he asked.

She didn't answer.

Later, when she was still not responding to his attempts at conversation, he burst out with: "What the hell's the matter with you today?"

By the time they were on the thruway, they all felt easier and Ethel answered Costa's questions with a story.

"When I was a little girl of ten, my class in school was sent for a vacation to a farm in the East. Our teachers and our parents thought we desert kids ought to learn about trees where they grow green. About half a mile up the hill from where we were put up, there lived a farmer and his family. They raised Concord grapes and McIntosh apples and black cherries and peaches with the most luscious golden flesh. They had all kinds of animals too —fierce roosters and lovely white Leghorn hens, baby lambs and a terrible-tempered ram, working horses and riding horses, goats and a herd of milk cows. One day the whole gang—the man was a Hunky or a Polack or something and he had nine children and five grandchildren—they all came down the hill in a procession, leading a cow. On her head they'd piled flowers, and around her neck they'd tied ribbons and hung little brass bells. They walked slowly past us and it was a sight to see, even if we kids had only a vague idea of what it was all about. They were all laughing, kidding the cow and giggling among themselves, the boys teasing, the girls blushing, everybody so happy! Except the bride-to-be. That cow plodded along, as dutiful as you please, belly and bag swaying from side to side. She had no choice except to go where they were taking her. Now, what were you asking me, Dad?"

"Hey, you Levendis," Costa said. "What you listening all the time from there?"

"I hear nothing. What she talking, a cow? Who cares about cows?"

"Now I'll tell you about another animal I know," Ethel said. "My father has a mare. Her name is Maria but she's called The Bitch because she's so downright ornery. She won't let anybody ride her except my father. But I noticed that while everybody calls her The Bitch, still they treat her with respect. They don't fool around with that mare, they watch out for her teeth and her sharp little hoofs. They give her the best stall in the stable and a saddle embossed with her name. They're not going to give her to any old stud; no, sir. Only to the best stallion in the West. She must know all this; you can see the pride in the way she carries herself. There is something in her eyes that those other horses don't have.

"Now, everybody told me, Don't get on that mare, stay the hell off her. But you know me: I had to ride her just to spite them. And as they said she would, she threw me. But then I spoke to her, I gave her respect, not a scolding, and I said, 'You're my sister, Bitch!' Then I got on her again and we had one hell of a beautiful ride and I knew that nobody had ever tied a brass bell around that mare's neck and nobody ever would.

"So tell me which you'd rather be, the cow or The Bitch?"

Costa yawned.

"Do I bore you, Dad?" she said.

"Sometime yes. If *paramythia* was true facts, life would be simple to figure him out."

"What was that—*para* what?"

"Fairy tales. Aesop Fables. Nothings. You're not a cow and you're not a horse. There are laws of Nature, which is part of God, and She don't give damn whether you like them or not. She don't ask your opinion. She don't wait for your all K. You must take her as she comes. That is your situation."

He put her on the plane.

fourteen

WAITING at the airport for Ethel's plane to set down, Teddy swept his hand under the car seat and found the crumpled tissue he'd seen Dolores throw down. One fold was stained with lipstick.

He looked at the electric clock on the dashboard, which he kept a quarter of an hour fast so he'd never be late for a duty, then turned on the motor to start the air conditioner. Teddy perspired when he felt guilty.

Ethel, trim and cool, kissed him briskly and got into the car without his help. She sat in the middle of the front seat, but never moved closer. On the way home, she offered a routine report on the health and disposition of his parents and what the weather had been in Florida. Hot. She was not hostile. Reserved.

Teddy suspected her. She had instinctive sources of information; her guesses were good. Had she guessed anything?

If it was only that she was tired, "not in the mood," that was all right; he could use the rest.

When they entered the short-leg seraglio they called home, her only comment: "Oh, look at this!" Had she actually forgotten what she'd done?

He'd brought Dolores there once. "She sure made a mess of this place," she'd said. "What the hell did you let her do it for?"

"She was so goddamn nervous that week—" he'd started to explain.

"Let's go to my place," Dolores had said. "This gives me the creeps."

Teddy heard a rip. Ethel had pulled a leaf out of her mimeographed curriculum and gone into the kitchen. He walked after her, stood in the doorway. He'd stood in the same spot a couple of months before and she'd come to him, putting her knee between his thighs, and tried to get him to bed. She'd wanted it quickly that night. Now she was making a grocery list. It was an affront to his pride.

"I know the place is filthy," he said. "What I needed here was a woman."

"What you needed here was a vacuum cleaner," Ethel said.

They drove down to the supermarket, which served four condominiums, twenty-four hours a day. He noticed she was buying things in limited quantities: half a dozen rolls, two frozen spinach soufflés, two frozen chopped broccoli, eight breakfast croissants, a dozen eggs; she took one in the morning he two. She was shopping, it seemed, for a precisely calculated number of days. Four?

When he called her attention to people from the base cruising the corridors, she was indifferent.

"You know they can pick you up here as well as in Florida," he said. "You're on every list now."

"I don't think their computers work that fast," she said. "They've still got me in Florida. By the time they catch on, I'll be gone."

So, Teddy thought, four days.

Dolores. He'd known her for a week. She'd filled the gap. A woman can't leave her husband by himself week after week without asking for it. Ethel had asked for it. So, Dolores.

She'd given him a nickname. Pasha. She said he was an Oriental prince. She had a taste for dark, cruel men. Once he'd hit her as she was coming. Or pretending to. Could you tell these days?

But Dolores could hold her own; she was number one secretary to Lieutenant Commander Bower, the ranking legal officer on the base. Her boss considered her the perfect secretary because, along with everything else, she knew the birthdays of his children. Professionally she was efficient, discreet and controlled. In bed she was a demon. Teddy's nickname for her was Crazylegs, because of the way she wrapped her legs around his back. Sometimes she'd drum him with her heels. Along with all that, she liked him. Or seemed to.

When he was through, she'd lay his penis along his thigh and admire it. Dolores always put a hand towel under their pillow, a habit from her second marriage, but she preferred tissues for intimate work. She had a thing about tissues. She'd pull one, two, three, and fondly wipe his part, gentling it in her cupped hand. "Pink as a baby," she'd say, "and so soft now." Then she'd get up, light a cigarette, pull a deep drag, put the cigarette into his mouth, let him pull on it, kiss him, taking his smoke, then take the cigarette back. And so forth. Games.

"No one since Livingstone has gone so deep into the dark interior," she'd said the night before. "I hope you get out in time to meet your wife's plane." Praise from a woman, Dolores knew, is the greatest aphrodisiac, so before long he was at it again.

"Do I please you?" she'd said.

"You please the shit out of me."

"If you want anything different, tell me what."

Despite all this very effective flattery, he didn't altogether like Dolores. For instance, she told him stories about other men, their failures and their failings. There's an old folk saying: "If they talk about others, they'll talk about you." So Teddy didn't trust Dolores.

But she sure filled the gap.

Ethel was much more at home in a kitchen now, Teddy noticed. The dinner was delicious, and accomplished with ease. "I'm going to take a bath," she said after they'd done the dishes.

He couldn't remember, did she ever take baths after dinner? Hadn't it always been in the morning? She'd certainly never taken one before when he was waiting in bed for her, certainly never stayed in the tub this long. He was falling asleep. Any minute. It would serve her right. No woman should dare to keep a Greek waiting in bed that long. Who the hell did she think she was? He looked at the clock. She'd been lying in that goddamn tub nearly half an hour. What was she doing in there? What was she thinking? Now she was coming out. Naked. She crossed to her purse, took something out and went back to the bathroom. He heard the door lock turn. When had she ever locked the bathroom door before? Was she off the pill, using something else? More time passing. Oh, fuck her! He'd be asleep when she finally did him the honor of coming to bed. If he wasn't asleep, he'd pretend. That way he'd preserve his dignity.

He led her to believe she had to wake him, acted groggy, kept his eyes closed as she caressed him. He remembered she used to say to him, "Don't. I'm not ready for you yet, wait a little longer, baby." But now the Pasha was running the show,—he was deciding who was ready and when. He was making her wait for it now. It felt good.

She used to say, "It hurts when you enter me that way." Actually he preferred that. It gave him the pleasure of rape. What he really liked was partial rape. He liked to force his way in, bit by bit, and feel her open for him, deeper and deeper, when he was in her.

Now he just might let her have it. He was ready now.

Then came the surprise. Ethel took it in her hand as if it were an instrument and inserted it carefully, quickly and neatly, and—a surprise! She was perfectly lubricated, all the way in. Then another novelty—what the hell was going on? Usually she'd make every effort to prolong his stay in her body, playing him, holding still, distracting his mind, everything that the magazine articles told a woman to do to get the satisfaction which was, they'd recently discovered, her birthright.

Now Ethel's effort seemed to be to bring him off as quickly as possible. To get it over with. And then it was. They were lying side by side, looking at the ceiling. He couldn't help thinking of D. No comparison! D. really wanted it. D. put a pillow under her ass. D. wound her legs around his back. D. arched her back to lift her cunt for him. D. wanted it to last forever. D. had a spectacular come. He wondered where D. was at that instant and what she was doing.

With Ethel, that night, it had been an exercise in mechanics.

To make matters worse, the first thing she'd said afterward was: "You've been with somebody else, haven't you?"

She said this without the least rancor.

"I haven't been with any such goddamn thing," he said. "What makes you say that?"

But he knew he was giving it away. He was perspiring.

"Isn't it awful hot in here?" he said.

"Just right for me," she said.

She lifted her head, gave him a lemon smile. Ethel was a tough girl to fool.

He wished he could control that goddamn giveaway. Even as a kid, when he'd done his light finger stroll along the drugstore counter, he'd be in a sweat as he was walking home, the candy bars in his pocket.

He'd told Ethel all about that once, in the days when they'd been talking truth.

Ethel didn't forget anything.

"I don't mind," she said. "If you have. Been with someone."

He flapped the sheet which covered them to cool his body and then, undetected, he believed, wiped his palms and the backs of his hands.

"Why don't you mind?" he said.

Should he tell her? She wasn't pressing him. If he told her the truth, maybe he'd stop sweating. He felt like a goddamn victim, in such a shamefully weak position. He resented her having this advantage over him.

"Because—I don't know," she said. "I wouldn't mind, that's all. I wouldn't blame you. We've been separated for so long."

"Have you been with anyone else?" he asked.

"Would you mind if I had?"

"Yes."

"Would you blame me? We've been separated a long time."

"I would blame you."

"Well, I haven't. Been with anyone."

"Why not?"

"There was no one I wanted."

He took the leap, felt better even as he did it.

"I didn't want the one I—"

She cut him off. "You don't have to explain," she said.

"Thanks," he said.

Then something unusual happened. She fell asleep. First. It had always been the other way around: he'd fall off immediately after he came.

She was breathing easily; she was not under stress.

Why the hell wasn't she? How could she take it all so calmly? Indifferently?

He didn't sleep well, got up before she did and went to his duty, then studied in a corner of the ed officer's office.

In the afternoon he found an hour for Dolores. His pride demanded it. As he left, he contrasted her cries of pleasure, her following murmurs of praise and gratitude, with the efficient way Ethel had introduced him into her body and hustled him to finish.

When he came home, he found that Ethel had spent the day scrubbing and cleaning the entire place. He'd let it go to dust and filth. Even the floor was waxed, every dish washed properly, the bottoms of the frying pans showed copper again, the shelves of his shirts and underwear reordered.

How could he complain?

That night it was the same. You couldn't call it making love. She was aggressive without being ardent, reaching for his member the instant it was erect, nudging him on top of her with her hand, guiding the shaft into her body, opening her lips for it, seeing to it that they joined neatly.

Again there was something unusual about the way she was lubricated. Generally she responded in two stages; that's the way it had always been. She had an outer door and an inner door, he used to say; first one opened, then the other. This time she was evenly and immediately ready, no pushing necessary. At once he was all the way home.

Then she urged him through the act. She didn't make a sound, whether of encouragement or passion, simulated or real. When he was through, he realized she had brought him off again as quickly as she could. While she . . . ?

She'd been a bystander.

Teddy wondered back over their lives. She'd been so passionate once.

Could all that have been pretense?

The next night, Teddy discovered a jar of lubricant on the table at the side of their bed. He didn't immediately understand what it was and why it was there.

"Do you use that?"

"Yes, I do."

"Why?"

"Because you come in before I'm ready and you hurt."

"Have you always used that?"

"No. I decided not to be hurt anymore. Do you mind?"

"I sure do."

"You mean you want me to hurt?"

"You know what I mean."

He was furiously angry, his pride offended. A man who couldn't bring his wife to the point of being ready and wanting him! That couldn't be him!

"You never complained before," he said.

"Well . . . do you really want to talk about that, how it used to be and how it is now?"

He said he did. But he didn't press. After all, he had Dolores and, like yesterday, anytime he needed proof of what kind of man he was, all he had to do was—

So he said he was sorry if he entered her too quickly and she said it was O.K., but when he did, it hurt. And they dropped the subject.

The next night it was exactly the same, perfect lubrication, a guided tour, a rush for the finish line.

But how could he complain? Under the circumstances? After all, he had been unfaithful. He'd even admitted it, sort of.

Maybe she read his thoughts, because she said, "You can't blame me for being a little tight, can you? After all, you were with someone else."

He was perspiring again. Suddenly. Heavily.

He was relieved when she slid off the subject. "This is my fertile time," she said. "These four days. I don't want anything to go wrong. Your daddy's getting impatient."

They laughed and she didn't bring up his infidelity again.

Two days later, she informed him that her fertile time was past and she was going back to Florida.

"I can't stay here," she explained. "Somebody's sure to see me. Then they'll take me in. It'll be a mess, especially for you. You want that?"

"It would be a mess," he said, "especially now when I'm bucking for a commission. But they're going to find you sooner or later; they always do."

"I'll think up some way they won't. Meantime I'll be with your parents, right there in your bed. Call me."

"I'll be home in seven weeks. It's between courses. And listen, I do understand what you were talking about, you know."

But he didn't. She'd shamed him.

When they kissed good-bye, light and quick, he said, unasked, "I'm not going to be with anyone else again, O.K.?"

"O.K.," she said.

Had he expected her to be grateful?

In a week he was back with Dolores. His pride demanded it. "After all," he said to himself, "I'm a man!"

What disturbed him most was that Ethel wasn't jealous.

She wrote him a month later to inform him she wasn't pregnant.

That's all she said. Nothing else.

A letter from his father annoyed him even more.

"You don't appreciate what you got," Costa had written in his crabbed hieroglyphics. "Every day she go to beach, sit by herself, read books. You hurt your eyes, I tol' her. Then she come home, help Noola give me dinner. Believe me, home-life best thing for woman. I wish you see her now, how beautiful, brown skin, gold hair, like angel. Right away then, I have grandson, I'm sure. I tol' her she must go to you, right away. 'Whatever you want,' she said. Fine girl! Miracle!"

Teddy didn't want her to come west again. In bed the night before, he'd decided, with no encouragement from Dolores, whose head was on his shoulder, to leave Ethel.

He found himself in a dilemma.

What Teddy did not want to do was offend his father. Ethel had completely won Costa over, so it was out of the question for Teddy, such a good Greek boy, to leave her now.

Another dilemma. Dolores had brought him the news that he'd passed his college boards and that, of course, he'd be admitted to Jacksonville University.

"But why go to Jacksonville?" she said. "There's a college right here which offers the same courses. I can get my boss to expedite the whole thing. You'll be a commissioned officer before you know it; leave it to me."

When she told him this, Teddy felt the power rise in him. He thanked her, then he fucked her.

Dolores, he decided the night before he flew east, was the kind of girl he should have married.

"Where's Ethel?" he asked Costa, who met him at the airport. Teddy, expecting she'd meet him, was rather relieved she had not.

"I tell you right away," the old man said in a conspiratorial voice, as he looked around for eavesdroppers.

As soon as they were in the car, Aleko Iliadis at the wheel, Costa told his son in a hoarse whisper what was troubling him. "You must give her order right away, stop!" he said. Then yelled, "Hey, you, Levendis, mind you business over there. Close your ears."

"How can I close my ears and drive the car?"

Costa whispered the news. Ethel had taken a job as secretary in the offices of a large marina servicing the huge new condominiums between Bradenton and Sarasota.

"How can she be a secretary?" Teddy whispered. "She can't type."

"I'm learning," Ethel said, "and shorthand too." They were talking before dinner. There was no crisis as far as she was concerned. It was a natural and helpful thing to do. She would be adding to their savings, for one thing. As for disrupting Costa's life, Ethel had made most of the dinner. When they got home, she was in the kitchen.

Still Costa looked worried. Ethel reassured him with kisses. The fact that he liked the dinner, a kebab of cubed lamb over purée of eggplant, rice at the side, certainly helped.

Later, as the women were doing the dishes, Teddy found out exactly what was troubling his father.

"Looks like you can't support wife," he said. "Disgrace over there!"

"Oh, Pop, come on. She can't lie on the beach every day of her life, reading books. Besides, we can use the money."

"Everybody talking," Costa said. "Not yet. Soon."

Teddy felt that his father was disappointed in him.

Should he have shown more command? Should he have forced Ethel to give up the job? Could he have?

"In the old country," Teddy told Ethel as they undressed, "if a woman works, it means her old man isn't bringing in enough money to put food on the table, so it's a public insult to him. Also, the only job a woman could get over there would be that of a menial, kitchen help or washing clothes or nursing babies."

"But you don't mind, do you?" Ethel said.

"I worry what they're going to do about it back there when they find out. They've sent your name out to be picked up."

"They sent my name to whom?"

"To everybody. The shore patrol at Orlando, north of here. The state troopers. Even the local police."

"How do you know?"

"I know the secretary in the law office on the base. They're old-fashioned back there too. They think I should have said, 'You can't do that!' And that if I had, you'd obey."

"You did tell me not to."

"And you did what you wanted. That's your business, I told them."

"You really told them that?"

"Had to. I told them I had no control over you."

"Did you tell them where I was?"

"Had to. I'm sorry. But . . . I had to."

"I've got a solution for that. I've moved. I have a place of my own now."

"You have what! Where?"

"Down near the marina. Where they'll never find me."

"Whereabouts will they never find you?"

"I'm going to take you there, Teddy, but I won't say the address or the name of the street. That way you can say you don't know. Look, I can't drive fifty miles to work every day, can I? Especially through Saint Pete traffic and back at night. I'd be worn out."

"What did my old man say?"

"I haven't had the nerve to tell him. I haven't moved yet. I've been waiting for you to help me—with the move, and especially with him."

Teddy wondered which was more important to him: that the Navy should feel they could trust him or that she should feel that she could?

The next day, after Costa and Noola had gone to The 3 Bees, Teddy and Ethel filled the car with her belongings and drove to the apartment. She'd already done some decorating, had kept the curtains from the previous tenant. It was beginning to look homey.

But not his home. Hers. He was nowhere in it.

She must have guessed what he was feeling, because she said, "I've got some pictures of all of us, being framed. The place will look more like home when I get them up."

Then they drove to the marina. "You can keep the car all day," she informed him, "if you'll call for me after work."

He nodded, but resented the favor. She'd made him dependent on her for transportation.

Again she must have intuited how he felt, because she asked, "Are you sore at me? About something? See, I couldn't discuss all this with you. I had to move quickly on the apartment. I figured you might be angry about that."

"You might have told me over the phone. Before you did it. I would have understood."

His mind went back to Dolores. He heard her song of appreciation.

"If you don't want to hang around here all day while I'm working, you can take the car," Ethel said. "I'll stay overnight. Call for me tomorrow night. It'll give you a chance to explain everything to Costa."

"I'll call for you tonight."

The marina was very big, very busy and still expanding.

"Who owns this place?" he asked her.

"A bastard and a company," she said. "My particular boss, the manager, is a Greek kid. His name is Petros something. Kid? Well, he acts like a kid out of one of those monster comics."

"You're late," Petros said as Ethel opened the door to the office. Then he saw Teddy following his wife. "Oh, I see. You been busy."

Then he laughed. Petros Kalkanis laughed at his own jokes, a sudden loud explosion which always ended on a high note. It didn't bother him that no one within hearing shared his amusement.

He bounded up to Teddy on goat's legs. *"Patrioti! Patrioti!"* he said. *"Posseeeseh?* You speak Greek, eh?"

"Not too well." Teddy decided to fib. Nothing embarrassed Teddy as much as a professional Greek.

"O.K., O.K., English." Then he turned to Ethel. "Very good-looking man," he said, rolling his eyes like a ethnic comedian. Teddy thought him ridiculous.

"Yes, he is," Ethel said neatly. She went to her desk.

"Why you let her work?" Petros asked. "You give her permission?"

"She didn't ask. This is America, you know. How's she doing?"

"No good." Petros laughed. "Can't type, no shorthand. Good for nothing." He looked at Ethel, who was separating the bills that had come in that morning.

"Why did you hire her?" Teddy asked.

"American people, they look at me first time, they get scared; they look at her, calm down right away." He studied Teddy for an instant. "He looks just like American," he whispered to Ethel, as if what he said was fraught with a special meaning. "Look at that nose! My God!"

Petros's nose, Teddy noticed, was half his face.

"Never mind that garbage," Petros said. With a grand gesture, he swept everything in front of Ethel into the wastepaper basket.

"Mr. Kalkanis!"

"No money to pay now, they send same bill next month. "Here." He found a contract form. "Mr. and Mrs. Lasky, berth number . . . ?"

"Twelve-twelve. I know where the Laskys are."

"They don't sign contract yet. So go get it signed."

"O.K." She was looking at Teddy. Clearly she wanted him to leave.

"What time do I call for you?" Teddy said.

"I finish at six," she said.

"You want her early," Petros said, "I let her go early."

"Be here at six," Ethel said. And left the office.

"Sit down, sit down," Petros said. "You want coffee?"

"No, thanks."

Teddy was looking at him as if he were sizing up an enemy.

"You look like your father now," Petros said.

"You know the old man?"

"Once he was going to kill me."

"What for? What did you do?"

"He was mad, come to me with big stick, call me, my friends, garbage. *Kalymniotico skoopeethi.*" He laughed. "Probably right, huh? But some of the other boys, they want to discuss the situation with him. I was brought up to respect old age, so I turn them around."

"Why did he get mad at you?"

"No reason necessary. You see what I am. Big mouth."

"Seems like you're doing very well here with your big mouth."

"Work twice as hard as everybody. American people, they don't work. I tell boss this place, you don't work, soon I own you. He don't care. For God's sake, sit down. Want something, coffee, something?"

"No, thanks; really."

"These people here, they don't appreciate what they got. America! *Paradisos! Paradisos!* You want to see marina?"

"I've got to go."

"Where you going? I don't have work. Come on."

"I've got to— No I don't. I don't have any work either. Let's go."

The boat owners respected Petros; Teddy could see that. He confronted everyone as an equal, playfully, boisterously, without asking favors, usually with a mock scolding.

"This here big owner," Petros said, introducing Teddy to one of two men playing gin rummy on the aft deck of a large cabin cruiser. "He will make me small partner soon, right, Mr. Roth?"

"You'll own me in a year, you son of a bitch," Roth said, not looking up from his hand, with which he wasn't satisfied.

"Look." Petros pointed to the foredeck. Two women, the same age as the men but looking considerably younger because their bodies were so burnished, were being served something liquid by a little brown man in a trim white coat. "The American good-for-nothing wife!" He turned to Roth. "Hey, Mr. Roth," he shouted, "why you don't put your wife to work? She's getting pretty lazy up there."

"Too late to do anything about her," Roth said.

"Hello, Peetie!" Mrs. Roth reared up, holding her bra front. "Pick me up a few pompano for tonight, will you, Peetie?"

"Go shopping yourself, for God's sake," Petros said. "I ain't got time for— All right, last time, special favor."

They walked out of ear range and Petros said, "I like everything this country, only the women I don't like."

"What's the matter with them?"

"They don't know their place. Useless, good for nothing. This woman, please pompano, Peetie! *Scada!* You know what that mean?"

"Shit."

"Shit is right. That poor son of a bitch, Roth, he come down after bad week stock market, poor man don't have time take off coat, she say, 'Darling, fix me Manhattan?' Then, 'Make one for Peetie, would you, Sy darling? Come on, Peetie, join us.' No, you bitch! But I don't say that, I don't want to hurt his feelings. Also he is my money. When he go back to New York, she gives me signal, she want my *nikolaki*." He pointed to it with a sweep of his palm. "I say to her, 'You wait rest your life, you bitch.' This I tell to her: 'If you my wife, I beat all that fat off your ass.' 'Oh, Peetie, Peetie,' she say, 'I'd like that. When you going to show me your boat, Peetie?' Never, you bitch. My boat for Greeks only, no women 'lowed. Look." He pointed. "There she is."

It was an old sponge boat, broad-beamed, sitting deep in the water with heavy, beautiful lines. Petros had refitted it to serve as his sleeping quarters. "No woman 'lowed down here," he said, pointing to some pictures on the cabin walls. "That's my father; over there, my mother. This here whole Kalkanis family, some dead now. I in America. They, Kalymnos."

Petros held Teddy before each photograph, explaining with genuine devotion who the people of his life were.

Teddy was impressed. Despite himself, he liked the man.

"My sisters." Petros pointed. "Two married, O.K., one not yet. I send dowry next year, that finish my problem."

"Then you'll get married?"

"But not with American, believe me. These women here, disgrace, shame. Hello, you say. Half hour later they explaining you how their husbands don't know how to fuck them."

Teddy chanced it. "My wife, though—what about her?"

"Tell you the truth, same thing. I mean, spoiled. But I am trying to teach her right way, O.K.?"

"Why did you hire her? The truth."

"I thought I'd like to *gameeso*—you know?" He clenched the fist of his left hand and slapped its end with the open palm of his right. "I didn't meet you yet. I have no idea she marry with Greek. Now I might as well fire her out, get good secretary."

"You know, you've really got a lot of nerve."

"Regular Greek."

"I was like you before I joined the Navy. But it takes it out of you, the service. You begin to match up to the rules, be careful what you say, all the rest of that."

"Don't worry, I don't do that business to Greek fellow wife."

"You think you can do it to anyone you please?"

"No comment. I know I look like animal. But woman don't care about looks. People make fun my nose, like handle water pitcher, they say, ears like hound dog, hang down. But my wife, when I pick her out, she will look at men here and say, 'Where's their nose, for God's sake? Show me one man with beautiful nose like my husband. And ears! Nobody has ears that big!' "

"Tell me one more thing: How will you find this perfect wife?"

"Main thing, no hurry. First I have to be rich man. If you don't have money this country, you are, like your father call me, *skoopeethi*. Meantime I am looking."

"You go to Greece and look?"

"I got my uncles Vassili and Spiro over there. They watch schools in Kalymnos. Now she may be nine, ten, eleven. Look that age, I tell them. And not so beautiful; beautiful girls give trouble. When she twelve, I go to father, make contract. Sixteen marry. Her legs never been open 'cept make water. Everything she will learn from me. Boom! Boom! Boom! Boom! Four sons. Don't give her time to get ideas. Then she has her work. Make no trouble. Every time she go out of house she has to have O.K. from me. If she wants newspaper, she has to explain me what she wants to read. Your wife, read, read, read. What she's going to be, professor? Tell her stop. It will make her sick, believe me. She get wrong ideas. Your wife, my friend, I don't understand what she want. You know?"

"Not anymore. I used to. I thought."

"I find out, I tell you."

Ethel and Teddy decided to break in the apartment, not drive north that night. Teddy called his father and created the impression that he and Ethel were in a little hideaway, enjoying a second honeymoon. He was granted the old man's blessing.

The next morning, Teddy drove Ethel to the marina. Petros was bouncing all over the place, a human pogo stick, and everywhere audible.

"You never told me what you thought of my boss," Ethel said.

"I liked him. But why does he say everything twice?"

"He does what twice?"

"Says everything. *Paradisos! Paradisos!* Twice. Once gets the idea over. Why does he push so? What makes him so anxious?"

"You think he's anxious?"

"He spent half an hour impressing me that he knows how to handle women and that I—mind you, I liked him—I don't. Maybe it's because he's so spectacularly ugly."

"He's that, all right. One nice thing about him is the way he feels about his family. Did he take you down into his boat?"

"He told me women weren't allowed there."

"I bring him his mail every morning."

"You trying to make me jealous? Look, here he comes."

"I didn't know I could—make you jealous."

"Rest easy. You can. Who's he fucking, anyway?"

"I've never seen him with a girl. They tell me you Greeks like cathouses."

"I never had to pay for a piece in my life!"

"Patrioti!" Petros shouted. "Hey, young fellow, you come here, work with me and your wife, I make you rich man, what you say?"

"Just make my wife rich. I'll live off her."

"You going to drive north?" Ethel asked.

"I haven't made up my mind."

"If you want to go, you can take my car," she said.

He decided not to go up to Mangrove Still. Just before six, he drove to the marina and found Ethel at a cocktail party on the deck of Mr. Roth's boat. Petros waved to him to come on board, but Teddy kept his distance till Ethel made her excuses and joined him. Laughter followed her; she'd made friends.

"I stayed around here," he told her later, "because I'll be damned if I know how to break it to the old man about what you've done. I can't pretend I gave you permission to take this apartment."

"I guess you'll have to heave it at him and duck."

"I figured I'd stall till we can go up together and maybe you'll tell him, with me clucking on the sidelines. If he can take it from anybody, he can take it from you. He'd just bawl me out for not controlling you."

Teddy stayed down the next day too. He saw a movie, went back to the apartment, read the old magazines the former tenant had left behind, went to see another movie, came home and waited for the working member of the family to be through for the day.

He took her to dinner. "I've only got two more nights here, then I'll have to fly back west. What will you do if Pop blows sky high?"

"Run for the woods," she said. "Honestly, Teddy, I wish you'd tell him; it's the only sensible thing. I mean, be tough with him. Isn't there a limit to how much we can go by what he thinks right? I will not drive one hundred miles a day, that's for sure!"

"You know he expects you to be pregnant any minute."

"To tell you the truth, I've stopped waiting for that. But if I am, all the more reason."

The third night, he surprised her, told her he'd make dinner. Hamburgers and onion rings out of the freezer. She told him she'd get one of the black men who worked around the marina to drive her home so he could stand by his hot stove. She was tickled that he was doing it.

When Teddy heard a car drive up, he looked out the window and saw that it was Petros who'd brought her home. The two of them sat talking in the front seat for over ten minutes while Teddy watched and waited.

"What the hell were you two talking about while my dinner spoiled?" he grumbled, only half a joke. "It's seven o'clock."

"He was telling me what he thought of you."

"What was that?"

"He likes you but he says no Greek should marry an American girl. Your mothers, he says, bring you up a certain way and you expect a wife to replace the old lady, right down to washing your Jockey shorts by hand

and cleaning out your ears in the morning. He was very interesting on the subject."

"I'm sure. By the way, did you know he gave you the job because he wanted to fuck you?"

"Oh, Teddy!"

"He told me that. Straight out."

"Teddy, everyone's always wanted that. It's nothing I ask for."

"But you knew it when you took the job."

"Don't be that way, Teddy."

"Tell me this and I'll shut up. Is he your next step?"

"To what?"

"To whatever you're up to?"

"Teddy, I've been working hard all day and I'm very tired."

"O.K."

"And goddamn it, you were with someone else, remember that? Not me."

Ethel congratulated him on the dinner, said he ought to cook more often. Then at precisely eight fifty-four, she fell asleep watching TV.

Teddy marked the exact time. He'd waited for her all day and they'd been together exactly one hour and fifty-four minutes.

The fourth day when Teddy went to pick her up, there were two men in business suits talking to Ethel in a corner of Petros's office.

Petros was watching from his desk.

"What's going on?" Teddy whispered.

Petros pursed his lips, pushed them forward, shrugged his shoulders.

Teddy couldn't hear what they were saying. He saw Ethel nod, then nod again.

"I'm her husband," Teddy said, walking up. "Petty

Officer Third Class"—he touched his sleeve—"Ted Ava-liotis."

"Sorry about this." The taller of the two men flipped a wallet to establish his identity. "We have orders to bring your wife in."

"In to where?"

"Orlando. To the naval investigators on the base there."

Teddy's reaction was relief; Ethel was about to be controlled. The problem was out of his hands.

Ethel smiled at him. "Don't worry about it," she said, "I've been expecting this. Hey, boss, how about some coffee for these men?"

"Sure," Petros said. "Coffee? Something? I got good whiskey."

"No, thanks," the tall man said, then, turning to Ethel: "Hate to hurry you, Mrs. Avaliotis—is that the way you pronounce it?"

"We've been up all night," the other man said. He sounded grumpy.

"So now what the hell you rushing?" Petros said.

"Peetie, this is not your business," Ethel said, "so shut up."

"A few minutes, for God's sake. Everybody have one coffee."

The tall man thanked Petros politely and the pair left the office, signaling Ethel to follow.

"Wait a minute," Teddy called out. The men stopped. Teddy took Ethel by the hand and led her to the agents. "I want you to tell my wife that I didn't give you her address."

"They don't have to do that," Ethel said.

"We got the address in the usual way," the tall agent said. "It was on our pickup sheet yesterday morning."

"I'll get my purse," Ethel said. She ran into Petros's office.

Teddy saw she didn't believe him, and he was about to go after her when he heard Petros speaking.

"You coming back? To Florida?"

"If I get lucky."

"Job here waiting," Teddy heard Petros say.

"You don't have to do that," Ethel said.

"You don't have to do nothing," Teddy heard. "Job here waiting."

Then Ethel was coming out. She took Teddy's arm and, walking close by his side, she whispered, "Don't worry about it. I don't blame you."

"But I didn't," Teddy said. "I really didn't."

"O.K.," she said. "You didn't. But I mean . . . how else could you run a navy?"

"May we get moving, please," the tall agent called out. He was standing against a tree, smoking a cigarette in the shade. The other man, less concerned about making a good impression, was leaning over the hood of their car; he seemed to be dozing; slumped in the back, asleep, was a man in manacles.

"I'd like to say good-bye to his parents," Ethel said.

The tall agent looked at his watch. "Where do they live?" he asked.

"Mangrove Still, just a couple of miles north of Tarpon Springs," Ethel said.

"I know where that is," the indifferent agent said, getting in behind the wheel. "It's a little out of our way. But so what? Let's go, huh? What do you say, miss?"

"You coming to Orlando with us?" the tall agent asked Teddy.

"He can't," Ethel explained. "He has to report back to San Diego in the morning."

"I'm on duty tomorrow," Teddy said. "But I want to say good-bye to my folks too. You can follow me up there."

Before she got in the car, Ethel put her arms around

Teddy's waist, pulled him to her and kissed him on the lips.

By the time they reached Mangrove Still, it had hit Teddy hard. His wife thought he was a liar and he was furious all over again with his father for encouraging Ethel's rebelliousness. It was because of that old fool's encouragement that she'd left the Navy the way she had.

Ethel, on the other hand, was in high spirits. She ran into the house to tell Costa the news. She had no doubt where his sympathies would be.

He stormed out of the house like a bull out of a pen. He saw Teddy first. "Why they bothering her?" he demanded to know.

"Because of you," Teddy said. "You encouraged her to desert. I warned you and I warned her. Well, now it's happened, so you straighten it out, go ahead."

This release of anger didn't dent Costa. He bulled over to the agent's car and demanded to know: "Why you bothering this woman?"

"Who are you?" the agent behind the wheel said.

"Come out from there, do me favor," Costa ordered. "I will explain you something. Family business. Come on, my friend, I don't want to be angry here."

The tall agent joined Costa.

On the porch, Ethel and Teddy waited while an intense whispered consultation went on. Costa seemed to be making a point about Ethel.

Noola brought them coffee.

Teddy spoke to Ethel. "I warned you," he said.

"Don't worry about me," she answered. "I knew what I was getting into. I can't imagine anything they can do that would bother me. Hey, look at your old man go!"

"He talked you into it; let him talk you out of it. And I'll tell you again, I did not give them your address. Maybe I should have, but I didn't."

"O.K.," she said. That was all she said; she still didn't say she believed him.

Now Teddy was even angrier and he walked off the porch to where Costa was talking to the tall agent. This man turned and looked at Ethel. "You mean take it easy on the bumps, is that what you mean, sir?"

"What I mean, her condition, why you bothering her this condition?"

"Sir, we have no choice. You can see that."

"I see nothing. I hold you responsible over here." Costa was no longer whispering. "If anything happen, government pay. Don't forget that, my boy."

"O.K., government pay," the man behind the wheel mimicked.

Costa was on him like a flash. "Don't get fresh with me, you!" he warned.

"Charlie!" The tall agent made a "Cool it!" gesture.

The opposition subdued, Costa walked away, stiff-kneed, grabbed Teddy by the arm and led him out of everyone's range.

"These are barbarians," he said.

"It's your fault," his son said. "They're just doing their job, but it was you encouraged her to disappear that way. You flattered her and spoiled her and made her believe whatever damn fool idea she had was O.K. I don't know what she's doing anymore or what she wants. She's out of control. I didn't tell you, she took an apartment in Bradenton, her own apartment! Took it without asking me! Why? She's working with that goat-head Greek, Kalkanis, took the job without asking me. Why? Every time I turn my back, she's into something nutty, and usually with your encouragement. What are you trying to do, Pop, break us up? Hey, Pop, I'm talking to you!"

Teddy had never in his life talked to his father this way.

Costa was shocked. "All right, my boy," he said slowly, shaking his head. "You leave this business to me. Her life, so forth, so on. I fix everything proper way. Don't worry." Quickly he went into the house.

The tall agent came up to Teddy and said, "My wife is pregnant, too, and she goes everywhere with me, fishing, camping—it's all superhighway now. She even bowls. Why's the old man so excited?"

"Ask him," Teddy said.

Ethel came running. "He's going with me," she said to Teddy. She was wildly excited. "Says he'll be out in five minutes," she told the agent.

The tall agent looked at his watch, then walked to the shade under the live oak and lit a cigarette.

"Teddy," Ethel said, "I'll call you tomorrow, tell you what happened."

"O.K. And—and I'm sorry. I don't know how to help you anymore."

That's all they said, standing side by side, not speaking, until, minutes later, Costa came out of the house, dressed in his shiny black suit and a dark-red tie. Noola followed him, carrying an old valise.

"Come on, we go," he ordered, walking directly to the car. There he saw the manacled man in the back. "Who's this criminal?" he demanded.

No one answered.

"You sit up here with me," he instructed Ethel. "You sit in the back with him," he told the tall agent.

Costa helped Ethel into the front seat, sat next to her, put his arm over her shoulder. "Ready!" he announced.

At Orlando's NTC, Costa sat impatiently in the waiting room of the naval investigator while Ethel was being questioned inside. Finally a secretary asked him to come in. He entered the office like an aggrieved king, sat, arms folded, waiting to make judgment.

"They've decided to dispose of the matter out there," the naval investigator informed him.

Costa frowned. "Who decide what?"

"San Diego. I talked to them on the phone," the investigator said. "They'd rather handle it out there. They're familiar with her record. It's serious, you see. Desertion means court-martial."

"So when we go?" Costa said.

"Oh, Dad, you don't have to come," Ethel said. "Teddy's out there. He'll take care of me."

"I hope so." Costa turned to the naval investigator. "When she going?"

"Now. There'll be a car outside—" He called to the outer office. "Bill! When's the airport pickup?"

They had a twenty-minute wait. At the end of the hall downstairs, there was an ice cream machine and Costa bought Ethel a bar on a stick. They found a bench outside, sat side by side to wait.

"How will you get home, Dad?"

"Don't worry, I take bus."

"Dad. You know what you told that man is not true? I'm not pregnant."

"How you know?"

"I know."

"So what's the matter? Something your family? Your mother, her sickness? Maybe you have same thing? A little?"

"I don't think it's anything like that," Ethel said.

"Teddy come near you enough?"

"Sometimes. Other times, I'm not sure he likes me that way."

"He has other woman, maybe?"

"I don't know, Dad."

"I speak to him, I straighten other-woman business out right away, that son of a bitch."

311

"I'm sure that's not it, Dad."

"You have to help him, you know, cook nice dinner, give him compliment, look at him certain way." Costa illustrated. "Like this."

"I do that. Not as well as you, but . . ."

Costa didn't get the joke.

"It's probably tension," she said.

"Six months' tension?"

"It's barely two months without, Dad. You know I want to make you happy more than anything in the world, you know that."

"You go see doctor," Costa said. "Let him look you over good. I pay everything."

"I'll do whatever you want, Dad, but . . . what do you say we give it another month?"

"O.K. One more month."

She finished her ice cream, slipped her arm through the bend of his and pulled up close.

He felt the side of her breast pressed against him. How could anyone not come near her every night? Costa wondered.

"Tell me," Ethel said. "What do they do in the country where you were born when a wife does not produce?"

"On island, Kalymnos?"

"They go to a doctor?"

"Doctor there, they know nothing."

"So then?"

"Whole family go to priest. Priest give *kukla,* means doll, small one, made from metal—silver for rich, for poor, tin. This size. Flat." He held his thumb and fore-finger three inches apart. "It has big belly." A gesture. "You understand? Our women wear this *kukla* under their clothes. Best place here."

He touched Ethel where her abdomen swelled.

"I write my cousin on island," he said. "I get you one."

312

"And that works, the *kukla* under the dress?"

"Better than doctor, guarantee that much. At same time, everybody in family pray. Every night. Gives more strength."

"Have you been praying?"

"Every night. I tell Noola too."

"She's been praying?"

"She do what I do. Prayers of mother very strong on this."

"Suppose," Ethel said, "despite the prayers and the pregnant *kukla* of silver or tin—despite all that, nothing happens. Then what?"

"You mean in the old days, what would happen?"

"No. Now. What happens now on your island if, after all that—"

"Change the woman."

"Jesus! Isn't that sort of drastic?"

"Women understand. Son is necessary. Who's going to bring in fish? Who will bring up sponge?"

"Would you change me?"

"What else could we do? Even you would say go 'head, change me."

Ethel thought for a moment, then she said, "Suppose it's the husband's fault?"

"How could it be his fault?"

Ethel failed herself.

"Of course," she said. "It couldn't be his fault."

A car drove up. It was olive drab; the airport pickup.

fifteen

IN San Diego, she was escorted to the long, low Spanish colonial building that holds the legal offices of the Naval Training Command. She found Teddy waiting there, but they didn't have a moment together because the chief lawyer, a Lieutenant Commander Bower, came back from lunch and immediately asked them into his office, a square room full of heavy oak pieces.

"Avaliotis!" He looked at Teddy sternly. "Why didn't you come to me months ago and tell me she couldn't take the military life, was getting tension headaches and nightmares and dizzy spells and all those other disabilities women are supposed to suffer when the fact is they're a lot healthier than we are?"

"Because I didn't have headaches or nightmares or dizzy spells," Ethel said. "What I had was a sudden impulse, early one morning, and I left."

"A sudden impulse!" Lieutenant Commander Bower inspected the young woman carefully. "I have your record here." He held up a folder. "It appears you were doing very well. What happened? Avaliotis, what happened?"

"I was doing well," Ethel said, "so don't blame Teddy, sir."

"Anyway, I'm afraid it's serious now." He turned back to Teddy. "She not only went UA, she didn't come back under her own power. She had to be towed back under guard. Am I right? Avaliotis, I'm talking to you."

"Yes, sir, you're right, sir."

"So it's no longer a matter of Unauthorized Absence. It's desertion."

He pressed a button on his desk. Dolores came in, looked at Ethel, whom she didn't know, nodded at Teddy, whom she did, and said, "Yes, sir," to her boss.

"Get that damned shrink on the phone," he said. "What's his name? The one whose mind is on tennis and —You still go out with him, Dolores?"

"Yes, sir. Captain Cambere, sir."

"Well, come on; let's see if you can get him on the phone."

He turned back to Teddy. "There is no indication anywhere in all this paper," he smacked his hand down on Ethel's folder—"that she planned to come back. Did she ever—Avaliotis, I'm talking to you! Did she ever show you any such indication?"

"Ask her, why don't you, sir?"

"Did you plan to return here, Mrs. Avaliotis? Ever?"

"Not ever," Ethel said.

"You see, Avaliotis? She'll have to go before the captain's mast. There has to be some kind of effective punishment. You can see that, can't you?"

"Yes, sir," Teddy said.

"If there were no punishment, everyone who had what your wife calls a sudden impulse would disappear and then who'd be left to man the ships?"

This struck Ethel as funny and she began to laugh. Lieutenant Commander Bower studied her.

A buzzer sounded. Bower lifted the listen key and they all heard Dolores: "Captain Cambere is playing tennis, sir."

"Well, there you are," Bower said. "We're not exactly at battle stations here, are we?"

He pushed the talk key. "Send someone down to the tennis court and get your boyfriend to a telephone immediately." He released the key. "I told them not to put tennis courts on the base," he said.

Then he looked out the window and sighed. "Yes, I'm afraid there has to be some show of force. Avaliotis, I'm talking to you. Your wife, she's sweet, or seems so; naïve, or so it appears; maybe she's just plain stupid. I can't make her out, can you? But we have one hard fact. She's a deserter. I don't know what good it would do to confine her, but . . . Would that make her a good Navy man? Avaliotis, answer me!"

"She'd be what she is," Teddy said, "no matter what you did to her."

"So what do we do, Avaliotis? I don't mean to put you on the spot, but you are her husband and to some extent you have to take responsibility——"

"No, sir," Ethel said, "he is not responsible. Not for anything I do. I'm responsible for every silly bit of it."

Dolores put her head in the door. "Captain Cambere on five-seven-five," she said.

"Where the hell have you been? Don't lie to me, because I know. You're not separated from the service yet, are you? Another week? Well, let's get our money's worth out of you. I'm sending you one white female, Seaman Apprentice Avaliotis. What? I don't give a damn about your rubber set. What? Desertion! That's what it amounts to. Now don't just put her name up top of the same report you've sent me the last ten times! 'This person has no

316

place in the U.S. Navy and so forth, signed, Captain whatever-your-first-name-is Cambere." Give me a genuine estimate of this person's personality. Because I can't make her out. When? Now. Look outside your door; she's there."

Captain Cambere was in his tennis clothes, a towel around his neck, still perspiring and in a sulk. He didn't rise when Ethel was shown in.

"Are you in some kind of hurry?" he asked.

"Not that I know of," Ethel answered.

"Now what does that mean, please?"

"Your chief seems to be in a hurry."

"Frankly I don't care. I'm going to sit quiet till I stop sweating. Get yourself a magazine; there's a mess of them in the corner."

He pushed his sneakers off, wheeled his chair so his back was to her, put his feet in their white sweat socks on the window sill and ran his palm over the soft hair that covered his calf. Then he proceeded to light a long, thin cigar, running the flame of the match up and down under its length before applying heat to the tip. He behaved as if Ethel weren't in the room.

After a moment of silence and smoke, he turned in his chair and pressed the talk key of his intercom. "Tell Bobby Frost," he said to the girl in the other room, "that I shall be back in ten minutes and—What? Where is he! Marian, will you try thinking a little before you ask a question? He's on the tennis court, the one I just left, and what I want you to tell him is that I will certainly play the third set if he'll stay put till I get back, which will be in ten minutes. You got it now? On the tennis court?"

When he looked up, he became aware that Ethel was examining him.

"You play tennis?" he asked.

"I don't play any game."

"Then you cannot have the faintest idea, can you, what it means to have an opponent on the run, particularly a man you've wanted to beat for months, then be jerked off the court, away from a victory you can taste."

"And what's even worse," Ethel said, "the reason is to examine a silly little cunt who's deserted from the United States Navy."

"What!"

"I don't blame you for being sore."

Captain Cambere couldn't tell if she was kidding.

Until she said, "You're a rude man."

"I can be rude, yes. What in particular made you say that now?"

"In particular! Everything you've done since I came in. You haven't even taken off your hat."

He pulled the visor of his cap down, reached for a yellow legal tablet, picked up a pencil, then looked at Ethel long and hard.

"Perhaps we can make this short," he said. "Do you want to stay in the Navy or do you want out?"

"Is it up to me?"

"Do you always wear a perfume this heavy?"

"Don't you like it?"

"Why do you assume I don't like it?"

"You've asked me three questions," she said. "Which one do you want answered?"

"I see you're married," he said.

She looked at her ring finger, posing her hand in the light from the window as a jewelry model might. "Yes," she said, in the manner of a TV commercial. "I'm a woman and I'm married."

"Happily?" he said, making a note.

"Does anyone really know? Are you married?"

"No. Why did you join the Navy?" He made another note.

"I thought it would solve my problems."

"Did it?"

"What would I be doing here if it had?"

"And what are you feeling now—along with resentment of me? What do you think of all this?"

"All what, please?"

"You're here because you deserted. The Navy takes a dim view of that. What do you think of the situation you're in?"

"It's like one of those scenes they have in desert movies, a mirage, something I don't understand happening somewhere else to someone else. I don't believe I'm here. I don't know why I gave you the right to judge me. I don't know if I should stay and take it or walk out that door and disappear from everybody forever."

"All this here is a mirage, you say?"

"A fantasy."

"Have you been kidding me?"

"No. I'm telling you the truth. Don't you want to hear it?"

"I want to hear whatever you want to say."

"My brain, or whatever you call it, seems to have turned into a comic book lately. I have these fantasies all the time. I'm going along fine, when all of a sudden I'm imagining something awful which I didn't mean to think about and don't want to think about."

"You are kidding me."

"No. For instance, suddenly I'm raising hell with a cop who's arrested me unfairly. I pull the handcuffs out of his hands and slash him across the face. Or someone has finally found out something terrible I did long ago. I'm dragged before a kangaroo court. What are they? Israelis. I detonate a bomb, destroying them all. Like a comic book. Or—this one came to me just this morning—I'm calling my husband's mother and explaining to her that I shot her son by accident, that it wasn't my fault he died. Isn't that ridiculous? But I warn you that—"

"Warn me? What have I got to do with it?"

"Nothing. But I'm warning you that I won't take it. I don't have to explain anything to anybody, and that includes you."

She seemed to be laughing, but he wasn't sure.

"Go on," he said, "though I still don't understand my connection."

"So then I'm pleading with whoever's judging me—the cop or the Israeli court or my mother-in-law—that I'm not as bad as they believe. I think I'm being forgiven, but I'm not, because these comic book scenes keep coming back, again and again. I've done something awful, escaped, then been caught, brought back, kicking and pleading."

She stopped. There were tears in her eyes.

"Still everyone seems to like me," she said. "In real life, I mean. But you know something?" She dropped her voice. "When people like me is when I don't respect them. They don't know my real thoughts. If they did, they wouldn't like me. If they weren't so stupid, they'd think the same thing about me that I think of myself."

"Which is?"

"Not much." She turned her face away. "I didn't tell you," she continued after a moment, "that I'm an adopted child. I should be used to that by now. But I'm not. I still feel bad about it. Real bad. Like today. I hate you all today."

"Us all?"

"Including you, yes. Everybody. Yes."

There was a long interval of silence. Ethel, unable to speak, was staring out the window.

Captain Cambere put down his legal pad, leaned forward and pressed his talk key. He spoke to his secretary in a voice she could barely hear. "Tell Frost, on the court, that I won't be coming down after all. And no calls until I tell you different."

Their interview lasted almost three hours, the light outside dimming toward the end. Forty-five minutes before her usual departure time, Captain Cambere's secretary came in, after knocking twice, and asked if she could go. She'd learned to do this if he remained with a female longer than an hour.

"Yes," Captain Cambere said, "you can go."

"I have to go too," Ethel said to the secretary.

The secretary nodded and left the room. She'd heard that before.

"But I feel better," Ethel said. "Much better." She was looking for her purse.

Captain Cambere took the purse off the desk, where she'd left it, but he didn't give it to her.

"Do you find," Ethel said, "that you can tell more to an absolute stranger than to someone you know well?"

"What blocks you from talking to your husband?"

"I don't know. Do you?"

"I have a pretty good idea. Tell me, why do people keep trying to solve their problems through other people when everyone knows it's impossible?"

"That's true. Why do I do that?"

"I haven't met your husband. Is he some kind of extraordinary man?"

"I thought so. The most trustworthy man I've ever met."

"Still you don't trust yourself to him."

"True. But why do I? I mean, what you said before —I've always tried to solve my problems through some man or another. Isn't that what you said?"

"You said 'man.' I said 'other people.'"

"Why do I do that?"

"I could find out in another talk or two."

"Now . . . I have to go." She stood up.

"Well, I'm here."

"May I ask you one more question?"

"No. Are you kidding? Of course."

"My husband, he doesn't come near me anymore and—how can I say this? I always have to start it. When we do. And yesterday, I looked in the mirror and I thought: I'm really very pretty! So . . ."

She waited. He didn't speak.

"I am," she said.

"What about you?"

"What? Oh. I like him. I even love him. And I used to get it off so quickly, so easily. But now, when we do it, nothing happens. At the end—there is no end. I used to pretend. Now I don't even do that. It's all dried up and I don't know what happened."

Her eyes were filling with tears.

"Tell me," she said, "are you supposed to always feel the same way about someone?"

"Perhaps you've simply stopped believing he can help you. And he, that you can help him."

"Yes, there's that. But it's more physical. You know?"

She suddenly turned her head toward the door.

"What?" he asked.

"I thought I heard someone out there."

"Our door is locked."

"I have to go." She moved toward the door. "Now you can take your shower. You must be good and gummy." She laughed as she reached for the purse he was holding.

"I'm worried about you," he said as she pulled the purse slowly through his hands.

"Oh, don't bother. Just one thing: You said before you had a pretty good idea what blocks me talking to my husband. . . . Every other way too?"

"When a god fails, it's not forgiveable. There is only one way you can find out what you feel about him—which is the problem, isn't it?"

"How?"

"Push it to the sticking point, then push it till it breaks. Or doesn't."

"O.K., I'll try." They stopped at the door, stood there, not speaking, not looking at each other.

"You've helped me a lot," she said.

"I could help you more." His hand was on the door-knob.

She turned and looked at him directly and without wavering.

When he leaned toward her, she held up her hand, stopping him.

"Don't do that," she said.

"Do what?"

"What you were going to."

He took her hand, simply held it in his. Perhaps she left it with him an instant longer than was appropriate.

Suddenly he opened the door. He'd heard something.

A man was sitting in the darkened waiting room.

"Oh," Ethel said. "This is my husband."

She noticed a sign that had been hung on the door-knob. CONSULTATION IN PROGRESS. DO NOT DISTURB. Captain Cambere's secretary must have put it there when she left for the day.

Captain Cambere shook Teddy's hand, but could not have said, later, what the young man looked like.

As soon as they'd gone, he locked the door and poured himself a drink. After a second swallow, he dialed the office of the legal officer.

"Does he have any idea," he asked Lieutenant Commander Bower, "what he's into with that girl?"

"Why do you think I sent her to you? Well, what's your verdict?"

"I like her. She is also the all-American ball-breaker, the one who comes on like a pussycat. I feel sorry for the man. Tell me, do you want him to stay in the Navy or not?"

"If he's not the kind of personnel we're looking for, who is?"

"If you want him in one piece, separate them. Only, when she goes, she must not take his entrails with her. Better let me talk to him, equip him with some psychological protection. Because any minute the ax will fall."

Cambere's interview technique with men was less penetrating, less intimate. When he was through with Teddy, the captain called his superior and informed him that he was right. "Avaliotis has precisely the right limitations on his intelligence and his imagination," he said. "He even has some backbone and it's beginning to stiffen. He's perfect material for the U.S. Navy."

"It's a shame to say that about anyone."

"I didn't intend it as a compliment."

"What did you say to that goddamn shrink?" Teddy demanded from Ethel that night. He hadn't been able to enjoy his dinner. "Did you tell him we were in some kind of trouble?"

"Aren't we?"

"I'm not."

"Even you. Somewhere in"—she touched his chest—"that place you don't tell me about, Teddy."

"I don't like you talking to strangers about what goes on between us," he interrupted.

"He's a psychologist."

"I don't care what he is. It's none of his business."

"Maybe he can help me."

"Do you need help?"

"Like a fire engine. Quick, to the rescue! So do you."

"Did you give him the impression you were thinking of leaving me?"

"Did he say I was thinking of that?"

"He got that from what you said."

"I have thought of it, haven't you? Considered leaving me?"

"Never seriously."

"You have many times. And seriously too."

"How the hell do you know what I think?"

"Because it's normal. Everybody has the same thoughts. But you don't let yourself know what you think. You're cut off from the interior. Listen, Teddy. Don't turn me off—listen. Whatever you think, it's O.K. now. Also, whatever you do. If you find somebody who really helps you, don't hesitate. The ship's going down. It's every-man-for-himself time."

They were in bed, side by side, face up, perfectly still.

"How did he help you?" Teddy asked.

"He told me to stop trying to solve my problems through another person."

"And that helped you? That idea?"

"A lot, Teddy."

"Any other person?"

"Every other person. I'm alone now. And I like it."

"What am I for?"

"For yourself."

It wasn't a court-martial, though it was called that, *pro forma;* it was a hearing. The facts were stated, Ethel confirming that they'd been accurately told. The judge shook off consultation. Then the room, full of heavy maple furniture, was cleared and the judge, a captain of supplies, faced Ethel.

"I have no choice," he said.

Teddy wasn't there; he worked hard all day.

When he got home, Ethel had a drink waiting and dinner in the stove. She told him what the judgment had been: thirty days confined to quarters, loss of a month's pay, reduction in rate. "But there was nowhere much to go down," she said. "I'm back at the bottom. E-One seaman recruit. Home by special dispensation."

They laughed together. Both were relieved.

"They were generous," Teddy said, "even to let you come here."

"They were. I'm disgraced but happy. So are they. I mean happy, not disgraced. They're rid of me."

"Now what?"

"I'm confined to quarters, which is here, I hope. Till the CO makes the final decision. Commander Bower has given him his recommendation, based on Adrian's report."

"Who's Adrian?"

"The shrink, Captain Cambere. He urged them to get me out because you were an asset. To protect you, the Navy should get rid of me. Isn't that cute! He's smart, that Adrian! Take your shower—go on, hurry. I'll get dinner."

"Now what do we do?" he asked, standing in the bathroom doorway, toweling himself.

"I'm going back home," she said. Her hands were in the flower-patterned potholder mittens they'd bought when they'd first furnished the place, long ago.

"Where's home?" he asked, as he'd asked before.

"Florida."

Teddy didn't react; that is, he reacted but concealed it. He went back into the bathroom, hung up the towel and slowly, thoughtfully, put on a blue terry-cloth robe.

He was trying to decide if he really wanted her, and if he did, how far he'd go to hold her.

"What were you thinking in there?" she said when he came forth.

"Nothing."

"Try saying what you think, Teddy, just for the hell of it."

"I don't really know."

"Sure you do. Say it. I dare you."

"Well, then——" He stopped.

"Go on, baby."

"Well, this means that we'll be living apart?"

Putting it as a question relieved him of presenting it as a conclusion he'd come to. It forced her to say it.

"That is correct," she said, Navy style.

"Why do we stay together at all?"

"Speak for yourself. There is nobody I like better than you."

"That is certainly a bass-ackwards compliment."

"It's saying a lot. I trust you. I don't want to look too far ahead. It's too confusing. There is only one thing I need now: an infant Avaliotis to give to your father. He really knows what he wants. We don't and no one else I've ever met does. It's the least we can do. Out of respect, to respect his wish. Besides, I love him. I really love you too. I'm not in love with you anymore, but I love you. I feel for you."

"Why don't you love me—I mean, what you said?"

"Maybe I haven't got it in me."

"You got it in you; I remember."

"Maybe it's because . . . I'm a little scared now, that's the truth. All I want is for someone to love me. Despite what I am."

"Baby, you'll be O.K."

"I hope so. Oh, Teddy, Teddy dear . . ."

The sexuality her voice promised was so entire, so soft and open, a plea from the bottom of a hungry soul. She touched his face, then put her soft, pale hand through the fold of his blue terry-cloth robe.

Once again he didn't doubt that he loved her and always would and that she loved him and always would. It happened that quickly!

Afterward she told him that it was precisely her time of the month to conceive.

They spent the whole next day in bed. It was something Ethel had always wanted to do.

The following morning the decision came down from the commanding officer. Ethel had been granted an administrative discharge. She was, they had decided, unsuitable for the Navy. That was final and it was official.

That night they made love again and again. Teddy had forgotten how much of it he had in him. Once again he discovered how fragile she seemed, how powerful her body actually was.

The next morning she left for Florida, and this time he drove her to the airport.

"I know I can go on to be an officer now," he said to her at the gate while everyone else was boarding. "I have to go to NROTC next, but I can do that in Florida, at Jacksonville U. I've applied there. When I graduate, I'll be commissioned. Would you like that?"

"I'd love that."

"I mean, in Florida."

She kissed him. They were in love again. So they believed.

"Better get on the plane," he said. "And write me, will you?"

"Hurry," she said, "and miss me, miss me bad."

Still in his arms, she whispered, "I won't take that job if you don't want me to."

"Which job? Oh. With the marina, Petros whatsisname? I don't mind; go ahead."

They walked to the gate, holding each other all the way.

The last of the passengers were hurrying through.

"Don't worry," she said, "I won't let him come near me."

"I'm not worried," he said. "Not anymore."

sixteen

THE next afternoon, in the "happy hour," Teddy went to the Ship's Bell and sat in the booth where Dolores had first come to comfort him. There he waited, prepared to tell her that he and Ethel were close again.

He saw her across the darkened public room, looking for him. "I need a drink," she said when she was at his side.

After she'd finished one drink, talking about this, that and nothing, she ordered a second and told him she was pregnant.

"Whose is it?" Teddy asked.

He was frightened but oddly pleased.

"Yours. Who else?"

"I don't know who else you been with," he said.

"Holy Christ! You fucking men!"

"Well . . . whose is it?"

"Sure I been going out. What did you expect me to do

—sit and worry how you and your wife were getting along?"

"What'd you think of my wife?"

"I can see what men find attractive about her."

"What?"

"She's the perfect victim and since all men are sadists, she must get one hell of a play. Did she sleep with Adrian Cambere?"

"No."

"You sure?"

"Sure I'm sure. What makes you think that?"

"Adrian doesn't see a girl twice unless he's aced her."

"She didn't see him twice."

"You sure?"

"And she didn't fuck him either."

"How was she after me?"

"Don't talk about her that way."

"So that's the way it is!"

"Yes, that's the way it is. We're going to have a kid."

"What about the one you're having with me?"

"You just said you'd been out with—"

"Going out with doesn't mean going to bed with, and seeing doesn't mean fucking. You're really such a prig. I got your kid in me. Now what do you want me to do about it?"

"Whosever it is, have an abortion."

"Good-bye."

She started to get up, but just then the waiter brought their order and Teddy said, "Have your drink. What's your hurry?"

An hour later they'd had four apiece and an hour after that they were in her bed.

The next morning, she looked wan. "I'm going to make arrangements to have it sucked out of me," she said.

"Sucked!"

"Pumped. Like that better?"

"Sounds brutal."

"You men! I'll need some money."

"Tell you what. Let's all chip in, all your lovers and all your prospective lovers; let's keep you circulation-ready."

She walloped him. But he didn't care.

"I don't want to see you anymore," she said.

Dolores's pregnancy had made him cocky. "You'll see me anytime I want," he said.

And she did.

A week later, as he was leaving to go back to his own place to spend the end of the night—and be there in case Ethel called in the morning—Dolores informed him that she was having the abortion that day.

"Just tell me one thing," she said, "and it will hurt me less."

Teddy was surprised to see tears in her eyes.

"Tell me that you believe me that it's yours," she said.

"I'll pay for it. Is that what you mean?"

"That is not what I mean. Tell me what I said. I'm carrying your kid and because you don't want it, I'm getting rid of it, and all I'm asking you is that you tell me that you know it's yours."

"O.K., it's mine. And I'm sorry for your trouble."

That noon, he found her eating lunch in La Cantina. He gave her ten twenties in an envelope and started to leave.

"Sit down for a minute," she said. "Try to be human."

Teddy went to the self-service counter, picked up a tuna-fish sandwich and a cola drink, and came back to her table. There he told her that he wasn't going to see her again.

"It's better that way," he said.

331

"You're really such a shit," she said.

"I don't want to see anyone who hates me, and you hate me."

"It isn't even that good," she said.

He finished his sandwich and left. He felt free of all obligation, congratulated himself on how he'd handled the problem.

A week later, he got a letter from Ethel.

"Bad news," she wrote. "I had a visitation this morning, a flow of blood. We don't seem to connect, do we? Your father is terribly disappointed. He watches me like a big cat, circling me, smelling for blood. Well, he found it. Now he insists I be tested. So I'm going to a doctor here and see if I'm O.K. Maybe you ought to do the same."

Then she told him about her job, that Petros kept coming on with her, not crowding her, rather offering himself and waiting for a signal. "Which he'll never get, not from me," she said. "If I ever leave you it won't be for him. When are you coming home?" she concluded. "I need some of those wonderful last days we had. Always remember, like I do, that it's there anytime we reach back for it."

Teddy was glad he'd knocked Dolores up; it was a comfort knowing that if there was a problem, it was Ethel's.

He also had a letter from Costa. "We have saying. 'Where apples fall? Under apple tree.' It's the same sickness her mother has, sure thing. When I first see this woman, I told you many time, remember I say American woman for pleasure, Greek girl for family? Your father knows from experience. Now she talk to Noola about adopting child and so forth. I told Noola tell her nothing doing, no adoption business this family!"

A week later there was a letter from Ethel. She enclosed the doctor's report. She'd been found O.K.

"So we just have to keep on pitching," he wrote his wife. "And that will be fun."

Then he had good news. He'd been accepted for the fall term at Jacksonville University. He wrote Ethel, told her the flight number and asked her to drive up in her car and meet him.

He went to see the Center commander to say good-bye and received the man's blessing. "I want you to know that I gave you the highest possible recommendation," the commander said. "I'm only concerned that nothing in your personal life derail your progress."

"What do you mean, sir?"

"Captain Cambere told me something of your wife. Are you still with her?"

"Of course. I love my wife very much."

"Forgive me for asking: Does she love you?"

"I'm sure she does, sir. I don't know what Captain Cambere can be referring to. I'm certainly going to speak to him and find out."

"He's no longer here," the commander said. "His term of enlistment ran out and he went back into civilian life."

"Where can I find him?" Teddy was furious.

"I could tell you, Avaliotis, but an encounter with him would be pointless. What happened between him and your wife—"

"What did happen?"

"I wasn't suggesting anything irregular took place."

"I thought—excuse me, sir—I thought you were."

"Women, it's been my personal experience, are far more skilled at deception than we are. I value you, so I'm speaking frankly."

"Please do, sir."

"A neurotic woman has ruined many a good naval officer. For instance, a woman can hate you and you'll never know it. If you're her meal ticket she can't afford to let you know it."

"Excuse me, sir. Exactly what did Captain Cambere tell you?"

"You see now, she's got you all upset."

"I'm not upset."

"Good. I'm sure you'll be able to tell at contact whether or not she's alienated—or ever was. Carry on."

Ethel met him in Jacksonville. They went to the university campus and Teddy was among the first to register.

When he said to her, "Why don't we start looking around for an apartment?" he discovered she had no intention of moving up with him.

"Why the hell not, Ethel?"

"I don't want to give up my job."

"I thought you didn't like your boss."

"I don't like him."

"Then why aren't you going to live here with me? Oh, fuck this. I don't want to visit my wife; I want to live with her."

He was so exceptionally aroused that within an hour she'd changed her mind.

They went apartment-hunting, didn't find anything they liked, decided to have a good dinner and go to bed.

The sheets of the chain motel smelled of disinfectant. When they made it, it wasn't the way it had been those last days in San Diego.

"It's always a fizzle the first time after a long drought," he lied.

"Were you with somebody after I left? Tell me."

He decided to give her the truth. "Yes," he said. "For a week. Then I knew I loved you most and forever. So there. I've told you the truth, which is silly, men say, but I decided to do what you asked."

It was a mistake. Even though she said she appreciated it, was glad he had told her, still she was cold. And next morning she took it out on him.

"I went to a doctor and I was tested. I did that for your father and for you and because I want it to work."

"I'm glad you did."

"Now what about you?"

"I'm O.K."

"How do you know?"

"I know."

"How? How can anyone tell?"

"Look, we'll be living together, we won't be in that terrible tension all the time and—"

"You knocked the girl up."

"That's right."

"Well . . ." she said.

"I'm sorry. But that's the whole story. We were together a week, and she got pregnant, and when she had an abortion I didn't see her again."

"O.K.," she said. "That happens."

"Right. Thanks."

"Who was she?"

"What's the difference, who?"

"Was it the girl who kissed you in the Ship's Bell?"

"Yes."

"How would you feel if I did the same thing to you?"

"Did you?"

"Yes."

"Yes?"

"No. But I could have."

"For chrissake, Ethel, will you drop the fucking subject?"

"O.K."

"Let's go look at . . ." He pulled a newspaper out of his pocket, folded to the Apartments for Rent section.

"And you want me to give up my job and come up here—"

"I don't want you to—I insist on it!"

"Well, the hell with you, brother! I'm going back."

335

"No you're not. What do you want that job for?"

"Because right this minute, if I didn't have it, I'd have to stay here with you whether I wanted to or not, and because I do have the job, I can stay where it's best for me to stay, and if I come back it will be because I think I can make it with you and not because I'm dependent on you for meat and potatoes. I don't have to ask you for gasoline and garage and car repairs and you're dependent on me for a ride, not the other way around."

"And that is the way you like it—me dependent on you?"

"At least not the opposite."

Three weeks later she wrote him from the marina, told him she'd forgiven him, that she hadn't been with anyone else, hadn't sought revenge that way. On the other hand, she still couldn't give up her job. If he'd come down there, she'd be glad to see him and promised never, ever, to mention the Ship's Bell.

It was the first weekend after his courses had started.

They were tougher than he had thought and Teddy didn't want to take the two-hundred-thirty-mile ride down to where Ethel lived. But he did it—for his father's sake, perhaps, or for his family's sake, or for his tradition's sake: Greeks don't divorce. They use up their wives breeding children, then take a mistress to blow the froth off the beer.

Ethel was true to her word; she didn't mention the Ship's Bell. She'd fixed up her apartment, made it beautiful. There were pictures on the wall, including one of him in uniform, another that she particularly loved of him at the age of eleven with Costa. There was also a funny old poster Aleko had given her, advertising sponges and showing sharks swallowing divers whole. Before each of the open windows she'd hung little Japanese tinklers made of glass bits which swayed and sounded as the wind stirred them.

"I love what you've done here," Teddy had to say.

"I'm glad."

Ethel seemed harder—not mean or filled with anger; just stronger and in control of her life. Her conversation was full of the events and characters of the marina, about Petros and the new owner—Sy Roth had gone broke and sold out—and about herself, professionally speaking. "I've learned shorthand and I can really type now," she said. "Sixty words a minute!"

After they'd done it a number of times, she told him it was her fertile time again.

He didn't see her for another three weeks. He could not commute that distance; his courses were too tough. He had also found several companions, girls, adequately pretty and very ready. Once again he was on the verge.

It was during these three weeks that Ethel had her first quarrel with Costa.

Costa had noticed that everyone in the area who had once been so delighted with Ethel's presence now seemed to have turned against her. He was no longer complimented daily on his daughter-in-law.

His friend Johnny Gonatos, when questioned, explained it to Costa this way: "She looks at the men now." It was a precise explanation.

Ethel was struggling with something she'd seen all her life but never really taken in before. When a man and a woman pass on the street, if natural curiosity makes them glance at each other, it is the woman who looks quickly away. A woman will not hold a look at a man for longer than the blink of an eye. It might be misunderstood.

Women, Ethel decided, behave on the street like animals being hunted.

She experimented, prolonged her looks, soon turned the tables, had the men looking down or away.

Costa called her on the phone to tell her of the change in the attitude of his fellow citizens.

"Why you look every *skoopeethi* on the street?" he asked.

"Where am I supposed to look?" she asked.

"On the ground!" Costa said.

"Even when I'm with somebody—another man, my husband, you?"

"On the ground! When they look you, right away throw your eyes on the ground. Otherwise, sure thing, they get wrong idea."

But Ethel wouldn't. Soon the talk stopped, which was the worst possible sign; it meant the attitude of the town was fixed in hostility.

One evening Ethel came home to her apartment to find Noola there, looking embarrassed. The two women made dinner and while they were doing the dishes, Noola revealed why she was there.

"He wants to know what's the matter."

"Tell him to ask his son."

"Last time I told him it was tension. What will I say this time?"

"Same thing," Ethel said. "This time I'm tense."

"He thinks you should be up there, living with Teddy."

"Tell him you don't like being his messenger. If he wants to know something, let him come down and ask me himself."

"He can't talk openly about these things."

"O.K., I'll drive up and I'll talk openly."

Late Sunday afternoon—Monday was her day off— Ethel drove north. Costa was waiting for her, sitting in the last of the light under the great live oak back of the house. As she came toward him, he indicated where he wanted her to sit, an old king receiving a subject come to plead a favor.

He didn't waste a minute. "I want you quit that job,"

he said. "It's bad for Teddy you be away from him like this. And I don't like you there with that fellow Petros. He no good."

"I don't want to quit the job, Dad," she said.

It was as if he hadn't heard her. "I tell Petros myself, son of bitch, I tell him you don't want his money, I go down clean everything straight right away."

"I like the job, Dad. I'm going to keep it."

"No, no; no good for Teddy. That's why every day tension over there. You quit now; it's enough."

"I'll talk to Teddy about it," she hedged.

"Never mind Teddy," Costa said. "I'm telling you. Quit the job."

"I won't. I will not."

She thought he was going to strike her. But he didn't. He reached up to a branch of the tree, one that was dead, tore it off and smashed it against the trunk. Splinters flew.

She waited, head down. She was very frightened. But when he'd stopped shaking, she spoke. "I'm sorry, Dad," she said, her voice husky. "It's not tension or anything like that. I went to a doctor the way you asked me to. He said I was O.K."

"So then, what's it?" Costa could hardly get his words out. "The problem?"

"It's Teddy's turn to go to a doctor."

She got up and went into the house, her knees still weak.

But she was pleased. This time she'd stuck up for herself.

In a few minutes she heard the screen door slam and his footsteps going past her room and on to his at the end of the hall. Then, after an interval, he knocked on her door, and when she said, "Come in," he did.

He looked his age now, drawn and pale; the fury, as it passed, had taken some of his strength with it.

He held an envelope in his hand. Its proportions were slightly different from the ones she was accustomed to. One side of it was almost entirely covered with stamps she'd never seen before.

He sat on the edge of the bed, where she was stretched out.

"O.K.," he said, "I tell Teddy to go. Doctor, I'm talking."

"He's probably all right," Ethel said. "He knocked up a girl out west."

"That's good," Costa said.

"It's all right for him to be unfaithful?"

"That's the way men are. I tol' you that many time. You can't change nature."

He was opening the envelope.

"You must forget all that," he said. "You must forgive him that."

"I told him that I have."

"You're a good girl."

"Because I let him off? No, thanks."

"I hear from my cousin," Costa said. "Remember I tol' you I write him our problem over here and ask his help? He went on boat to Lesbos, big island north our small island, and there is priest, Orthodox Church, fine man, very old, near finish his life from where he can see clear ahead to the end."

He held the envelope open now and carefully pulled out two packets wrapped in tissue paper. Putting the envelope to one side, he placed one packet gently on his lap and began to open the crinkly folds.

"This old priest, he listen what my cousin ask and he say one time he had same problem, one of his daughters, she brings out nothing. And he give her this."

Out of the packet of tissue paper he pulled a thin chain, a loop of about two feet.

"This is of silver," Costa said. "So thin, so light, like

sea shell. See." Hanging it from two stubby fingers, he held it up to the bedside lamp with its pink silk shade. "You see. The old priest bless it at the altar, his church."

"For me?"

"Wear it around your middle. When it don't close, you're a mother."

"It's beautiful." Ethel made it sway gently before the light. "So delicate! Can I really keep it?"

"We got it for you. Then my cousin find donkey and he go, day's journey, to old cathedral, Aghia Paraskevi the name, she sits on top of mountain in middle of the island. There they still have old customs and there is another old priest, older than the first one. This man is not educated, so forth, so on, but he has done many surprising things. He brought out all of these here, I show you."

Costa was unfolding the other little packet of tissue paper.

"For different sicknesses, we have different figures," he said. "An arm, a heart, an eye, a leg. My cousin buy this one."

Costa revealed a small figure, stamped out of cheap flat tin and about three inches long.

"What is it?" Ethel asked.

"A woman with child in her belly. You will wear it under your clothes. The peasant womans over there believe in this."

Ethel took it, turned it over, held it up.

"You believe in this, Dad?" she asked.

"Can't do any harm," he said. "My cousin over there give priest money so he bless it at the altar. Yes, I believe."

"Then I'll wear it. Every day."

Costa got up from the bed and walked to the door.

"I ask you now for last time," he said, his back to her. "I don't ask again. Quit that job."

"O.K., Dad," she said. "I'll quit the job."

"When?"

"Tomorrow."

"Good," he said, and left her room, closing the door softly.

When she came in to dinner, Costa embraced her, held her at arms' length, then embraced her again.

She didn't respond. She knew she'd betrayed herself.

Costa was up at six the next morning to see her off and remind her of what she'd promised.

"I'll tell him today," Ethel said. "Give him two weeks to find someone else."

When she got to her apartment, she found a telegram informing her that her mother had died "in her sleep, peacefully."

Vanished without a whimper, Ethel thought.

She reserved a seat on a plane west from Tampa, told Petros she was not sure when she'd be back.

"Hurry up, I need you here," he said. "Goddamn busy week—Whatsa matter?"

She was breaking down. She hadn't known she'd loved Emma Laffey.

Petros came to her and embraced her, gently. "Whatsa matter?" he repeated, like a boy who sees his mother crying for the first time and doesn't know what to do.

She walked to a corner of the office and stood there sobbing. "Get away from me," she said when Petros came near.

Fifteen minutes later she turned around, dry-eyed.

seventeen

DR. Laffey drove Ethel straight to the funeral home. Emma had never looked better. Her hair, which had thinned so that scalp showed, had been curled and teased. It lay on top of her head like baker's twirls and covered the small embroidered baby pillow she'd always had on her bed. Her face had been filled out by some undertaker's gimmickry, the creases eased, the grimace of anxiety on her forehead relaxed. On her lips was the smile of compliance and she was dressed in blue, the color of tranquillity.

Ethel swore she'd never wear blue again.

As they drove home, she noted that her father was thriving. He'd filled out around the shoulders, slimmed his hips, now suggested a former athlete, perhaps a football coach.

A car was leaving their driveway. "I want you to meet Margaret," Ed said. He signaled her to stop.

She immediately liked Margaret, a big woman of perhaps thirty-five, who was bound for the tennis court. "I came by," she said to the doctor. "Thought you might want to play, take your mind off things. Well, don't worry, I'll find a game at the club. Hello there." She waved to Ethel. "I'm glad to meet you finally." And she was gone.

"She plays one hell of a game of tennis," Dr. Laffey said. "Beats me most of the time. She's coming around the world with me."

"Around the world!"

"Everywhere I've never been."

"What about your practice?"

"I'm abandoning it."

"What are you going to do?"

"Not a damned thing. Nothing!"

They had dinner on the terrace. "It's O.K. with me if Margaret comes," Ethel had said. But he wanted to be alone with her.

"I turned fifty-five last week," he said when the table had been cleared for coffee, "and I don't care anymore what anyone thinks of me. Except you. I want to keep a bond with you. So later, if you come to believe that I've been heartless with your mother, remember that she was dying for eight years and that I was here every day and every night and that I did the best I could. But now it's happened and—can you understand this?—I'm celebrating my release."

"You don't have to explain," Ethel said. "I hope this doesn't sound terribly superior, but I'll say it anyway. You have my blessing."

"Thanks." He kissed her. "That's all I wanted."

To celebrate, he had Manuel bring out a bottle of smoky Spanish brandy, Pedro Domecq. "I've been keeping it for an occasion," he said, "but there's never been one I wanted to celebrate. Till now."

Ethel smiled and nodded, took her brandy and re-membered the woman dressed in blue laid out in the teak box, and the smile of compliance on her face.

Many people were at the memorial service for Emma Laffey; many people shed tears.

Ethel noticed a coolness toward her father. Everybody knew about Margaret. To make sure that there was no misunderstanding about her attitude, Ethel stayed at her father's side throughout, held his arm whenever she could.

When they got home, Margaret was there. Ethel liked her even more. She was of a longer-skirted tradition. "Mistress" did not describe Margaret.

Together they finished the brandy.

"What are your plans?" her father asked.

"I don't know."

"Going back to Florida?"

"Not for the time being."

"But eventually?"

"I have a debt to pay there."

"I know it's none of my business," Margaret said, "but your father has told me about your husband and his—"

"Don't say anything bad about his family!" Ethel warned. "Either one of you. It's the only family I've ever had."

Before she looked away, she saw this cut Ed Laffey.

The next morning, she'd disappeared; she was on a plane to San Diego.

She'd wired Adrian Cambere, asking for another in-terview.

He met her at the airport.

"I want to take you up on your offer," she said.

"Which offer?"

"To talk to me again. You helped me before. Did you get me a room?"

345

"At the Rodeway Inn."

"You look different."

She'd noticed he wore a toupee, remembered that at their first encounter he'd never taken off his tennis cap.

"I'm a civilian now and it feels great," he said. "I'm also writing a book."

He went on explaining the changes in his life as he helped her check in. All through dinner, he talked a streak. His professional technique—prodding others to talk—had fallen away.

When he drove her back to the inn, he asked if he might come up.

Once they were settled, she in the maple armchair, he on the side of the bed, there came a moment of uncertainty. Ethel was feeling the wine; they'd emptied a bottle and half of another and what she truly wanted was to go to bed, alone. He was smiling at her in a way she'd seen many times before, the instant before the charge. She knew she'd have to get up an awful lot of energy to hold him off; this tennis player had made her aware all evening how strong his grip was.

It occurred to her that perhaps the simplest thing would be to let him do it; it probably wouldn't take long, he was that worked up. Then she could go to sleep in peace.

He was shaking his head in a kind of premature disappointment—or was it a warning?—a tactic she also recognized: softening the woman up by making her feel guilty in advance for even considering to refuse him. Well, she thought, here it comes.

"The most revealing thing about you," Cambere said, "is the mask you wear."

"That's real heavy shit," Ethel said. "Tell me what it means."

"Why did you come back here? Come on, the truth!"

"To talk with you. You helped me."

"Well, I'm flattered. Is that the only reason?"

346

"I'd like to have a talk with the girl my husband was seeing."

"I'll arrange that for you. And that is all?"

"What I particularly wanted to ask you is . . . remember I told you it had stopped between my husband and me? This puzzled me."

"Why? It's perfectly natural."

"Because I still like him, even love him. But nothing happens. To me. And I used to . . . so easily. For a time I pretended, at the end. You know?"

"Millions do."

"Then I even stopped that. What I was going through or not going through didn't seem to concern him. So I just lay there."

"Yes," he said. "I know." His eyes sparkled. "Now what do you want from me?"

"Only your opinion. Is there any way back from that? Or should I give up?"

He got to his feet, frowning professionally.

"Are you in a hurry?" she asked. "We can talk tomorrow."

"No, this is a very good time for me. First, let's strip away some of the mythological clutter—the bullshit—from around the sex act." He paced back and forth. "No one will admit what is perfectly obvious," he said, "that sex and love are separate, that novelty is a turn-on, that conquest is equally pleasurable to both sexes, that the need to quiet anxiety about one's sexual worth is urgent, that love is not singular, that a person can love more than one person at a time and usually does, that there is nothing wrong with going to bed with a number of one's friends—on the contrary, promiscuity is enriching—that most women in our society marry for a meal ticket and most men for sexual convenience and both stay married, after all interest has collapsed, because they dread the prospect of dying alone—"

"Don't do that."

He was on the floor at the foot of her chair, and he had parted her knees with his hands.

"I want to fuck you," he said.

"I know. When I want you I'll let you know."

He persisted. Urgently aroused, as she could see, he pressed on up her dress. His hands were around her buttocks and he was pulling her forward so her legs were being parted by his body.

"This is really quite good," she said.

She'd lifted the toupee off his head.

All struggle stopped.

"So that's why you kept your tennis cap on that day?"

Dr. Cambere was furious. "Be careful of that," he said, getting up off his knees. "It's fragile and damned expensive." He pulled the hairpiece out of her hand, folded it carefully and put it in his coat pocket. His scalp gleamed.

"Look, Adrian," Ethel said, "I'd really like to talk with you. Could we? Tomorrow? I'm awfully tired now. All that wine's made me sleepy. It's been a long day, for both of us. Sit down. Relax a minute."

"I'm tired too," he said. He sat on the edge of the bed, and after a moment for deflation, consulted a little notebook and said, "I have between two and three open tomorrow."

"Tell me," she said, as she showed him out the door. "When it's all stripped away, the bullshit you were talking about, what's left?"

He smiled at her in a way he hadn't before and in a way that she liked. "Something quite nice," he said.

The next afternoon they had an excellent talk. "Your whole history," he told her, "is one of self-betrayal. Sacrifice of self to authority. The Navy, for an example. I advise you to cultivate the Christian vices. Selfishness above all."

When she shook his hand at the door—there was a patient waiting—she said, "May I come see you tonight?"

"I have a group session between nine and eleven, but after that I'm free and I'd be glad to see you."

"By the way, were you able to locate the woman my husband . . . ?"

"Oh, yes. Dolores. She's available at five-thirty and will be glad to see you. Well, that's an exaggeration. Let's say she's willing to see you. In the Ship's Bell."

It was a lovely afternoon and Ethel had an hour to kill. The breeze off the harbor reached the playground in the residential area where Adrian had his office. Everywhere mothers watched their kids playing in sandboxes and jungle gyms. Infants slept under netting in their carriages.

There wasn't a man in sight, not a father to be seen.

Ethel, sitting in the shade, took it all in, then closed her eyes. There are levels of sleep. Did she dream or did she wonder? If I could somehow make a kid without a father, I'd give Costa a present.

She met Dolores, whom she remembered from Bower's office, in the same booth where she and Teddy used to sit and where Dolores had kissed Teddy with "what he thought was love"—which is how Ethel recalled it to Dolores.

There was no pretense of cordiality.

"There were a few days," Dolores said, "just before you came back the first time, when he used to tell me, 'You're the right girl for me.' That's what he used to say."

"You believed that?"

"You should have seen his face when he said it. I thought: Oh, all my dreams are coming true! My sex dreams, I'm talking about. He's really gorgeous, or have you forgotten? He's what I always wanted. But he doesn't seem to care for it much. Does he?"

349

"Sometimes. And tell me, he asked you to marry him?"

"Many times. I used to practice my new name. What it was going to be. Dolores Avaliotis. It sounded good."

"He thought so too? He liked the sound of it?"

"He didn't stop me saying it. He really doesn't like you, you know."

Ethel didn't answer that—if it was a question. "And when you became pregnant," she said, "the child you aborted—was it his?"

"It could have been. But who knows? When you came back the second time, I saw you walking around together, hand in hand. It wasn't anything like the relationship he'd described to me. I thought he was such a liar."

"He probably felt different ways, different times."

"So I got fed up and I did other men—well, your boyfriend Adrian Cambere for one; he does everybody." She laughed. "I even got my boss one afternoon."

"But you made Teddy pay for the abortion?"

"They all paid for it."

"They chipped in?"

"No, they all paid."

"Each paid?"

"The full amount."

"You made a lot of money on that deal."

"Three times two hundred. You can't have too much money, you know."

"How did you manage that?"

"Scares the shit out of them when you tell them you're knocked up. They give you the cash and run. I could have got more."

"Who was the third again?"

"My boss. Commander Bower. He took exactly two minutes."

"To pay?"

"To do it."

"And you have no bad conscience?"

"Bad conscience! Have you any idea—of course not; Teddy told me you were born rich—still, have you any idea what they can do to you when you have no money in the bank?"

"What who do to whom?"

"Men! To us! Money, my dear, is freedom. Without it, you're a nothing. I have nice tits too, so they tell me. But how long before they droop. Oh, fuck it. Is that why you came all this way—to hear this? You must have guessed it all."

"It does me good to hear it. From you. Thanks. I don't like you, but I appreciate your speaking to me this way."

This conversation convinced Ethel. Her instinct had been true. Teddy was sterile.

The night with Adrian was a disaster.

She did like his body; it was compact, with nicely rounded muscles, and free of heavy hair. But he was unexpectedly anxious. All through the event he kept up a running stream of admonition and instruction, which amounted to urgent requests for appreciation.

"You like this?" he'd ask. "You like it this way, baby? Tell me," he'd say. "Here? Eh? Say something. Tell me what you want."

But when she reversed the flow of exhortation, just what she expected happened: he went soft.

As soon as she was silent, he was up again and at her.

Ethel, for once, was glad to be a woman. That was one anxiety—the anxiety of the performer—she didn't have to go through.

"Oh, you like that! Well!" He pumped and pumped. "You going to come on your daddy? Eh? Say something! What's the matter? Don't you come?"

She was relieved when it was over. She still wanted to talk to him.

But he fell asleep. Immediately. Just like Teddy.

"Hey, don't fall asleep." She shook him. "I want to talk to you."

"What about?" he murmured.

"You never answered my question. Once you start to fake it, can you ever feel it again?"

"When you find out," he said, "let me know. Now will you for chrissake go to sleep. I have a tough schedule tomorrow."

But she couldn't sleep. For one thing, he snored, and this kept her awake. But mostly because she was on edge, unsatisfied. She didn't want to wake him again so she went to the other room, the one he used for consultation, and masturbated.

That night she had a sex dream. It was about Costa and it was graphic. Next morning, she was horrified, but at the time she'd gone with it. She'd been particularly aware of the distinctive odor of his person. It still affected her when she remembered it.

Adrian was pretty cocky in the morning, making coffee, bringing it to her in bed. "Just like the movies," he said.

Meantime he continued the lecture he'd started the moment he woke up.

"What attracts women to men has nothing to do with their looks," he said, and there was no edge of uncertainty to his voice.

"What then?"

"Power."

"What kind of power?" asked the dutiful pupil.

"Any kind." He pointed to the loci. "Head, fist, pecker, pocket."

"Which kind have you got, Adrian?"

"All except the last." He slapped his pocket again. "By the way, you can help me!" He announced this as if he were about to do her a favor, not ask her for help. "I'm writing a book," he said, "quite well into it, actual-

352

ly, and there's one chapter I'm having trouble with, not conceptually but in respect to detail. The point I'm trying to make is that the instant most saturated with the basic characteristics of each individual male is the instant of orgasm. That is when he reveals himself truly. Hidden qualities are exposed. The essential takes the place of the customary. What do you think of that?"

"You'd know better than I."

"That's an evasive answer. I need corroboration. Obviously you've been with a lot of men—"

"What do you mean, obviously?"

"Obviously means clearly. I wish you'd describe some of the orgasmic behavior of the men you've . . ." He reached for pad and pencil.

"There haven't been all that many, and as I say, I don't remember."

"Why don't you want to help me? Are you angry at me?"

"Of course not. I don't think most people are watching one another then. Except you."

"Good! Start with me."

"You keep a pad and pencil by your bed."

"Go on."

"Maybe that's why your hands are cold."

"Cold!"

"Well, cool. O.K.?"

"Not O.K.! Obviously you're angry at me. I can't imagine why. Forget it. I've got to run now. Will you be here tonight?"

"No, I'll be gone."

They had a touching scene at the door.

"You on the pill?" he asked as he was showing her how to fix the latch so it would lock as she left.

"Not anymore," she said. "It puts weight on you. Have I got it right, the lock?"

"Yes. Fine. What then. What do you use?"

"Nothing. Well, many thanks and I'll be seeing you."

"Nothing! You might have told me!"

"On the other hand, it's a strange time to ask that question."

"Jesus Christ!"

"Looks like you may be almost a father again. Dolores tole me about her abortion."

"Well, I'm not paying for any more abortions. Don't look to me for money."

"Let's worry about that when it happens, O.K.? And thanks again."

She closed the door on his anxious face.

"Bitch!" she said of herself after he'd gone.

Back at the inn, she packed, then went to the bank and closed her savings account. She'd decided not to go back to Florida yet.

On the flight to Mexico City she didn't feel like reading or listening to the plane's stereo, so she asked for paper and began to doodle, drawing little figures of pregnant women, like that tiny tin cutout Costa had given her to wear under her clothing.

She hadn't taken the pill since the day, months ago, when she'd surrendered her little blue case to Costa. But it didn't concern her. "Ishallah!" as Aaron used to say. "What will happen will happen when Allah is ready."

In Mexico City, in the dirty, heavily scented air, she felt completely alone. Which was what she wanted. She decided to stay awhile, at least until her father had sold their home in Tucson; he might need her help to empty it.

What she wanted now was a job. "Money is freedom!" Dolores in her wisdom! Ethel had good Spanish from a long line of Chicano nannies. The secretarial skills she'd learned for Petros now served her well. In three days she had what she wanted, a job in the office of a great mining company, organized to take out of the earth the fluorocarbon from which the propellant for shaving creams and deodorants is made. This substance, it was said, is found only in the Sierra Madre mountains of Mexico and the company had a near monopoly. The produce was sent north to Big Brother.

From the beginning, Ethel found herself greatly valued, not only because she could take dictation in Spanish and type letters in English, but because she was an attractive interpreter and companion for visiting gringo industrialists. They all had letters to send back to the States and needed someone understanding and friendly to dictate to. Ethel received many tokens of appreciation, had more dinner dates than she wanted.

It soon became evident to her that the office was an intricate web of sexual relations. Every secretary there, except for a few older women who did the important work, seemed to have been chosen because some man in a strong position had asked for her. The place was bustling with pretty girls who knew that they earned their paychecks by making visitors feel at home and executives of the company feel cared for.

Ethel wondered which man had spoken for her.

The usual started: she was pursued without intermission. Again she began to feel like a game animal. Holding off the predators took more energy than she wanted to spend. In the end, it seemed to her that the simplest thing to do was accept one of the men and so get rid of the rest. If the man she chose was powerful enough in the company structure, he'd protect her from the constant come-ons, the leers and innuendos, the laying on of hands, that now harassed her.

So she looked over the field—coolly. "Be just like a man," was her motto. There was one special qualification she sought—just in case. Her choice should be a biologically premium male.

She'd had the evidence that Adrian hadn't done the job. She was open for help from another.

The man she settled on was a young executive of thirty-one, Arturo Uslar, beautiful to look at, educated at Williams College in New England, therefore able to show off perfect English. He sported a wardrobe of suits from Savile Row, monogrammed shirts and bespoke shoes, was in superb condition due to the squash he played every afternoon, and was, so she'd been told, a respected collector of fine paintings. In private, she found him ardent but gentle, romantic still amusing, kind, yet, when the time came, possessed of ample macho flair—in short, the perfect Latin lover.

Arturo was destined, so everyone said, to be president of the company. The reason? He was married to the daughter of the founder—"my Isabel," he called her—a woman somewhat older than himself, who had inherited the greatest fraction of the company's stock. The fact that she was plain did not affect his life. Arturo had given her four fine children, and was home often enough to satisfy her needs. The aura of her wealth enhanced her appearance, as did the very expensive clothes she wore. With this connection, there was no end in sight for Arturo—unless he made the one serious mistake he was often on the verge of making. So everyone said.

Arturo seemed bolder and more careless than was necessary. Ethel learned that his flirting with danger was part of the tradition of his culture. He took her with him to public places, particularly when he had to entertain a gringo client. Even though he was careful that a third person should come along, people began to talk. Arturo didn't seem unduly concerned. Ethel wondered whether he wanted this notoriety; was it a kind of swagger?

He was very proud of her, mostly, she felt, because so many other men wanted her. He showed her off like a race horse, a great purse winner, that he owned. Actually he loved her more in public than in private. His mind tended to wander back to himself when they were alone.

One weekend, when his wife had gone to Acapulco, he drove Ethel into the suburban hills above the university and showed her his home. The walls were covered with paintings by the great Mexican painters, calls to revolution now the property of the very rich. When she admired them, he offered her one he had in his office.

"I don't want presents from you," she said.

"But I'm your lover," he protested. "They're from me!"

"Because you're my lover," she said.

It perplexed him that Ethel, unlike his previous mistresses, would not accept money. It even offended him.

Arturo had a small secret apartment high over Chapultepec Park and insisted that she move into it. There she found out what the siesta is for.

As they began to grow easy with each other, she discovered that things about him she'd once thought charming now made her uncomfortable. As his guard dropped, she respected him less. For instance, more than any man she'd known, he was fascinated with his image in the mirror. A trivial thing—but it bothered her.

"Do you think I've put on weight?" he asked one day as he was dressing to go home. "A pound or two, perhaps? I have to be careful." He was standing before the mirror, turning this way and that, sucking in his gut, then letting it hang out, squeezing and kneading the flesh at his waist.

Ethel, watching all this from the bed, couldn't remember if there was a mirror anywhere in Costa's house or whether she'd ever seen him look into a store window as he walked by, as most men do some of the time and Arturo did without fail.

"Ethel! Are you listening to me?"

"I don't know if you've put on weight. I've only known you five weeks."

"You must make me diet. Before I knew you, I used to spend these hours every day on the squash court."

"Well, you still can. Why don't you?"

He leaped on her, took her in his arms. "How can you say that, *mi vida?* You're so cold! Don't you know that you are the reason I live? I'd rather be with you than with anyone I've ever known."

He saw her every afternoon, except when he had an appointment for a fitting with his tailor or shirtmaker. These dates were sacred.

"You know what Mr. Richards of Allied Chemical said about me? Did I tell you?"

"Yes."

"No I didn't. Why do you say yes? Don't you want to hear?"

"Well, then, tell me again."

"He said I had the charm of a Latin, the devotion to business of a *norteamericano* and the cunning of a Jew. He should see me now, eh?"

"Why?"

"He left out lover. Are you asleep, Ethel?"

"I'm listening."

Later that afternoon, he asked her to marry him. They were under the sheets, their arms and legs wrapped around each other, speaking in whispers.

"I want to be with you all the time," he said, "I enjoy you so much."

"I'm married," she said.

"Is that important?"

"Yes. And so are you. And so comfortable the way you are, why spoil your life?"

"You're right. Besides, you're a bit of a bitch, no? I

love that now, but in my old age, you wouldn't stand by me."

He took many pictures of them nude, standing side by side. He had a camera with a delayed-action shutter which he would set for fifteen seconds. That gave him time to dash to her side and shake out his penis so it would look as long as possible.

"You know I'm very brave too," he said to her the next Monday. He'd been reading about the Sunday bullfight.

"Are you really?" she said.

"How can you doubt it? I only mention it because it's actually a fault. It is the cause of all my scars. You have noticed the scars on my body?"

"Just the one across your shoulder."

"I have, *mi corazón,* five large scars on my body. No one has ever not noticed them before. I am surprised, *mi tesoro,* that you have not. But then, of course, when we make love you are watching yourself, not me. You know what you are?"

"Tell me. I've been wondering."

"A narcissista. Is that how you say it? That's what you are."

She didn't contest it.

About a week later, he gave her a present, a recording he'd made, unbeknownst to her, of their love-making. It was certainly an impressive dramatic exercise from his side; he'd been in great voice that day. She was hardly on the tape.

"You see," he said, "you do not have the orgasm."

Ethel knew what he'd been wanting her to do, but she was past faking now. She guessed that when Arturo decided to drop her, whatever reason he gave, her failure to respond to him as he thought she should would be the real cause.

"You will also notice," he continued, "that I enjoy the experience despite your coldness. I give you this tape so you will always remember me."

Ethel prepared herself for the breakup, watched with devilish curiosity how Arturo would choose to bring it about.

The next day, the following conversation took place:

"Ignacio Alvarez was asking about you again today," he said. Señor Alvarez was the company executive in charge of personnel and placement, the man who'd engaged Ethel. "He says that the moment he saw you, he knew you had to be a member of our little circle. Since then there hasn't been a day that Nacio doesn't inquire how we're getting along. I believe he is waiting for you to tire of me."

"You're talking about that little man with the glasses? He's waiting?"

"Yes. With those thick glasses. He is the one truly intelligent person in our office and so the only one who can perhaps understand you. I admit he looks like an office animal, a professor of science perhaps, but the fact that he cannot see clearly without the aid of those lenses is not a handicap in his personal life. I have been told by some of the friends we've shared that he is a *jefe* in the bedroom and comes equipped with an exceptional sword."

"I have the feeling," Ethel said, "that you are trying to pass me on."

"How can you say that, *mi vida?* It's simply that I want you to be aware of all possibilities and of the desolation you cause in the souls of men."

A couple of days later, he was again recommending Ignacio Alvarez. "He does look like a man of continuous calm," he said, "but I have been informed by those who've had intimate experience with him that he has elements of exuberance combined with a sexual terror of the kind that appeals to constrained women. It's possible that he may be the precise choice to shake free your orgasm—the thing I am embarrassed to say I have been unable to do."

"Don't let that bother you," Ethel said. "It doesn't me."

"Well, who knows? It occurred to me that perhaps, in time, you will wish to give Nacio his reward. You do appreciate that you owe your job to him? And that he gave it to you at a time when we didn't need more secretaries? Of course, he then made the error of introducing you to me. But hasn't he been sufficiently penalized for that mistake? Despite this long, painful wait, I am sure, *mi tesoro,* that he has never lost hope, that he has been, in his soul, more than faithful to you."

Ethel changed the subject. "By the way, don't you think I have developed into a pretty damned good secretary now?" she said.

Arturo brought the subject back. "Even your enemies say that. Nacio confided to me the other day that he is giving consideration to raising your salary."

When it became apparent that these hints had failed, Ethel waited for Arturo to come more directly to the issue. He did. He told her that his wife, Isabel, had found out about them.

"It's a disaster for me," he said. "I am painfully in love with you. But now—with Isabel aware—it's become impossible. Are you following me, Ethel?"

"You're following me, Arturo."

"I shall probably die without you. Certainly very soon look much older."

"Oh, now come," Ethel said. "It may be a disaster, but it's a disaster you will survive." Who sounds like the man now? she asked herself, as she turned on top of him.

"I've come to the conclusion that you only like me for my body," Arturo said after they'd made love. "Ethel, are you listening?"

"Always."

Actually she'd been having more and more difficulty maintaining attention. When he talked longer than a sentence or two, her mind would wander. Arturo bored her.

"Of course," he went on, "we can't afford to think of anything as permanent, can we, *mi vida?* Or else life would be a series of painful disappointments, am I right?"

"No doubt. So tell me. When I'm gone, what will you do?"

"Work, work, work."

"What else?"

"I will play squash, resume my exercises, restore my body."

"What else?"

"I will look after my children. I will keep company with my son. Because of you, I have deprived the boy of my company."

"Oh. Sorry. What else?"

"I will be a good husband."

"For how long?"

"Until I judge the time right—" He'd broken up laughing.

"Right for what?"

"To find another little friend."

"Then?"

"I will say, 'Why aren't you like Ethel?' and beat her."

"No you won't."

"I may. I may kill her."

"Tell me, will you bring my replacement here?"

"Yes. And as my wife found out about you and caused

this painful occasion, she will find out about the next one."

"You could be more discreet next time."

"That phone call I made to you from my bedroom—I knew how insane that was, especially with my wife in the house."

"But that happened before. You told me. With someone else."

"Yes. I never seem to learn my lesson."

"Perhaps you want to be found out."

"What are you talking? I'm not a masochist."

"Well, now, before we part, tell me: was it worth it, all this intrigue?"

"How can you ask that? One minute of our love was worth everything. Besides, what choice did I have? I live for love."

"But you don't love your wife and you're going back."

"How can you say that? I love my wife very much. Only her."

"Well, then, you're doing the right thing, getting rid of me."

"Who knows? But I have come to recognize this: that there is one thing worse than to be lonely, and that is to be poor. I must not allow myself to forget that my Isabel owns and controls by far the greatest share of the stock of our company."

"You hold and control a pretty good hunk yourself."

"But she has more."

The truth was that Arturo Uslar, as the weeks passed, had found Ethel strong in a way he wasn't accustomed to and didn't like. "In her soul, she's a man," is how he put it to himself. "And in love, cold." Of course, Arturo would never never forgive Ethel for not responding to him, as so many others had, with a volcano of feeling. He was relieved to call it quits.

Ethel went to meet him for what was to be their last rendezvous. When her key opened the door, she found not Arturo, but sitting in his place, smiling eagerly, his eyes magnified by his thick lenses, Señor Ignacio Alvarez.

"Arturo was required this morning to make the long journey to Monterrey where our processing plant is located," Señor Alvarez said. "He told me to tell you how unhappy this has made him, how deep his pain is that he is unable to be here with you this last time. He sent me in his place and told me to do my best."

His glasses threw off a dazzling reflection.

Ethel didn't inquire further into the depths of Arturo's pain. She packed what she had in the love nest over Chapultepec Park, said a cordial farewell to the more than faithful Ignacio and left.

In the morning, she didn't go to the office but wrote a note of three sentences to Arturo and dropped it in the mail.

Then she vanished.

eighteen

"I HAVE a piece of bad news," Ed Laffey said. He'd picked Ethel up at the airport and they were having a drink on the terrace where Emma Laffey used to eat her supper from a tray.

"It's your mother's will," he said. "Well, here, I'll read it to you." He reached into the pocket of his denim jacket and produced a lady's letter written in longhand on pink notepaper. "I found it, I must tell you," Ed said, "quite bizarre. Even shocking."

"What could Mom possibly say that would shock anybody?" Ethel asked.

"You'll see. It's in the form of a letter to Martha. Remember I told you about Martha? And me?"

"I remember," Ethel said.

Ed put on his half glasses and, controlling his hurt or his anger, Ethel couldn't tell which, began to read.

DEAR MARTHA:

I want you to be the executor of my will. I haven't seen you for many years but then I haven't seen anybody for many years. And we were once pretty good friends, you and I.

I'll be brief. I don't feel that in this, my last word to the world, I need explain anything.

I want you to supervise the disposal of my worldly goods. As follows:

First, to my husband, Ed Laffey, I leave nothing.

Then, to my adopted daughter, known as Ethel Laffey, I leave only this: my love and good wishes. In the will I drew up two years ago my bequest to her was more material. But since that time, dear Ethel has written me such a touching letter, asking that I not leave her one cent. "I want to be on my own," she said, then went on about how much that meant to her. I have always felt that Edward spoiled Ethel. I'm so glad to see her trying to right herself.

To Manuel and Carlita, my husband's servants, I leave the sum of one thousand dollars. This would have been more if I hadn't felt for many years that they have been, by Edward's orders, spying on me and manipulating me.

Everything else of value I own in the world, including the house where I have lived all my married life and where I am writing what you are reading, I leave to the Saguaro Garden Club. I happen to know that they need a new headquarters and meeting place; I hope they will find our residence suitable.

I must prepare you: this house was put in my name by my husband, Edward Laffey, for tax reasons. He may regret that now.

He may, of course, keep the furniture in his study and his bedroom. I don't want to inconvenience him.

Now if you are wondering why I have chosen you to be the executor of a will which deprives my husband not only of his home but of the Treasury bonds my brothers left me, here are the two reasons.

The first is that I wanted very much to do one unselfish thing with my wealth, put it, however tardily, to a decent use. Since I didn't earn one cent of it, I have always felt guilty that I had it. This act relieves me.

The other reason you know and I know, but I shan't embarrass you by putting it into a letter that others must, sooner or later, read. I do want to say, though, that while I haven't been able for several years to stay in touch with what was going on around me, I had the blessing of a few concerned friends and I could still use the telephone.

I hereby deed you the sum of one thousand dollars for the services I am asking you to perform in my behalf.

Do excuse the pink notepaper. Isn't that little squirrel up in the corner darling?

Ed put the letter down. "She signed it," he said, "and got Diego, the yard boy, and Eddie, the TV repairman, to witness it. Here are their signatures. This is a legal document."

"Why were you so shocked?" Ethel said a little later. They were walking through the last light in the cactus garden Emma so dearly loved. "On account of the money?"

"No. Though I had been, I suppose, unconsciously counting on it. It comes to considerably more than a million dollars. And it's not the house. I'm through with this house. It's that her letter is so full of hatred against me. I had no idea that . . ."

"But what did you expect? Mom was not stupid. And she had to do something with her anger. Have you told the garden club people?"

"I wanted you to see the will before I did."

"It's fine with me."

"I've been having trouble with it," Ed said. "For instance, I haven't given the letter to Martha. Need I? I suppose so. Better me than a lawyer. But sooner or later I'll have to show it to a lawyer. In this community, it's bound to get around. I suppose I shouldn't care. But . . . damn it, it's embarrassing that my wife hated me all her life long and I—"

"I'll do it for you."

"Do what?"

"Everything. Show it to Martha, after you've gone. Consult with a lawyer and try to keep his mouth zipped. And whatever there is to do around the house—"

"Would you really? Take it over? I'd be so grateful."

"I'd just as soon stay here a few weeks to see if—to see what develops, if anything."

"What do you mean?"

"I want to be alone for a while. Don't ask questions."

"That would be such a favor, Kit. I don't want this damned furniture." He kicked the desk with his toe. "Even my old desk. Sell everything she left me. I'm not going to continue living in this community. It's poisoned for me."

"The horses?"

"Sell them. I'm only worried about your living. . . ."

"I've become a damned competent secretary. Don't worry about me."

"Oh, thanks, thanks," he said, and kissed her. "Come on, let's have another drink. Where did you learn to drink tequila neat, Kitten?"

"In Mexico. I took a lover there. He taught me."

"Took a lover?"

"That's the word. It was my doing."

"A Mexican?"

"Part Indio. Very educated, very rich. To be precise, his wife, as sometimes happens, was the rich one."

"Going back there?" He gave her the tequila. "Here's the lime."

"And the salt, please. No. I don't think he gave me what I wanted."

"You mean you didn't like him."

"I liked him. I liked the others too." She drank, closed her eyes, drank again.

Ed Laffey laughed nervously. "Which others?" he said.

Ethel didn't answer.

"Where are you going now? To Florida, of course."

"I don't think so, not for a while. I do have a debt there I mean to pay, but . . . I won't go for a while."

"I talked to Teddy. He called and wanted to know where you were. Said if you showed up here to call him instantly. Want me to get him on the phone?"

"No."

A week later, Ethel again found evidence that she was not pregnant.

When she called the gynecologist, he told her that it sometimes takes a few months to escape the power of the pill. "Keep trying," he said.

A few days later she saw her father and Margaret off on the plane for San Francisco and Japan. She kissed him good-bye and, with the same degree of affection, Margaret. Ed had become a stranger whom she wished well.

The next day, she called Martha, made a date, called a lawyer, made a date, went downtown, saw them both. Neither showed surprise or shock, if indeed they felt any.

Ethel had a week to wait for her fertile time. Day after day, she oversaw the final disposition of her childhood environment, made sure it was in perfect order and, as Emma would have wished it, broom clean for the Saguaro Garden Club.

Late one afternoon, she showed up at Ernie's place, just as she used to, uninvited and unexpected.

She found a terrible change in Ernie, tracks of anxiety and rage on his face. And why? He cared more about somebody else than she did about him. Ernie went on and on, telling Ethel about this person, what an evasive little bitch she was, how promiscuous, how he couldn't tell where she'd been or where she was going, what she was up to or with whom.

This girl treated Ernie as he'd treated all the others.

The next morning—it was two weeks now since his call—she decided to write Teddy.

"Father tells me you called," she wrote. "If anyone cares to know when I'll be back, tell them that you don't know. Because I don't know. Or say that I've done one of my vanishing acts again. O.K.? I'll be back when I'm ready. I guess it's important every few years to look yourself over again, decide who you want to be, not who you are, how you want to live, not how you've lived, what you want for yourself, not what people want of you. In other words, return to self-interest.

"I guess that's what I'm doing."

She signed her name without the "love."

She attached a postscript. "I suggest you do the same thing," she wrote. "I'm not the right girl for you. Maybe someone like Dolores is, maybe you were right when you told her that. Surely you'll find someone where you are now who would be proud to be an officer's wife and spend her life taking care of you."

And another. "Tell Costa I pay him respect every day."

She depersonalized Ernie, had intercourse with him coolly and mechanically. She mounted him, inserted him in her body, then, in the slow, regular rhythm of an oil well, pumped him dry, waited for him to resupply himself, then pumped him dry again.

When he tried to reverse their positions, she wouldn't let him, spreading her knees so he couldn't turn her over. When he complained about it, she told him to shut up and fuck her.

Like Cambere and Arturo Uslar, he would be glad when she left.

One morning, when they were in bed, his girl friend came by.

Ethel was shocked. The girl may have been seventeen, but she looked an untouched thirteen, dewy.

She was not at all embarrassed. "You want me to go or you want her to go?" she said.

370

"You bitch," Ernie said. "Where have you been?" He looked rather frightened.

"None of your business."

He jumped out of bed and, stark naked, went for her.

Ethel used the door to the backyard to escape. The last she saw was Ernie's face, bleeding from long scratch marks.

The next morning, she drove her white Mercedes to the bank, withdrew all her money, stuffed it into her purse, then drove the car to the Mercedes dealer and asked him to sell it for her.

That was it, the end.

Tucson, good-bye! The plane flared into a uniformly blue sky, leaving behind a vast crumble of red and brown rock. The plane came down through soft, heavy clouds, landed in a driving rain. Tampa.

She wondered how she'd greet Teddy. Part of the "it could be anyone" process was Teddy; she wanted it to be possibly his too. She didn't know if he'd want to go to bed with her now, but she suspected he would and she'd do it, without guilt.

Her little place in Bradenton looked good to her. No one was in it.

By the time she drove to the marina, the rain was over but there was mist moving across the water and heavy drops falling off the edge of the office eaves.

As she came up, Petros opened the door of the office and put his head out. He was looking at a flock of girls in their teens scooting along one of the long, narrow piers. Their clothes were soaked; they'd been running in the rain.

"Ever notice," Petros said to her, "girls run in the rain more than boys?" He was speaking as if she'd not been away.

"Never noticed that," she said.

Now he looked at her. "You got thinner," he said. "How come?"

"Attrition," she said.

"What the hell is that, a disease? Come on in."

She hesitated in the doorway. "I see you got a secretary."

"You stayed away three months. I'll fire her."

"Oh, don't do that."

"Mind your business. I mind mine."

He'd ripped out the wall behind his desk and put in a picture window. Turning in his chair, he could see the whole layout. It had prospered while she'd been gone.

"You seen him yet?"

"Who?"

"The big shot." He pointed.

There was Costa rolling along a dock, swaggering as he must have long ago when he was the number one diver of the Greek community. She could hear him roar instructions to a small boat that was coming in on its auxiliary. When the owner tied off, Costa undid his knot and tied it correctly, instructing the tyro all the time: "Like this first, gentleman, please, then like this, it's easy, all right, remember?"

"The bank got The 3 Bees," Petros said.

"They took it away from him?"

"With great regret, they say. Some Greeks on the board, too. He borrowed money for something, putting up the store with the bank. Now he can't make the payments. So he's out. The shop sits there, doors closed. America, America!"

"What's that on his head?"

"I bought him a captain's hat. He's my new dockmaster. Runs their ass to a frazzle, that old boy. He's tough, I'm telling you."

372

Costa had seen her. He broke out a kind of Balkan salute, throwing the flat of his hand against his captain's hat, then shooting the hand up into the air. Then he was running toward her.

"Money buys anybody," Petros said. "Wait till you see—we're friends tight like glue now."

"He's a good boy," Costa said, coming up to them and throwing his arms around Petros's shoulder, confirming what the man had said.

"Your mother die," Costa said, "I hear. Too bad. Fine woman! Well, I'm next, right? But not yet. Where's my kiss?"

She kissed him. "I'm sorry about the store," she said.

"We don't talk that," Costa said.

Close up, she noticed he looked younger; he was close-shaved, his hair was carefully arranged and he smelled of the sea. Petros had done something good for the man.

"You talk to Teddy?" he asked her.

"I just got in," she said.

"We call him. Hey, boss, blow us phone call maybe over there?"

"Talk two hours," Petros said. "I'm going into Saint Pete's."

"She look beautiful," Costa informed his son. "Here." He handed her the phone.

"Where've you been?" Teddy asked her. "For ten weeks?"

"I wrote you," she said. "I was tired and I thought I'd take a vacation."

"Where'd you go?"

"Mexico."

"What's there?"

"Mexicans. I want to live there someday. I like it."

"I can't come down for a couple of weeks. We've got exams and—"

373

"That's O.K. Come when you can."

They were competing in coolness. Indifference versus indifference.

"Unless you want to come up here," Teddy said.

"I've been traveling a lot and—"

"So why don't you rest up?"

"That's what I figured."

"Are you O.K.?"

"Never felt better."

"Me too."

That was all. Nothing to it.

Costa had forgotten his insistence that she quit her job; now he was there too.

Petros was pressing her hard. Not in any physical way —he never touched her—but she could feel him every minute when they were in the same room, desiring her.

"What's the matter?" he asked when he invited her out Saturday night and she refused.

"If you gave me this job because you wanted to go to bed with me, call in the other girl. I'm not attracted to you that way."

"Bull," he said.

She could see that she'd made him want her more. The perversity of men!

The next day she had a letter from Teddy:

I'm sorry about our talk last week. The phone is so cold. I want to know all about your trip. And about your mother. I don't know whether you knew it but I liked her. If there are sides to something like this, I was on her side.

I have to ask you something embarrassing. It's easier to do by letter than face to face, but it's pretty damned hard this way too.

During these years of college training, the Navy pays tuition and the cost of textbooks. Then they give you $100 per month to live on. I got a room with another guy because it's cheaper. That's why I didn't ask you to hurry up here. We pay one-sixty per month, which leaves me twenty dollars for food and so forth, like clothes, which I don't need anyway, but like an occasional beer, which I do. I can't ask my father for money. You know they lost the store. So—well, here it is.

Could you spare me a little out of your salary? I'll keep track of it, and pay you later. Christ, this is embarrassing but—I said it. I love you and miss you a lot and if you say you can't spare any, don't worry, I'll find another way. I'm doing O.K. in my studies and I think I'll be a good officer. I have the temperament for it, don't you think?

They work the hell out of us, day and night, so I don't have time for fun and games. By the time I get through doing my assignments each night, I am ready for nothing but a solitary bed.

YOUR TEDDY

So, Ethel said to herself, he's got a girl.

She thought of writing him and saying, "Let your girl friend feed you." Instead she decided to send him twenty dollars every week.

The Saturday following he came down. He wore dark glasses and didn't take them off when they embraced. He kissed her like a dutiful husband.

While he showered, she looked at his clothes. His shorts were pressed. Even the socks were ironed. Whoever it was took good care of him.

Why had he rushed down? Gratitude? Money does wonders.

She fucked him before they ate.

She did not pretend anything.

Afterward they lay together. She told him about Emma's funeral and about the will and about Margaret, and a little about Mexico, but not that she'd worked there.

What struck her was that he didn't ask anything beyond what she chose to tell him. She decided he didn't want her to ask questions either.

The next morning they did it again. He seemed mechanically much better, as if he'd been practicing. He came later than he usually did and apparently at a time he chose.

Again she did not pretend. Their union was no more than what Adrian had called—an act of friendship.

Monday, Petros asked her how it went. He knew Teddy had come down. She could see he was eaten up with curiosity.

"Fine," she said, cutting his interest off.

"Who you kidding?" he said.

Two weeks later she advised Teddy that she was driving up to see him. She gave him time to clear away his dates.

"I got us a room in a motel," Teddy said when she arrived.

He'd put an overnight bag into the back of the car he'd borrowed from his roommate.

"Drive around a little first," Ethel said.

"I'll show you the campus," he said. "It's pretty."

It was. The buildings were simple and modern and neat. There were female recruits everywhere and blacks in good number. Ethel didn't see any of it.

"Drive to the beach," she said. "Is there a beach?"

"Yes. A beauty. Ponte Vedra. On the way, there are two big Navy installations and—"

"I don't want to see them. I want you to take me to a place where I can tell you I'm pregnant."

"Terrific!" he said. "How great!"

"Yeah," she said. "But then there's this: I doubt if it's yours."

He didn't say a word.

"You might be the father," she said. "But not likely."

"Then whose?" he said after a moment.

"I don't know."

"What do you mean, you don't know?"

"I mean I know but I won't tell you. The point is it's not yours."

He had nothing to say, it seemed.

"Aren't you going to fuss about it?" she asked. "Even a little?"

"What can I do? It's happened."

"O.K., then?"

"No, it's not O.K., but . . ."

"But what?"

"Nothing."

"Nothing again? Well, then, take me to the motel."

"Whose could it be?"

"I'm not even going to ask myself that question."

He drove around aimlessly.

"There's one more thing," she said. "I'll get rid of it if you want."

He didn't say anything.

"I know why you can't say anything," she said, "and I'm going to tell you. But first I want to say that I don't hold anything that happened against you. I don't think we're for each other anymore. That time's passed. This is the end, do you see? And if you want me to get rid of it, I'll do it. It's up to you."

He didn't answer.

"You've certainly developed that officer's reserve they tell about," she said. "What are you thinking?"

"I don't know what I'm thinking."

"Did you ever go to a doctor?"

"Yes."

"And?"

"My semen count, whatever you call it, is low."

"Why didn't you tell me?"

"It's embarrassing—for a man."

"Not for a woman? Well, forget it. I'm asking you again, do you want me to get rid of this kid? You have to tell me."

377

"Now?"

"Why not? The only thing I want to do before I leave here—and you—I'd like to give Costa what he wants. I love your father and . . . I sort of love you too. So I'll do this for you and him—I'll go through this for eight months or seven or whatever it is. I will give him his kid. I'll do that if you tell me to. If you don't, Ill leave tonight."

"Let me think about it."

"O.K. Let's say tomorrow, O.K.?"

He drove her back to the motel.

"You want to come in?" she asked.

"Why not?"

He sat in the chair and she lay on the bed and they were silent a long time. Then he got on the bed with her.

He made love to her with more feeling than he'd ever had before. Losing her made him more passionate. He devoured her.

Afterward, he didn't roll away. He held her close.

Then he was at her again. He'd never before come back so quickly.

Was he apologizing this way? she wondered. Saying what he couldn't say in words?

They dozed. When they woke, it was dark and very quiet.

"Look, Teddy darling," she said, "we can be friends, so tell me. You have someone here, don't you? A girl."

"Yes," he said.

"Good. And you like her?"

"Not as much as I like you."

"Well, naturally," she said. "Who's as good as me?"

They laughed and suddenly it had happened. They weren't married anymore; they were friends.

"O.K.," he said, "give the old man the kid. It'll be our secret. What the hell, why not? It's all a mess anyway."

"No it's not. If you could produce a child, I'd do anything you wanted. But the kid he wants, it might as well be mine. He likes me, doesn't he?"

"He's in love with you, the old bastard. You're all he talks about. Ethel this and Ethel that, when is Ethel coming back, did you get a letter from Ethel?"

"I should have written him!"

"I covered for you. I told him you were taking care of your mother's funeral and so on. I made up a lot of stuff."

"Then let's make up one thing more."

"O.K. with me."

When she woke in the morning, he'd gone. She vaguely remembered that he'd slipped out in the first show of light and that she hadn't tried to stop him.

He had parade that day and she saw him in his whites, handsome and stern, very much the officer. Maybe it was tough for him now, knowing what he knew, but she believed that his career in the Navy was more important to him than anything else and that he'd be a damned good officer.

She waved. He came running to her when it was over.

"You look handsome in your uniform," she said. Also very distant, she thought.

"Thanks," he said.

"About last night—still feel the way you did?"

"Yes."

"Want me to keep it?"

"I think so. Yes."

"Well, then, I will. And . . . I'm glad you decided what you did."

So, she thought, it's over.

nineteen

IN Saint Petersburg, the traffic was like a tangle of wet string. But to the south, there's a great bridge thrown over the mouth of Tampa Bay, a span so long and so high that it seems much narrower than it is. The incline is steep but a car will take it without diminishing speed and it gives a driver the feeling he's lifting out of the fumes and frustration below.

As Ethel rushed to the top of this fling of metal, she was filled with a mysterious confidence and the exhilaration of strength that came with it.

"There isn't anything you want to do now that you cannot do," she told herself.

From the crest of the bridge, she looked over the side at the silver chop below and saw, moving toward the open gulf, a small freighter, an old tramp, once clad in white, now dressed in the gold thrown by the setting sun, her smoke a veil. She looked like a dream, not plowing the water but sliding over its surface. She was flying the flag of Mexico. Bound for Veracruz, Ethel guessed, or Tampico.

She remembered something Teddy's education officer, of all people, had once said: "Oh, to be eighteen again and have everything you own in a sea bag. Then you're invincible!"

That afternoon she felt, if not invincible, self-sufficient, complete, ready for anything.

She spoke to the old freighter, saying, "Soon, soon."

There was only this: For seven months more she had to pretend that what she was carrying, what she couldn't yet feel, was Teddy's.

She'd pay off her debts that way, to Teddy, to his father and to her past. She'd give Costa the child and disappear.

No, she thought, I won't disappear. I'll simply go.

She found music on the radio and slipped down the long incline into Bradenton. She was recalling the men she'd been with, the pleasure she'd had with each, the excitement of experiencing a new person, coupling for a time in midflight, giving the gifts of her nature, taking what they had in return. There would be others; a world was waiting—friends, lovers, equals.

She only had to hold the lesson she'd learned with Teddy, to know when it was over and move on.

Her room was quiet as the space under the trees of a pine forest. She raised the windows. The curtains were of ruffled cotton and the breeze off the Gulf lifted them in white fluffs, then let them slowly settle. The Japanese glass tinklers made their thin clean sound.

Her dress was soaked through where it had been pressed against the seat back, so she pulled it off. Her undergarments felt tight, so she freed herself, scratched where they'd bound her, under her breasts and across her waist, relieving her skin.

She'd made her bed with sheets only. She didn't part

them now, lay on top, spreading her legs, throwing her arms up and out.

The breeze caressed her.

All sound came from a great distance.

She had nowhere to go, no one to meet. She wasn't anxiously waiting for a man. That night, no one would require her to "get him off." Nor did she require anyone's service to make her feel complete. Her body was in a transport of good feeling, deeper than sexual. She didn't need the act of love to convince herself she was alive.

Or to pass time away. She was jealous of her minutes.

Even her breathing had altered. It was soft and even and measured. It was exact, it was normal.

In seven months, she thought, I'll never have to lie again!

She closed her eyes and savored her own presence. She didn't want the silence broken; it didn't threaten her. She didn't wish for the sound of a human voice, didn't need the news of the day. It didn't matter to her what time it was.

When she began to doze, she invited dreams.

She saw herself as a naked babe. An old Orthodox priest was carrying her to a brass ceremonial bowl, chanting ritual as he moved. He dunked her three times in the blessed water, which was warm as piss. Then he lifted her, reborn.

Later she was a small sun, with the rest of the universe whirling around her in tracks far out of reach.

Though she was half asleep, it was a time she remembered to the end of her life, her interval of purity when compromise and accommodation and deceit were no longer necessary.

The night after she returned, Ethel went out to dinner with Petros. They drove to a seafood place near Sarasota. A mass of people, senior couples all, waited in line for the privilege of eating in this place. Petros, flashing his power for her, walked past them all and took over a booth that had just been emptied. The waitress in that territory nodded and smiled.

"How do you get away with that?" Ethel asked.

"She and I"—he indicated the waitress—"we used to . . ." He rubbed his forefingers together.

"How does she get away with it?"

"She goes with the boss now."

As Petros ordered a dozen oysters for himself and stone crabs for her, Ethel examined the waitress. The woman was in her thirties, clean, neat, respectable; she looked like what she was, a Midwestern housewife, now, for whatever reason, on her own. There was nothing flirtatious or coy about the way she related to Petros. Sexual diversion, Ethel guessed, was simply one of several practical problems the woman had had to solve for herself.

Petros was looking to see how Ethel would receive the intimate information he'd given her.

"I like her," Ethel said. "I'm glad you go with her."

"I don't go with her," Petros said. "That was last winter when it was raining every day—remember those two weeks?"

She looked at Petros's face; it was all thrust. The nose broke its space in two. The hairline was low, the face said action, not contemplation. Petros was not a reflective man.

"Whom do you go with now?" Ethel said.

"You," Petros said. "I go with you."

"I'm pregnant, friend," Ethel said. "I'm a married woman and I'm pregnant and I'm quitting my job end of this week."

"You're pregnant? Since when?"

"What do you want, the day and the hour?"

"Who's the father?"

"Teddy. Who do you think?"

"I think it happened when you were away seeing the world. You saw it, all right. But you don't look any different."

"You can't tell yet when I'm dressed."

He looked at where her breasts pushed out her dress. "They look just the same, very good."

He was silent through dinner, seemed to have forgotten her announcement. Then he made up his mind. "I don't care," he said. "I'll wait. You're still who I'm going with."

"Petros, I'm married; don't you understand that?"

"Listen, bitch, you think I'm dumb? If you were married and working at it, you'd be with your husband wherever he is. Shit, I know when a woman's married."

"I'm quitting your job Friday," she repeated.

"Like hell you are."

About that he was right. Ethel was paid good money, had a favored position, was relied on to provide Teddy with twenty dollars a week. On Friday Petros raised her salary ten dollars. He didn't tell her; the money was in her envelope.

When she asked about it, he explained: "We're doing pretty good here. I take a raise, you take a raise."

"Persistence," Ethel told herself, "will win any girl, so watch out."

Until this time Petros had kept his private life private. Now he opened his address book to her. As his secretary, she was asked to make his arrangements. When, for instance, he decided to put off one girl in favor of another who was suddenly available, he asked Ethel to do the dirty work over the phone. Each morning he'd summarize what had happened the night before, sometimes in graphic detail, then indicate to his social secretary whether he wanted a repeat performance.

What made him believe that this would attract Ethel? Perhaps he thought she'd beg to be allowed to pull her nose out of his sheets, so indicate her interest in reverse?

If he thought this, he underestimated how tough Ethel's hide had become. She enjoyed playing procuress for him. She laughed at his naïve efforts to humble her, scolded him unmercifully when he allowed a teen-ager to attach herself to him.

Finally he gave up. "O.K.," he said. "No more *gamo!*"

"What's that, *gamo?* Something good?"

"Who knows? Greek word for marriage, *gamo,* also Greek word for the business." He slapped the side of his clenched fist with an open palm.

"How primitive you heathen are!" Ethel said.

"O.K., I give up. I ask nothing. I expect nothing. I am a monk."

It was a long, hot, humid day. September on the west coast of Florida produces days and nights with nothing to recommend them. That was the first night Ethel spent in his bed.

She dropped the suggestion on his desk at the end of the afternoon when she picked up the mail he'd signed.

"If you still want me to, I'll stay with you tonight," she said, and walked back to her own desk to put the letters in envelopes.

What surprised her was that he didn't rush her, didn't even acknowledge her offer by kissing her or touching her anywhere he hadn't. Instead of saying, "Let's go to bed," he said, "Let's go eat." He took her to a restaurant where they'd been before, they ate what they'd had many times, her favorite stone crabs, his sand dabs. The only indication that it was a special occasion: he ordered an imported Chablis.

"What happened to you all of a sudden?" he asked after his first gulp of the wine.

"Since it means all that much to you, I thought—"

"Don't do me favors, Miss Laffey," he said. "Bitch! Why you smile?"

"You're supposed to sip that wine, not swallow it a glass at a time."

"I'm nervous," he said.

"Don't undress yourself," he said to her later. They were in the boat and it was dark in the hold. "I want to do it."

He went to the hatch and looked out. "Air coming from the west now," he said. "It'll rain." He closed the hatch.

She turned off the bed light, the dark to ease his nerves. It used to work with her, she remembered, when men did it.

Side by side on the bed not touching they talked of several things—and she waited.

"I want to give you something," he said, going to a locker. "Been saving it for this night I never figured would happen."

"Who's it of?" she asked when he came back with a stiff-backed photograph.

"My family. On our island." He switched the bed light on and tipped up the shade. "There! My mother. In the middle!"

"Where's your father?"

"My father damn fool, went into army, nineteen forty, and—can you imagine?—the Italians kill him. He is only Greek Italians kill in that whole goddamn war. These my three sisters, two marry now."

"Who's this here?"

"Your friend. Five years old."

The fierce little boy held his mother's hand as if to reassure her there was no reason to worry with him around. The woman in black with the stockings of coarse black yarn looked at her only son as she might at a redeemer.

"Her hope's on me," Petros said. "I send dollars every month."

"That your house behind that pile of rocks?"

"That's what we got there, rocks. Only olive trees grow."

She looked at his jagged face, into his black-olive eyes.

Which was when he touched her.

"You have most beautiful breasts here," he said as he released them from her bra.

His touch had a delicacy she hadn't expected. It was a caress, not a squeeze.

"You still scared?" she whispered a little later.

"More than before," he said.

It was hot inside the cabin; they were covered with a film of moisture.

What she wasn't prepared for was how it made her feel when he slid into her. "Oh!" she gasped, her intake of breath a convulsion of surprise. "Oh!"

"At last," she heard him say.

Only when it was over and they were still did she realize that although she had entered into their sex so casually, it was the first time in months she'd finished. And not because of anything special he'd done. He'd shown her a photograph.

After he came, he kept looking at her, an urchin who couldn't believe his good fortune. "I never thought it possible," he said. "A girl like you."

When he came for the second time, his cry chilled her. He'd called out, "Oh, M*ama*! M*ama!*"

Then he passed out, asleep, and she held him like the mother he'd called for.

It began to rain. The boat rocked gently.

She knew that in the morning, she'd look at him and wonder what she was wondering now: why with him, why with this little man with the hatchet nose and the disproportioned body, this "white nigger," as the black dock hands called him, "Mr. Five-by-Five"—why with him and not with the others who were so much more "attractive" and so much more sure of themselves?

Adrian had pumped and pumped and finally, in exasperation, had demanded, "Don't you come?"

But about his book Adrian was right. What happened with men at the end told the story. So often it was a surprise, seemingly a contradiction.

Adrian's eyes, narrowed to a glint, hadn't warmed when he came. He was neither sympathetic nor concerned nor even personal.

Aaron, the democrat from Israel, had fucked her like an autocrat, his orgasm a reward for her good services.

Ernie revealed what he truly felt only then. "You're a spoiled rich bitch," he cried out, his voice a vent for the hatred he habitually concealed.

Teddy, a concerned man generally, was at that moment apart, perhaps even relieved that it was over; it brought him sleep.

Julio did it for revenge. "Where's your popi now?" he'd screamed at her. "Hey, you, *puta!*" Or was he screaming at his departed wife?

Arturo showed off like a bullfighter, waited for her to award him the ears and the tail. Despite all the flattery, the compliments and the constant offers of presents, she could have been any one of a crowd.

Petros, the swaggering master of a great marina? No, a homeless boy in a rocky landscape crying for his mother.

She could write a book about them all. But not Adrian's book. Hers would be with sympathy. She saw them as pathetic, these members of the "strong sex."

Once she wished she'd been a boy. But no longer. They were so much more vulnerable than women, constantly called upon to perform an act that would reveal what they lived their lives to conceal. Women could, if they needed to, hide.

"I don't want to belong to any of them, not ever again," she said to herself. "Not this one, not any of them."

Which, of course, Petros did not hear, but answered.

"I'll never let you go," he said, waking. Then he fell asleep in the fold of her arms.

But Ethel stayed awake, held him and felt for him and for all the others. For while she didn't love any single one of them, she loved them all.

Her only concern now was that Costa not find out. Since Petros and she were together, they could more easily behave, publicly, as if they were not. And Petros made a tactical concession: he waited each afternoon until Costa had taken the bus north before coming near her.

She was concerned about Teddy. She wouldn't want him to hear about it from anyone else, a rumor. She called him in the morning and suggested he come down to Mangrove Still for a "council of war."

She told him the facts in plain words. She also told him a truth she'd not told Petros, that she would disappear as soon as she'd delivered the infant, would hand it over to Costa, feeling perfectly certain it would be well taken care of.

"That you can be sure of." Teddy laughed at the thought. "That old fool will devote his life to nothing else. Of course, Noola will do the work."

Ethel interrupted to tell him something Costa had informed her of only the day before. "Your mother took a job."

"A job! What kind of job?"

"Making one hundred and twelve fifty per, that kind of job. Which is a hell of a lot more than they used to make together at The 3 Bees. She's working at that stocking factory between here and Tampa, that one along the canal, you know. And she's wearing shoes every day, I'll bet for the first time."

Teddy got the details later from his mother.

He'd taken off three days, so on Sunday night he drove

down to Ethel's place with her. They'd become better friends than they'd ever been before. That Monday night, Ethel made two dinners. She made Petros his, leaving it on his stove with instructions, then she went to her apartment, where Teddy and Costa waited for her, and fixed theirs.

"That son of a bitch," Costa griped. "He keep her late over there on purpose, aggravation to me! He knows!"

Even Teddy noticed that Costa was physically overfamiliar with Ethel, touching her, fondling her. It was embarrassing to watch, the old man was so unaware of what he was doing.

Since there was only one bed, she fixed Teddy a bed on her sofa. In the middle of the night, he crossed over.

"Don't be silly," she said. He didn't persist.

Petros, of course, believed they'd "done the business."

"Bullshit!" he said when she protested. "He's his father's son, a *vlax* makes a *vlax,* one big stuck-up shithead Greek from wrong side our island. I kill him one day, both of them!"

"What's it got to do with which side of the island? What wonderful side of the island are you from, brother Peetie?"

"I'm from the side of the island facing my *patrida;* that's big difference. His village close to Turkey; they got all kind mixed-up blood over there. You watch someday he get mad, start speaking Turkish, you watch that!"

"Who cares about that stuff now, Peetie? We're all the same—"

"We're not all the same. From my side we are merchants, businessmen, modern people, educated, going somewhere! His side? All they know, go down bring up sponge. Sometimes the *melteme* wind, she blows three weeks from the north. Three week they sit in front of coffeehouse, cut their nails, spit and complain. Here the same thing, all day they sit in the *kentron,* good old days, good old days. D.fferent country, same talk. Believe me, on dry land they're use'ess! Under water, O.K., maybe. But how many important thing in life happen under water? What've you got to say to that? Hey, you! Wise guy! I'm talking, you're walking circles!"

She gave up.

On the following Friday afternoon, she gave the old man the big news.

He'd just received his pay for the week. Immediately he sent out for liquor, appropriated the office telephone. The first person he called was Aleko the Levendis. "Bring car here!" he commanded. "When? Now, what you think? Now!"

With Teddy he was hysterical on the phone, shouting his praises and thanks, putting Ethel on while he poured for all. A prince was going to be born.

"Isn't he being a bit premature?" Teddy said to his wife. He sounded nervous.

For the moment they were both glad they'd decided what they had. Looking at Costa, his joy deepened by drink, who could deny the importance of that much joy?

When Aleko arrived, Costa ordered Ethel into the car. She and Petros had an understanding about dinner that night and afterward too, but Costa's celebration was a torrent that swept everything before it.

They drove north, Aleko at the wheel, humming one tune after another, she and Costa in the back, his arm around her, his eyes straight ahead.

He recalled the birth of Teddy from the announcement forward. He told how he'd known immediately that the infant forming in Noola's body would be a boy and that this boy would, in time, produce another boy who would be named after him and would stay by his side, "pro er way," till the day he died.

He told her about his own grandmother, a person he'd

never mentioned before. She could tell, this old woman, employing the science she'd learned from the women in black who'd raised her, the lore of the Dodecanese, what sex a baby would be from the first swelling.

"She taught me, so I tell you. Soon. It is going to be what I want!"

They stopped before the church of Saint Nicholas. It was the first time in years that Costa had entered the territory of the bingo priest. There was a scattering of old women in black.

Costa led her to the icon of the Madonna. The Mother of Christ waited calmly for their approach. Costa fell on his knees before her, pulled Ethel down beside him. As Costa bowed his head, Ethel bowed hers.

For a long time, Costa spoke his praise to Mary in a tongue that Ethel couldn't understand, of course. It was Greek that a Greek would have had trouble following, heavy, archaic, out of general use.

Then he reached into his pocket, took all the paper money he had, and finding an opening at the top of the glass that shielded the Mother of Christ, he stuffed the money down so that it fell between the glass and the image.

Finally he allowed Ethel to get off her knees.

Someone had told the young priest that the old man, once one of the vicars of that transplant cathedral, the man whose publicly proclaimed alienation had hurt the priest's feelings as well as his community standing, was in the church. So the bingo priest himself had come to meet them. Standing in the back of the nave, not knowing what to expect, he was prepared to be snubbed again.

Costa raised both his arms in a greeting of forgiveness and joy healing all, marched toward the young Greek-American, enveloped him in his arms and embraced him in a way that made local history.

"Only one thing. The money I leave over there, it is

not for the church, it is for Her Majesty, the Queen of Heaven; it is for the poor over whom She watches."

"That is the one purpose for which it will be used," the priest said.

Costa kissed him on both cheeks.

"Kiss his hand," he commanded Ethel.

Ethel didn't hesitate. The young man's hands smelled not of beeswax or the holy candles; they smelled of Dial soap.

At a large tray in the back of the church, Costa threw all his change down and took two candles. One he gave Ethel and she did as he did, lit it from the flame of candles that were already burning in the shoulder-high candelabra.

Now again Costa performed a shopping ceremony. At the dock he asked for fish, chose a large grouper, demanded an oath that it was fresh. He paid nothing; fishermen don't pay fishermen. At the wine store he bought—on credit—three bottles of Hymettus, a wine imported from Athens.

Everywhere he went he announced the coming event. "A savior will be born," he seemed to be proclaiming. "A redeemer!"

Suddenly Ethel was ashamed; she wished she had not done what she'd done. What had made her believe that she could play this way with this kind of person? She wanted to run away from it all, but she could no longer do that.

Stuffed with food, rich in wine, heavy with child, she slept in the bed where Costa's father had died, the bed which was now Teddy's. Waking in the night, she choked down an impulse to get out of bed and run. In the morning, she decided there was nothing to do but see it through.

She passed Sunday morning with Costa, visiting his father's grave, listening as he spoke to his father's image (did he hear a message in return?), watching Costa cut the grass around the stone (who else, she thought, cares for their dead this way?), then take out his little whisk broom and sweep the cuttings off the stone. Logically it was absurd. Still, the devotion itself, the feeling exercised, was a value she could not scorn.

The afternoon was hot and muggy. Ethel, sleepy with the heat, was content to sit in the yard under the shade of the live oak and read.

But not Costa. As she fell into a sleep, she saw him going across the street to a neighbor's place. When she woke, he was back, now dressed in white sailcloth bib overalls. He was still, she could see, a heavily muscled man.

On the ground lay the pick and shovel he'd gone off to borrow. Alongside was a box of old household string and cord and some stakes he was bringing to a point with a hand ax—the sound that woke her.

Now, as she watched, he drove the stakes into the ground, making a double rectangle, one just inside the other, the wall of his bedroom serving as one side. This done—"What are you doing?" Ethel called—he began to stretch pieces of the twine, different lengths tied together, from stake to stake, around the double perimeter's parallel lines.

"I put new room here," Costa said. "Nice porch, screen wire, so forth, he can sleep with me in open air, very healthy for boy, understand, no mosquitoes, clean!"

He was singing to himself in Greek. She couldn't hear the words and if she could have, wouldn't have known what they meant. But the song she understood. It was a hymn of yearning for a land long lost. It kept the memory of fatherland alive, it memorialized a civilization.

The rectangle of string finished, Costa took the pickax and broke ground with a mighty "Harumph." Then another. And another, all around the perimeter between the walls of string. Then, with the shovel, he began to dig a three-sided trench. "Here I put concrete, hold room steady," he explained.

"Isn't it too hot to work?" she asked.

"Yes," he said, "very hot." He laughed with pleasure as he wiped his forehead with a handkerchief and mopped under his brows where the perspiration had come down, stinging his eyes. "Very, very hot."

She had made him a happy man. Now she was glad. It was worth the gamble, she decided drowsily, and she dropped off again into the sleep of a summer's afternoon.

twenty

BUT the evening turned sour.

First of all, it became obvious to Ethel that Costa expected her to quit the job at the marina immediately. It wasn't even something to discuss.

Ethel stepped gingerly. "Teddy wants me to work," she told Costa. "He doesn't want me fat and lazy; he wants me to be like a Greek peasant woman on your island, working to the last day."

"No, no, no." Costa brushed her aside. "Boy doesn't understand what is right."

"Nevertheless," Ethel said, "it is his wish."

"I explain him everything," Costa said, going for the phone.

But Teddy was not at home, so the matter dragged on and the issue softened.

Ethel told Costa she was sending Teddy thirty dollars a week. The U.S. government did not properly support the members of its officers' training program, she complained, so it was up to her.

Costa frowned, pursed his heavy lips, nodded, spit.

"He wants me to save as much money as possible," Ethel said. "He has three years more when he'll be needing money from me——"

"I give him," Costa said.

"You have other uses for it," Ethel said. "Besides, Teddy wants to support his own family; he doesn't want charity."

"From his father! That is not charity."

"It is how he feels," Ethel said.

"What you feel?"

"I do what Teddy tells me," she said.

This was talk Costa respected and for the time being it held him.

Besides, he had another problem: Noola wouldn't give up her job at the stocking factory. Ethel heard them quarreling that evening from the room across the hall, Costa shouting, Noola's voice always even, always controlled, never yielding. In the morning, Costa was not talking to his wife.

He and Ethel drove south together; both were late for work. As they walked into the marina, Costa accepted her reasons and her resolve.

"You must do what your husband wants," he said, "but I shall probably kill my wife, maybe next week." He laughed at the thought, but he added, "On my island —oh, my grandfather! oh, my father!—what they would do over there!"

Noola had discovered what Ethel had, that independence comes from the possession of money. Having tasted that tonic, she wasn't about to give it up.

"My wife," Costa said, as they separated, "she forgets who she is."

"Who is she?"

"She is Greek woman, she is my wife. I will teach her again, with this." He showed Ethel his great hand, an unclenched fist.

If his new job, dockmaster to the boss, had swelled his sense of self-importance, the announcement of Ethel's pregnancy made his ego boil over. People began to complain about his arrogance. The job irked him now and he vented his impatience on everybody, stormed up and down the piers of the marina, making the customers feel what they were, incompetents in the crafts of the sea.

"Don't pay him attention," Petros advised those boat owners who didn't see the humor of this arrogant old fellow. "He's just been told he's going to be a father."

Not altogether a joke, Petros complained to Ethel.

"Tell him to keep his hands off you," he told her.

"Oh, come on, Peetie—"

"I don't want him pawing you all the time."

"He's an old man, Peetie. Besides, you and I, we're not married. I didn't give you the right to order me around, so don't talk to me that way!"

"One minute more, I wallop you down."

"No you won't. I may knock you down."

"Every time I see you, he's rubbing you or touching you. What the hell is that?"

"He's just happy."

"When you're both sitting and he leans over and whispers, puts those big ham hands on the inside of your legs, not your knees I'm talking about, up here where you feel it, what is he whispering, tell me that?"

"He says, a hundred times a day, he says, 'It will be a boy, I will name him Costa, grandfather to grandson, the name goes that way in my family, grandfather to grandson.' That's what's on his mind."

"He doesn't look like he's saying that stuff. He looks like he's got a big ratchet screwdriver in his drawers!"

"Well, suppose he has. What am I supposed to do—throw a pail of cold water on it?"

"All right, I'll fire the son of a bitch out!"

"Peetie, you haven't got many brains, use what you have. You act funny one time like that, he'll become suspicious. . . . Well, he would—why are you making that face?"

"Sooner or later—"

"Not sooner, not later. And stop looking so mean every time he puts his arm around my shoulders."

"Shoulder, shit! He's feeling your tit on the other side, like this."

"Cut it out, Peetie. I know where it is. He wants to see if they're getting bigger."

"Let him ask me; I'll tell him."

The fact was that there was no way to stem Costa's joy. He soon became impossible to control and his arrogance fell on Petros.

"You're working her too hard!" he bellowed. "She's tired!"

"I don't do that. That's the way she is," Petros protested.

"Fix a place she can lie down when she tired or I take her off the job, boy, tell you that much. I take her home."

"She can lie down in my boat," Petros was miffed enough to say.

"Be careful, my friend," Costa warned. "I get mad at you, I kill you, guarantee, so I don't want get mad at you. Be careful!"

Petros caught hell from Ethel.

People around the marina noticed a change in her manner before seeing any physical alteration. Ethel began to daydream. In her thoughts she became a New Yorker. She had a secure, well-paying job, lived alone in a sunny apartment, led an orderly independent existence.

She would spend afternoons in Petros's office planning her furnishings or making up an imaginary calendar of activities, the entertainments she'd go to, the classes she'd take, the books she'd read, the kind of clothes she'd wear.

Then she'd bang up against the real problem: finding employment. She bought the *New York Times,* studied the want ads, considered her qualifications. She wrote a college acquaintance who'd made it in the big city, hoping to revive a friendship so she might, later, ask her help.

One afternoon, an opportunity presented itself from an unexpected source.

The new owner of the marina was the president of a conglomerate who had clustered around the original drug firm (inherited from his father) the following enterprises: a paperback house (featuring textbooks); a TV production company which operated in Glendale, California; a nationwide shoe line based in Switzerland (with special interests in Greece); a frozen king crab cannery in Alaska; and a brassiere business (the Whisper bra, the Promise), whose offices were in New York but whose products were manufactured in Puerto Rico.

With more money than he knew what to do with, he'd bought a large cruiser and named it after his mother. The *Sara* was a long, broad-beamed boat, so he had trouble finding a mooring in the sun belt near an airport. Hearing that the owner of his marina was in trouble, he made him an offer. In the three months since he'd bought the marina, he'd been too busy even to meet his staff (Petros had made one quick trip to New York), but he'd managed to keep the cruiser occupied most of the time (so its expense would be deductible).

On a particular afternoon, the afterdeck was covered with creatures Petros called *poustis,* male homosexuals. They were uniformly handsome (except for one old bitch) and their bodies were in much better shape than those of their heterosexual contemporaries. Their hair was touched with Glint of Gold (trademark), a product of one of the conglomerate's firms.

This group, most of whom had something to do with the brassiere business, hated to spend time in Puerto Rico, where their factory was (they found the poverty depressing), so they'd fly to Sarasota and their conglomerate boss would let them use the *Sara*. Ethel had met the queen of the bra line, a man with the dubious name of Robin Bolt; she'd taken him messages and telegrams, and—what had brought her on board that particular afternoon—cashed his checks.

"Say, Ethel, did you ever consider modeling?" Mr. Bolt asked. A friend was spreading Sunsoother (trademark) on his back.

"What could I model?" Ethel asked as she gave him an envelope fat with cash.

"How can you ask, dearie?" the friend said, turning Mr. Bolt over.

"I'm pregnant," Ethel said. "That's why they look so good."

There was a hosannah chorus of congratulations.

Ethel told Bolt those big boobs had been an embarrassment to her since they first appeared.

She laughed away the idea.

The time came when everyone could see that Ethel's belly was filling. "You got a soccer ball in there?" asked Petros, a soccer fan. He resented what wasn't his.

And now Costa again began to insist that Ethel quit her job and come home to live quietly like any proper Greek mother-to-be. When she still wouldn't obey him, he got on the phone to his son, crowded him so hard that Teddy finally agreed to drive down for a confrontation.

Ethel found Teddy very much on edge.

"I got a ton of work up there," he said.

She walked him out back, told him she was saving money for her own purposes and that there was no reason she shouldn't work. "It's up to you to handle your father," she said.

He nodded brusquely, turned in place the way he'd been trained to, and marched into the house.

Not wanting to see or hear the scene, Ethel stretched out under the live oak and waited. The sounds of quarreling reached her.

First she heard the father shouting his demands in words she'd heard again and again. Then the son doing exactly what his mother had done a few weeks before when Costa had demanded she quit her job, saying the same thing over and over, keeping his voice even and low so it reached Ethel only as a murmur.

And Costa shouting.

And more murmur.

Then she heard Teddy, the officer-to-be, speak in the voice of command.

"I want her to work," he said, sounding like a line officer delivering final instructions to an unsatisfactory crew. "This is America, Pop, and I'll decide when it's time for her to quit, not you. She's my wife, Pop, not yours."

"What you mean that remark, boy?"

"You act like she's yours. You're stuck on her, or something. O.K. It's O.K. But I'm telling you, it's for me to say how long she works and when she quits and anything else she does or does not do— What? Oh, I was kidding about that. But please, just mind your business, will you, Pop?"

Costa created the crisis he needed in another direction. He cornered Noola, his face clenched like a fist, and ordered her to quit her job. "If you don't," he roared, "I put you out."

Noola went into her room and began to pack her bag. When she came out she asked Ethel to drive her to the home of a friend who worked in the stocking factory.

Ethel said of course she would.

"You see!" Costa roared. "You see who's together?" He pointed to the two women. "One worse than the other! Your wife start this, talk to her, damn fool!"

When Teddy didn't intervene for him, Costa snatched the suitcase out of Noola's hand, flung it against the wall, breaking the glass of Teddy's graduation photograph. Then Costa followed the suitcase, predator on prey, ripped the top off its hinges, lock and clasps flying through the air. Now he went for the entrails, scattering the Sunday dress, stockings, toilet articles, underwear, even breaking a toothbrush, hammering at everything he could crack with Noola's silver wedding-present hairbrush, screaming oaths in Greek and a few in Turkish, spitting at the contents, stamping on them as though they were living things and he was eliminating all signs of their life.

Noola wept quietly at the side of the room.

Then he went for her. "Now get out," he shouted "Go live with those bitches in the factory."

When she didn't move, he reached for her. He was going to literally throw her out the door.

Till Teddy stood in his way.

"That's enough, Pop," Teddy said. "Step back, please."

Teddy didn't get out of the way when Costa ordered him to with a gesture. So Costa struck him across the face with an open palm, the classic assertion of old-world authority.

Teddy didn't budge. "O.K., Pop," he said in the same clear, controlled voice. "That's enough now, Pop."

Costa couldn't believe it.

Again he started toward Noola.

"Stay back," Teddy said. "Please. I don't want to touch you, Pop. But if I have to, I will. Why don't you go wash your face now, in cold water. Leave her alone. You've done enough."

Dazed, breathing hard, his lower lip trembling, Costa stood staring at his son.

"My house!" he said. "Get out! Both. You. I put you. Out!"

There were tears in Costa's eyes.

"My son!" he said. "You! I never want to see you again."

He was quiet but still pulling in air with difficulty.

"I expect nothing," he said. "From anyone here. Only Ethel!"

Then he left the house and didn't come back.

Late that afternoon, Teddy prepared for the long drive north.

"You're going to be an officer, all right," Ethel said. "You sounded like top brass today, kid."

"I hurt the old man," he said.

"You had to. Who knows what he would have done?"

"Yeah, yeah, but . . . see him crying?"

"You're a very sweet human being, Teddy."

"I know. It's been my problem." He looked at her. "Hasn't it?"

Then he kissed her on the cheek, as is proper between friends, and said, "Well, you got what you wanted, didn't you? And he'll get over it. I guess."

Ethel nodded and smiled. "Yeah, you're going to make it. I'll promote you right now. Captain Avaliotis."

"You're nuts," Teddy said. "You know that?"

When he'd gone, Ethel found Noola. "You want me to stay here with you, just in case?" she asked.

"Just in case what?" Noola asked.

"He goes crazy again."

"Not necessary."

"I think he means it this time," Ethel said, "about quitting the job and all."

"Well, this is the biggest thing in his life," Noola said, "but—excuse me—it's not the biggest thing in my life. I'm the biggest."

Then Noola said it. "Thank you."

"I didn't do anything—you mean the child?"

"I mean the idea of working. I got it from you. It changed my life, that little thing."

"The independence, you mean, Mrs. Avaliotis?"

"You can call me Noola now. No, I mean the money."

They slept in the same bedroom that night. There were twin beds there and in the first years after Noola and Costa had married they had used that room.

The night was quiet.

At five-thirty, when it was still dark out, both women got up, made coffee and toast, chewed and sipped silently.

"You're not worried about him, are you?" Ethel asked.

"Sure, I'm worried. He goes crazy like that sometimes. Then he can do anything. It passes, but while he is with the devils of his nature . . . you saw!"

Ethel drove her to the factory. Fifty-odd women, most past their middle years, filed into the old ivy-clad building.

Noola joined them and did not look back.

When Ethel got to work Costa was there, very drunk. He'd announced his retirement to Petros, who'd protested not at all. Now he was packing his gear. Aleko the Levendis, sad and sleepy, was outside, waiting in his car.

Costa looked at Ethel a long time, as if making up his mind what to do, then came up to her, head bowed like a naughty schoolchild, and said, "Noola all right?"

"She's fine."

He nodded heavily. "She turn into donkey," he said. "Stupid!"

"She's waiting for you."

Costa nodded his head and swayed.

"You hear what damn fool son said yesterday?"

"No," Ethel lied. "What?"

"Better you don't hear these things."

Then Ethel did something naughty. She went over and kissed the old man on the cheek. "Don't let it bother you," she said.

"Oh, yes, oh, yes," he said. "He do what he want, Noola do what she want, you and me, we do proper way. I quit job here today. Don't be afraid from me. I love you. Understand that?"

"Noola is waiting for you."

"I don't love Noola. I will live without her." He looked at Ethel, cupped his hand under her chin, lifted her mouth and kissed it. He was very drunk. "I thank you what you do for me. I don't forget that. I was getting worried over there. And don't worry, I take care new boy, I raise him proper way."

"I trust you to do that. Proper way."

"All K., then. He's mine?"

"Yes. And mine. But you can raise him. I trust him to you!"

"Guarantee!" Costa said. "One more question. You come see me; I don't frighten you away?"

"I like men who get mad; the kind I don't like is men who don't when they should."

"Then you come see me many time." He laughed. "Right away again."

"This weekend."

Again he kissed her on the mouth. Then without saying good-bye to Petros, who was of no further consequence to him, he left for home.

"Where you going?" Petros demanded on the next Sunday afternoon.

Petros had decided to behave like a man who was being taken.

"Up north."

"I don't believe you."

"That's your problem."

"Who you going to see up there?"

"The old man."

"You're not going all that way to see an old man."

Ethel walked out of the office, got into her car and drove off.

She had the eerie feeling she was being followed. She thought she saw Petros's car behind hers, all the way north.

Costa had put down a cement and cinder-block foundation, on top of which he'd laid down four-by-fours, fastening them to bolts he'd imbedded in the concrete. He'd ripped out the side of the house and made a bridge in the foundation. He was working without plans, but it was obvious he'd thought about it a long time.

She watched him work, ran errands for him, brought him a fresh supply of three-inch nails, made his supper.

At night Costa slept in the half-finished room, the big old bed with its great headboard visible to anyone on the street who passed that side of the house.

Ethel accepted the stance he'd assigned her, indolence, waiting. Costa had padded the day bed under the live oak and brought her a portable radio. She looked up at the hanging moss and listened to country music. From the house she heard his hammering.

At night, Ethel and Noola occupied twin beds in the same room—Ethel's suggestion. She felt sorry for the woman and, unaccustomed to the kind of violence Costa had shown, thought Noola might need protection. She had even tried to ease Costa's feelings about his wife, but had not succeeded.

Costa considered Noola a traitor. All his concerns were for Ethel.

He worked part of Sunday, then knocked off. He washed himself carefully, shaved his face and anointed himself with a perfume that smelled a little too sweet.

Then he walked up to where Ethel was stretched out and put his hand on her abdomen.

"I teach you," he said. "Boys"—his hand moved up gently and reassuringly—"like this, here, high. Girls" —he moved his hand down—"lie like this, here, my grandmother taught me."

She didn't pull away from his caress.

Petros didn't say anything when she returned. She was openly his mistress now, slept in his boat, cooked his dinner, did her duty. It wasn't going to go on much longer, so Ethel determined to do right by him while it lasted. Apparently he had followed her, because he no longer complained when she disappeared weekends.

She knew she was walking the rim of a crater, a precipice on both sides.

Time went by. She spent every weekend at the old house. The new room was finished and she drove Costa to antique stores, where they inspected the remnants of old households. She helped him select a crib and a chest of drawers. At Sears they bought a layette.

She read Costa books about baby care. He was learning everything carefully, laboriously. He had never studied before—anything.

They stocked paper diapers, filled a shelf with talcum powder and baby oil.

Everything was in place, waiting.

Afternoons Ethel spent in the backyard, a pumpkin in the sun. As the day cooled, Costa joined her under the live oak, withdrawing into reverie as the earth turned away from the sun. A faint but perfect smile lifted his lips at the corners. His eyes revealed the contentment he was knowing within.

At sunset, Ethel would bring him his *aryan*, yogurt thinned with water, flavored with cucumber strips and stirred into ice cubes. He didn't acknowledge her service until he'd had a first sip. Then he'd pay the girl with a nod and a smile.

It made her happy to be the attendant at this daily ritual. Costa, during those perfect weeks, was her presiding Buddha, a god of reassurance, benign, perfect.

Physically, he had become increasingly familiar with her. She'd mentioned her concern that her belly might be streaked with stretch marks. He reassured her, rubbed her abdomen with olive oil, another of his grandmother's old-time techniques. He told her to do the same to her breasts, which were now enormous.

There was a contented familiarity between them, a total physical trust.

Whenever Ethel was there, she made dinner. Noola, as an accredited wage earner, accepted this service. Costa expected it.

Ethel was serving as his wife in every way except one.

When she walked from her resting place under the live oak to the house, from the kitchen to the dining room table, she felt him watching her movement and her carriage.

He lived through those weeks with her, waiting as she was waiting.

When the child began to stir, he'd place a heavy open palm on her belly and measure the strength of the life arriving, make a fist and say, "That little bastard has a hell of a kick!" Then, addressing the child directly, he'd say, "Hey, you, tough guy! I wait, I wait, now all of a sudden you're in a hurry?"

Every weekend he pushed her again to quit her job.

Finally, when her time was near, she told him she'd done so.

Petros had not objected; the reason was obvious.

Her time was measured in weeks, then in days. Costa became impossible to talk to, always seemed about to fly off the handle.

Only with Ethel was he gentle and patient.

Ethel wanted to have the birth in the house, but Costa insisted on the hospital. "Everything the best," he said. It was an argument Ethel did not need to win. It was his child; he should have this detail as he wanted it.

It was the time of Teddy's first sea duty, a feature of the break between the first and second terms at N OTC. After explaining the problem to Ethel on the phone, he asked to speak to his father.

When Costa spoke to his son, Ethel heard a new respect for Teddy in the old man's voice.

They spoke for a long time. Ethel imagined Teddy was telling his father what he'd told her: how important the exercise at sea was and that he didn't want to miss it.

When he was through, she heard Costa say, "Don't worry, my boy, I take care everything here perfect."

Costa was left in command of the field.

twenty-one

THE contractions were coming more frequently. What patience Ethel had left was disappearing. She wanted to be alone and battle in silence. But ever since she'd arrived that morning, Petros had been calling her on the bedside phone as if it were one of his office extensions. And Costa, standing astride her doorway, glared at any passer-by who talked above a whisper while he complained about everything in a voice everyone could hear. At the slightest shifting of her body, he'd look at her anxiously and call for a nurse.

She decided not to put up with it and, between contractions, pressed the call button.

"I'll have your phone plugged right away," the nurse said. "And tell me, do we have to have that big old man blocking the door? What is he, a detective or a member of the Greek Mafia?"

Costa, who'd been out of view for a few minutes, came back and gestured for the nurse to get out. Which she did, in a hurry. He seemed all wrought up again, closed the door, then whispered to Ethel, "I find out."

"You found out what?"

"Your doctor, he's Armenian. His name, Boyajian. You see his nose, how it turns? Like this?" He twisted his own nose grotesquely.

"For chrissake, Dad, what the hell has his nose or his nationality got to do with his ability as a doctor? I mean, what kind of reasoning is that?"

"On this I don't need reasoning." With his pursed fingertips, he pounded his chest, which he believed shielded the seat of his instincts. "I know here. He is no good. I'm going to change him."

"Like hell you're going to change him. It's my body and he's my doctor." Then she began to break up. "Stop it! Cut it out! I've got these damn contractions now, Dad, and I don't need a lot of fussing and feuding here, I want it quiet here, for chrissake. Can't I have it quiet here for a change, Dad, I mean just for today? I mean, will you stay the hell out of here now till I pull off this stunt and produce you a child?"

"Whatsa matter?" Costa said. "I been like a mouse here, so quiet."

"Go take a walk—will you take a long walk? And when the doctor comes, you damn well better give him respect, because I like him and if you're rude to him, I swear to God, I'll bring out a girl and she'll have two mouths and one eye. You hear me?"

"I hear and I'm going. But I tell you one thing. If anything happen to the boy, I will kill him, this Armenian!"

"There is no boy yet, Dad. We're spinning a coin here, Dad."

"Don't worry on that," he said as he stalked out of the room, head thrown back, knees stiff. "On that much I'm sure."

He stayed away for over an hour, but he must have had her door under surveillance, because when Dr. Boyajian came in with his crew to take her to the delivery room, Costa followed after them.

"Please forgive bad thoughts, Boyajian," he said.

"What bad thoughts?" The doctor was bent over Ethel, examining her.

"All forgotten now. You are great doctor, I'm sure, also scientist." Again he pounded his sternum with his stiffened fingertips. "I trust you with my life."

The doctor acknowledged the compliment with a slight bow.

Then Costa added, "So better be careful!"

He flanked the small white procession all the way to the elevator. Ethel was relieved when they wouldn't allow him to go farther. As she waved good-bye through the closing grate, she was figuring out what she'd say if it was a girl.

The first time Ethel saw her child, he was in Costa's arms.

Her first visitor was Petros.

"So," the jealous man said, "he got what he wanted, a boy."

"He believes," Ethel said, "that it's God's payment for his faith."

"He's crazy," Petros said. "Say, you look much better without a belly."

Suddenly he was on the hospital bed with her.

"What the hell are you doing?" she cried. "Get off here! Go away!"

She shoved him so he fell off the bed.

He lay on the floor laughing.

"You're some powerful bitch!" he said as he got up. "When'll you be back?"

413

"Never."

"I give you one week. Then I'm coming for you. Then also I stop pretending."

"Go on, get out. I'm through with all of you."

He laughed. "Some powerful bitch!" he said. "I got a good surprise for you one of these days soon."

"I don't want it. I don't want anything from you now."

"Not now. That's what I mean, a surprise. But hurry, I'm waiting."

The new fact—she was the mother of a son—had little effect on Ethel at first. Between feedings it seemed she forgot about the boy. She was guarding her emotions, holding them back.

And she had other concerns.

The pincers were closing. In a day or two she'd be leaving the hospital. Petros's promise of a surprise was a threat, Costa's worshipping and possessive looks another. Would they allow her to "vanish"? Ernie and Aaron and Teddy and the others were boys. These two Greeks were men from another, a tougher, world.

Even if she succeeded in disappearing, where would she run? Her father was gone.

She swallowed the panic. Mexico had proved she could find a job and hold it. The first step was to pick a time for flight. Soon. While there was still an opening she could squeeze through.

Something else worried her. Arturo's man, Ignacio Alvarez, had given her a job only because he wanted to fuck her. Petros had said as much to Teddy. Matter-of-factly! Could she get, or hold, a job without that?

Of course she could. Not every working girl had to peddle her ass.

Did they?

She had to train herself quickly, improve her mechanical skills—no, do more than that: school herself in some special capability, bookkeeping or tax preparation, otherwise face the fact that when a man hires a secretary who's pretty, he expects her favors.

Late that afternoon, Noola came to see her son's son, the traditional mother-in-law visit. She wore her best mortgage-payment-day hat, sat watching Ethel nurse the child. "Looks like you got plenty milk," she observed. Noola's breasts had withered.

At regular intervals Costa walked by the door, checking that Noola was still there. His nerves—what was it about this time? Ethel wondered—had everyone on edge.

When the nurse took the little boy back to the sterile room, Noola reached for her hat with the startled feathers. "They've been talking about your boss getting married," she said.

"Petros! Who to?"

"No one knows. It's a surprise. Must be somebody pretty good because he's taken an apartment in the Gulfview group, a three-year lease."

After Noola left, it occurred to Ethel that she'd come fishing.

Costa had a new worry. There were a dozen infants in the sterile room and, "Maybe they get mix up, who knows?" He wanted a separate space for their child, so he was waiting in Ethel's room when Dr. Boyajian came by for a visit.

With a hint of impatience, the doctor informed Costa that what he was asking was impossible.

"Then my boy and me, we go home," Costa said.

"Not for another day, please," Dr. Boyajian said. "There's a thing or two we have to finish here."

"What's this, a thing or two?" Costa demanded to know.

"Something you can't do at home." Dr. Boyajian turned

415

to Ethel. "You're in great shape," he said. "Let's say late tomorrow afternoon, shall we? They need the space here."

Costa had found something ominous in Boyajian's manner as well as in his words, so he followed him into the hall. Ethel couldn't hear what was being said there, but to judge by the rumble, Costa was not getting satisfaction.

After a minute, she heard him accost another new parent. This man mistook Costa for a *landsman,* spoke of circumcision as *bris,* and moved on.

A nurse entered Ethel's room with Costa close after her, raging.

"You tol' them they can do this?" he demanded of Ethel. He drew his forefinger like a cutting edge across his genitals.

"I think they just went ahead and did it," she said. "I mean, I believe it's done already. But if they'd asked me, I'd have said——"

Costa was gone.

"That it was all right with me," she called after him.

She knew it was up to her to control Costa; no one else could.

It was her first time on her feet.

In the corridor outside Dr. Boyajian's consultation room, Ethel saw nurses crowding a door and heard cries of fear and of outrage. She moved up as fast as she could. "He broke into the sterile room," a nurse told her. "When he saw it had been done, he went berserk."

In the doorway of the examination room, they made way for Ethel. She saw a black woman sitting on a gynecologist's table, holding up the dress she'd dropped for her examination. Crouched under the table, the gentle and distinguished Dr. Aslan Boyajian was shouting for the police. Costa was kicking at him, trying to drive him from cover. Apparently one kick had broken the man's eyeglasses, for the doctor was clutching them in his closed fist.

"Costa," Ethel called, "Costa, stop it!"

Lifting the black woman off the table, he thrust her into Ethel's arms. "Take care this poor woman," he said. Then, before Ethel could do anything—her arms were full—Costa picked up the examination table and flung it against the wall. He had the doctor at his mercy.

By then Ethel had passed the black woman on to a nurse and rushed between Costa and the doctor on the floor.

She's learned from Teddy how to handle Costa.

"Don't be a *vlax*, Costa," she said in an officer's voice. "This is America. Wha he did is the custom here."

"Never mind customs here," Costa said, his eyes blazing. "He's my boy. You see what he did to him, this Armenian?"

"Now, Costa, really, you're acting like a donkey."

"He should have asked me, what the hell! *Vlax!* Donkey!"

"About that," Ethel said, "you're absolutely right. Isn't he, Dr. Boyajian?" She turned to the doctor, who still was on his knees. "Say it, Doctor, say he's absolutely right."

The doctor got the message. "About that," he said, "yes. I suppose he is."

"Never mind 'suppose' business," Ethel said. "He's absolutely right. Say it. Say those words to him!"

"You're absolutely right, sir," Dr. Boyajian said.

"You should have asked him first. You know that now. So say it."

"I should certainly have asked you first," the doctor said to Costa.

"What's the good of this now?" Costa said, throwing his hands up.

"Tell him you're sorry," Ethel said. "Say it to him."

"I'm sorry, sir," Dr. Boyajian said. "I apologize."

Ethel turned to Costa. "I know how you feel about this, Dad," she said, "and I'm sorry. But now . . . Costa, I don't feel so strong. Hurry! Take me back to my room, Daddy."

"What?" Costa said. "What's the matter?"

"Hold me," she said, falling against him, grabbing his arm for support. "Hold me."

The police came looking for Costa. They found him in Ethel's room, asleep on the bed across from hers.

"He's had an exhausting day," Ethel said to the officers of the law. "You can see he's not a young man."

"We just want to tell him," one of the men said, "that the doctor decided not to press charges."

When the cops were gone, she crossed over and sat on the edge of the bed where the old man was sleeping. Gently, she stroked Costa's head. Their happy times were over.

She nursed the infant for the last time before taking him home.

Young Costa, she'd noticed from the beginning, had a strong character. When he looked at her, his eyes fixed in a penetrating stare; they did not waver.

She'd spoken to the doctor about this and he'd said the child couldn't focus yet so he wasn't really looking at her, not particularly at her. She found this expert information reassuring, but nevertheless she continued to feel that little Costa was looking at her, particularly at her, and that his eyes were accusing her.

"What do you want?" she'd ask as she gave him her tit. "Ouch!" she'd say when his hard gums found her nipple. "You think you own me, don't you, you little bastard," she said when he clasped her thumb in his hand and, with strength that surprised her, held on like a monkey. "What are you worried about, monkey? Your mother's not going to drop you out of the tree."

But she knew she was.

There were things about him that were babylike: the smell of his well-powdered body, the faint perfume of urine, his perfect pink nails, as delicately colored as precious stones, the sweet drool she had to wipe from his lips, the way he moved his legs as if he were still trying to kick his way out of her belly.

But the main thing about him was the unwavering demand in his eyes. It gave her the eerie sense that the child knew she was planning to betray him, make of him what someone had made of her—a parentless child. "Why are you going to do that to me?" is what Ethel read in that stare.

Which was silly, of course . . . to see a thought.

But was there anger there? Already? It did seem so.

When the child wasn't at her side or in her arms, these feelings of guilt eased. "Why should I take on another life when I haven't really started my own yet?" she'd ask herself. "Costa will take good care of you," she'd say to the child. "He'll do a damn sight better than I would."

Sometimes she believed that, sometimes she didn't.

At home, Costa kept track of the baby's feeding time, by day and by night. Five minutes before, he would knock on her door and say, "Get ready. He's waiting!" When the boy was through, Costa took him—being careful, she noticed, not to look at her breasts—and held him up to burp. He was concerned every other way too. He boiled the sheets. "Lotsa germs in the world," he said.

Exactly what Ethel wanted was happening. Costa was taking the child away from her.

But it was evident she couldn't pull out as early as

she'd planned. Little Costa had to be weaned; he pulled at her nipples with his hard gums, making them bright red. His needs were absolute. It might be some weeks yet. Costa had made it clear he expected her to nurse the little one as long as she had milk. "My mother, same way," he said. "But Noola. Formula! That's why I'm stronger than Teddy. You see?"

When Petros paid a visit that weekend, Costa refused to let him into the house. "You dirty," he said. He did offer him a peek at the heir to the family temper through the wire screen of the new room.

"He acts more and more like he's the father," Petros said. Then, despite Ethel, he called through the wire: "Hey, you, *vlax,* I take a shower three times a day. How many you take? I change my underwear every morning. When you change yours last time?"

"You're still dirty," Costa said.

"I can smell you from here. I feel sorry for that boy. He will grow up thinking it's normal for a man to smell like a dying sponge."

"Go on, go home, before I get mad." Costa pulled a plywood screen around the sleeping boy.

"People at the marina still talking how you leave stink behind. They're praying for a hurricane to blow your smell away."

Costa came to the screen. "Get out my property," he shouted.

"The niggers there smell better than you. They're perfume to your shit!"

"Last chance. Get out quick. Before I kill you."

"Once too often you said that."

They were nose to nose at the screen.

The baby slept peacefully through it all.

Ethel had to pull Petros away. Even after he was in his car, sitting behind the wheel, he was trembling.

"When am I going to see you?" he said. "I'm going nuts down there by myself."

"Get yourself another girl," she said.

"You're my girl. Come on, Ethel, I need you. Can't you see I'm all worked up? I'm going to kill that old bastard, I swear, unless you calm me down. Ethel! Come on!"

She paid him a quick visit, taking the infant with her in a small laundry basket lined with a blanket. Petros showed her the "surprise," the Gulf-view apartment. She'd never seen him so anxious about anything.

The place had been completely furnished by a Greek interior decorator, a recent arrival from the motherland. The furnishings were not Greek; they were international middle-class parlor furniture, respectable and uncomfortable.

Petros watched her face as she walked around the place.

"O.K., O.K.," he said. "I don't like it either. It doesn't go with you. I will change everything."

When she walked into the bedroom, she looked out the window and directly into the bedroom window of the condominium next door. An old wrinkled lady with golden hair was looking at her. The effect was eerie, a time mirror.

Petros jerked the shade down hard. It broke off the roller.

He closed the brocade curtains.

The bed creaked so that she got the giggles. He had to laugh too. It was impossible for them to make love with steel springs complaining under them.

"Next time," she said. "I shouldn't, anyway, for another couple of weeks."

But he threw her on the floor and took her.

It made her angry but she didn't say a word. She was leaving soon.

Costa was furious. But not in his usual out-of-control manner. No, he was lovelorn, he was betrayed. So, he declared again and again, was little Costa. How could she do that to his grandson? Take him to see that pig?

"Tell the truth, you ask him come here before, that time?"

"Yes," Ethel said. "I suggested it."

"I don't want that man here again."

"O.K., Dad."

She was making absolutely sure that before she left, Costa would have mastered the intricacies of baby care.

"What's so hard?" he boasted as he was powdering the baby after his bath. "You women make big deal from that, but I learn perfect two weeks. Wash! Powder! Dress! Everything clean! That's it!" He lowered his head, big mouth wide open, into the soft belly of young Costa, wallowed there. "Guwhaguwhaguwhaguwha," he said. "I eat you up!"

"If I had tits," he told her, "I do better than you. Maybe I grow tits next. What you say to that?"

Then he'd look up at her coyly; he was flirting with her.

But mostly he treated her with the reverence due a madonna; gave her presents, inexpensive, dearly chosen trifles. He lowered his voice when he talked to her. He was never unaware that she was near, and when she nursed the infant, he'd turn his face away.

She received a letter from her father, who was back in Tucson. Ernie had killed his girl friend—or so the police believed. The girl's naked body had been found with twenty-eight stab wounds.

The neighbors reported violent quarrels. They knew the girl was giving Ernie a bad time. But twenty-eight thrusts with a knife! What could justify that?

This dreadful news depressed Ethel. She knew her son was Ernie's; he had the same sleepy eyes, too heavy, they seemed, for their sockets. He couldn't be Teddy's and she was already pregnant when she began to sleep with Petros.

Oh, drop it! Little Costa was who she'd wanted him to be. Hers alone!

It occurred to her that she could always go back to her father. It might be humiliating, but she was glad that last resort existed.

The time had come to prepare the first step away—in whatever direction.

She told Costa one morning that the child had to be weaned now, her milk was drying up. It wasn't true, but there was no way Costa could find that out.

So they worked out the formula—what it was, how to prepare it, the feeding and then the sterilization process.

Costa was glad to take this over too.

Then she told him she was going back to her job, would come home weekends. She waited for him to blow up.

"I don't want you working for that man," he stated.

"When you get a job, Dad, then I'll quit mine," she said.

Costa was very hurt. Because he had no answer.

"I have to take care the boy now, proper style," he said, "make sure everything O.K., he don't get sick, so forth. No? What?"

"Sure. And you do a good job. But meantime somebody's got to pay for the groceries. You won't take money from Noola. My savings are going fast. Teddy is waiting for thirty dollars every week from me."

"Boy shouldn't ask that from you."

"I don't mind. But that is why I have to keep the job."

"Then why you have to look at him all the time? Bad enough you take his money—why you have to look at him? That way?"

"Which way?"

"The way you were looking at him when he was here. You suppose to look at human being that way. That fellow—don't you see his face?—he's animal!"

"Well, what can I do?"

"I told you. Look on the ground when he's near."

"I can't work for the man and look at the ground."

"All right. But I'm telling you, one day he will get wrong idea from you, then I will have to kill him."

At the marina office, she found another letter from her father. She read the enclosure first, a piece from the Tucson paper which informed the community that Ernie had surrendered, admitted his crime and was going to be tried for murder. The reporter reminded his readers that the deterrent the State of Arizona had for a crime this serious was the gas chamber.

Ed Laffey had no comment. He had other news.

"After seeing the rest of the world," he'd written, "Tucson seems mean and narrow to us. So we've decided to make a big move. We're leaving the day after tomorrow to find a new home. It will be on an island—Majorca, Ischia, Capri, Ceylon (now named something I can't spell), the Seychelles, who knows? So, Kit darling, I'm afraid we're abandoning you—"

Apparently Margaret had snatched the pen out of his hand and written: "Like hell we are! When we find our magic island, you will be our first guest."

Then he'd written: "As you may have guessed from that very firm correction, Margaret and I are now married."

And she: "And it hasn't ruined out relationship."

And he: "Not yet."

424

They both sent kisses.

Ethel had neglected to inform them about the birth of her boy. And now, when she could have told them on the telephone, she didn't. A call would inevitably become a call for help. "Crawling," Ethel called it. So she didn't and a day went by, then another, then it was too late. She didn't know where in the world to reach them.

Ethel stayed in her own apartment, visiting Petros, as she used to, on his boat. One day, he took her to see another apartment. There were great bunches of flowers in every room, an extravagant welcome. Petros had not only changed apartments, he'd changed the furniture. He'd gone to the extent of engaging a designer from the community theater in Sarasota, given him one instruction: "It's for my woman. If she like it, I like it." The place had been done with this single requirement in mind. In the kitchen there was a microwave oven, in the bedroom romantic prints on the walls, in the dressing room an enormous mirror framed with nymphs and swans and cupids.

"Owen," Petros said to his decorator, "change anything she wants."

"Owen," Ethel said, "who could ask for anything more?"

When she looked out the bedroom window, there was nothing in sight except the aquamarine water of the Gulf of Mexico and the long curve of a perfect white beach with Casey Key in the distance.

Petros had gone to fantastic lengths—and expense—for her sake.

Her milk dried up in a few days, but she still had the instinct to nurse. The baby was weaned; she was not.

Petros had demanded she stay with him that weekend —in fact, he'd ordered her to. But when Sunday came, she had a bad feeling about the little boy up north, felt guilty for the first time and told Petros she was going. When he protested, she defied him.

It was a very humid day and the temperature was to reach 102 degrees. On the way up she had a near-accident. Her mind had wandered and she crossed the median, turned back, just in time, by the angry blare of horns from all sides.

She'd been telling herself, at that instant, that she should not sneak away this time; she should, for once in her life, tell the truth and face the consequences.

She walked into the house at four o'clock, the heaviest and hottest part of the afternoon. No one was in sight. They were probably asleep, she thought, so she tiptoed to Costa's new room. Opening the door soundlessly, she saw the old man and the baby naked on the bed, taking their afternoon nap.

Between his legs, Costa was large, his scrotum bigger than any she'd ever seen. His chest was a barrel that swelled and fell, evenly and slowly, taking more time than the average to fill and empty.

Then the child was awake and kicking his legs.

This woke Costa. He looked at the boy with complete adoration. Then he turned to the door where Ethel stood, looked at her without covering himself.

She closed the door softly and went into the dark, cool parlor. She looked at the old fading photographs on the walls, the family history, browning with age. Closing her eyes, she sat very still.

Then she got into her car and drove south.

The next day with Petros was a stormy one. He'd decided that she would divorce Teddy immediately, marry him and move in, child and all.

"You're eating my enemy's bread when you go there,"

426

he said. "I want you here with me, next week, finish. The boy too."

"I can't take the baby away from the old man," she said. "I made it for him."

"I will take it away. I'll enjoy doing that."

"What will you do when he comes after you? You know how he is, a madman."

"I will kill him. He's always talking about how they do on our island. That's how they do."

She knew she was egging him on, pushing him and the other man toward a terrible crash. But she couldn't seem to stop. Am I enjoying it? she wondered. Do I want them to fight over me till one kills the other?

"I will never again not have a place of my own," she said.

"You're going to do what I say, so make up your mind."

"Fuck you."

"When?"

A joke. But it really wasn't. It was a technique. Whenever he felt she was getting out of line, that's what he did, his solution to every problem. He believed he could always quiet her that way.

The time had come. There was no reason—or way—to put it off anymore.

The next afternoon, Costa called her at the office. Over the phone he seemed a different person.

"Come right away," he said.

"Where, Dad?"

"Where? My house. Where! Come on. Tonight."

"But, Dad, I—"

"Come on, come on, I'm waiting. Teddy coming too. Good-bye."

And he hung up.

She was annoyed. He'd been so peremptory, his voice so harsh. But then—perhaps something had happened to the child. She took Petros's Olds and rushed north.

Costa was under the live oak, holding Costa the younger against the side of his hip. He showed her how the baby could hang, clinging to his thumbs. "Like gorilla, strong," he said proudly. "This boy be admiral, sure thing."

"Or an acrobat. Is this what you rushed me here for?"

"Big day tomorrow," Costa said.

"What big day?"

"I call Tampa. Priest ready. Teddy too, he's coming morning plane. That bitch Noola, she don't give up day's pay. So we baptize little Costa without her. 'Bout time, right?"

She remembered the old man had been waiting for his son to return from sea duty for this event.

The next morning, she left Costa and the child at the old church in Tampa and went to pick up Teddy at the airport.

He really looked like an officer now. Since his explosion at Costa, he'd become another man, dealing with the problems of the rest of the world as he did his own, with an unassailable confidence that he had the right answers because they were the ones in the manual.

As they drove back to the church, Ethel told him, "I can't go any further with this. I'm not sorry, I've done it, but it's come to an end."

"Will you tell them? Before you go?"

"If I have the guts. If not, I'll just go. What do you advise?"

"Don't ask me that. I can't say. About the old man, question number one: Does he know how to take care of the kid?"

"Wait till you see!"

Whatever significance the ceremony had for Costa, for Ethel it was her ritual of farewell to her son.

The old church was crumbling from lack of bingo. The hairy old priest had deteriorated too. There was a moment when they saw that his eyes had completely failed. They had moved all together down the center aisle of the church and arrived at a battered brass basin on a tripod. An old woman had filled it with warm water, then rolled up the sleeves of the priest's robe. Ready, he reached out his hands to Ethel.

"What's he want?" she whispered to Costa.

"He wants the little one," he said.

Costa was holding the child. "Don't drop him, you old son of a bitch," he whispered to God's deputy as he gave him the naked child.

"May you populate the earth with Greeks," the old priest said in conclusion. Later, as he saw them to their car, he spoke of the birth rate of the Turkish people. "They reproduce like rats," he observed.

She drove the men back. In Tarpon Springs, Costa made her stop at the side of the square, said he wanted to go into a liquor store. But what he wanted was to walk slowly and gravely, carrying his grandson, through the *kentron,* where the old men of the town gathered every afternoon. Ethel and the officer he'd given the Navy of the United States walked behind. Costa stopped everywhere for compliments.

He bought some port wine—that is, he selected it, and Teddy paid for it with money that Ethel slipped into his hand. At home Costa sipped it down slowly, holding the sleeping child on his lap. "May he live for his parents," was his toast.

Teddy was going to be O.K. with the boy, she saw. He'd taken a whole pack of Polaroids.

They excused themselves early. Costa held Ethel like

429

a lover when he said good night. "You make me happy man," he said, stroking her face.

Teddy saw Noola look away.

"I know," Ethel told him when they were alone. "She hates me."

"You really believe that?"

"I know it. She acts the way she was brought up to act, discreet no matter what. But she will never forgive me."

"Then what you're planning to do is the only solution. Just disappear. Go!"

Ethel was surprised to hear him say it so plainly.

There was only one bed in their room, Captain Theo's. He held her in his arms, but he wasn't aroused. He had a girl now, he told her. "You saw her when you came up and you liked her. Remember the one who thought you were so pretty? She's an officer candidate too and just as ambitious as I am. At least! To move up in the Navy, I mean. I think I have what I need now. Finally."

They planned the divorce.

"No, he didn't touch me," she told Petros when she called him from a phone booth next morning. She was on the way to the airport with Teddy.

"You sleep in same room?" Petros demanded.

"Yes,"—then she lied—"but there are twin beds there and—oh, the hell with it, Peetie. I didn't give you the right to talk to me that way. We're not married."

She hung up.

"I won't be here next time you come down," she told Teddy as she got back into the car.

Before they parted, she gave him two hundred dollars out of what she'd saved.

"Won't you need it?" he said.

"I could give you more," she said, "but your father has no income now, you know that. So from wherever I go, I'll have to send him money every week. As soon as I find work, that is."

He kissed her. "I'll pay you back, for him and for me," he said.

She walked him to the gate.

"I made up my mind last night," she said. "I'm going to tell them both that I'm leaving."

"That will be some explosion. Want me and a couple of sailors here that day? I'm not kidding."

"I don't want to be helped through this one," she said. "Or through anything else. I particularly don't want that."

"Well . . . need I say it? Good luck. I really love you," he said.

"*Episis,*" she said, Greek for "likewise," one of the few Greek words she'd learned.

As she watched him walk through the gate and out of sight, she felt she was losing her last refuge.

That night she slept in her own bed. Alone. She woke with a plan. She'd give notice to the landlady that morning. That would give her two weeks to get rid of everything she owned, keeping only what she could pack in the big suitcase her mother had left behind. Everything else she'd clean out of her life.

"I gave notice on the apartment," she told Petros. He had been waiting for her, spoiling for the fight of his life. "I'll be out of there in two weeks."

He'd been keyed way up; now he was let down.

"In two weeks"—she elaborated the deception—"we'll have a party at your place. We'll be there together. Then everyone will know."

"Everyone knows now. Only you don't know."

"I know. I told Teddy yesterday."

"Between fucks?"

"He's got another girl."

"That never stopped a Greek."

431

"The only one who doesn't know is Costa."

"I'll tell him."

"Please, Peetie, let me do this my way. I'm going to tell Costa. Please."

Looking at him now, his lips tight as a half-healed knife cut under the great bone of a nose, she could see she was not getting out an instant too soon. He was a dangerous person.

Still she'd decided to tell him and she was going to. Costa too. She was not going to be ashamed of herself again.

She went on making Petros believe her lie, telling him about Mexico, about the guacamole and the margaritas and how happy she'd make him in the warm, soft nights, what clothes she'd buy, yellows and pinks and whites, nothing sad, nothing blue.

Till finally Petros was carried away. "O.K.!" he said. "That's it then. First we'll have a party like you say, then Mexico! Quiet and happy. I'll give you everything you want there."

"Thank you," she said. "Oh, Peetie, thank you."

She didn't believe in miracles but she found herself wishing for one. Her disaster fantasies grew more frequent and more intense. She'd be going along, thinking of "nothing," when all of a sudden she was imagining a bloody scene with Costa: he was cutting her everywhere as Ernie had his girl. Or—and this came on her the same day—she was locked in a room with Petros, who'd just found out that she was planning to disappear. Or, worst of all, that the child had been destroyed by Noola, who'd found out whose it was.

These sudden, complete takeovers of her mind, instant psychological strokes, were now coming one on top of the other.

"Miss Laffey, would you come up here a minute, please?"

A voice, half remembered. Robin Bolt was on the aft deck of the *Sara,* surrounded by his fellows. He wanted a check cashed, and while he was filling in the numbers, he asked her, "Ever think about my suggestions?"

"Mr. Bolt, thanks, but I really couldn't."

"You'd start, right away, at, let's say, three-fifty a week. If you turn out to be good at it, you'd soon make considerably more."

"How could I be good at it? These just sit here."

"It's not your glands I'm interested in. Most young boobs can be made to look good in one of our products. It's the contrast."

"What contrast?"

"You have—Emil, listen." He spoke to an assistant, who was sketching. "I was about to say she has the *poitrine* of an eighteenth-century royal concubine. How about that for the name of a new line? Royal Concubine! No? O.K." He turned back to Ethel. "And the face of a Tintoretto baby angel. That contrast, between your figure, which is voluptuous, and your face, which is pure jail bait, can be, I believe, highly commercial. Your face would be featured, your breasts covered by one of our best numbers. By the way, are they more or less as they were before the event?"

"I haven't looked at them." She laughed. "Professionally, I mean."

"Come to my cabin."

"Oh, no, thanks. Thank you, Mr. Bolt, but really no."

Later in the day Ethel fantasized living on three hundred and fifty dollars a week.

The next morning she made up her mind. She'd tell Costa first. He was the least dangerous. "I'm leaving

433

here," she'd tell him. "It's not your son's!" she'd tell him at last. Then she'd tell him everything, close her eyes and blurt it out. When he said, "I don't understand," she'd tell him again. When he said, "I don't believe you," she'd say it over. When he began to pale and tremble and puff, she'd tell him once more, then again, then again, then beg his pardon— *No!* Fuck that! She'd done nothing wrong; she wouldn't beg anyone's pardon!

After Costa, Petros. He was the dangerous one.

Then she'd tell the facts to the whole world, to anyone who cared to know, anyone who asked. What a relief that would be, to have it out!

Her motives through all this had been honorable. Even generous.

They deserved thanks. Not the opposite.

At last! She was eager to come out with the truth.

Someone beat her to it.

twenty-two

THE one person Costa would never forgive was his wife. Just to see Noola in her new independence infuriated him. When she came home from work, he turned his back to her. If he was in his room when she came home, he kicked the door shut so she'd hear it slam.

Ethel had guessed what Noola must be feeling. But since Noola had been influenced by Ethel's independence, Ethel hoped she might finally feel some bit of admiration for her, even a little gratitude.

Not so. Noola thought Ethel had destroyed her family. Lately she'd found a new reason to hate the girl.

One of the women at work had a cousin who put in half a day every day cleaning Petros's Gulf-view apartment. She told Noola what was going on.

Noola thought of it as a punishment for her husband. She accepted an invitation to take dinner and spend the night with the woman whose cousin worked for Petros, called Costa to tell him she wouldn't be home that night.

"You stay out tonight," he said, "you don't come back in here tomorrow."

"Whatever you want," she said.

But the next night—where was she to go? No one wanted her to move in with them. She'd considered getting a place of her own, a furnished room near the factory, but she wasn't ready for that yet. So she was in no mood when she got home to hear Costa say that the only woman who'd done anything for him in his life was Ethel: Ethel had given him a grandson.

"Go listen to what they're saying about her," Noola said.

"Keep your tongue quiet!" Costa roared. "Don't insult what's left here, whore!"

"Your dear daughter-in-law is the whore," Noola said.

He whacked her across the face. "I will clean her name from your dirty factory women," he said, ready to strike her again.

"Clean it from herself first," Noola said.

When he struck her again she fell into a chair and stayed there, prepared to defend herself against the attack she knew was coming.

"I don't live with you," Costa said. "Get out!"

"You get out. I made this house as much as you! If you don't want to live with me, go live somewhere else."

Then she told him plainly what she'd heard.

He said he didn't believe a word of it; it was women's malice speaking, he said.

"Why is she not living with Teddy?" Noola asked. "You know she should be with him; I heard you tell her many times. Why do you think she lives down there?"

He didn't answer. For a long time he looked at her as if she was betraying him. Then his eyes wavered and he left the room.

About half an hour later, she heard him on the phone, ordering Aleko to bring his car to the town square.

Ten minutes later he left the house, carrying the child.

It was late afternoon, the hour when the old-timers gathered in the *kentron*, to pass and pick up gossip.

Costa sat apart, on a stone bench, holding the baby in his lap.

When he saw Aleko drive up, he went to meet him. Opening the back door of the car, he wrapped one blanket around the infant and put the other down on the back seat, composing the child for sleep. Then he took the key from his friend and locked all four doors.

Now he took Aleko by the arm and led him into the circle of benches and shrubs in the heart of the park.

There he stopped and put his arms on his friend's shoulders.

He was, the Levendis could see, in desperate pain.

"Aleko, you my friend?" Costa asked.

"Yes, of course. You know that."

"So then, tell me."

"Tell you what?"

"Tell me what they're saying."

The men in the square were watching.

"I don't know what you're talking," Aleko said.

Costa fell to the ground, clasped his friend at the knees. Aleko tried to lift him, but Costa appeared to be without control of his limbs, a dead weight.

"I know," Costa said. He was sitting on the ground. "I know," he said. He looked around at the other men. "I always knew it," he said.

"Knew what?" Aleko said. "Get up, Costa!" he whispered.

Costa sat still, his head down, not moving. "Why don't you tell me what you know?" he asked. "Can't you see

—look at me—you can tell me now. Since I know. Come! Come!"

He heard some men whispering at a bench nearby. One of them, looking at the spectacle of the old fool sitting on the ground, had started to laugh.

Costa had him by the throat. Shaking him, he shouted, "It is not true. You all liars here. I never trust any of you! You are not my friends if you believe this."

"It is not I who say it," the man he was shaking got out. "They say it."

"Who? Where?"

"South of here. In the new marina in Bradenton, they all say it there."

"Say what? Damn fool, say what?"

"Go ask them. Let go my neck—you're killing me!"

"No! I ask you. Say it. Say it, then I let go. Come! Come!" He shook him.

Another old man, speaking gently and calmly from another bench, said it. "What they say, your daughter stays every night with the boy from Kalymnos, Petros, the beast with the money. She is his woman."

Costa released the man he was holding by the throat, didn't follow him with his eyes when he ran off.

Then Costa began to walk in a circle. The men seated on the benches in the heart of the square did not dare move; they did not want to call attention to themselves.

"You heard that too, Demosthenes?" Costa whispered to an old man he liked. "You heard it with your own ears?"

"Not from anyone down there, Costa," he said. "Nobody heard from there."

"Where then?"

"The barber," someone said. "Go talk to the barber."

The town barber was the town dandy. Born in Kalymnos, he had refined his personality by spending five years in Athens before emigrating to Florida. It was inevitable that he should take exception to some aspects of American culture. Particularly, it would seem, the shoes ("for mountain climbers"), because he sent back to his favorite shop in Athens for sharp-pointed, two-tone shoes with built-up heels, his favorites. You didn't have to lift your head to see who was coming when it was the barber.

Barbering provided this man with his bread, singing fed his soul. He had a tenor voice, and at weddings and other celebrations, he sang the old songs and led his happy patrons through dances which the young people of the modern Greek community had not properly learned. He was, in this way, a cultural leader, his barbershop a center for the arts of the people—among them, gossip.

Common gossip, of course, is not an art; it takes a considerable man to bring it to that level. The barber did. When he found a subject worthy of his talent, he would elaborate it in song. His verses were quoted everywhere.

Despite his height—under five foot six—the barber was also a *palicari,* a strongboy. His weapons were his razor and his rages, barbers, like cooks, being disposed to violent outbursts of temper. It seemed he had also distinguished himself in the war against Italy. Captured Italian muskets hung on the walls of his shop. Here, too, were less colorful but more practical weapons, those the barber used for his other enthusiasm, the chase. Among these was a Swedish hunting knife with a handle made from a piece of elk horn. Costa had always admired this blade and several times tried to buy it. The barber had responded to Costa's offers with the kind of scorn which suggested that Costa, in his opinion, was nor worthy of so fine a piece of Scandinavian steel.

For this reason, as well as more instinctive ones, Costa never liked the man. Now, when he and Aleko entered his shop, Costa did not hesitate to pull the barber by the elbow, away from the customer in his chair.

The barber resented it. "What you want, you?" he protested in Greek. He'd been shaving an American, an old county pol.

"What's there to shave here?" Costa answered, also in Greek, pointing at the tax collector, who was bald, with a hairline mustache and a fringed scruff. "Come, come, I must speak to you for a minute or two."

"Wait till I get through with this customer, you!"

"I wait for shit! Mister, go on, get out, come back maybe fifteen minutes, O.K., mister?"

The old cracker didn't want to be there if the barber took up his razor for nonprofessional purposes. He rose and ran out, found a phone booth and called the sheriff's office. The barber was notorious for his quarrels and rows.

"Now sing for me, pig," Costa said. "Sing for me what you been singing behind my back."

"What kind empty foolishness you talking?" the barber said.

"You know what I'm talking, my son's wife I'm talking. Who gave you the right to mention her name, little pig with the sharp shoes!"

"Who gave me the right? I need a right to talk here? This is a free country, you didn't hear that yet?"

"Now I remember, you are friend of Petros, am I right?"

"I'm not his big friend. What the hell, I come from the same part of the island, but I'm not his cousin. But let me tell you, on his worst day he is better man than you!"

When Costa went for him, the barber's razor flashed.

No one found out immediately whether the razor had touched Costa, the cut was so fine. Costa had the man by the throat and was knocking his head against the metal headrest of the barber chair. "Now sing, you son of a bitch, sing, sing for me."

"Yes, yes," the barber gasped.

Costa relaxed his grip a bit. At the same time he put his knee between the barber's legs, so held him to the back of the chair, stretching his neck over the headrest.

"Let me hear, let me hear everything." Costa shook the man again.

"How can I talk when you squeeze my neck? Let go, for God's sake."

"Look out the razor, Costa," Aleko said. He moved quickly and took it out of the barber's grip.

Now, disarmed, the man talked.

"I can't talk," he said.

"You can talk. I understand you very well now. Come on. The subject of the song, your friend Petros and my daughter! Sing!"

"That is right. Your son's wife and Petros. *Boom, boom, eat his bread! Oopa, oopa, in his bed.* She works for him, right? *Takes his money. Gives her cunny.*"

When Costa left the shop, he took the Swedish knife off the wall.

Driving up the street, he checked the child in the back of the car. It was getting dark, time for the boy to eat.

"Where we going?" Aleko asked.

"Time to feed boy," Costa said. "We go home."

As they crossed the main street, they saw the police car racing the other way, siren shrieking.

As Costa the younger was finishing his bottle, the police pair, one a cracker, the other Greek, came up on the porch and knocked.

"Shshshsh!" Costa said.

The police tiptoed into the house.

Behind them Costa saw the barber. "He don't come in," he warned.

The policeman who was a cracker spoke first. He dealt with the Greek cases, the Greek took care of the cracker cases—till either got difficult, then they switched.

"Now, Mr. Avaliotis," the cracker cop said, "we are old friends and I'm sorry to say I got a complaint against you. Aggravated assault."

Costa held up his arm which had been under the child. There was a blood-soaked cloth, part of a pillowcase, wrapped around it. "I have complaint too," Costa said.

The cracker cop looked at the barber standing in the porch door.

"You ought to carry him to the hospital," the Greek cop said to Aleko, who was sitting in a corner of the room.

"If I go to hospital, I have to explain where I get this. Tell me, you, cop, barber use razor unfriendly way on customer, that O.K.? His license, so forth, so on, tell me that much."

Both police turned and looked toward the barber, who'd backed to the edge of the porch.

"You going to press your charge?" the cracker cop asked.

"He forget, I forget," Costa said.

The barber nodded and started down the porch steps.

Then the Greek cop got to the nub of the matter. "You must do nothing now," he said to Costa in Greek. "Promise me or I'll—"

"You what?" Costa replied in their language. "Get out here quick, before the devil eat you. You are Greek, you heard what's been happening. My son, himself, he not here. You know I must do something, never mind what, I don't know myself what, but something I must do, it is my duty to my family, you know that."

"What did he say?" the cracker cop asked his Greek partner.

"He said the incident is over."

Costa had a few more words to say to the Greek cop as he left. "When these things happen," he said, "we are back where we came from. Their laws here mean nothing! You know our laws."

The cop said good-bye in English, and in Greek he said, "Good luck."

About an hour later, with the child fenced in the back seat by his folded playpen, Costa and Aleko drove south. The sky was darkening, the road full of end-of-the-day traffic.

Aleko stopped his car in front of the marina's entrance. There was light from the office and some of the boats. They could hear a pleasant murmur from the cruisers that were lived in. People were eating their supper.

Leaving his friend to mind the baby, Costa walked slowly down the ramp to the water-level office. He was an unimpressive figure, his left arm in a sling, his middle too heavy, his thick black hair disordered, his rolling tread pigeon-toed. But he seemed completely self-possessed.

He didn't expect to find anyone in the office. "Hello, Mr. Avaliotis," the cleaning woman said.

"Hello, Clem." He smiled at her. He appeared to be, she was to say, the same as usual.

He walked across a stringer, then along a narrow pier, the shortcut to the old sponge boat that Petros had fixed for his living quarters. From its hold, a night light showed.

There was no one on the boat either, but Costa did find some bits of Ethel's toilet—a robe, her hairbrush, a front-clasp bra hung to dry, a half-used box of tampons.

"We are going to stay here tonight," Costa told Aleko, back at the car. When his friend complained, Costa suggested he go to a motel. But Aleko would not leave him, said he'd lie down on the front seat. Costa gave young Costa his bottle, changed him, then laid him out to sleep, locking the car door from the outside. Then he went to Petros's office and stretched out on his sofa.

The moon was lopsided, waning.

All three slept soundly.

It is difficult to maintain a rage through a night's sleep. If the emotion Costa was riding had been a simple anger, it might have cooled by morning. But waiting on a bench outside the office, the rising sun in his face, Costa was even more confirmed in his intention. So what he was feeling would have to be called something else—tribal responsibility perhaps, or obligation to his family. It was duty! Still no one who passed him that morning noted any sign of agitation in the man.

Arriving with Petros and Ethel was the barber of Tarpon Springs. He saw Costa first. "There, I told you," he said to Petros. "I told you he'd be here."

Petros turned to Ethel. "O.K.," he said to the girl, who had not slept. "You can't put it off anymore."

It was Petros's intention to go about the business of managing his marina while his girl had her scene with the foolish old man.

"Be careful, I'm warning you," the barber whispered. "He took my knife from the shop, my Swedish—"

"Oh, go home, will you," Petros said to the barber. "You think I back off from this kind shit?" He turned to Ethel. "Go ahead," he said. "Now!"

Costa, still seated, his face still warmed by the sun, didn't appear to be watching them.

"First I have something to tell you, Peetie," Ethel said. "I'm leaving you. I'm leaving this place and I'm leaving you. Him too, but you too. I'm not going to be with you anymore. Last night was the last night."

Petros stared at Ethel, the shock so total he could not respond.

"So," Ethel said, "there! Now I'll do what you want. I'll tell him too."

Slowly she walked down the inclined boardwalk to the odd man who loved her, her walk uncertain, a totter. She stood before him.

He didn't get up, sat, arms folded, like a judge.

"What they're saying about me," she said gently, "that . . . I know you heard it from someone else and I'm sorry—but that bad talk is true talk. I have been with him, the one you're looking at—yes, Petros."

She turned. Petros was still standing where she'd left him, just as she'd left him.

"I told him now that I'm leaving him," she said to Costa. "But Teddy—I left Teddy long ago. I pretended for your sake. Now, something else . . ."

The old man's expression had not changed. He seemed to be waiting for something that had not yet happened.

"I do not know whose he is," Ethel said. "Little Costa, I mean. But he is not Teddy's. Are you listening?"

Costa nodded. Watching Petros.

She turned and saw that Petros was slowly walking down the incline, and behind him, the barber. They were acting casual.

"There have been other men," she said. "I don't know which of them is the father of the boy."

The old man seemed to take it calmly, nodded his head several times.

She could hear Petros and the barber on the wooden walkways behind her.

"But if you ask me"—she was whispering now—"it's ours. It's mine and it's yours. I made it for you and it doesn't belong to anybody else."

The old man didn't appear to have heard. As Petros approached closer, he dropped his head.

He seemed inert, without resolve.

Petros was next to her now and the barber right behind.

"When you're all through with him," Petros said to her, in a low voice, "I want to talk to you."

Then he looked at the old man. "Hello, Costa," he said.

Costa nodded his head, not raising it. He seemed to be studying the barber's sharp-pointed, two-tone shoes.

Petros shrugged and walked away. It had been as he thought: no danger. He smiled scornfully at the barber before he left. Then he was striding down the narrow pier toward the Gulf. He either had or pretended he had some business with the large cruiser in the last berth at the end.

"You stole my knife yesterday, you son of a bitch," the barber said to Costa, who sat there head down, taking the abuse. "Give me my goddamn knife, you dirty old thief—"

Ethel watched the old man shift his weight, slowly heist one buttock and reach into his pocket for the elk-horn handle of the Swedish knife. As he slowly pulled it out of his trousers, he cocked his head and sighted down the pier. Petros was approaching the end berth where the large cruiser was docked.

"You mean this one, barber?" Costa asked. He showed him the knife.

"Yes; give it to me."

Costa nodded slowly. He seemed lethargic, heavy in the head, even stunned. "O.K.," he said, looking at the blade, then at the barber, then once again to where Petros was walking along the pier.

Now Ethel knew what Costa was waiting for.

Then Petros was at the end of the wooden walk, where there was nothing ahead but the water of the Gulf, and Costa was charging down the narrow way at a speed that was unbelievable to see.

"Look out!" the barber screamed. "Petros!" He started to follow the charging old man. But Ethel, exhilarated by Costa's sudden action, blocked the barber. For those seconds Costa needed.

When Petros faced around, he found Costa charging, head down, falling forward on his feet with the momentum of his hurtling weight. Petros, unable to side-step on the narrow stringer, was hit.

The barber slapped at Ethel with his open hand and got past her.

She turned and saw that Costa had driven Petros off the end of the pier. They were falling into the water and as they did, she saw—so quickly she wasn't sure what she saw was real—that Costa had clasped Petros with one of his great thick arms, and clamped his teeth into Petros's shirt front. Holding him so, he struck at his wriggling prey with the blade of Swedish steel he held in his heavy crook-fingered hand.

Then they were out of sight, both bodies, dead weight, gone into the water of the Gulf.

Ethel followed the barber, running down the pier.

Men were coming from all sides. Once there, they didn't know what to do.

It was like watching two great marine creatures. Nothing that was happening between them was clear in the swirl of harbor water and the cloud of sand and mud rising from the bottom. Something terrible was going on down there, but no one could tell what it was.

The end of the pier was crowded now. Men shouted at each other, suggestions, instructions, cautions. Several prepared to jump in, others held them back.

Then they all saw a plume of blood rising from the

447

bottom where the bodies struggled, the deep red mixing with the cloudy blue swirls of bilge fuel from the back of the docked cruiser.

Now Ethel could see that Petros was struggling to get loose while Costa, in his element, the one he knew well, the one he did not fear, was striking again and again at the younger man.

Costa came up, gasping and blowing, knife in hand.

He looked for Ethel, found her.

He had wanted, above all, for her to witness what he'd done. It was his answer to what she'd done.

He climbed onto the dock. At the end of his strength, he slowly got to his feet.

Men were jumping into the water from all sides.

Others tried to detain Costa, but he threatened them with his knife. They knew he was capable of anything because he feared nothing.

Petros was brought up.

He was in a state of shock, bleeding from many wounds. He had no fight in him.

He lay on the bloodstained planks where so many fish had been cleaned.

At the head of the walkway from the marina office, the Chevy waited, door open, motor running. Costa, staggering, then at the end on his hands and knees, climbed into the front seat.

The last Ethel saw of him, he was turning to check the child in the back. Then the car was gone.

Petros was bleeding from many cuts. But the worst wound, a quick inspection at the hospital made evident, was to his pride.

He would not look at Ethel.

The police searched for Costa. He wasn't at home. His wife, Noola, said she had no idea where he was and the police believed her.

They went looking for Aleko the Levendis. His wife gave them their lead. "Try Mrs. Achillea in Clearwater," she said.

There they did find Aleko peacefully eating his breakfast and studying the racing form in the Saint Petersburg *Times*.

He received them cordially. "I don't know where he is," he said.

"Weren't you driving him?"

"I let him off in front of his house."

The police didn't believe he was telling the truth.

Sitting at a window, feeding an infant, was Mrs. Achillea. One of the police made a guess.

"Yes," the Levendis said, "he told me to bring the boy here."

The child seemed easy in the care of Mrs. Achillea.

The police consulted. "He knows where Costa is." The cracker cop indicated Aleko.

"Sure he knows," the Greek cop said. "But what can we do?"

"We can sure as hell make him talk. There are ways to do that."

The Greek cop looked at the Levendis, who was offering them coffee, eggs, toast, jam—anything except information.

"We'll be talking to you later," the cracker cop said. "Don't take any sudden trips."

"I'll be at the track," the Levendis said. "O.K.?"

The police drove to Ethel's apartment. They found her on the bed, dressed to travel. On the floor, partly packed, was a large old-fashioned suitcase.

"Where you going, Mrs. Avaliotis?" the police asked.

"I haven't decided," she said.

She wanted to know the latest on Petros. One of the police went out to call the hospital.

"If you find out where Costa is," she said to the other, the Greek, "let me know."

"Where would he be?"

"Ask Aleko?"

"Either he doesn't know or he won't say. Your little boy, we saw him there. With Mrs. Achillea in Clearwater. You know her?"

Ethel didn't answer.

"She's taking good care of him," the young cop said. "So don't worry."

Ethel stared at him.

"Is your husband coming down?"

"He's at sea."

The Greek cop continued to question her, but sometimes had to repeat himself. "Are you hard of hearing?" he asked.

She'd written notes to each of the principals. They were spread out on the round table in the window alcove, where the sun's rays fell.

The cop saw to whom they were addressed. "Do you mind?" he asked, indicating the letters.

"Do what you want," she said. She hadn't moved off the bed.

When the Greek cop, a sentimental boy, had read them, he looked at her with pity.

"I better cover these," he said. "If he reads them"—they could hear the cracker cop coming up the stairs—"he might take you in for questioning."

"Do what you want," Ethel said.

The cop covered the letters with a magazine just as his partner entered the room.

"He's off the critical list," the cracker cop said. He waited for Ethel to say "That's good," but she didn't.

"Well, Mrs. Avaliotis," the cracker crop said, "maybe you better not leave town for a couple of days." He didn't know what else to say.

twenty-three

DRESSED to travel, uncertain where or when, Ethel Laffey sat at the window, looking through the haze of heat at evenly spaced telegraph poles and the motel signs in the distance: VACANCY . . . VACANCY.

When she began to tremble, not with cold but with fear, she got into bed as she was, fully clothed. Pulling a blanket over her, she clenched up as she used to when she was in her teens and felt alone and without hope.

She'd lived more than twenty-two years and had never been close to that kind of violence before: those two men had been pitched to murder and she'd been the cause. She huddled lower, knees to chin.

On her dresser, wedged between the mirror's frame and the glass, she saw the Polaroids Teddy had taken of her son. The infant had stared at the camera as he had so often stared at her. Accusingly.

Could she really leave this child with the old man

she'd seen scrambling out of the water, a knife in his hand, his front soaked in bilge and blood?

But she'd promised Costa the boy was for him.

She was shivering again.

She decided to soak in a bath, ran the water as hot as she could take it.

Ed Laffey had told her about finding his wife in a tub where she'd stayed so long that the water was cold. He'd had to lift Emma out, a dead weight.

I wonder where Ed is now, she thought.

But Emma had no reason to live, had no child, no husband, no capability, no interest to pursue, no talent for pleasure. Emma had to die before she could express her true feelings.

Ethel pulled herself up out of the bath. The scalding water had brought her blood up under the skin; her body was pink. With a towel she wiped the steam off the mirror attached to the bathroom door and looked at herself. She could find no change, no stretch marks across her belly where Costa had rubbed the olive oil, her breasts no smaller, no way limp. Her neck was firm and smooth, it hadn't turkeyed anywhere. There was no evidence that she'd given birth.

"You look beautiful," she said.

Her voice was defiant; she was impatient with herself. Why the hell did Robin Bolt's proposal repel her so? Ethel Laffey, who'd been in Julio the metalworker's bed! Three hundred and fifty dollars every week would change her life!

She decided to put on a different dress, a bright, perky number, fresh from the cleaners. Pulling out the tissue paper, she mashed it into a ball and flung it across the room into the wastebasket. The dress was crisp and cut to her figure; putting it on made her feel better.

She decided to collect her things from the office and

from the Gulf-view apartment. That would be a first step. To whatever.

Before she left, she looked at the letters on the table, then tore them up. She wasn't going to leave notes behind, not this time. She'd go to the hospital and see Petros, find Noola and submit to her spite, track Costa down and face his anger. She'd take her punishment.

When she came out, it was into a glare of light. The heat was so heavy there seemed to be a fog over the area. She had difficulty keeping her mind on the road and the cars coming the other way. She turned on the radio to keep herself alert, then turned it off, dreading what she might hear.

Her key went into the lock of the Gulf-view apartment, but it wouldn't turn. "Mr. Kalkanis sent someone to change the cylinder," the super told her, "half an hour ago. Yes, I have a key but the man said I wasn't to give it to anyone. I know, miss, I know. I'm sorry."

At the marina, she saw Mr. Bolt, wearing a peppermint-striped robe, alone at breakfast under the awning that shaded the aft deck. He was reading the morning paper, clearly didn't wish to be disturbed. Not quite ready to take that step, she was relieved.

The office looked abandoned. Quickly she stuffed everything from her desk into a shopping bag. As she did, she became aware of Petros's bookkeeper, a dark-skinned Greek from Alexandria, watching her from the doorway.

"Collecting my things," she explained.

He didn't respond, turned his back as she left.

She started toward the *Sara* to speak to Mr. Bolt. But now he was surrounded by his friends, all chattering and laughing. It wasn't a good time, she decided. She'd drive to Clearwater, see her son, come back to the *Sara* in an hour.

The Levendis was asleep, Mrs. Achillea told her.

"Last night, in the middle of dinner," she said, "he laid his head on the table and that was his good night."

"He's been under a strain," Ethel said.

"It's been terrible," Mrs. Achillea said, "the strain."

"I want to ask him just one thing," Ethel said. "Please wake him."

Mrs. Achillea was about to refuse, but she remembered Ethel's first visit and the Mozart, "Dalla Sua Pace," and how, as she was singing the last note, she'd turned to Ethel and the girl had said what no one else had, that Aleko and she were beautiful together and must never part.

So she called out: "Alekooooo! Oh, Aleko, my heart!"

The reply, when it came, was a grumble. "What you want now, for God's sake?"

Mrs. Achillea smiled fondly. "My angel is up," she whispered to Ethel. "Ethel has come to see you, darling," she called. Then, dropping her voice, "Anyway, one good thing came out of it. The first time in eight years he's slept here overnight. Imagine! These Greek men! And his wife has said—are you listening?"

"Yes."

"She won't take him back. A friend called to tell me. You changed my luck."

Aleko came forth in a bright-orange terry-cloth robe that belonged to Mrs. Achillea's college-age son. Across the back was printed SWIM TEAM.

"I'll tell you the truth, Ethel," he said in answer to her question. "I know where he is. But he asked me not to tell anyone."

"Just me," Ethel pleaded. "I'm leaving forever. Tell me and no one else."

"Especially not you," he said. "Excuse me, I don't want to hurt you."

"If you don't want to hurt her, why do you hurt her?" Mrs. Achillea said. "Look what you did to her. Look at her face."

The Levendis raised his voice to that autocratic level built into all Greek men at birth. "Mind your business, woman, or I go home."

"I'd like to see the boy before I leave," Ethel said.

"He's in the backyard," Mrs. Achillea said. "I borrowed the carriage from my neighbor." She showed Ethel through the kitchen door.

"Where you going now?" the Levendis complained. "You wake me up, so where's my coffee? Piece of toast, something, for God's sake?"

"I'll run make him quiet," Mrs. Achillea said.

The boy's face was in the sun. Ethel turned the carriage. With the movement, he opened his eyes, looked at his mother steadily from under heavy lids, then closed them with a tiny sigh.

How could she leave this boy behind? No matter what she'd ever said to Costa. She'd take Mr. Bolt's goddamn job, go to New York, find an apartment, furnish it, make it beautiful, and when she'd found a nanny to take care of the boy, she'd come back and steal him away.

Mrs. Achillea was back. "That Aleko!" she said. "Put something in his mouth, he's quiet. Just like a baby."

Side by side, in silence, they admired the child.

"He's a beauty, all right," Mrs. Achillea said. "And a boy as well, thanks to God. He looks just like his father."

"Just like," Ethel said.

It could happen, Ethel thought. "You can start on salary right away," Mr. Bolt had said. If he said that again . . .

"Tell me," Mrs. Achillea said. "Teddy hasn't seen him yet?"

"When he was baptized, of course."

"He must have been so proud!" Mrs. Achillea said. "He's a *lokoum,* this boy, made of honey. Oh, how I wish he was mine."

Ethel looked at Mrs. Achillea carefully. "Do you?" she said.

"Look at him smiling! What secret is he smiling at?"

"We'll never know," Ethel said.

The child made a sound.

"He's having a dream," Ethel said.

"Yes, he does! Very serious ones. Like he's having business troubles. But such a good boy; he never cries."

"He hasn't really had anything to cry about yet, has he?" Ethel said.

Yes, she thought, if Mr. Bolt was kind, if he repeated his offer, she might even do it tomorrow, take the child, not wait at all.

"When his teeth come in," Mrs. Achillea said, "then we'll hear."

Goddamn it, she owed the boy that. He was her son and she'd given him a bad start in life. She had to make up for that! She mustn't do to him what someone else had done to her.

"Wipe your eyes," Mrs. Achillea said, "Aleko's coming. Here." She pulled a tissue out of her apron pocket, turned and called out, "Aleko, my heart, bring me a cig, do me that little favor. They're in the bedroom."

"You see, Ethel," the Levendis said as he turned back toward the house, "her intention is to make me a servant."

"Why do they call him the Levendis?" Ethel asked, as she used the tissue. "Does he really live only for pleasure? He always seems so worried."

"Worry, that's his pleasure. Why were you all of a sudden crying?"

"The opposite of him. I was crying because all of a sudden I was happy."

"What I don't understand—forgive me—is how you can give this child up. Some other little beast, all right —I'm not a fool about children. But this one! Look at him smiling again. As if he has a secret."

"He does," Ethel said. She looked at the house. Aleko was not in sight. "Can I trust you?" she said.

"If it's about this boy, you can."

"I want you to hold him here for a day. Don't let him out of your hands, no matter what happens. Find some reason. Invent anything. I will come tomorrow and take him. Will you do that for me, Mrs. Achillea?"

"With sorrow at losing him, with joy that you are doing the right thing. My name is Anthea."

"Anthea. I have some things to do, then—"

"He's coming back," Mrs. Achillea whispered. "You don't have to say any more. I'll hold the child against anybody."

"Don't tell Aleko."

"I don't tell him anything important."

"What are you talking?" the Levendis said as he came up. "You women, always whispering."

"Women's foolishness," Anthea said. "Nothing."

"A person doesn't whisper nothing," the Levendis corrected her. "Not even a woman does that. What were you saying so I couldn't hear?"

"That you're afraid of Costa Avaliotis."

"It's only reasonable. He's a crazy man. On the other hand, I'm not afraid of him. I'm not afraid of anybody."

"Whenever he calls, you run with your Chevy."

"Quiet, woman, or honestly God, I go home."

"Anthea, I'm leaving," Ethel said. "Walk me to the car."

As they passed through the gate of the garden, Anthea put her arm around Ethel's waist, a pledge, and Ethel returned the caress in thanks. Just before Ethel drove off,

Anthea leaned into the car and kissed her. "Be careful," she said.

Then she returned to the backyard, sat by the carriage, brushed a fly off the netting.

The Levendis spoke. "You notice she didn't even lift the child," he said. "Not even once in her arms. These American women! Hearts like ice! A cat worries more."

The *Sara* was gone, its mooring empty. No one Ethel asked knew where it had gone or when it would be back.

"Like the birds," she reassured herself, "all boats return."

But when she looked at the rectangle of fouled water where the *Sara* had been, she began to wonder.

In the hospital corridor she encountered Petros's bookkeeper again. He turned his head away, then, when she'd passed, he called out in a hysterical tone, "Nurse! Nurse!" The one who was passing turned. "He doesn't want to see her." The bookkeeper jutted his finger at Ethel.

"But I want to see him," Ethel said. "Nurse, please go into his room and ask him. Tell him it's Ethel. Ethel."

Ethel! Ethel! The morning after the first night, they'd made love again and she remembered Peetie had asked her to put her arms around his neck and, sitting up, he'd lifted her so she was straddled across his thick thighs. With her there and he still inside her, he'd got to his feet from the side of the bed, his hands under her, holding her close, and carried her to the mirror. "Take a good look," he'd said, "so you don't ever forget who you belong to and what's going to be from now on. Look and remember."

She did look and thought the image in the mirror grotesque, even ludicrous, but when she looked at his face and saw how much having her meant to him, she stayed where he had her, didn't smile. "Ethel," he'd said. "Ethel, Ethel!" as if they were the only words he knew.

"He doesn't want to see anybody." The nurse was back.

"Tell her the truth," the bookkeeper said. "He doesn't want to see her. Not just anybody. Just not her."

Circling him quickly, Ethel entered Petros's room—and wished she hadn't. His wounds were not deep but they were many. The single discolored bandage across his neck was the least of it. An antibiotic in a sterile solution was being introduced into Petros's bloodstream with a tube. It had been, after all, a blade used for skinning animals. Two wounds, still open, were packed with gauze pads and medication and being drained. Petros's body was belted to the bed so he couldn't move and dislodge any of the bandages.

The bookkeeper came up behind Ethel and started to pull her away, but a gesture from Petros's free hand ordered him to stop.

Then Petros motioned Ethel to approach, and when she did, to bend to his mouth so he could speak to her.

She leaned close and whispered, "Try to forgive me, Peetie, please try to forgive me."

She was looking straight into his eyes when he spit in her face. After which he continued to look at her in silence.

She kept her head bent, accepting the punishment.

The nurse, who'd been watching from the door, led Ethel out of the room.

At Costa's, no one was home. Ethel, feeling like a stranger again, waited in her car two hours for Noola to come.

Noola saw the girl, passed her by and entered the house.

After a few minutes, Ethel forced herself to walk

459

up the cracked pavement, through the shrubs and the blooms Costa had transplanted from his father's grave.

The door was locked. Ethel knocked.

She heard footsteps in slippers. She heard them stop.

"You can't come in," Noola called through the door.

"Just for a minute, Noola, please."

Noola opened the door, didn't wait for questions or apology. "Now I know what I always knew," she said, and shut the door.

"Where is Costa?" Ethel called. "I want to speak to him. For only a minute. To say good-bye. Then you won't see me again."

"You ruined everybody here," Noola said. She slammed the bolt too.

At the same hour, that same afternoon, Teddy came in from sea duty. He dumped his gear into the hatchback of his Pinto and, instead of driving to where he was billeted, drove to where his girl friend, Betty, lived. She wasn't home but he had a hunch where he might find her. She was in the neighborhood's laundromat.

"We're getting married," he told her as they walked back to her apartment. "To quote my old man, 'I made up our mind.'"

Betty, as careful and controlled as Teddy, was astonished at this recklessness. But she knew it was a good time to kiss him.

They decided to give themselves a weekend on nearby Ponte Vedra Beach. They found a lovely room with a window over the water. The motel, made of coquina mortar, was shimmering pink in the afternoon sun. Hand in hand they walked along the beach through the twilight. Then went to bed.

Ethel spent that evening rinsing out her underwear and panty hose, washing her hair, packing her belongings into the large old-fashioned suitcase Emma had left behind. It was after eleven when she was done. She decided to go to the marina. If the *Sara* was coming in that night, it would be there now.

Walking down the broad entrance ramp, she could feel the damp and the chill that come over the water with the dark. When she rounded the corner of the deserted office, she saw that the *Sara* was tied off at its mooring. The night lights, bow and stern, were on and there was a glow from the portholes. The ship was absolutely still.

Ethel knew it was a bad time to come. She hesitated, walked a little, stopped, walked on until she came alongside the boat. Then she heard whispering. On a wide deck lounger, she saw what seemed to be two people, covered with a blanket. Totally occupied with each other, they hadn't noticed her approach.

Now her eyes were fully accustomed to the dark and she saw that there were two human forms, but the head of only one, that of a very young boy whom she'd never seen before. Some kind of love play was going on; she had a good idea what it was. She turned and started away.

"Hey, you." The boy had noticed her. "You! What are you looking at?"

The hidden head came up into sight. It was Robin Bolt.

Now that she'd been seen, it was as impossible to walk away as to stay. Besides, if she was leaving the next day, this might be her last chance. The *Sara* might go out again in the morning.

She turned and again went close to the ship.

"Mr. Bolt," she said, "I'm sorry."

"Who is it?" Bolt said to his companion.

"Some little cunt," the boy said. "Did you have a date with her or something?"

"I don't know who she is," Mr. Bolt said.

"It's Ethel, Mr. Bolt, Ethel Avaliotis, remember?"

She could see that they were both very drunk, their movements uncoordinated, the boy falling off the side of the lounger as he struggled to get to his feet. He didn't adjust his clothing as he got up.

"Go away, you silly bitch," he said, waving his arms. "Go peddle your ass somewhere else!"

"Just two sentences, Mr. Bolt," Ethel pleaded.

"Go on, you leaky old cunt," the boy said. "Find your own meat!"

"Ethel?" Mr. Bolt said, and his speech was blurred and indistinct. "Yes! Mrs. What? Something. Don't you know better than to disturb a man after business hours?"

When Ethel didn't move, the young boy picked up a wicker stool and flung it at her.

"What are you doing, Andy?" Bolt said, laughing. He seemed delighted at the boy's extravagant show of jealousy.

"I'm chasing her ass. Go on, you old cow!"

He picked up the wicker table, held it over his head, balanced it, then ran to the rail and flung it at Ethel. But his aim was uncertain and the table tumbled into the water.

Bolt fell into a fit of laughter. The boy's wildness thrilled him.

Ethel stood still, waiting. She could feel her cheeks burning.

"Come on, Andy," Bolt said. "It's chilly out here." He took the boy by the hand and pulled him toward a door. "I said, come on, Andy, leave her alone." Andy was looking for something else to throw at her. "She's a nice girl. Now come on."

"Fuck her," Andy said as he finally covered himself. "She was standing there watching us and I don't know for how long."

"So what?" Bolt said. "It's not the first time that's happened to you. Come on."

They were gone.

Ethel didn't walk away.

She was ashamed of herself, begging that way, humiliating herself, all for that stinking job! Did her future really depend on a few chance words, an accidental show-off remark that Robin Bolt had made? Did her life hang by that thread?

She picked up the wicker stool and threw it at the only window along the deck that was lit. Then she ran up on the deck of the *Sara,* picked up a large silver tray of glasses and ice, drinks and mixer, and ran at that lit-up window and crashed the tray against the pane.

Sounds of outrage came from within.

Ethel charged off the boat and up the stringer, past the office and up the broad entrance ramp.

She was furious, not at Bolt and his boy; at herself.

She was raging. Why the hell did she value herself so cheaply?

Hell, she was a damn good secretary. The men she'd served at that Mexican chemical company had fought each other for her services!

She didn't want Bolt's goddamn job. She didn't have to peddle her tits any more than she had to peddle her ass. She was able.

She got into her car and slammed the door.

Was Arturo smarter than she was? He was an infant, a spoiled boy!

Petros? Smarter than she was? Like hell. More cunning, perhaps. Tougher. Yes—that, yes. But she'd damn well get tougher. After being cuffed around all day, having doors slammed in her face, being spit at and told to disappear, she'd be damn tough, damn quick.

She gunned the car.

Fuck them all. Big and small!

The anger pumped her blood. It was wine in her veins. She made the car jump to her rage.

She turned onto the main highway and didn't know why she took the direction she did.

That night, after they'd made love, Teddy expressed to Betty some of the resentment of Ethel that he'd always choked down. "I've lived in tension ever since I met her," he said. "I can't remember one easy week, a single really quiet day. Like it is now, here, with the surf outside. It's so nice and quiet here with you up against me, breathing in and out. This is what I always wanted." Betty reached up and kissed him sympathetically. "Life with her was an everlasting crisis, everything going great, then all-of-a-sudden sulks and mysterious fits and those crazy disappearances. Christ, I still don't know what that girl's about!"

"But honestly, Teddy," Betty said, "you must have been wild about her once. She's so damn pretty in that photograph."

"Once," Teddy admitted.

"And so sexy! Come on, Teddy, you can tell me. That part of it must have been great."

"I had enough of that too," Teddy said. "That supercharged sex. That's not love. That's some kind of neurotic thing, eating at her and eating at her. You can't satisfy a crazy girl. I want a normal life. Orderly! Like knowing where I'd find you today, in the laundromat. That was wonderful!"

Betty told him that was the kind of life she wanted too. Now, how would he like a nice cup of tea? She'd brought tea bags and her tiny heater coil.

"It's funny," Teddy said over the mint tea. "Now that I've broken off, I know how to handle her."

He raised a fist.

The car radio was tuned to the station she favored. The DJ was grooving on the Grateful Dead.

Louder than the rock, louder than the sound of the racing motor, was Ethel's voice.

"What did I ever do bad to you, Peetie?" she yelled as if he were there in front of her. "I didn't want to become involved with you in the first place, goddamn it." She shook the steering wheel. "You crowded me and crowded me! I never said, 'I love you,' did I? I was careful with that, I was honest. I told you from the beginning that it was only for a while. That was your idea, that forever-and-ever scene in the mirror. What right have you to spit in my face that way? You should thank me, not spit in my face." She pounded at the wheel. "And Noola, you miserable old bitch! Bolting the door in my face! What the hell do you mean—now you know what you always knew? I gave you the idea of working! I told you a check every week would make you a free woman! What right have you to hate me? And Costa, you telling people that you don't want me to know where you are? I gave you the one thing you most wanted in the world. What your son couldn't! I tried with Teddy, God knows, I tried! It was for you, Costa, for you. Because I loved you. More than anyone in the whole damned world, I loved you. And still do, only you—"

Then she heard the siren. The cop was a portly man, comfortably seated on a heavy black motorbike. She'd noticed him following her hundreds of feet back and thought nothing of it.

She stopped the car. In his own good time, the officer walked up to her window.

"May I see your driver's license, please?" he asked in a surprisingly gentle tone of voice.

"It's in here." She gave him her purse.

"Would you mind digging it out, miss, and giving it to me?"

"I can't—don't you see? I can't."

The motor cop looked at her distraught, tear-stained face. Probably on something, he thought. He'd seen hundreds like this one. Such a pretty girl!

"We're not permitted to do what you're asking," he said. "Take your time, miss; we're in no hurry, are we now? Find your license and I'll have a look at it."

Her voice soothed her. She rummaged in her bag till she found the flat black wallet and opened it for him.

"You were breaking sixty," he said as he examined the license. "I should give you a ticket, but you've got enough trouble already. Aren't you the young woman who was mixed up in that stabbing at the marina?"

"Yes. Did you say I could go?"

"I used to tie my twenty-footer up there and had some run-ins with that old Greek when he was dockmaster." He still held her license. "I'm talking about the one who stabbed Mr. Pete Kalkanis. I want to tell you that—"

"Are you going to give me a ticket or not?"

"He was the most arrogant, and all-around stupidest old man I ever—I had a hunch he'd do something like this someday. I just hope he gets what's coming to him. But he won't. It's revolving-door justice in this country now!"

"Will you give me that goddamn ticket and shut up!"

Suddenly she started her car, pulled the gear bar down and stepped on the accelerator. She'd forgotten to release the hand brake, so the car stuttered before she got it to take off.

Two hundred yards down the road, he cut in front of her, with a roar of his motor. When she'd stopped, he parked his motorbike against her front bumper.

"I hadn't finished talking to you," he said in the same quiet voice he'd used before. "All those Tarpon Springs Greeks, they'd do better to stay north of the Tampa Bay bridge," he said as he eased his pad of summonses out of his back pocket. He seemed to be taking as long as he possibly could to fill out the form. "This is a summons to appear in Judge Burley's court," he said as he gave it to her. "I'll be waiting for you there." Then he let her see how angry he was. "I see what everybody's saying about you is true," he said.

It was after two in the morning when she got home, but she called Anthea, badly frightening her.

"I know, Anthea, I'm sorry, forgive me. No, no, no, I'm all right. No, thanks, that's dear of you, but I don't need you to come all the way here. Isn't Aleko with you? Good. Yes, I'm going, my plans haven't changed. The only thing I want is to talk to Costa before I leave. If you could ask Aleko, please, to speak to Costa in the morning, he knows where he is, and beg him to let me know where I can meet him. Tell him I know I behaved badly. But I have a plan now and I want to tell him what it is—Oh, I'm keeping you up; go on, go back to bed, I'm sorry, I'm sorry. Just beg Aleko to get Costa to call me, will you do that? Good night."

Ethel slept fitfully through the night, talking to Costa in her thoughts and in her dreams, playing again and again the scene she hoped to have with him. Once she woke and wrote a letter to the Mercedes dealer in Tucson, asking him to get what he could for her car immediately and send the check to her care of Costa Avaliotis, Mangrove Still, Florida, and put "Hold till Arrival" on the envelope.

This made her feel better and she fell into an edgy sleep, waking every so often to look at the clock. She was waiting for eight o'clock: she had so many errands to do in the morning.

She went to the bank, drew out everything she had, went to the ticket office of Easten Airlines, bought a ticket on the eleven o'clock plane that night and accepted their offer to reserve her a hotel room for one night in New York. Then she went to Lazy Louie's, the used-car place she used to pass driving to work every day. It was lit day and night by a blazing perimeter of naked light bulbs and always jumping with loud music. The owner barely looked at her car, but he did look carefully into a loose-leaf notebook, there found listed the make, the model, the year and, opposite, a number.

"I can give you seven hundred and ten dollars," he said.

She accepted the offer without hesitation, told him she'd surrender the car at eight that night, wanted cash.

"We stay open till nine," he said. "I'll have the papers for you to sign, I'll give you cash, lady. I'll even drive you to the airport; it's on my way home."

Ethel was glad to see that whatever she had that made people eager to help her was still working.

Back in her place by noon, she called Anthea and confirmed that she'd come by for the boy at eight that evening. Could Anthea please go out and buy some jars of baby food and some condensed milk? "I'll pay you for everything when I see you."

"I don't want money from you," Anthea said. "Have you got a place to stay in New York?"

"For one night. Forty dollars! Tomorrow I'll find something reasonable."

"But why go in the middle of the night?"

"I'm staying on the chance that he'll want to see me. Did you ask Aleko to talk to him?"

"He made a call this morning, then left the house. He was very upset and cursing. I don't know who it was to."

"To Costa, I imagine, wherever he is. Have you any idea where? Please tell me if you know."

"I don't. May I—may I say this?"

"Anything. You're not only my best friend here, but now my only friend. What?"

"Don't go near that old man."

"In other words, you didn't say anything to Aleko this morning and that's why you didn't?"

"Yes, I am afraid. He's crazy, you know, not normal. About you. Please, just get on your plane. And go. Isn't there an earlier one? Later, write him from wherever you are. Explanations that are written might make him mad, but he won't be able to do anything about them. You know how he feels about that little boy you're going to take with you? I remember how he watched over you right from the beginning—as if your belly belonged to him. Then he gave up his wife for you, didn't he?"

"That's why," Ethel said, "I can't do what you say."

Late that same afternoon, Teddy's roommate finally found the happy couple. They were enjoying a picnic of chips, jack cheese and beer on the perfect powder sand of Ponte Vedra Beach. He informed Teddy that his mother had been calling and that she'd sounded frantic.

Over the phone Noola told Teddy as much as she knew: about the fight in the water, that Petros was in the hospital, that Costa had disappeared and the police were looking for him. And that she didn't know where he was but she was frightened about what might happen.

"I'll take care of it, Mom," Teddy said.

He rushed Betty home. "That's what I mean," he said as he left her at her door. "She led them on and led them on; one victim wasn't enough, she had to have two. So now look! I'm going to beat hell out of that girl."

He kissed Betty fondly. "Take care of yourself," he said. "I need you."

Then he turned his car south.

twenty-four

WHEN they'd left the scene of the fight, Aleko had driven his friend to the grapefruit and orange lady's ranch. It wasn't Costa's instruction; Aleko could have taken him anywhere without his objecting.

The old man had cracked.

Twenty-four hours after the tragedy, he still hadn't slept. He was violently penitent. Alternately, images of Ethel and Petros together prodded him to his feet, where he stamped the ground and struck the walls with his fists.

Grace, the big bachelor woman who owned the citrus ranch, was kind and she was patient, but he was getting to her. Every time she fell asleep, there'd be a new outburst from the bedroom next to her own, another self-immolation at the feet of the Lord God of the Orthodox Greek.

At first light, she heard him leave the house, and there was a silence. Grace slept. But within half an hour, he was back and at it again. Grace gave up; she dressed, brewed coffee and took it to his room.

"How you think I eat now?" he demanded, waving her off.

Then he caught her arm and pulled her back.

Then was when she saw the snake.

It was a small snake, perhaps three feet long, a young racer mottled with dusky peach and traces of blue. It was laid out on the floor before the chair where Costa had been sitting and to which he now returned. He explained that he'd almost stepped on it when he'd walked to the pond to see the sun rise. When it curled and hissed, he'd killed it.

"I hit him with rock," Costa said.

She watched him play with the slim, supple body, using a willow twig to arrange its length in long curves.

"See what I do to head over there?" he said.

"He was a beauty, all right," Grace said.

"This milk snake," Costa said, "no harm on him." He lifted the snake on the twig so its limp length hung evenly on either side. "I kill him—like that! -without thinking. I see him, I kill him. I never been this way, Grace. I call God witness."

"With Petros? You had good reason."

"Not for what I do. No reason good for that."

"Don't blame yourself; it was all her fault."

"We don't speak on her now, Grace. She is my family, my problem. I know what to do over there. But Petros! Man who give me job when goddamn bank take my place—why I kill him?"

"He's not dead, Costa; he's in the hospital."

There was the sound of a truck and voices speaking Spanish.

"My Puerto Ricans have arrived," Grace said.

"If someone religious as me can kill man like he is

animal, me who make cross every day when I pass Saint Nicholas, then Bible is right. We all have devil inside." He poked at his chest. "Waiting to come out."

"We're taking grapefruit today," Grace said.

"I am criminal, Grace. I am no good."

He dropped his head and beat it with his fists.

Grace left. She had a day's work to do.

Alone in the house, he was quiet. When the phone rang, he disguised his voice till he was sure who it was.

"You seen the paper?" Aleko asked.

"How I see paper, damn fool? No store here. Here is swamp. Anyway I know, something bad happen. He die."

"Breathe the air in peace. You don't have to hide from the police anymore. I'm coming right out."

He brought the morning paper with him. It contained a short bedside interview with Petros, which Aleko read out loud.

"I will bring no charges against that temporarily crazed old man," Petros was quoted saying. "I understand why he did what he did."

"He's good man," Costa interrupted. "I will go to hospital, fall on my knees and ask him forgive me."

" 'Everyone knows whose fault it was.' " The Levendis read on. " 'She should leave this area. And quick!' "

"That son of a bitch!" Costa said. "Why he mix up my family business?" He pulled the paper out of Aleko's hands and began to shred it. "He didn't do enough, now he's telling who should leave town! And quick he wants, too. I should have killed him in the water, that donkey-fucker!"

Breathing hard, he fell back in his chair and was silent. For a moment his brain stopped working, the links which make meaning broke, his mind was a blank.

"My family, my problem, my family, my problem," he kept muttering.

Then he came back, again aware of where he was and that his friend was watching.

"What they say?" he asked. "In the *kaffenion?*"

"Those old men in coffeehouse, you know how they are."

"So what they say? About me?"

"You want me to tell you?"

"I don't care what they— What?"

"That you can't control her, that she does anything she wants."

Costa nodded. "What you say?" he asked.

The Levendis took a chance with his life. "Same thing," he said.

"Everybody know my business better than me," Costa said.

"I saw you with her on the boat, and remember how you hold hands when Anthea sing? Remember that day?"

Costa got up and walked out of the house. The Levendis, blessed with a narrow escape, watched him disappear into the orange grove.

When Grace came in for lunch, Aleko was still there.

"What's he at?" she asked him.

He pointed to the pond. "Making himself more crazy."

Costa was walking along the shore, head down, hands punching the air, talking to himself as to an antagonist.

"He's a cuckoo, all right," Grace said. "Crying on and off all night—I can't stand to hear a grown man cry. Why's he take it so hard? Petros will recover. He's already giving interviews to the newspaper like a politician."

"Not Petros. The girl. The disgrace on the family. You know what they'd do on our island in a situation like this? You want to hear some stories?"

"Not while I'm eating."

Costa came back. "Aleko," he commanded, "six o'clock. Bring car."

"Costa, for God's sake, I got important things—"

"Never mind track today. Car! Six o'clock."

"It's dark at six o'clock—you know that?"

"What you think, my brain don't work? Go 'head, go 'head."

When the day's work was done and the light had begun to thin, Grace paid off the Puerto Ricans and came into the house. She found Costa in the bathroom, wearing her bathrobe and shaving slowly and carefully with the lather off a bar of Palmolive soap and the razor she had for her legs.

"Press my suit, right away," he said. "I was wearing in water."

He watched her put the hot iron to his garments and the steam sizzle through the shiny dark fabric.

"Don't go see her," Grace said.

"Grace, do me favor, mind your business."

"I liked that girl," Grace said.

"I like too," Costa said. "But one thing we know from Bible, Grace, you Catholic, you understand this. We must pay for what we do wrong. When we pay, God forgive us. Right?"

"Only remember you're not God."

"I am man this family. Teddy is boy. My job clean family name."

Dressed in his black suit, he sat on the front porch and waited for the sun to set. A headache was coming. He recognized the buildup of pressure behind the eyeballs and the first throbbing at the temples.

After Ethel had come back to her place, she'd done the last of the wash and hung it on the cord grid over the tub alongside what she'd done the night before. Then she wrote a letter to the landlady, instructing her that everything left behind was to go to the Goodwill except the small round table she'd admired; she could have that.

At four, discouraged and disconsolate, she called Anthea and said she'd given up.

"I know he won't come now," she said.

"So take a nap," Anthea said. "You have a long night
ahead. I'll make sure the boy gets as much sleep as he
can. At eight, he'll be waiting for you, looking beautiful.
I'll call you at seven-thirty, maybe, just to make sure
you're up."

Ethel put on a short white gown and a light robe
and got into bed. She was asleep when she heard the
heavy knock on the door, a command.

The patriarch walked in, bringing the possibility of
redemption.

He sat in the armchair and didn't look at her.

"Close door," he said. "And lock."

She did what he asked, then sat on the edge of the
bed and awaited his judgment.

She saw that he'd immediately begun to perspire. The
room had been overheated by the setting sun. He took
off his suit coat, sat again, raised his hands and, with their
fleshy heels, pressed his eyeballs gently into their sockets.

"Headache?" she asked.

"No."

She'd never seen him so hollowed out or so severe.

"I came to talk to you," he said.

"I've been waiting to talk to you," she said.

"I hear people speak 'gainst you," he said. "They say
you are bad person."

She seemed content to accept this judgment.

"They forget you are my family, it is my business what
you are and what you do. They forget we are together on
this."

"On what?"

"Our problem. Family, I'm talking. Why I come talk
to you."

475

That seemed to be all he had to say for the moment.

The light from the street lamps fell on her, but his back was to the window so he was in the dark. Only his eyes glowed. He'd noticed the suitcase on the floor, prepared for departure, but said nothing about it, moved his attention to the bed, stayed with that long enough so Ethel began to wonder what he was thinking. She remembered he'd never been in her place.

Now is the time to tell him I'm leaving, she thought, now, while he's quiet.

"How is Petros?" she asked. Instead.

"He spoke in paper 'gainst you," he said.

"Saying what?"

"He will put no charge on me, he said. Imagine that! Son of a pimp. Only 'gainst you he talk."

Now, she thought, tell him now.

"I can understand why he would," she said.

" 'Everybody know whose fault this is,' he say. He mean you."

He was looking at the suitcase again.

"You ready to go," he said. A statement, not a question.

"Yes," she said, again urging herself to tell him the whole of it, her resolve and her program, all of it, now.

"Aleko outside waiting in car. Take us home," he said. "But first I must explain you certain things."

"I suppose it is," she said, "what Petros said: my fault."

"You don't throw him in water, you don't put knife in his body. Why he don't put charge 'gainst me? Hah? Tell me that much."

"I don't know."

"Because when he don't speak 'gainst me, people think what wonderful man over there, and when he speak 'gainst you, everybody think same way now. I'm not fool. I understand these things."

Her robe had come open. As she folded it over her legs, she was aware how closely he was sensing her.

"You are my problem," he said. "I will tell you what you have to do, not Petros. You understand what I say?"

"Yes, but—"

"Yes, but nothing. No but business. You are my family. I protect you now."

Whatever he was thinking, as he studied her furniture, the bed and the suitcase on the floor, was more important, she could see, than what he was saying.

"That table over there," he said. "We take her home with us. I like that little round table."

"I promised it to my landlady," she said.

"Then what the hell, give it to her, give her everything. The bed too. We need nothing from here."

He looked at the bed for a long time in silence.

"You have no problem be 'fraid from anybody," he said. "You understand that? I am here."

His eyes were like hummingbirds, darting here and there, hovering, then darting to another place, picking up inferences, suspicions, doubts.

"I'm afraid of only one person," she said.

"Don't worry, I fix that fellow, guarantee you."

"Not Petros. You."

She rose to her feet and went to where he sat, got on her knees before him. He still wouldn't look at her, so she took his head in her hands and gently turned it toward her. But his eyes remained averted.

"Costa, dear," she said, "look at me. Please."

"Where you do it?" he asked.

"Do what?"

"With Petros. Here?"

"No."

"Then?"

"Costa, what's the difference where? He has an apartment."

The heels of his hands went to his eyes again and pressed them back gently. He was pale and tense and in need of relief, not what she was about to tell him.

"Costa," she said. "I have to tell you something."

"On the boat too? His boat?"

"What's the difference, Costa?"

"If no difference, why you don't tell me?"

"I don't want to hurt you."

"Now you worry on that?"

"I always did. That's why I was so careful."

"Same bed. You sleep in—?"

"Costa, don't ask me that stuff anymore, please."

"He make you do bad things?"

"Just the usual."

"What is that, the usual?"

"I will not talk about this anymore, Costa, so stop."

He dropped his head.

"Now listen," she said. "Please, listen."

He shook his head like a young boy who'd been hurt.

In a measure of desperation, to win him back, she kissed him on the forehead, holding his head so he couldn't pull away.

"I know you have a headache," she said.

She kissed him softly on each eye where it hurt.

He turned his head away as soon as she released it.

"Tell me the truth," he said. "He force you?"

"Oh, God no, nothing like that."

"Then how you go to him?"

"Of my own free will. I decided to be with him. Then I decided not to."

"But he make you do bad things."

"No! He's not a bad man."

"I know those animals, how they do."

"Like all the others; no different."

"All the others?"

"Yes. They're all the same." Her voice was frantic. "Why do you ask me all this?"

"Because I want truth. You must not lie to me anymore."

"I don't lie to you."

"You lie. Many time. You never tell me anything about this before. Every day, you wait for me to go north, right? Then you go with him. Every night. In the boat. Here. In goddamn Gulf-view. You don't think I know everything?"

"So all right, it's true."

"Every day you make other shame for my family. True?"

"True."

"So now you must pay for bad things you do. To my son and to my family. The people here must see you are 'shame yourself."

"But you haven't listened to me!"

"I hear you enough. Now you listen. You dirty my family. You must clean shame you made. When you confess sin, God will . . ."

His speech petered out as his attention wandered to the photograph over her bed, the one taken years ago on the deck of the *Eleni*. There was Teddy, a gleaming boy of twelve years with his hand on the tiller, and at his side, Costa, with his arm around the boy's shoulder.

"You see picture over there?" He pointed. "The *Eleni*. My boat. Two week before I sell her. The red tide come at that time. All sponge sick. We had no bread to put on the table. So, like always, I talk to my father. I imagine" —he touched his forehead with a fingertip—"you understand, what he would say. He told me red tide stay ten year. Long time no work, I say. So sell boat, old Theophilactos say, open shot for bait, boats, so on, small place. That way you make living. O.K. It's what I do. Now 'bout

479

you, same thing. I imagine what he will say. What is custom my people on island? I am not American these things, you understand? Citizen, yes. But in these situation I am still from other side. For us, there are three things possible when wife do what you do. You listen me?"

"Yes."

"First possibility. Head family kill woman. Done many time. Now less. Not for me. Only animal kill each other. So, number two. Send woman back to her family. You have no family. Mother, fine woman, dead. Father teach you nothing. Hopeless case. So, number three."

"What is that?"

"Tell Teddy take you back."

"Teddy doesn't want me back."

"Teddy do what I say, best thing for family."

"Costa, he doesn't want me anymore."

"I straighten Teddy out on all that there. I tell him you are good girl. Do bad things, but good girl. Maybe."

"Teddy has another woman."

"Because he mad at you. I would do same thing."

"Please, please, don't think that way."

"We are all you have, damn fool. Don't you know that? Who give damn 'bout you in world except me?"

"Nobody, Costa."

"Who will look after you if I don't? Who will take care of you now?"

"I will. I will look after myself."

"Look after yourself! Look what happen when you look after yourself! How could you be with all those men if you care 'bout yourself. One pile top the other! How could you do that?"

"I don't think I can explain it to you," she said, "but I'll try. Can you listen to me now? Just for a minute?"

He was silent.

"Teddy can't make children," Ethel said. "You know that."

"Only God knows that."

"And the doctors. Ask Teddy. Well, then . . . the others? I did it for you. I would have done anything for you then. And I did."

"All those men. One pile top the other. For me?"

He wasn't reprimanding her. It was a lover's reproach.

"Don't you like little Costa?" she said. "Isn't he what you wanted?"

He had no answer ready.

"They were decent men," she said. "All of them. Friends. I liked them all. But you're the one I loved."

She pushed close to him, her body between his knees.

"I gave nine months of my life to you, Costa," she said. Exhausted, she dropped her head to his knee. "I just can't talk about all that anymore." Her body began to shudder and to tremble. "Goddamn it," she said as she began to cry, "I didn't want to do this."

He pulled her close and his voice was gentle. "I protect you now," he said. "You do what I say and I protect you." He stroked her hair. "Maybe, like you say, you do it because you like them all. Maybe that's truth this time."

Which made her cry harder, that he was trying to understand what had happened as she'd explained it.

"Maybe you are not girl we can trust that way," he said. "Maybe you need someone watch you all the time."

"Maybe," she said, willing to admit anything. Then she said, "I did it for myself too. So I'd be free of you all. That's what I want now. That's why I'm going away. Are you listening? I said I'm going."

If she hoped this would reach him, she was wrong.

"I don't understand why you saying," he said. "But it don't make difference now. Be quiet. Here. Look up."

She did.

"Don't cry anymore. I take care of you now."

He kissed her cheeks, which were wet where her eyes had flooded.

"I'm going," she said. "Please, please, try to understand that."

"You not going anywhere," he said. He was kissing her all over her face now. "No reason to run away. I am here. You are with me. Safe. You belong to me."

She saw that he hadn't heard her—or couldn't—or wouldn't.

It was then that she made up her mind.

The only thing left was what she'd always done—not try to explain what she was going to do but simply do it, disappear without a word, without a signpost pointing to where she'd gone or a note left behind to explain why.

She didn't have strength left to do anything else except vanish. There was no understanding on his face now. She could only see what she'd seen so many times on so many other faces.

She didn't have to guess what was happening to him. She knew it before he did.

The idea came to her that she should put space between them. Quickly!

"Costa, dear," she said, putting her palms on her knees, "I'd better get up now."

She started to rise up off her knees. But his hands were on her shoulders, gentle but heavy, soft but unyielding, preventing her.

He shook his head, his eyes full equally of reproach and longing. He wanted to say something but had no vocabulary to say it.

She came close again, now asking his permission to leave him, saying, "Please, Costa, please, good-bye for now."

Again she tried to rise, but he held her where she was.

When he spoke, it was with difficulty. His head down, his breath coming short and hard, he had to struggle to say what he said.

"Proper way. Don't worry. I explain everything. To Teddy. He take you back. Don't worry."

"All right," she said. "Fine. Thanks."

"Good boy. Family boy. Obey his father. I tell him. What is right. Straighten out Teddy boy. On this."

"I know you will, Costa, O.K., O.K."

To make him believe her, she kissed him a quick good-bye and tried again to get up. But he held her close.

She could feel his arousal, tried urgently to free herself from what she'd caused.

"Costa dear, please." She was begging now. "Let me up. And I will write you from wherever I am and you will write me how the boy is, so let me up now. And on my vacations I will come down and be with him and with you, see how nice it will be, and bring him gifts and you too, I will be here every Christmas, I have to go now, Costa, and in the summer we will go sailing together, all three of us, Costa, see, I have a cramp in my leg now, so please, let me up, and we'll go to your father's grave and sit there all three and you'll tell the boy what you used to tell me, all about the family. All right? All right?"

When she looked up at him to beg him again to release her—that was all that was left for her now, to beg—he kissed her on the lips, his own lips heavy and enveloping.

"You are very wicked," he said, softly.

Again Ethel had that aroma from him, Eastern and pleasantly sour.

"But I don't care," he said. "I don't give fuckin' damn!"

She didn't move when she knew she should.

Because she also knew that if she rejected him now, she'd have to thrust him off with all her strength, wound him in a way she didn't dare to.

"You are so wicked," he said. "So wicked."

His body was trembling and he was kissing her on the mouth again and again, kissing her out of the need which exists at the end of life, only then.

"Call me Dad," he said. "Call me Dad like you used to call me."

"Don't do that, Costa," she pleaded in a whisper. "Please don't, don't—please, Costa, please."

"Say it, say Dad."

When she began to struggle, it was too late.

"Costa, stop. I don't want that!"

Sliding off the chair, he was on the floor with her.

"Costa," she begged, "don't. Please, don't."

He clasped her so there was no way she could free herself.

"I don't want you that way, Costa," she pleaded.

On top of her now, he wasn't hearing.

All there was for her now was to wait.

He didn't do what she expected, didn't reach under her cover, didn't try to free himself. Like a young boy, he simply pushed against her with all his strength.

If he needs it that much . . . she thought.

Then he began to pulse.

"Jesus, help me," he said at the end.

She closed her eyes.

"Jesus," he said, "I'm dying."

twenty-five

NEITHER moved.

She felt an impulse of guilt: she so cool, he destroyed. His hold relaxed so she was able to breath, but his dead weight was still on her body and his face was buried in her neck.

Silence.

Her mind wandered.

Might she have gotten more for her car? The used-car dealer had said she could try other places, but she'd been in a hurry to have matters settled so she'd agreed to what he'd offered. Seven hundred and ten plus what she had in the bank minus the air fare—she'd arrive in New York with almost fifteen hundred dollars. That should keep her for a while.

What time was it? Anthea had said she'd call at seven. No, seven-thirty. And at Lazy Louie's Used Cars the man had said, "We stay open till nine. I'll have cash for you," he'd promised, "and I'll drive you to the airport."

But she had to go to Anthea's first and pick up the boy.

She needed a look at her wrist watch.

"Costa," she whispered, "you're heavy."

Slowly he lifted his bulk off her disordered body and stood. Turning his back to her, he walked to the armchair where he'd left his jacket. As he sat, he spread it across his lap. Now he was still again, head bowed, lips parted, breathing in gulps, a man bewildered.

Still on the floor, she drew up her legs as far as she could under her robe, then stole a quick look at her watch: 7:03. She'd told Anthea she'd be there at eight. She still had time. But not much.

"Are you all right?" she asked.

He didn't answer.

She remembered that he'd only been in her place once before and indicated the bathroom door. "It's in there," she said.

He shifted his jacket farther up on his lap, then lifted his head and looked at her. There was a curious smile on his face, one she hadn't seen before.

"What are you thinking?" she asked.

It was, she thought, the smile of a boy apprehended in a crime.

"Me too?" he asked.

"What? You too what, Costa?"

He made a gesture with his hands, raising them a little, then parting them, palms up.

"Now you got me too," he said. "Raise 'im up, put 'im down."

He kept nodding his head, reaching, it seemed, his special understanding of what had happened.

"My son," he said, "he is weak on these things."

"What do you mean, Costa?"

He indicated the place on the floor where they'd been. "Now I know why," he said. "You make him weak."

"I don't know what you mean, Costa. Teddy's not weak."

"Oh, yes. On these things, yes. Let you run here, there."

"And I didn't make him weak."

"My son and Petros and God knows, all your life, how many more you brought down. Now me too, you think?"

"Costa," she said, "you've done nothing wrong. It just happened. One of those things."

"Then why you so nervous? Sitting there so quiet?"

"I'm just waiting for you to—"

She'd almost said it, that she wanted him to go.

Getting up, she walked to the bureau and looked at herself in the mirror. She arched her back where it had tightened, pushed back her shoulders and stretched her arms. It felt fine, as if she'd been trapped at the bottom of the sea, many fathoms down, then been suddenly cut loose to shoot to the surface.

She studied her face in the mirror, touched her hair.

"Tomorrow!" she promised her friend in the glass.

She shifted her eyes to Costa. He looked ashamed and he looked angry.

What could she say to help him?

"I'm glad you did what you did," she said.

And wondered why she'd said it. It wasn't true.

To her surprise, she was feeling the most normal of all appetites. She hadn't eaten in more than a day.

"It showed me how much you felt," she said as she went to the fridge. "I'll always hold that memory."

Which also wasn't true. She was saying things she didn't mean.

"Sure you always remember," Costa said. "Because now . . ." He hesitated.

There was some cheese, a bar of processed cheddar, which she broke open and bit into.

"You pull me down with you," he said.

"Oh, Costa," she said, "come off it." There were a few apples in the vegetable tray. She picked the best of them and closed the door. "It's nothing like that," she said.

"Yes," he said, "down in the dirt. With you."

"Costa, stop being silly. Here. A good apple. Take it. And cheer up. I'm not upset; why should you be?"

He stared at her, making no sign.

Actually, she thought, there was truth in what he'd said. He was suddenly "down in the dirt" with the rest of the race.

And he knew it. That's why he was so angry.

Was it at himself? Or was it at her?

She wished she was dressed.

When he looked at her, she turned her back, but moved enough so she could see him in the mirror.

Unaware that he was being observed, he lifted his jacket, looked quickly at the stain, then immediately turned his head toward her.

She shifted her eyes just in time, picked up the hairbrush she'd left unpacked and pulled it through her hair.

Despite what was so threatening in the old man's manner, Ethel felt relief. Whatever had held her in constriction all those months had been loosened. She could feel it in her body; it felt light and springy. If Costa hadn't been in the room, she might have laughed out loud with joy. She was about to be free.

"I can't go back now," Costa said. "I can't go back live at home."

"Oh, of course you can."

"You spoil things, Noola and me."

"Nonsense," she said, brushing her hair, making the roots tingle. "Noola hates me but she will always love you, no matter what she says." The brush was metal and it made a bristling sound as she pulled it through her long fine hair.

She turned in place. "Costa, believe me, Noola will always—"

"I don't want her," he said. The tone of his voice was final.

She took another bite of the cheese and sneaked a look at her wrist watch. Seven-fourteen. She'd have to go soon. Anthea would be waiting. Outside, the last of the light was fading. As soon as Costa left, she'd dress and—

How would she get him to go?

"I'm leaving tomorrow, Costa," she said.

"You're not leaving," he said. "Forget that stuff!"

She choked down her reaction, turning her back to give herself the moment she needed. She could see him in the glass, straining his neck over the back of the chair, stretching out the tension, then pulling his head down on each side. She heard the click of the vertebrae.

It occurred to her—for no reason she understood— that she might have to run.

She picked up the last of the apple. As she chewed, she found a blue bruise on the underside of her arm and made a little sound, part admiration, part scold.

"You're so strong," she said, turning to show him the place.

The transformation she found on his face alarmed her. She had to finish packing. It might soon be too late.

She walked quickly to the wall where the photograph of the *Eleni* was hanging, the one she liked, father and son at the tiller, pulled it off its little hook and put it, along with the hairbrush, face down on top of the pile of clothing in Emma's suitcase.

"Who you going meet now?" he asked. "With that suitcase ready?"

"Meet where?"

"Where you going?" he said. "Now."

"I don't know."

"You don't know where you going?"

"No. But I'm not meeting anyone."

"But tomorrow maybe. Someone? Sure."

"I have no plans like that."

"You lying again," he said. "I can see these things, the way you—" He made a series of quick gestures with his hand, flipping it from side to side to describe her quick, nervous movements.

Was she moving like that? Like a fish in panic?

"I can see you lying," he said.

"I am not."

"You telling me you don't know where you going?"

"Only in general. North. And I don't lie anymore. Not to you, not to anybody."

"So if it's true," he said, "what you say I go with you? North."

A suggestion she hadn't anticipated, didn't know how to answer.

"You don't want that?" he asked.

"No," she said, "I don't want you to go with me."

"If there's no one waiting, what you care?"

"I want to be by myself. With no one."

"Sit down," he said. "Because you're not going anywhere."

She didn't know what to say. To break the spell, she knelt by her suitcase, folded the bag over, tried to push the halves together so it could be buckled.

"Truth is," Costa said, "you going meet somebody."

She didn't have the patience to deny it again. She pushed the sides of Emma's suitcase together. Her body tensed. This goddamn suitcase, she thought, is too full. She laid it over on its side, got up on a corner and pressed down with all her weight. She heard the glass of the framed photograph shatter. She looked at Costa. He hadn't noticed. She had to close those clasps and fasten them. Quickly.

490

"Look out," she heard him say. He was on the floor with her, still holding his jacket across his front. He put his other hand on the bag.

"Why you closing this now?" he said.

She looked at the window. Night had fallen.

"Where you think you going, middle of night, like crazy woman in nightgown?"

God, yes, she still had to dress. But that would take exactly two minutes.

"Ethel, I'm talking to you."

The phone rang. Anthea. It must be seven-thirty. It rang again. She didn't pick it up. It rang and rang.

He was watching her.

"Why you don't talk to phone?" he said. "Hah?" He pointed to the telephone, waited. "I know why," he said. "That's the one, calling you, right?"

The phone rang again. His eyes didn't move off her. "Answer," he said. "Answer! Why you don't answer phone?"

She pressed down on the suitcase again.

The phone was quiet.

With his free hand, he pulled the bag out of her hands, opened it and jerked it around, scattering the clothes and bits of glass over the floor.

Then at last she felt relief, and knew what it was. Anger. She was on the edge with him.

But he must not see it. It could be incendiary.

Quickly she began to reorder the clothes he'd scattered.

"Tell me," he said, "who know what you told me, that it's not from Teddy? About little Costa I'm talking."

"Teddy and you."

"You sure on that?"

"Yes."

"Petros, nothing?"

"Only what happened with him."

"Teddy and me and—only you? Only? Tell the truth."

"That's it."

"How I know that?"

"Because I tell you."

"How I know later, sometime, you don't tell somebody, new man maybe?"

"You don't know."

"Never mind those clothes now. Sit quiet and speak truth for change."

Again she had to choke down her anger.

"Whom would I tell?" she said. "And why?"

"Whoever man you going to."

"I have no one I'm going to."

"Sooner. Later. Someday."

"I hope so. I'm going to lead a normal life."

"What's your idea, normal life?"

"I don't know yet. I'm going to find out."

"You lie sometime, right?"

"Sometimes."

"Many time."

"But not about this. I will never tell anybody that it's not—Oh, fuck this!"

She got up and looked at the door. She didn't want to be bullied anymore. She wished she was dressed. She went to the window and turned her back to him.

The homebound traffic had died out. All was quiet on the highway. It was twenty-four minutes to eight.

"Costa, why don't you go now?" she said.

He was walking toward her.

She passed around him, back to the suitcase, knelt on the floor and began to repack her clothes. A piece of broken glass stung a finger and she put it to her mouth and sucked.

He was watching her.

When she finished packing, she folded the bag over—

aware that he was watching every move—and tried the buckle again.

"Tell me," he said, coming toward her. "Petros, sure he know something about little Costa, who he is?"

Straining over the bag made her breath come hard. "I think he believes," she said as evenly as she could while thrusting all her weight down. "He doesn't know but he believes—"

At last! She had one buckle closed!

"That's he's not from Teddy," she said. "And that is all."

The other buckle wouldn't come together.

She paused, out of breath, sucked on her finger. The cut was not deep, but it hadn't stopped bleeding.

"But before you say he know nothing," Costa said.

"He doesn't know anything. He believes. How can he know if I don't?"

Again she tried the buckle, almost had it, when it slipped out of her grip.

"You don't know either?" Costa said.

"I told you a hundred times."

"Tell me hundred times more and I don't believe."

The phone rang again.

Quickly she looked at her wrist watch. It was twenty-one before eight.

"Come on," he said, looking at the phone. "He's waiting for you."

The hell with the bag. The phone rang. She would break out now, dodging Costa, out the door, down the stairs, out the building, in her robe, into the car. The phone rang. All she really needed was her purse. The ticket was inside. She'd snatch it up on the way to the door. The phone rang.

Costa picked up the cord and, with a yank, pulled it free of the wall.

She ran into the bathroom and locked the door.

She turned on the light, turned it off. On the rope grid over the tub she had seen, by that flash of illumination, the wash from the day before. There was a favorite dress, drip dried, ready to wear. And panties, bras, even a pair of espadrilles.

There wasn't a sound from the other room.

Over the tub was a window and outside a vision, a picture of the kind of existence she'd never had and never wanted, a still life, despite one moving figure.

Back to back with her condominium was another exactly like it, and in its backyard a swimming pool, set alight by a submerged fixture. It glowed like a jewel in the night.

A single swimmer, a young man, swam slowly from one end to the other, there jackknifed, turned and swam slowly back. She imagined he'd come home late from work and was relaxing before dinner. At the end of the pool, on its lip, was a drink. He went to it, coming up on target out of a shallow dive, took a long swallow, then resumed swimming.

Perhaps ten feet back of the pool was a kid's swing. Sitting in it, watching the swimmer, was a young woman, in a light blue housecoat, swaying to and fro, slowly, sensually.

Ethel imagined the scene which was to follow, the dinner taken from the stove and put on the table, the meal savored with loving talk, early to bed, no covers in the heat, no nightclothes, slow intercourse, deep sleep.

It looked like a print titled "Contentment," banal and commonplace, but it was what she longed for now.

She saw herself as the young wife in the swing.

Would she ever make it?

Just beneath her window was the parking lot for her building. Leaning forward, she could see the car she'd sold. The key would be where she always left it, on the floor under the seat. The drop from the window was a story and a half. If she hung from the sill, it would not be more than ten feet. Could she manage that without danger? It was worth the chance.

Quickly she dressed. Then she listened at the door of the bathroom. Whatever Costa was doing, he was doing it quietly.

Communing with his father, no doubt: Costa, the god abandoned, consulting with his own deity, asking for instruction how to return her to that absolute devotion which she'd given him until—until the episode on the floor.

No. More likely plotting how to make her cower again, move fearfully by night, hide by day, a beast pursued, running in terror for its life until it found a hole deep enough to vanish in.

There was a time, minutes before, when she'd believed that to run and disappear was her only recourse.

Her image in the mirror challenged her. How could she shame this living person again?

What she had to do was convince Costa that she was going to do what she'd said, that she was really leaving, really going elsewhere.

But the truth was that she had no plan. Except "elsewhere." What sounded like a lie—"I'm going but I don't know where"—was true. She didn't know what she'd do after tomorrow morning. How could he be expected to believe her if she wasn't able to say anything more definite than that?

The truth was unconvincing. It was of no use. She was dealing with a madman, so she had to be absolute to be believed.

And she was dealing with a bully. She'd crawled for him. That hadn't worked. A bully, she decided, needs a bully.

She unlocked the bathroom door.

He was waiting for her.

"I'm going now," she said, walking to her suitcase. "I wish you'd leave. Right now, please."

"I make up my mind," he said.

"Never mind that. Please go."

How easily the other buckle closed now!

"I don't let you do bad things again," he announced. "You will live in our house, serve your family, proper way, use your life to pay for your sin, that way God forgive you."

She pulled the suitcase up and set it on its bottom.

"I'm not damn fool," he went on. "I know your idea now. Running-away business again. So listen here to me! If you try that stuff, watch out. I take boy, he's not my blood, so I take your boy and I give to nigger family, they live upriver, have many children, one more, what's the difference? How you like that? Hah? If you don't take care boy and do your job like mother, proper way, that's what I do."

"I'm taking the boy with me, Costa," she said. "Tonight!"

"Where you taking? The boy? You have nowhere to go."

Then she was saying the unbelievable, but it was the only plan she'd ever had and the only one she could think of then.

"You were right," she declared. "I am meeting someone. Mr. Robin Bolt. Remember him? On the *Sara?* He is waiting for me with a job. He's going to pay me three hundred and fifty dollars a week. How do you like that? 'You're a beautiful woman,' he told me, 'I will photograph you,' he said."

The fantasy exhilarated her; she was laughing wildly.

"And the way Mr. Bolt talked," she said, "I may not settle for three hundred and fifty dollars. I may hold out for five hundred dollars. He has an apartment for me in the big city and he said he'd find me a wonderful nurse to look after the boy when I'm at work. A black woman —decent people don't call them niggers. You want to know my future? There it is. Not sitting in your home, under guard, a goddamn slavey. What do you think of that?"

Out of breath, she had to stop.

Finally, she could see, Costa believed her.

Ready for anything now, she pulled on the sweater she'd left out in case the night air was chilly.

"Who you be with? On that boat?" Costa said. "Who's waiting for you there? Not Mr. Bolt. He is *poustis*. Who's on that boat? Waiting for you? Hah?"

"That, goddamn it, Costa, is none of your business. But he is not a *poustis*. Of that you can be sure. I am going to lead a normal life. Not the life you're talking about, which is the life of a servant in your house."

"Normal life? What's that?"

"Like your son. Fucking who I want when I want. That what you wanted to know? So there! Now leave. Go!"

She turned her back and, trembling, waited for him to be gone.

He went to her, and putting his heavy hands on her shoulders, he turned her around to face him.

"You will never be with anyone else," he said.

"Let me go, Costa," she said. "You're hurting me."

"You gone crazy, I see that now," he said, gently. "But don't worry, I take care of you."

"Costa, let me go, goddamn it. Let me go!"

She saw there were tears in his eyes.

"I make you O.K. woman again," he said. "Don't worry. I make you behave proper way."

He shook her, gently at first, but when he felt her resisting, harder.

"I take care you now," he said.

497

"Stop it. Stop it, you're hurting me."

"You must understand this: You will never be with anyone else. You hear what I say?"

"Let me go," she said, wrenching her shoulders out of his grasp.

"Not in this life," he said. "You will never, in this life, be with other man."

He'd forgotten his jacket; his hands were free. When he reached for her again, she threw up her hands to meet his and push them off.

"No more cheap stuff," he said. "Not while I am living."

"They weren't cheap stuff."

"Sure, I know, you like them all."

"I loved them all, every goddamn one."

It was something to say in a quarrel, like what she'd said about the *Sara*. She'd wanted to hurt him and she could see that she had and she was glad.

But now, when she said it again, she thought it was true.

"I'm glad I was with every one of them," she said. "I wouldn't have missed one of them. I loved them all."

"I see the Devil has come into you," he said.

"That's not the Devil speaking," she said. "It's me speaking."

"You crazy now," he said. "Crazy!"

Then there was more but she didn't hear it because he was coming for her again and she was yelling at him, "No, Costa, no, stay back, Costa, stay back!"

"I will save you," she heard, "because the Devil is speaking in your mouth."

"I am speaking in my mouth," she said, as she backed away. "I loved them all. As I loved you, Costa. Can't you understand that? Like a human being loves a human being."

He was coming for her.

"Don't put your hands on me again, Costa. Don't! Don't!"

But he had her.

She tried to pull loose. But he was stronger than anyone she'd ever known. His strength was unnatural, it frightened her. The tears in his eyes were part of the terror. She couldn't move.

"I don't want you talk anymore," he said. "Finish this business."

"It's not up to you what I do. Let me go."

"No more talking now," he said.

His hold moved to her neck.

"Let me go, goddamn it! Stop that."

She struck at his hands and at his face. But he didn't seem to notice. Except that he tightened his hold.

"Business finish now," he said. "Stay quiet now. Quiet."

And she was. In his hands.

"You will never be with anybody more. You understand that?"

"I will, I will," she said; but her voice was thickening, grating.

He shook her. "You must understand that now. You belong to me."

Now she struggled for her life, spending all her strength.

Holding her by the throat, he lifted her off the ground, her legs flailing from side to side, her hands struggling with his. He held her there, off the ground, until she gave up and was still.

"Now," he said, "you understand what I want from you? Say!"

This was her chance and she knew it. If she would say what he was waiting to hear, if she would yield to his will, agree to his terms, he would believe that she'd be what he wanted her to be, accept that and turn her loose.

"So?" he said, loosening his hands enough so she could get her voice out. "Say!"

"I don't care what you do to me," she said, and it hurt her to make any sound at all. "I don't belong to you and I never will."

When he tightened his hold, she turned her head and bit at his hands.

He wrenched her head around and she cried out in pain.

Then the room was quiet.

Her mouth opened as she tried to pull in the air she needed.

The knowledge of what was happening to her eroded her will and softened her resolve. She stroked his hands as best she could, saying as best she could, a whisper, a murmur, a gasp, "Dad, listen, please, stop it, please, Dad, stop it now, Dad, I don't want to hate you, Dad, so stop it, now."

But he'd passed beyond hearing. The fact that she was still moving her lips was enough for him. He tightened his hands.

She could see that he was insane.

Some seconds later, she tried to claw at him.

Again he held her up off the ground until she was limp and hung in his hands.

And now he was possessed, God's host, having his righteous way with a transgressor. "You will never be with anyone else," he pronounced, his eyes flaming with the light of revelation. "That's it! Finished!"

"I will, I will, I will," her lips spoke. But there was no voice.

He saw her lips moving and stopped that too. "Make up your mind," he said. "What I say is how it will be."

"Fuck you," she wanted to say. And couldn't. It was too late.

"So that's it, quiet," he said. "The best thing for you. You see? When you don't talk, everything O.K.?"

Her lips moved for the last time, and his arms locked.

There was a choking, as when a piece of food is too big to go down.

He wasn't strangling her; he was holding her so she couldn't get away. It was an act of love.

A sound came from her throat, but not of her making, a snap, like the sound a chicken bone makes when it breaks.

And she was his, as he wished her, silent.

After a little, there was a slight seeping of blood from one nostril.

The breeze off the Gulf raised the dainty white curtains, fluffed them, then let them fall.

An hour later, Teddy let himself in with his key. The room was dark. What light there was came from a street lamp through the branches and leaves of a pepper tree. When the breeze freshened, these shadows stirred over the bed. And the body. And the back of a man, silhouetted.

Now Teddy began to see more clearly. Costa was sitting in a straight chair at the side of the bed, where Ethel's body had been composed. Her eyes were closed. Her hair was spread over a pillow and neatly reordered. Her dress had been smoothed over her long, slim legs. Her knees and ankles were together like those of a well-brought-up child. One of her hands rested at her throat, the other on her chest between her breasts, the fingers softly curled, at ease. The picture was reminiscent of certain religious paintings of the blessed dead. She was lovely and she was at peace.

Only when Teddy leaned closer did he see the marks on her neck and that the mouth, so welcoming in her loving hours, so moist then, so warm and soft, had coarsened, the lips dry and crusting.

The breeze caught the little Japanese tinklers and they made their thin clean sound.

Costa had not moved. His posture suggested he was waiting for someone he loved to wake.

The county medical examiner's report was brief.

"The victim revealed faint semicircular marks on the neck overlying the right and left mastoid muscles. Incision of the neck revealed hemorrhages in the thyroid cartilage with fractures of the hyoid bone. The trachea had been collapsed. Examination of the oral cavity revealed that the tongue had been pushed upward and backward, occluding the nasopharyngeal passageway.

"Cause of Death: Asphyxia by manual strangulation. Homicidal."

twenty-six

A GUT trial takes no time. Instinct judges in a flash. The verdict? Guilty.

Ethel, not Costa.

But the formal trial was another matter. To begin with, it was postponed. Costa was remanded to an institution where he would undergo an examination to determine if he was fit to stand before a jury. For some reason, this took several months.

Meantime, sure of its ground, Morality spoke. Sermons were rung out, community leaders rediscovered rectitude, the media anticipated the jury, intellectuals examined the ironies of guilt, the ethnicity of the Greek community was reaffirmed.

But soon these exercises in Right and Wrong died out. There were new, equally lurid headlines, fresh issues for concern and debate. By the time Costa was believed able to face trial, people had lost interest. Even the prosecution believed—privately—that Costa had been driven out of his mind by a demon. It was simpler to think of the event that way. It relieved the soul. It solved the case. There was nothing left to do. She was dead. Who needed the hazard of defending her publicly?

There were no complaints when Costa was judged not guilty by reason of temporary insanity. He was released, a hero.

Whereas the trial marked Ethel publicly as a woman who'd ruined the life of every person she touched.

But in the memories of those whose lives she'd touched, time, as it passed, unsettled this verdict.

Petros, for instance. A few months after the trial, he bought himself a splendid summer's wardrobe, a ticket to Athens and on to the isle of Kalymnos. There he found that his uncles had not exaggerated the beauty or the virtue of the sixteen-year-old *despina* who'd just reached her time of nubility. She was sought after by every family who had a ready son. Petros got her. After an island wedding that took almost a week, he whisked her to Florida, where, in proper time, a doctor pronounced her pregnant. Another son followed the first. There was no reason Petros could see why this harvest should not continue.

Because of her steadfast, orderly character, Petros became a changed man. He sold his interest in the marina, invested his moneys in motels and condominiums, plowed back the profits. Recently he has taken a financial position in shipping. Within these few years he has become one of the richest and most admired men in the sunland, lives in an exclusive residential park on Casey Key and is a patron to any worthy charity.

Able now to enjoy leisure, he has found time for reflection. He is able to appreciate how close he came to ruining his life by marrying Ethel. And in his secret heart, he feels a curious gratitude to the "monster" who, time after time, resisted his pressure, fought off his threats

...nd finally knew better than he did what was best for ...im. When he thinks of her now, it is to bless her for ...er good sense.

Petros is not the only one.

Off the coast of an unfamiliar continent, thousands of ...iles from our shore, the officer in charge of the detection ...ystem of a great carrier died in his sleep. His deputy, ...heodore Avaliotis, received an on-the-spot promotion. ...t the brief ceremony, the commander of the man-of-war ...oted how pleased he was that Lieutenant, now Captain, ...valiotis had worked his way up through the ranks. He ...as, this piece of brass declared, a model Navy man.

On the mirror of his quarters, Teddy has a photo-...raph of his new wife, Betty, a land-based ensign. It was ...thel who, encountering on her visits to Jacksonville the ...arious possibilities, had turned Teddy away from one ...oung woman ("She's just like me! You don't want to go ...hrough all that again, do you?") and guided him to Betty.

When they are apart, Teddy and Betty write letters ex-...ressing their longing for each other, vowing that they're ...nore in love than ever. They aren't together enough to be ...ried by the usual strains of the marriage bond. From this ...lateau of peace and order Teddy looks back and won-...ers how he allowed Ethel, that destructive woman, to lay ...vaste so many years of his life and what there was about ...er that intrigued him for so long.

Whatever it was, his second wife doesn't have it. ...fter two weeks on shore, Teddy can't wait to get back to ...ea.

Noola, more than the others, has reason to hate Ethel; ...he girl truly disrupted her home. On the other hand, ...ecause of what happened, Noola, for the first time, can ...onestly call her life her own. Living alone and apart, she ...emembers without regret of loss the long evenings she spent listening to Costa rave. "He's a stupid man," she confesses to her friends. Noola misses her old life not at all. But it is not within her capability to admit that Ethel upset her life—for the good.

After he was freed, Costa had some bad months. People would point him out on the street and the stories they told got back to him. Nothing unkind; hell, they were all on his side: how generous he'd been with Ethel Laffey, how goddamn generous. People particularly remembered the day Costa proudly showed her off to the village for the first time and how often he'd taken her to his father's revered gravesite. Everyone felt sympathy for Costa, and at first this irked him. It was not the kind of regard he enjoyed.

Then he saw he'd become a sort of hero, even a legend, and as the months passed, he learned to enjoy it.

Moreover, it had its commercial advantages. The bank, smelling opportunity for gain, returned The 3 Bees to Costa; after all, they had to find someone to operate it. A word from Petros behind the scenes helped.

Working by himself, slowly, carefully and with pleasure, Costa redid the front of the old store. Above the narrow porch which fronted the place, he had painted, in prominent letters: COSTA AVALIOTIS, HEADQUARTERS FOR TOURISTS, so announcing to all passers-by that the old man who'd killed his daughter-in-law with his bare hands was there, selling sponges, shells, sharks' teeth, all manner of curios and novelties. You could come in and, for the price of a trinket, have a long look at this murderer, finding him, as everyone did, ever so gentle. You could even allow yourself to admire him for taking the law into his own hands and wonder if you'd have had the courage to do what he did.

On Sunday mornings, the Headquarters does not open.

The old man can be found on the road to Tarpon Springs with a fine-looking little boy straddling his shoulders. They spend the day together. Morning? Church. Yes, Costa has gone back. Afternoons, the store. While the old man tends counter, the boy plays along the water's edge. Everyone in the area knows him and looks after him. At the end of the day, the old man prepares dinner. They eat alone. It is there and then that Costa tries to instill a regard for the "proper way" virtues in the little fellow. After which they retire to their bedroom on one side of the house and so to sleep.

Costa has a perfect life, which is to say, the one he wanted. And, as he admits only to himself, he owes it all to Ethel.

As for the little boy, he is the happiest of all. Everyone understands that he is the son of Captain Theodore Avaliotis, on active duty with the U.S. Navy. The boy gets beautiful postcards from all over the world. He has not yet confronted the mystery of his mother. Whatever happened before a time he can remember has brought him only loving concern. Nor does he miss a female presence in his life. In this sympathetic community, little Costa has a score of surrogate mothers who do everything for him that a proper Greek mother would, and much more than Ethel Laffey could have done.

The simplest reason for the kid's being so adored, however, is because he has the same soft, sleepy eyes, the identical taunting smile, that Ernie had. Along with these, there is something more deeply affecting, which he owes to his mother. His complexion is so brilliant, so changeable, his skin so transparent, that they reveal his slightest change of feeling. People who meet the little fellow say he seems to be searching for someone, and everyone hopes she or he is the one he wants. This power, to make people fall in love with him, the boy is well aware of; he knew of it as soon as he knew there were other people in the world.

These are the bounties Ethel left behind.

So she endures. By a few gratefully remembered.

Her photographs, the last physical evidence of her existence, soften by the chemistry of time. People who look at them wonder how anyone so fair could have done so many terrible things.

THE BEST OF BESTSELLERS FROM WARNER...

SCRUPLES
by Judith Krantz   (85-641, $2.75)

The most titillating, name-dropping, gossipy, can't-put-it-down #1 bestseller of the decade! The fascinating story of one woman who went after everything she wanted—fame, wealth, power, love—and got it all!

BLOODLINE
by Sidney Sheldon   (85-205, $2.75)

The Number One bestseller by the author of "The Other Side of Midnight" and "A Stranger In The Mirror." "Exotic, confident, knowledgeable, mysterious, romantic . . . a story to be quickly and robustly told and pleasurably consumed."   —Los Angeles Times.

A STRANGER IN THE MIRROR
by Sidney Sheldon   (81-940, $2.50)

Toby Temple is a lonely, desperate superstar. Jill Castle is a disillusioned girl, still dreaming of stardom and carrying a terrible secret. This is their love story. A brilliant, compulsive tale of emotions, ambitions, and machinations in that vast underworld called Hollywood.

STAINED GLASS
by William F. Buckley, Jr.   (82-323, $2.25)

The United States must stop a war with one man and one man alone. His name: Blackford Oakes, super agent. His mission: Kill his friend for the good of the world. This is Buckley at his spy thriller best, with the most daring, seductive, and charming hero since 007.

SAVING THE QUEEN
by William F. Buckley, Jr.   (92-109, $2.25)

Young Blackford Oakes, the most impossibly brilliant and dashing spy since 007, is assigned to London after World War II to find out who is leaking American secrets about H-bomb development to the British. A tour-de-force spy thriller, filled with the celebrated wit and sharp humor that have made Mr. Buckley an American institution.

THE BEST OF BESTSELLERS FROM WARNER...

ANNA HASTINGS
by Allen Drury   (81-603, $2.50)

With the speed of a wire service teletype, Anna Hastings
—a tiny, pretty reporter with a mind like a razor and an
iron will—shot out of the press gallery to become the
founder of Washington's leading liberal newspaper and
a media empire stretching from coast to coast. But she
paid for her legendary success . . . for the rest of her life.

THE BLACK PRINCE
by Iris Murdoch   (81-719, $2.50)

A cold private, fussy, 58-year-old man tumbles rapurously
in love with a girl of twenty. A searching tragi-comedy
of suicide and murder against a backdrop of desperate
love.

THE SACRED AND PROFANE LOVE MACHINE
by Iris Murdoch   (81-830, $2.50)

A powerful novel about a man and two women: The man
torn by unresolvable conflicts of love, duty, and preference; the women, by pride, need, and the awareness of
their roles.

BLUE SKIES, NO CANDY
by Gael Greene   (81-368, $2.50)

The tantalizing erotic bestselling novel that reveals bla-
tantly, nakedly, and relentlessly the fact that women are
fully as capable as men of feeling and experiencing
powerful sex drives.

THE PARTNERS
Louis Auchincloss   (59-714, $1.75)

A haunting novel that takes place behind the doors of a
respected law firm. An esteemed partner in that firm is
suddenly faced with the new breed of lawyer—young men
who are as desirous of love, power, and money as the
clients they serve. And the result is shattering for all of
them.

THE BEST OF BESTSELLERS...

THE WAR BETWEEN THE TATES
by Alison Lurie   (81-955, $2.50)

The witty, brilliant, best-selling novel of a marriage under siege by young sex, middle age, and old dreams. "A thing to marvel at . . . all that the novel was meant to be" said the *New York Times Book Review.*

THE WORLD OF APPLES
by John Cheever   (89-645, $1.95)

Ten new short stories by one of America's greatest writers. Each one seduces you into a world that only Cheever could create and present. "An extraordinary book" .   —*The New York Times*

P.S. YOUR CAT IS DEAD
by James Kirkwood   (82-934, $2.25)

It's New Year's Eve. Your best friend died in September. You've been robbed twice. Your girlfriend is leaving you. You've just lost your job. And the only one left to talk to is a gay burglar you've got tied up in the kitchen. P.S. your cat is dead. . . .

AN AFFAIR OF STRANGERS
by John Crosby   (89-280, $1.95)

He meant to murder her! In 1.5 seconds he had killed her three companions, but she escaped him. He was an Israeli agent. She was an Arab terrorist. When they met again, they would be conspirators in an international plot, working together but toward opposite goals, lovers and enemies in AN AFFAIR OF STRANGERS.

NIGHTFALL
by John Crosby   (89-354, $1.95)

For five years FBI agent Hawkins has tracked the young terrorist Geraldine Colt. Now she is in Spain and his obsession to arrest her has changed into a bizarre and disquieting love. An absorbing novel of the hunter and the hunted—and the erotic ties which bind them.